M000313813

The
Silver Linings
Wedding Dress
Auction

The Silver Linings Wedding Dress Auction

MARY OLDHAM

Copyright © 2021 Mary Oldham

All rights reserved. This book or any portion thereof may not be reproduced or used in any manner whatsoever without the express written permission of the publisher except for the use of brief quotations in a book review.

Kindle ISBN: 978-1-7377839-0-9
ePub ISBN: 978-1-7377839-2-3
Paperback (5.5" x 8.5") ISBN: 978-1-7377839-3-0
Paperback (5" x 8") ISBN: 978-1-7377839-1-6

Any references to historical events, real people, or real places are used fictitiously. Names, characters, and places are products of the author's imagination.

Story Editor
Edits by Sue, Sue Grimshaw

Cover Art by Lynn Andreozzi

Book design by Tamara Cribley at The Deliberate Page

Wedding Dress Sketches by Mary Oldham

Author Photo by Tanith Dean

Printed in the United States of America.

By-Creek-Ity Publishing
Portland, Oregon

First printing, 2021.

www.maryoldham.com

*For my mother, Caroline Snook Oldham, the strongest woman
I have ever known who told me to never stop writing, and
for my father, Wayne Oldham, who adored strong women
and told me that with the DNA he and Mom had given me, I
couldn't be anything but successful. I miss you every day.*

*And for the real Leslie. May there be many pieces of beautiful
jewelry and much happiness in your future. Thank you!*

Trudel's Wedding Boutique PROUDLY PRESENTS

THE 1ST ANNUAL SILVER LININGS WEDDING DRESS AUCTION

NOVEMBER
· 18 ·

The Portland Art Museum

THE PARK BLOCKS
PORTLAND, OREGON 97201

Benefiting Rachel's House, a shelter for women in need, this unique auction will feature fifty designer wedding gowns graciously donated by former brides from the Portland Metro area.

INDIVIDUAL TICKETS: $250
TABLES OF TEN AVAILABLE FOR $2,000
COCKTAILS AND SILENT AUCTION BEGIN AT 6 P.M.,
DINNER & DRESS AUCTION BEGIN AT 7 P.M.

TICKETS AVAILABLE AT: THESILVERLININGSDRESSAUCTION.COM

TITLE SPONSORS: WEDDINGS BY MILAN, BUDDY'S FLOWERS,
PORTLAND LUX PROPERTIES, AND SAUVETERRE JEWELERS

Present Day

FIVE days before the Auction

"Now, with a sweet story of happy endings, let's go to Hannah who is shopping until she drops at the Portland landmark, Trudel's Wedding Boutique. Hannah, take it away!" the news announcer with the too-bright teeth said as he set up the story for his reporter in the field.

"Thank you, Jeff. I'm excited to be here so bright and early to bring you this story that is bound to have fifty happy endings!"

"Well Hannah, that is a pretty tall order," Jeff replied with a wink.

"Jeff, it is all but guaranteed," Hannah announced with her own big toothy grin. "On Saturday night, Trudel's Wedding Boutique will be hosting a wedding dress auction in the ballroom at the Portland Art Museum like nothing ever seen before in our city. Benefiting Rachel's House, the local women's shelter, this large wedding dress auction is raising money for a great cause. Before I show you a couple of the dresses up for grabs, I want to introduce someone special.

"We are here with Trudel herself and the most beautiful wedding gowns you've ever seen," the reporter said, turning to Trudel, a small statured woman who was dressed in her customary black dress and large pearls. "Trudel, I want to thank you for getting up so early to meet with us this morning to talk about your first Silver Linings Charity Auction."

"Thank you, Hannah, I'm happy to be here with you showcasing this fabulous event."

"Great, great! Now, tell us how you came up with this idea."

"Well, you know that love is not a straightforward journey for everyone. Sometimes a beautiful wedding dress makes it down the aisle and the next step in life begins. For others, it is the collateral damage that sometimes gets left behind. A gorgeous gown can become a bride's nemesis after a broken engagement, which is such a waste."

"Really, Trudel, I never thought about it that way. Have you seen it happen a lot over the thirty years you've been running your boutique here in downtown Portland?"

"Most of the time, everything goes off without a hitch. But there are those times when everything that can go wrong, *does* go wrong. That is how I came to have such a glut of beautiful inventory. And in some cases, people have glorious gowns they will never wear again or give to another family member to wear. Well, the gowns aren't doing anyone any good just hanging in the closet! But they could! That's when I got to thinking that an auction could help those who aren't lucky in love and Rachel's House at the same time. Also, these dresses could help women who find themselves in a difficult financial position, but still want to have a designer dress for their wedding day."

"That's so great," Hannah said as she smiled at the camera. "Such a lovely thing to do."

"Just to give you one example, I have several elegant wedding dresses I will be putting in our sale from a lady who hasn't made it down the aisle yet!" Trudel confirmed.

"Wow, now *that* sounds like a good story."

Trudel shook her head to the contrary, her smile turning to a grimace. "She is a very sweet person, but she has been engaged many times and yet never married… And she is like a niece to me, so she knows the importance of ordering a dress at least six months in advance. Unfortunately for her, several times, just when the dress was ready for the first fitting the engagement was a thing of the past."

"So, it was this reluctant bride that gave you the idea for the auction?"

Trudel nodded and continued, "Most of the time it was unfortunate circumstances for this particular bride, if memory serves me right, but I do believe there was a time or two that she realized this was not 'the one' for her. On some level, she was my motivation for the Silver Linings Wedding Dress Auction. It is just so sad to see all those wedding dresses hanging in her closet. She doesn't need to be reminded of those situations, either. It isn't like I can resell all of her dresses because they've been altered to fit her. She has generous curves," Trudel recalled the jilted bride's figure as if she was divulging a dirty little secret, "So her dresses could fit smaller women who aren't as curvy."

"I'm curious, just how many dresses does she have in her closet?"

"I think she has at least a half dozen! One for each new fiancé!" Trudel exclaimed with a laugh.

"My goodness," Hannah's astonishment got Jeff chuckling at the studio and probably many of their viewers, too. "What does she do that she meets all those men who propose to her?"

"She is a realtor, they just meet *everyone*," Trudel said with a sarcastic laugh. "I can tell you she has some beautiful dresses though, a Paris Germaine, and several James Casper's, who I think is her favorite designer. Overall, we are excited to have nearly fifty dresses from almost every major name in bridal fashion."

"That's wonderful, they should raise a lot of money for Rachel's House."

"That's what we are hoping!"

Hannah looked into the camera and said, "Now, if you have a dress you don't want, and it doesn't need to be a Paris Germaine, you know who to call. They should call you, shouldn't they, Trudel?" she asked turning back to the store's owner.

"Yes, or they can just bring the dress by the shop. We are known for our designer gowns, but as long as the dress is in good shape and only worn once or not at all, we will take it. We are hoping to have enough gowns for a second auction next spring."

"So, if you have a story similar to Trudel's honorary niece, I'm sorry her name escapes me," Hannah nonchalantly asked Trudel, as if she was trying to finagle some tidbit of gossip.

"Leslie Westcott," Trudel blurted out, as she looked into the camera with large, frightened eyes, the realization hitting much like a cornered rabbit looking up the long barrel of a shotgun.

"Yes, if you have a story like Leslie Westcott's, Trudel of Trudel's Wedding Boutique would love to hear from you. Okay, thank you, Trudel, and thanks again for getting up with us so early this morning. Now, in our next half hour, you're going to see me in one of the dresses from the Silver Linings Auction. Who knows? Maybe it will be one of Leslie Westcott's cast-offs. Okay, see you in a bit. I'll send it back to you, Jeff."

"Thank you, Hannah, great story," Jeff said. "Let's hope Leslie Westcott's dresses bring a lot of money for such a great cause. Now, we'll turn to Rhonda for the latest in traffic."

Leslie Westcott stood naked in the bathroom doorway with a towel wrapped around her wet hair and a toothbrush dangling out of her mouth as she watched the morning news in horror. First, she *was* Trudel's niece, but since Leslie's mother had died, Trudel always treated her like a second daughter. And Trudel's daughter, Suzie, was like a sister to her and her best friend. That honorary stuff was crap. This woman, who had just blurted out her name on the morning news, *was* her blood relative.

Second, they had all agreed that if Leslie decided to participate, her dresses would go into the auction *anonymously*. She knew when she'd mentioned this last, important detail that Trudel hadn't been listening—or as the family liked to think of it, she was *projecting*, but not *receiving*.

Aunt Trouble strikes again!

Had Leslie believed this whole charity auction wouldn't come back to bite her in the ass? No. She had just hoped it wouldn't be so personal. Aunt Trudel had been so crazed with auction details it had been difficult to be around her.

Leslie stepped back into the bathroom and rinsed her mouth. She held onto the edge of the granite counter and counted to ten, reminding herself to breathe. As the words Aunt Trudel had said repeated again and again in her mind, Leslie cringed, her stomach doing flip flops.

This was going to be trouble. She couldn't murder Aunt Trudel. She didn't need the hassle with the police, but then she had connections in the police department and a good lawyer, but still, it wasn't worth it. And it wasn't like Trudel meant any harm. She was a very sweet person with a big heart and the attention span of a gnat. To be fair, that reporter was a bit sneaky in her questioning; Leslie could see it in her eyes and then especially in her aunt's when she realized what she'd said.

Her cell phone began buzzing and a number she didn't recognize registered on the display, and then there was a chirp and a second number appeared, and this time her caller ID snared the caller—it was the news station that had just interviewed Trudel. No doubt they wanted Leslie for a follow-up story, posing in one of the gowns. Not going to happen.

And, just to be clear, she had not yet agreed to put *any* of her wedding dresses in Aunt Trudel's Silver Linings Dress Auction. No, all the garment bags holding clues to her torrid, tumultuous, and controversial past were still in the guest room closet like white encased corpses. And she was quite content to have them stay there.

Leslie's sweet Vizsla, Daisy, raised her head off the bed, her amber eyes big and tender, as Leslie dressed. If her dog could talk, she'd no doubt be saying, "Are you mad at my Aunt Trudel? Is she coming for a visit? She gives me treats even when you tell her to stop."

"You sweet girl," she said as she placed a kiss on Daisy's head. "Be good while I'm gone. I'll try to be home early. Got to run to a closing. Who else is going to keep you spoiled in doggy biscuits? Take care of the house."

It was obvious to Leslie that her clients had watched the morning news. As she took her seat at the conference table, their wary, suspicious expressions asked many unspoken questions. She wanted to reassure them that she only had five wedding dresses in her closet and a very nice cocktail dress that was too significant to her past to ever wear again and too expensive to ever give away. But truly, they didn't need to worry, because she could explain everything. She was a good realtor, and they had acquired an excellent property. Their *dream* property.

Instead, she settled for the thick silence that seemed to permeate the room like fog.

Was it her imagination or was Mrs. Peters giving her a dirty look each time she smiled in the direction of Mr. Peters?

Just two painful hours later, Leslie was out the door, finished with the awkward closing on the Peterses' new 1.2-million-dollar home in the prestigious West Hills of Portland. What should have been a celebratory experience for them both was nothing more than an uncomfortable transaction, all because of her aunt. On her way to her car, Leslie turned on her phone and listened to more offers from news stations and other local media wanting to interview her. The one person she'd hoped to hear from hadn't called, which wasn't a total surprise. She was starting to accept that after all they'd been through, he wasn't going to marry her; he was going to ghost her. She spent the next ten minutes freeing up her voicemail and blocking all the unwanted numbers she'd hoped to never hear from again.

She needed to call Aunt Trudel and discuss the interview. The longer she put this off the worse it would be for both of them. She just didn't feel like letting her off the hook yet.

Perky Peggy, the overly friendly office receptionist and notorious gossip, hopped up from her chair as if it had springs, and rounded the large mahogany reception desk to stop Leslie when she arrived.

"Lessslie!" she announced. "Oh my god! I saw your Aunt Trudel on the news this morning. She was talking about all your broken engagements. That must have really gotten to you. I'd be so embarrassed."

"Good morning, Peggy," Leslie replied as she tightened her hold on the mail and tried to remember to keep a handle on her words. "Yes, I think everyone was watching the news this morning. I'm doing fine. I just hope the auction raises a lot of money for Rachel's House. It is an excellent resource to women in our community."

"You have eighteen messages, and your voicemail is full," Peggy informed her.

"Great, thanks, I'll take care of it," Leslie said as she took the messages, turned, and tried to make a run for her office.

"Have you really been engaged like a half a dozen times?" Peggy asked. "I mean I remember a few of them—"

"No, I haven't been engaged that many times. It just feels like it. Bye-bye…"

"Who are you dating now?"

"No one," Leslie said, thinking that she wasn't sure what she was doing with the man she'd just realized she loved. She hadn't heard from him in three weeks. It didn't take a relationship expert to analyze what was going on. His inaction spoke volumes, and Leslie didn't like what he was saying at all. He didn't love her. Not like she loved him. And she had only herself to blame. It had taken her too many years to see what was right in front of her. And he'd witnessed everything that was her life. Obviously, it was all too messy for him and he didn't want to deal with her past.

"I can't blame you, not after that good-looking guy married someone else instead of you," Peggy said with a tilt of her head.

Leslie just nodded, not wanting to rehash old news or protect what was left of her bruised self-esteem–which Peggy seemed hell bent on kicking until it was dead. She walked toward her office without another word.

"What should I say to the reporters when they call?" Peggy asked as she followed.

"I like, 'no comment.' I think it gets the point across nicely, don't you?" Leslie responded as she shut her office door not waiting for Peggy's answer.

She leaned against the door and shut her eyes for a brief reprieve. This was going to be a long day.

Dropping her mail on the desk, she looked at her cell phone and gave a sad smile. In all the drama, she had a missed call from "Suede" aka Samuel Winston Drake. Finally, an oasis in a shit-storm morning. She hit redial and waited for her lawyer friend to answer. He was the older protective brother she'd never had.

The one man she'd never marry despite the lovely dress he'd purchased for her.

"Hello, baby, how is my beautiful today?" he asked after the first ring.

"You don't need to butter me up. I know you saw the interview," Leslie said. Sam had been a friend of hers since a very complicated time in both of their lives. They were now connected. Not only was he one of her closest friends, but he was also her attorney, and knew what each dress in her closet had done to her heart.

"Try not to let it bother you. It says more about Trudel than it does about you. Remember what they say about relatives?"

"What?" she asked.

"If you shoot them, it's murder. If you push them down the stairs, it's an accident."

"I'll keep that in mind," she grumbled as she briefly envisioned Trudel rolling down an elegant staircase in her perfect black dress and pearls.

"As your lawyer, we never had this conversation."

"Thank you," she said, and smiled genuinely for the first time since she'd seen the interview.

"How else are you holding up?"

"I'm good, but Peggy just reminded me that my last fiancé was that good-looking guy who married someone else."

"Oh Peggy," Suede laughed. "You know, every time I set foot in your office, she looks at me as if I'm a juicy filet mignon. I worry she will bite me someday."

"I kind of hope she does and I'm there to see it," Leslie said with a sardonic chuckle.

"Have your little laugh at my expense. But, let me ask you a question, Ms. Westcott. Just who is this new man Suzie has been telling me about? Some mysterious love affair that has the cool, put-together Leslie turned inside out." She wasn't comfortable with the new Sam and Suzie closeness. He was her friend, and Suzie needed to keep a tighter zip on her lip. And she didn't want to talk about it.

"I don't want to talk about him. No jinxing, no discussing, no obsessing. Not yet," she said into the phone. "Besides, there is nothing to tell." Except that he was in some far-off land on business and hadn't called her for several weeks. And she was finding it hard to eat or sleep which was totally ridiculous for such an evolved woman as herself.

"Except that you are in love with him."

"Please Suede, if you care about me at all, you will stop this conversation. If you saw the news this morning, you know that Trudel's niece falls in love all the time."

"Because she is a wonderful woman with a big, open heart."

"This isn't helping, but thank you," Leslie said.

"Okay, I know you're having a hard day today, so I'll take it easy, but I did have a couple of details on the auction that my sweet husband, Milan, asked me to iron out with you. Do you have a moment?"

"Suede, for you, I've got all day, but I don't want to talk about my dresses. I haven't decided what to do yet. Tell Milan to cool his jets."

"That's Suzie and Trudel's department. I just want to know if you'd like to have cocktails before the big event. We could get our copper fur babies, Ginger and Daisy together. Mother and daughter haven't seen each other in a bit."

"Want to come to my place?" Leslie asked.

"Sure, we'll bring the champagne and the hound. Now then, keep a handle on it. And remember, Trudel Strudel really does love you, I love you too," he said and ended the call.

Leslie glanced down at her mail. Among the assortment of catalogs and bills was a thick ecru envelope, similar to a wedding invitation. Inside was an elegant reminder for the dress auction. She had RSVP'd two months earlier, but she got the reminder with a personal note from Suzie, who was supposed to be her best friend, sister from another mister, and—not to forget—cousin!

I haven't heard how many dresses you will be adding to the show. We need your dresses by the 15th! I'll call you for pickup.

Had nobody listened to her? She'd said she'd "think about it." Had Trudel and Suzie just assumed she would be donating all her dresses to the show? Well, that was a huge assumption, and she wasn't sure how she felt about it. She was upset by the lack of regard for her feelings. Yes, she would probably donate a couple of dresses, but all of them? No way. They were her battle scars and they couldn't be more personal to her.

Each one of the dresses represented a different part of her life, a chapter that was both a learning experience and a lesson. Those dresses were hard won trophies, and she wasn't about to give them away without careful consideration. She just didn't know how much it might cost her to revisit the past.

Why was this so hard? It wasn't for other people… She just wanted to be happy, to love the man she married, to feel protected, adored, and to know that when she woke up each morning, that the man next to her loved her with all his heart. But was that too much to ask? Maybe you only did get one chance at true love in this life. Maybe she'd had her chance and it was time to give up.

PART 1

Five Years Earlier

The First James Casper

Chapter One

"I've waited for this day for so long," Trudel exclaimed as Leslie, her father, and stepmother stepped inside Trudel's Wedding Boutique as customers for the first time.

"You and me both, Aunt Trudel Strudel," Leslie said as she smiled and hugged her aunt. Leslie had been in love with Jordan Slater since she was sixteen years old. He'd appeared in her life at a difficult time just when her mother had been diagnosed with cancer. He'd been there for her throughout her mother's illness and death. It was as if she'd lost the person closest to her and been given another person to help fill the void of her loss.

Jordan had been the first boy to ask her out, the first boy to kiss her, and the only man who'd made love to her. And in the nine years since they'd started dating, they'd been best friends. And now, they were planning a life together, complete with a little house and soon, she hoped, children. She felt nothing short of a princess in a fairytale. At twenty-five they had their entire lives ahead of them.

Lucky for Leslie, her aunt had *the* wedding dress shop in Portland. Anyone who was anyone in the Pacific Northwest, bought their dress at Trudel's. And, if they didn't, they probably went to San Francisco or New York for an inferior selection not influenced by Trudel's amazing taste.

Leslie, along with her cousin, Suzie, had worked every summer at Trudel's Wedding Boutique since they were fourteen and dreamed of their very own special day.

Trudel's Wedding Boutique had proven to be Leslie's escape as a teenager and through her college years. When her mother died and her father remarried, she'd gotten closer to her cousin and her aunt. Trudel's had been salve to her deep sadness like nothing else.

How many hours had Suzie and Leslie spent discussing their future weddings? Enough to know exactly what they wanted. They took playing dress-up to a whole new level, but that was to be expected—they had access to hundreds of dresses just waiting to be tried on.

Ever the shrewd businesswoman, Trudel encouraged them and would complete their look with veils, jewelry, high heels, and flowers. Then she'd photograph them for her ads and website. It was the ultimate in fairytale dress-up and never grew old.

But today was different. Leslie couldn't take a deep breath with her stomach full of butterflies, because today this was for real.

Throughout the morning as she'd prepared for her appointment, she'd had to blink back tears, thinking of her mother and how much she would have enjoyed this day. Leslie knew she should be thankful for the people she did have in her life: her father, her aunt, and her cousin. Her relationship with her stepmother Denice was still formal and strained despite the years she'd been a part of Leslie's life. The woman had done her best to get close to Leslie, but the fact that she was only fifteen years older than Leslie hadn't done their relationship any favors. Parents and children shouldn't have the same fashion sense or like the same music. It just wasn't normal.

Suzie was being groomed to take over the bridal shop when Trudel retired, which would probably never happen. Married the previous summer to her college sweetheart, Timothy, Suzie had set the bar fairly high when it came to having a beautiful wedding dress.

Working with her father and taking on more and more of the business, Leslie was quickly making a name for herself in the luxury real estate market. She wished she could say she'd done it all on her own, but her father had been selling real estate for almost thirty years—or as she liked to think of it, since Denice had been a child.

With Leslie handling the business, her father and Denice had more time to escape to their new passion, winter in Palm Springs. Leslie didn't mind. She liked the idea of them being in another state. But on a more personal level, there was still a part of her that hadn't gotten used to seeing her father with another woman not her mother. She was getting better with it, but it hadn't come easily.

Sitting on the richly upholstered serpentine couch in the VIP area, Leslie tried to relax as Trudel's assistant asked, "Would you like some champagne or orange juice or a mix of the two? How about we have a little mimosa to start off the appointment this lovely Saturday morning?"

They all opted for champagne, and Aunt Trudel pulled up a chair to start taking notes in her special little black moleskin book using a silver, bejeweled Tiffany pen. All the ladies at Trudel's wore black and carried moleskins with their bejeweled Tiffany pens. And they all dressed like Trudel.

Trudel's petite frame rocked an elegant black dress with black sheer stockings and high heels. A triple strand of pearls completed the look. Aunt Trudel once commented that she liked the elegance that wearing black spoke without saying a word. It helped that Aunt Trudel was barely five feet tall, had a gorgeous figure, and white-blonde hair. Leslie's mother had been a blonde as well, a soft, ash blonde—a little more natural than her sister-in-law, Trudel. And unlike Trudel, Leslie and her mother were natural blondes. Leslie inherited her mother's Swedish looks but had her father and aunt's quick German mind.

Denice was the exact opposite of all the women in the family and had dark brown, almost black hair with olive skin and a tiny figure that put Aunt Trudel's curves to shame.

"I think I know the answer to all the questions I'm about to ask, but I want you to have the full bridal experience! Now, is there a specific silhouette that you're looking for today?"

"Aunt Trudel, you know I've seen hundreds of brides come through here. And I've tried on every silhouette possible. The best thing I can do is to be quiet and let you and Suzie pick some dresses for me that you both feel will be most flattering to my figure. I will add that I'm not sure about strapless and bare arms. I'm not a fan of too many ruffles or tulle. The rest is up to you. Oh, and I don't want to look like Cinderella in a ball gown."

"But a ball gown would look so pretty on you," Denice offered, unsolicited. The other women ignored her as Leslie wrinkled her nose in displeasure behind her stepmother's back. Suzie gave a half laugh and then caught herself. Denice's opinion did not and would not factor into any decisions today.

"We raised you right," Aunt Trudel said with a nod to Leslie's father. "Normally, I'd ask you about the venue, but I know! What a lovely idea! A wedding at a lighthouse. And yes, you can definitely wear bare arms."

Leslie and Jordan were getting married at Heceta Head Lighthouse along the rocky Oregon coast. Leslie had been going there since she was a child. She liked standing on the bluff and looking south at miles and miles of coastline. Some of her fondest memories of her mother and father came from those trips to the beach. The memories were so dear that she could sometimes feel the pain of the loss as if it were a physical tug at her heart.

Leslie liked to think that since the lighthouse was one of her mother's favorite places that she would be happy about her daughter's choice to marry there.

Their reception would be at the large, white Victorian caretaker's house that was now a bed and breakfast just to the east of the bluff. The day after the ceremony, they'd drive back to Portland and catch a plane to Paris for a two-week honeymoon.

"Now, is there a price range your dad is comfortable with for his only child who happens to be a daughter and is only going to get married once in her life? Might I also add, the last single girl in our little family?"

Leslie's father, George laughed, and said, "Whatever my girl wants is fine, Trudel, but I expect a family discount, sis."

It felt like an hour passed before Suzie and Trudel returned, but when Leslie glanced at the clock, only fifteen minutes had gone by. Leslie highly doubted Trudel would be giving any family discount. She was just a wee bit cunning and hadn't quite accepted Denice into the family. It amused Leslie that she, Suzie, and Trudel were united in solidarity against the woman her father had married. They were nothing but nice to her, but they never let her get too close. Leslie knew her aunt and cousin were following her lead and it warmed her heart.

Leslie knew it was a bit unfair to Denice, but it had little to do with her new stepmother and much more to do with how quickly her father had remarried. They'd never forgiven her father for moving on just months after Sally's death. When he'd introduced them to Denice, he'd been so smitten, acting like a teenager. Leslie had cried to Trudel and Suzie that it was unfair that her father had gotten over her mother so quickly, while Leslie was still in so much pain.

"It is so odd to be on the other side of this," Leslie said, trying to keep her excitement at bay. When she and Suzie were young, Aunt Trudel called them "young consultants in training." They had learned to be careful with the dresses, treating them like valuable treasures.

"You've waited twenty-five years, and I couldn't be happier," her father said, bringing tears to his daughter's eyes.

"Your dad is so proud," Denice managed as she took a big swig of her champagne and then observed, "Trudel really does have a beautiful shop."

"How many years has it been since you've set foot in this shop, Dad?" Leslie asked.

"Oh, I suppose I picked you up a time or two when you worked here in the summer."

"Only ten or so years ago," Leslie said with a laugh.

"Trust me, honey, nothing has changed," he said with a smile.

As Leslie predicted, Aunt Trudel's excellent taste was on full display. All the dresses she selected fit Leslie's 5'8" curvy frame. But it was the Alexandra lace bodice dress with silk trumpet mermaid skirt by James Casper that brought tears to her eyes when she slipped into the cool, ruched fabric. It was perfect for an outdoor, summer wedding.

Aunt Trudel nodded in satisfaction and then nudged Suzie as if to say, "Nailed it!"

"I think this is it," Leslie said as she spun around in front of her family, thinking of Jordan standing on the cliffs at Heceta Head, watching as she walked toward him.

"It hugs you in all the right places," Suzie added. "Jordan will pass out in awe. It's just that beautiful on you."

"Your hair is so exquisite long, have you thought about wearing it down?" Aunt Trudel asked.

Jordan liked her hair worn down. He spent hours just running his fingers through it as he called her, "My little Viking princess."

"Down, but if it is a windy day, I'll need to wear it up. I'm hoping for down with maybe a few flowers in the headband or veil."

Gardenias would be the only choice. She loved them with their lemony almost tropical scent. And the first corsage Jordan had given her on their first date in high school contained three gardenias to complement her dark green dress.

"I think that would be lovely," Denice proclaimed as she dabbed at her eyes with a tissue. Leslie tried to ignore that the woman was crying. It wasn't as if Leslie was her daughter, but thankfully they hadn't had additional children, so really this was the closest Denice was going to get.

"What do you think, Dad?" Leslie asked.

"You look beautiful. I think Jordan is one lucky man. I just hope he is worthy."

It was an old joke between them. "After all these years, seriously? Yes, Dad, he is worthy. I promise."

There was no point in looking further. All her time in this boutique had culminated to this moment. And Leslie felt as if a missing piece of the puzzle of her life had slipped into an empty space, completing the picture. This was her dress, and in six and a half months, she would wear it as she walked across a cliff side meadow to her future husband. How had she gotten so lucky? She could barely speak; she didn't want to take one misstep and wake up from her lovely dream.

They left the shop after picking out her veil, shoes, and a garter with a blue ribbon on it. Suzie promised to take care of all the packages until Aunt Trudel called them back for her first dress fitting in four months. In two weeks, they'd all meet again with the bridesmaids to select dresses.

"So…" Jordan began and then stopped. Leslie knew he was waiting for her to disclose some small detail from her afternoon at Aunt

Trudel's. She'd never been good at keeping secrets from him, but who could blame her? He was gorgeous with thick, unruly brown hair, and the sweetest blue eyes that seemed to look through her. He only needed to glance at her, give her a small smile, and turn up just one corner of his delicious mouth to churn her insides to mush. It had always been this way between them, this attraction that was so strong, yet so familiar, it was almost as if they were part of the same soul.

But discussing her dress—this was different. This was secret wedding stuff.

"Don't even try. You aren't getting a thing out of me," she said and helped herself to another bite of marinated vegetables. Jordan liked to grill, and even though it was January, he had been out on their back patio grilling steak and vegetable shish kebobs in the cool air. It was one of her favorite meals, but she still wasn't going to tell him anything about her wedding dress. Call her superstitious; she was playing by the rules.

After refilling her wine glass, he said, "Oh come on! I've seen you with wedding magazines ever since this summer. Is it a full ball gown or fit and flare?"

"No way, you've been watching too much 'Say Yes to the Dress.' And you sound just like Denice. She tried to influence us, but we ignored her," she said, spearing a piece of marinated filet.

"I feel a little sorry for her. She tries hard, and I think she genuinely cares about you," Jordan said.

"Okay, okay," Leslie said. She offered, "For you, and you alone, I'll try to be nicer to Denice."

"That is very cool of you. A cool woman like that, well, I want to marry that woman. Now, tell me about your dress."

"That is secret bride stuff. You don't get to know until the first Saturday in July. This isn't a negotiation. I want you to be surprised."

"Did you at least say yes to the dress?"

"Yes, I did, thank you very much."

"What if I told you that I have a little surprise for you?"

"What is it?" she asked, taking the wine glass and sneaking a small sip.

"I picked up a little something downtown."

"From where downtown?" she asked.

"Sauveterre Jewelers."

Her heart beat a little faster. Her mother's engagement ring had come from Sauveterre Jewelers thirty years earlier, and someday, hers would as well. She touched the heart-shaped diamond from her mother's ring that she now wore on a platinum chain around her neck. It was her most treasured piece of jewelry. Her dad had given it to her when she graduated from college. They'd thought of using it for their engagement ring, but Jordan had other ideas. He wanted her ring to be something he'd designed.

But the ring was temporarily on hold. They'd discussed this when they got engaged. Jordan didn't have enough in savings to buy her the kind of ring he'd wanted to, so they'd decided to hold off on an engagement ring for several years and opted to buy their first house instead.

It was the right, financially responsible, mature decision for two, young, professional people to make, but Leslie still secretly coveted the idea of an engagement ring. Something she could show people when she told them she was engaged. When you told someone you were engaged, their eyes immediately looked at the third finger of your left hand. She'd always had to explain that her diamond was in the form of a three-bedroom, two-bath, mid-century ranch-style home in Raleigh Hills that they were lovingly restoring. But the disclosure of a house never had the same excitement as a sparkly ring, a purely sentimental indulgence.

Jordan gave an exaggerated sigh. "I picked up a little something for you, but I don't want you to get your hopes up. Remember, it is only a little something."

She wondered if it was something cute like a silver heart bracelet. There had been an upcoming Valentine's Day display in Sauveterre Jewelers' window last week, and it had featured heart jewelry. And that would be just like Jordan. He was incredibly sentimental. She had several heart bracelets and earrings from Valentine's Days past, and never grew tired of them.

As she thought all this over, Jordan stood from the table, dropped to one knee before her, and opened the little black velvet box that had materialized from a pocket.

She didn't understand. This wasn't supposed to be happening right now. They had a house to finish renovating. But below Jordan's smiling face was an open box and a diamond ring. It was too large, too expensive for their budget. What had he done?

Leslie could see the beautiful ring in the dim candlelight, a sparkling, impressive diamond bracketed by two beautiful stones.

Speechless, she leaned forward out of her chair and all but fell into Jordan's arms to kiss him. Jordan pulled back from their kiss to place the ring on the third finger of her left hand.

"How did you do this?" she asked as they faced each other, both on their knees in their cramped little dining room.

Ignoring her question, Jordan asked, "Leslie, I've loved you since the day you agreed to go to Dairy Queen with me after school. Remember? It was after seventh-period physics class. I hated that class, but I loved sitting next to you. Would you please spend your life with me, marry me, and be my forever partner in crime?"

"Yes!" Leslie answered, crying for the second time that day. "But how—"

He answered her with a kiss and one little word, "Surprise!"

How could she be happier than she had been that morning? Just how much better could it get between them? She loved Jordan with her heart and soul. She knew how lucky she was. She felt it in her heart as she looked at him and saw his love for her reflected in his eyes.

They made love that night in the newly redecorated master bedroom of their little house. It smelled of fresh paint, the soft sage color of Italian cypress trees, and the new comforter and dust ruffle that smelled a little like the department store they had come from. Later, as Leslie looked through the skylight in the vaulted ceiling of the master bedroom, she saw the moon and smiled. What a perfect night! What a perfect day! Nagging little questions about the beautiful ring continued to poke at her. How could Jordan have afforded this diamond? What would it do to their budget? He had to still be making payments on it. She didn't like the idea of having the ring belong more to the jeweler than to them.

"Hey there," Jordan whispered as he spooned her from behind. "Is your ring too bright in the moonlight for you to sleep?"

Turning toward him, she smiled, and said, "It is so beautiful! The diamond, I don't want to ask, but I have to know how did you afford this? What about our budget?"

Jordan was a high school science teacher, and she knew that he didn't make a ton of money. In fact, she made almost twice what Jordan had their first year out of college. It didn't matter; her money was his, and vice versa. They were partners in this life. She loved him, and she didn't want to burden him with the debt of an engagement ring despite how much she wanted to wear his ring on her hand.

"The diamond was on my grandmother's hand for over fifty years. My mother gave it to me at Christmas. And the sunstones, well, I got those on our trip to Eastern Oregon in August."

"When you proposed?"

"Yes."

"But I didn't see any sunstones like these. The ones you had were cloudy and more orange. This is red and pink and fiery! You found this?"

"Yes, I didn't show you the *big* rock I found because I wanted it to be a surprise. It was a hard secret to keep from you, but I didn't think you'd hold it against me. The jeweler cut it for me and faceted the stones. I think he did a great job."

"It's… so… beautiful," she said, tears streaming down her face. The ring was perfect, a huge diamond with two brilliant, deep pinky-tangerine sunstones framing the diamond and emitting all the other colors of the rainbow. If she had asked Jordan for her dream engagement ring, he couldn't have gotten it more right.

"It was made for you, my ray of sunshine. Now stop crying and kiss me."

Chapter Two

"I want you to think of this as my bachelor party," Jordan said as he inspected the ropes and other assorted climbing gear that littered their living room floor.

"Cave diving? Seriously?" Leslie asked, looking at what would become Jordan's lifeline in the cave he was diving into two weeks before their wedding. "I think, no, scratch that, I would *prefer* you getting lap dances in Vegas as long as you kept all your clothes on, and your pants zipped up."

"Honey, you need to relax. You know I've done this many times before. I don't take chances, and I'm careful," Jordan said, pulling her into his arms. "I love you, and I'm not going to do anything to jeopardize my safety. Besides, I might bring you back some pretty rocks to play with, maybe make you a necklace of fluorite or more sunstones. Who knows what treasures I'll find in that dark cave?"

She hated it when he was away from her. She didn't sleep well, and even food didn't taste as good. There was a deep loneliness that always made its presence known, a kind of irrational insecurity that never felt good. In fact, she could count on one hand how many times they had been apart in the last few years because he felt exactly the same way. When he was away, she felt like a part of her was missing. She supposed it was a weak female response, but she couldn't help it. Jordan completed her.

She didn't need any damn fluorites. She needed Jordan.

"But why now? You're going to be gone this weekend climbing Mt. Hood, and next diving into a dark, scary, rocky cave. And I don't need a fluorite necklace. I just need you."

"And you will be stuck with me for at least fifty years if you're lucky," he said, winking at her. "You know I don't like being away from you, but I've promised the students since March. I can't miss Mt. Hood, besides it is only a day thing. Easy peasy. With any luck, I'll be home in time for dinner. In fact, make a reservation at the Indian place for eight. I'll be hungry after the climb."

Ignoring him, she said, "I will worry because that is what I do." He passed by her and gave her behind a playful swat.

"I would expect no less."

This year, one of the kids in Jordan's geology class started talking about climbing Mt. Hood, something Jordan had done eleven times. Eleven times she had waited for him at Timberline Lodge and eleven times he had successfully climbed Mt. Hood and made it back to the lodge in time for dinner. Only this time, she had too many wedding details to arrange and wouldn't be waiting at the lodge.

Jordan being Jordan, he'd arranged for an end-of-school celebration trip planned with ten students, a couple of teachers, and a bunch of parents. She was thankful she was marrying a giving, caring person who couldn't say no to his students. She was just glad he hadn't asked her to climb or jump into anything. Besides, she was terrified of heights, and he knew it.

But the cave jumping—looking for more rocks to fuel the rockhound in him was all him. He'd planned the trip with three of his closest buddies. That was a good thing.

"Well, I guess I will be busy writing thank you notes for my shower gifts, while you're diving into dark depths to the center of the Earth. Just don't think I'm letting you off the hook on the wedding gifts. You're writing those notes with me, especially to your Aunt Betsy who gave us the bacon-of-the-month subscription."

He kissed her cheek, "Thank you, baby. I love you, and I'll miss you like crazy."

"You'd better," she said.

She needed to check on the flowers and start making a list for their honeymoon in Paris. The caterer was giving her grief about choosing entrée selections, and she had her final dress fitting at Aunt Trudel's. And she had promised Denice a spa day because she was trying to take Jordan's advice to heart. She was trying to be nicer to Denice.

"You're getting the trackers and stuff for Mt. Hood, right? And the cave, right?"

"Yes, for the tenth time, honey. I'm picking them up here, and they will work both on the mountain and in a cave. You need to relax."

"How about my Mophie for your cell phone? You know it holds four full charges?"

"I know, and I have power bars, and little blankets, and flares, and extra batteries for my headlamps, and duct tape. I have everything anyone would need for survival. I could survive on the duct tape alone. I could be trapped for two months and walk out with a nice full beard, but I'm taking my Leatherman tool, to shave just for you."

"Stop it," she said, placing her hands over her ears, "Just humor me and tell me you will be okay."

"I love you. I'm not going anywhere. I'll be the guy in the monkey suit at Heceta Head marrying you, so you'd better be ready because I can't wait to start the rest of my life as your husband."

"I can't wait," she said with a smile. It was just so easy between them. They never fought. They talked, but it was never hostile. They understood each other. "And I can't wait for Paris. Did you find your passport yet?"

He went to a drawer in one of the end tables, opened it, and held up his passport. "Good for five more years. Start planning. I want us to explore someplace new every summer."

"Paris is a great start."

"What do you say to Italy next year? Maybe the Amalfi coastline? Positano?" he asked, putting his arms around her. "Or we could go someplace exotic like Fiji or Bora Bora."

"I don't care where we go, just as long as we go together," she said and kissed him. "And as long as you don't make me climb any mountains or jump off any cliffs."

"You might like it."

"Stop it." Leslie was scared of heights, and always had been. Even standing near the top step of a ladder could make her fingers and toes start to tingle painfully. It was bad enough that Mt. Hood sacrificed several climbers a year, but they were nameless. Her fiancé was the most precious part of her life.

"Relax. I would never want to do anything to the love of my life that would make her feel uneasy. Trust me, honey. I will take care of myself, so I can come back to you. You are a motivation like no other."

They talked around Leslie as if she wasn't there. She'd heard the front door opening and closing all day. Sometimes they came into her bedroom, creeping softly down the hall, and looking in at her. If she was awake, they whispered soothing, comforting words to her, and then to each other as they left the room in shifts. They placed plates of food in front of her that she ignored. They tried to make her drink everything from water to vodka, offered her every kind of pill from an aspirin to a Xanax. Eventually, they would fade away to what they thought were quiet places in her house, the house she had bought with Jordan, to talk about her as if she wasn't there.

The only problem was that she could still hear them talking from where she hid in the master bedroom. The house wasn't that big, and with the hardwood floors, vaulted ceilings, and no other sound but voices; she knew exactly what they were saying, and it was all bad. Worst of all, she couldn't turn them off.

Denice talked to the reporters who had camped out on the front lawn and tried to get them to leave. But Denice felt sorry for the poor young reporter who looked about eighteen, she told Leslie's father. Maybe they should take him a sandwich.

God help her, she was so clueless sometimes—she completely missed the point.

Her father suggested they call the police and have all the reporters removed, including the kid.

Leslie wanted to yell, "Shut up! Everyone shut up!" She barely had the energy to raise her head off the pillow, and when she did, she was dizzy and nauseous.

Denice reasoned that the reporters, as well as all the rescue people, had worked very hard for three days keeping Jordan's story alive. Three long and horrible days that were never-ending torture until finally they were able to rescue Jordan's body from a crevasse, where he'd fallen eighty feet to his death on Mt. Hood.

Leslie was thankful for the people involved in the rescue, the Black Hawk helicopters, and the mountaineering teams. She only wished she could pay back all the people who had helped.

She heard snippets of the people talking in her living room. Apparently, public opinion didn't want taxpayer money funding the recovery of Jordan's body from the crevasse. A GoFundMe page had even been established to help pay back the bill.

Leslie had been at Timberline Lodge at the base of the mountain when word had come in that the rescuers had gotten a look inside the crevasse, the rescue turning into a recovery of bodies.

Leslie only hoped that both Jordan and the student who had caused the fall, had died quickly, on impact. The story of how the student slipped and fell into Jordan, taking them both into the crevasse was hard enough. The thought that Jordan or his student might have lived for hours or days and suffered—

She couldn't, wouldn't go there.

And now, anytime she shut her eyes, she pictured Jordan's shattered body lying on the ice, his arms and legs twisted and broken. Or she pictured him frozen, his skin a lifeless blue-gray.

She'd been worried about a cave when she should have been worried about a mountain. A mountain he told her he knew like the back of his hand. An old friend, he'd once said. In actuality, it was his worst enemy.

She heard Aunt Trudel say to Denice, "I've put her wedding dress in storage at my shop. And a few months from now, if she doesn't think she could wear it if she ever decides to get married again, well, then I'll just sell it in my fall blowout sale. It has been altered to fit her, so it won't be an easy sale, but we'll get something for it. It won't be a total loss—"

Denice responded, "I think I've called everyone: the florist, the caterer, and Heceta Head Lighthouse for the reception. Then there is the honeymoon. I don't know how to ask her about that. They have plane tickets and reservations at hotels all around France."

"Maybe she will still want to go," her father said. "It might be good for her to get away."

"I have a feeling your daughter won't want to go on her honeymoon by herself," Denice said, censuring her husband.

"George, sometimes you just really show that you are lacking a sensitivity gene," Aunt Trudel snapped, being a little less politically correct. "I can't believe we were raised by the same parents."

"Really Trudel? Is that necessary?"

"Yes, it is," Suzie chimed in.

Denice to her father: "Can you believe that Jordan's mother is already planning a funeral? Don't you think she should consult with Jordan's fiancée? I never thought she liked or valued Leslie enough. She didn't think Leslie was good enough for Jordan. They should have been beyond thankful that their son met Leslie. Of all the nerve—"

It was the first time she'd ever heard Denice defend her and she didn't know what to think of it. Denice was stepping up, she couldn't deny it.

Her father commented to Denice, "My God, Leslie didn't die. It's like she's in a trance, it is like talking to a zombie. I don't know, Denice. We might need to send her somewhere for help if she doesn't snap out of this. I wish her mother was here. She always knew how to get through to Leslie. I think she might be having a mental breakdown—"

Then she heard Suzie, beloved Suzie, the closest person she had to a sister, closer than most sisters. "Excuse me, but would everyone shut the Hell up? For God's sake, my poor, tender cousin is in shock. She isn't having a mental breakdown. She just lost the love of her life for fuck's sake. She needs time to cry or to scream or to eat cheesecake for the next week and not be judged. She needs time to come to grips with what she has lost. She needs us to leave her alone until she figures this out or asks us for help. She needs those reporters to stop stepping on her flowers and get lost. They aren't going to get a photo of the grieving fiancée who isn't going to be a bride. Those fucking vultures want to exploit her sadness to get more followers on their news stories, their Twitter, their Facebook page. They need to get lost. Hell, she needs us to get lost—"

Those words were the first that made sense to Leslie in the last four horrifying days of her life. Suzie got it. Suzie understood. Leslie lifted her head, the dizziness from hours of sobbing and tears getting worse by the moment. Sitting up, she slowly put her feet on the floor. Eventually, she made it into the master bath, where she brushed her hair and teeth, and then made her way out to where they all waited to see the devastated fiancée. She wouldn't disappoint them, but she would kick each and every one of them, but Suzie, out of her house.

Jordan would have hated the funeral, Leslie thought as she rode in the backseat of her father's big black Cadillac Escalade. This was the car he liked to take home buyers around in. He called it, "The Whale Mobile." As she rode in the backseat, she felt small, like a little child, the tag-a-long in her father and Denice's life.

Today wasn't going to be fun; Leslie knew it like she knew that the next two hours would be worse than anything she'd endured in the last week.

Her prediction was right. The cold funeral had not even been about Jordan.

They had once talked about what kind of sendoff they would each want. They agreed it would be light-hearted and fun with people telling stories with memories of happy times. They wanted photos and happiness, a celebration of a great life. Not sadness. They wanted liquor and laughter. They wanted joy.

There was an hour and a half church service arranged by Jordan's mother, Anna, which hadn't been fun or light-hearted. There was one photo of Jordan, one that Leslie didn't like, adorning the altar. No one spoke of Jordan's humor or desire for adventure. They didn't say he died doing something that he loved. They didn't mention Leslie or the fact he should have been getting ready for his wedding which would have been less than a week away. The priest talked about welcoming him into Heaven. They prayed and prayed, but they didn't know him. Not like Leslie had.

Big surprise for you, Father, Leslie thought, Jordan believed in reincarnation, not Heaven. It had been a hard concept for Leslie when Jordan had discussed it with her, but she had listened and agreed that he made some good points. She still believed in Heaven. She had to because she needed to think of her mother there, watching over her. But the sendoff Jordan got would have made him angry. He'd once said his mother didn't know him. He was right.

So, when she prayed in the church, she spoke to Jordan. She told him she knew he would think this was utter bullshit. He'd be incensed that his mother had commandeered everything and taken over when she should have asked Leslie for input. And the fact she hadn't made her an A-number-one bitch to the highest degree.

It didn't matter. Their love had been real. It was still real. She'd never lose his love. That was all that mattered. His domineering mother couldn't take that away from Leslie.

The weather for late June was unpleasant, a cold rain descending on everything for an entire week starting with the discovery of Jordan's body right up to and including the funeral and graveside service. All the rain fit Leslie's mood perfectly as if the world was crying with her.

Several rolls of thunder boomed at the cemetery as they were about to commit a box holding the body of the man she loved into the cold, wet dirt. A part of her wondered if all the metal framed umbrellas shielding her were a good idea. If lightning struck, it would be a painful death, but she didn't care. It would be quick. In fact, maybe she could fall right in on top of Jordan and save all the people the cost of another funeral and box. They could just shovel the dirt on top of her and be done with it.

Over a hundred and fifty thousand people die every day around the world. But when Jordan died, Leslie thought the world should have stopped to take notice, but still, people went to work, walked their dogs, made breakfast, took trips, got speeding tickets, had babies, bought groceries, and complained about their jobs. The world went on, despite her life crashing in around her.

Leslie didn't hear the words as the priest committed Jordan's body to the cold, wet earth.

He's not there, she thought as they lowered the casket. That is just his physical remains. Jordan left this world ten days ago when he fell into the crevasse.

Denice and her father stood on either side of her offering their unspoken support.

Leslie had chosen a black sheath dress with matching bolero jacket. It was one of Jordan's favorite outfits on her, and she knew he'd be proud of her for not lashing out at his mother or creating a scene. Oh, how she wanted to create a scene.

As they walked back to the Escalade, Jordan's mother asked for a moment to speak to Leslie. Denice handed her one of their large black umbrellas, and Leslie stepped to the side, standing on the edge of the grass feeling her heels sink into the soggy sod as she waited to hear what Anna had to say.

"Thank you, my dear. I know this is a hard day for you, too," Anna began.

"A hard day for us, both," Leslie replied.

"Yes," Anna said, pointing to the ring finger on Leslie's left hand.

Leslie looked at her engagement ring and felt her heart tighten. It represented every dream and hope in her life that wouldn't come true.

Anna started again, "About your ring, my dear—"

"What about it?" Leslie asked.

"You see, that is a family diamond. I gave it to Jordan because he was my eldest son. We weren't as close as I am to my other two sons but I felt it was the right thing to do. Now that Jordan has passed, it is only right that I give it to his younger brother."

Leslie froze. The old bat wanted the ring back. There was no way she was going to part with her ring. The old lady could have the diamond, but not the sunstones, they were hers.

"You want the diamond," Leslie clarified.

"Why don't you give me the ring and I'll have the diamond removed."

"No," Leslie said, her hand making a fist to hold her ring tight. "I'll have the diamond returned to you, but I'm keeping the ring."

"Why don't you just let me have it—"

"I said no," Leslie said ready to strike this woman with her umbrella if it came to that. Maybe there would be a scene after all.

"I am only trying to make your life easier. I just planned the funeral—"

"Without my input. Jordan would have been horrified by that church service, and you know it. It was disrespectful to his memory."

"Well, I'm not going to stand here in a graveyard and have an argument with you on the day we buried my son."

"Good, then we're done here."

"Leslie, we have a few other things to discuss… Now about his things—"

"Seriously? I just lost the love of my life, and you want to discuss 'things'?"

"Now Leslie—"

"Anna," Leslie said, pulling her anger inside and reminding herself that this woman didn't matter. "I'll box up his 'things' and get them back to you in the next couple of weeks. And I'll call you when the diamond is ready."

Not waiting for an answer, she turned and walked across the drenched lawn to meet her father and Denice, biting hard on her lip until she tasted blood. It took everything in her power not to turn back to Anna and say, "Don't ask me about the ring again, you'll get back your damn diamond when and if I feel like it, you nervy bitch!"

She didn't look back at Anna and hoped she'd never have to talk to or see the woman again.

Leslie refused to go the reception at Anna's house. She was done with the whole ceremony of death. No one, especially not Anna, could know what she was going through. It was time for Leslie to take care of Leslie. Screw what everyone else thought.

"But honey, you have to go," her father said, "He was your fiancé. People will talk."

Like he suddenly cared what people thought, Leslie mused. What a hypocrite.

"No," Leslie replied, curling up into a ball on the too-short couch in the living room of her father and Denice's riverfront condo.

"Leslie, honey," her father pleaded. "It just doesn't look good. It is disrespectful."

"No, not after what I just saw. Not after she degraded Jordan's life to a church service and a burial in the rain. Forget it."

"But what will we say?" her father asked.

"Lie, tell everyone that I'm sick," she said and then, narrowing her eyes, she added, "Tell his mother that it might be morning sickness."

"Oh Leslie," Denice asked, "Are you—"

"I'm not pregnant. There wasn't time. We wanted children though. We couldn't wait," she said, giving them a pointed glare.

"Okay, okay, we can go, and say you weren't feeling well," her father explained.

"What can I get you, honey?" Denice asked.

"Fast-forward my life. Let me know how it all turns out," she replied bitterly.

Chapter Three

Leslie had aged ten years in a week and a half. She no longer cared how she looked. She had something to do, and the faster, the better. And she didn't trust anyone to do it for her. Trudel, Suzie, and Denice had all volunteered, but this was an errand that only she could do.

She stepped inside elegant Sauveterre Jewelers and recognized the matriarch of the business, Caroline Sauveterre, who approached her with arms outstretched. Leslie didn't think. She didn't just get a greeting from the other woman; Leslie sank into her arms and let herself be hugged. Caroline and Leslie's mother had gone to high school together. Leslie's family bought all their jewelry from Sauveterre Jewelers. Caroline had pierced Leslie's ears when she was fourteen so she could wear the pair of pearl studs that Aunt Trudel gave her for her birthday.

"Oh Leslie, I couldn't believe it when I heard the news. I'm so very sorry."

She hadn't cried in a few hours, but with Caroline's words and the fresh reminder of her mother, she couldn't seem to stop. And then, the little speech she'd rehearsed on the way over forgotten, she started blabbering about her ring.

"It's going to be all right. We'll take care of the ring, I promise," Caroline reassured her.

"Will you take care of the diamond?" Leslie asked. "Jordan's mother wants the diamond back. It was a family heirloom, and now that Jordan is dead, she's going to give the stone to his younger brother. But I want the ring and the sunstones. They are mine. I don't want it destroyed. It is all I have left—"

Caroline dried her tears with tissues and patted her back with a genuine comfort that only mothers seemed to know how to provide.

"Of course, don't worry, we won't hurt your ring," Caroline said softly to soothe her. "It's going to be alright. Come on back, and I'll have Charlie help you. You remember our son, Charlie, don't you? He is a few years older than you, but he was around the shop when you used to come in with your mother. He is the one who designed your engagement ring with your fiancé. He's the one who cut the sunstones. Did you know that? He's become quite a gemologist in his own right. I don't think you've seen him in years. He will be able to help."

The other woman was talking to fill the space, talking to distract Leslie. And even though she knew what the other woman was doing, she listened and let herself be led to the back of the store where a man straightened at their approach and set aside his tools.

When Charles Sauveterre had been in the store when Leslie was a child, she had never liked him. He'd always looked angry and stared at her as if she were a mutant.

As a six-year-old, she remembered complaining to her mother, "I don't want to go to the jewelry store with you. Please don't make me go. Charles hates me."

Sally had laughed a little, not so much as to totally discount her daughter's feelings, but she had said, "Darling, his mother tells me he is painfully shy. I think he actually likes you quite a bit. And I'll let you in on a little secret, I think he might even have a little crush on you."

"He hates me," Leslie had repeated, ignoring her mother.

"I really don't think he does. I'll make you a deal. You come with me to the jewelry store, and I'll make sure he doesn't look at you like he hates you. Then we will go get ice cream. Deal?"

She'd gone and been rewarded with ice cream. That had been one of her mother's strengths, always thinking the best of a person or a situation. Her optimism hadn't rubbed off on Leslie. She never felt comfortable around Charles.

Now, all these years later, he was the man who had not only designed her engagement ring but had cut the stones.

Had Jordan told her that? She couldn't remember—she didn't think so. She would have remembered a detail like that because of her past association with Charles. But the thought that she would forget anything Jordan had said burned deep. She wouldn't be able to ask him anything, ever again. What other small details about the love of her life would she forget? Would it someday all just mist over and be a distant, fuzzy memory? The thought, the very idea that she could lose more of Jordan had her sobbing into her tissue.

Charles had his mother's brown eyes and that same aloofness to his expression that Leslie remembered from her childhood. She couldn't believe her mother had thought it was a crush. Her mother had missed the mark. He wasn't shy, he was surly. None of his mother's warmth had rubbed off on him. Not even a grin. Of course, he'd be the one she'd have to deal with today.

Was it her imagination or had his expression hardened at the very sight of her?

Regardless of how uncomfortable he made her feel, Leslie did have to admit that aside from the scowl, everything else about him was quite a bit different than she remembered. He was tall and broad shouldered; he had grown out of the scrawny boy he'd once been. He now assessed her with a square jaw, high cheekbones, and those unsettling brown eyes. He had an aquiline nose that looked like he'd been chiseled to resemble Michael Angelo's David. Yes, the stars had aligned when it came to handing out looks on the day he was born. His unruly brown hair was now wavy and thick, no doubt tousled perfectly because he was an unnaturally lucky bastard.

And then Charles met her eyes, and she didn't imagine it, he flinched. So, he still looked at her as if she were a troll. This time he was probably right. Her hair, which she'd washed and styled sometime in the last few days, was flat, in an untidy ponytail. She hadn't worn any makeup, why bother? And when she looked in the mirror, she was shocked by the creature who looked back at her with purple circles under her eyes and a gray, unhealthy pallor.

"I was very sorry to hear about Jordan," Charles said, sounding sincere as he shook her hand. "We had discussed going rock hounding sometime in the future. I liked him, he was a real good guy."

"Thank you," Leslie managed.

"I don't want to upset you further, but I have to tell you, Jordan was so happy to be engaged to you. I admired his enthusiasm. I want you to know how much I enjoyed working on your ring with Jordan. It was a fun project getting to cut such beautiful sunstones. It is rare that I see someone so much in love. And I see a lot of couples buying rings."

"Thank you for saying that," Leslie said.

"It's the truth," Charles said.

Leslie looked back at Caroline who was helping another customer. "Your mother is wonderful." And then she added, "I don't think I could have done this without the greeting she gave me. I felt like family coming in the door."

His demeanor changed—the coldness replaced by a warmth she hadn't expected.

"Your family has been coming here for years. You are family." She nodded, hearing the emotion in his words. He was the last person she'd have thought would understand, let alone sympathize.

"How can I help today?"

Leslie's voice cracked as she tried to hold it together, but then she thought of Jordan's mother and her obscene request. "Jordan's mother wants the diamond back, which is insulting enough, but the thought of destroying this beautiful ring that Jordan wanted me to have, that Jordan had made JUST for me… I can't, it's just killing me. Is there anything you can do to save my ring? I'm begging you. I know this sounds crazy, but I feel like it is the last part of Jordan that I have left. Can you save my ring?"

Charles got it. "Yes, of course. I can definitely do that."

Well, at least they agreed on something.

They ended up sitting across from each other with an antique table between them. Charles held out his hand, and asked, "May I?"

Leslie reluctantly placed her left hand in his.

"It is beautiful. After all these years of designing, it is one of my personal favorites," Charles said as he gently set her hand on the table.

"I didn't know you were a designer."

"I've been cutting stones since I was fifteen," Charles said.

"I can't lose this ring," Leslie said, the words tumbling out of her mouth with little grace or elegance.

"It's going to be all right. Pardon me for just a moment. I want to get something to show you." He disappeared from the table for a few moments and then returned with a small manila envelope.

"I don't know if Jordan told you about these," he said as he poured the contents of the envelope on a black velvet cushion. Three reddish-pink stones tumbled onto the velvet.

Leslie saw the fire and the color. "Are they sunstones?"

"Yes, the stone Jordan brought in was large enough that I was able to cut three from it. He was going to come in for these later. We discussed making more jewelry for you… Over time," Charles said, looking uncomfortable. "I think the largest stone will fit nicely in the center space of your ring once I've removed the diamond."

He was waiting for her to speak, and she found that she didn't know what she wanted to say. She nodded, and after one, long, painful moment, Leslie handed him her ring. "I think that would be lovely. Thank you."

"I promise, I'll take very good care of this and call you when it is ready."

"What about the diamond? When will it be ready for me to pick up? I need to get it back to Jordan's mother as soon as possible."

"Anna Slater is a client," Charles said.

Leslie couldn't tell if he meant it to be a warning that Anna was a good client and he thought she was justified in asking for the diamond back or if he was telling her just to fill the empty space. "I mean that I'll take care of getting the diamond back to Mrs. Slater. I don't think that is a detail you need to be bothered with. Just be gentle with yourself."

It was a lifeline she wanted to cling to.

"I'd really appreciate that," she said. She didn't want to have to do one more thing. She didn't want to have to see Anna ever again in her life. The relief this brought to her made her tear up all over again. Charles handed her a tissue, which she thanked him for.

After some more small talk, she left. And then she realized it was all done. The final chore. There was no longer any physical tie to her being Jordan Slater's fiancée. She reached for her left hand and felt for the missing ring that she knew was not there. She was amazed at how attached she had become to it. Now if only she could get her heart to let go as well.

As June passed into July and the weather turned to the warmest of summer, Leslie spent a lot of time in her backyard looking at the flowers she and Jordan had planted only two months earlier. Their roses were spectacular, and Leslie wondered again what had motivated Jordan to plant a rose garden. "We need one," he'd said at the time when she balked at the care and time roses took. He'd surprised her again when he special ordered roses bearing the names of Marilyn Monroe, Diana, Princess of Wales, Jubilee du Prince de Monaco, Ingrid Bergman, and Queen Elizabeth.

"What is all this about? You got a thing for lady roses?" she had asked as he chipped away at the hard clay soil to make room for his lady roses.

"Elegant ladies for my elegant lady," he'd said with a sexy smile, and had resumed his mission.

Now, bouquets of roses filled the house. Jordan, thankfully, had seen the first blossoms, but not the true glory of the pinks, reds, and peaches they were now producing.

Her father had been as understanding as he could get about their real estate business.

"Let me help," he'd offered, surprising her by all but taking over her current clients. "Give yourself some time off." What he probably meant was, "You look so horrible, you are scaring away clients. No one wants to buy from someone who is depressed."

She had lost her fiancé, not her love of real estate, but her father was treating her delicately, and she wasn't sure how she felt about it. She also knew that in a couple of months, her father and Denice would be heading to Palm Springs. She needed to have a handle on her life by then. While he was being patient now, she suspected within a few months he would expect her to have moved on, just as he had when dealing with the loss of her mother. She needed to be ready to take over the business.

Real estate might just be the right distraction. It was 24/7 stressful with no rest or break from the tension. If you weren't at the top of your game, you could lose the sale. She wasn't mentally there yet, didn't want to deal with sellers who wanted more than their property was worth. She didn't want low-end buyers who wouldn't look at anything that didn't have slab granite.

They didn't get it. These were all just things that could be bought and sold. She couldn't replace Jordan like a failing roof or fix her broken heart like someone might fix a broken seal in a window. So, would she ever move on?

Their life had been planned out—marriage, children, travel, and most of all, love. Now what was she supposed to do? Someday when her biological clock was ready to quit, settle for close but not good enough? Was that what the future held for her? Maybe she was forever damaged and would never love again. She needed to toughen her skin. Jordan would want her to move on, but what did that look like?

And maybe the busy workload that real estate would demand of her would be therapeutic.

She knew one thing for sure, she was tired of being treated like a porcelain doll.

The doorbell rang and snapped her out of her thoughts. She hoped it wasn't a reporter wanting a follow-up story. There were already enough sad stories of this bride whose fiancé died two weeks before their wedding. She felt like a martyr. She couldn't even go to Starbucks without getting hugged by complete strangers who expected her to replay her grief over and over again. She wondered what they would do if she said, "Enough already. This really isn't helping."

Maybe it was another delivery of flowers. She'd had a lot of bouquets and had only just finished on the thank you notes a few days earlier. She was getting good at thank you notes, all kinds and for all occasions.

"Thank you for the lovely place setting of our china. We will enjoy them on many holidays to come—"

"Thank you for the lovely champagne flutes. They are gorgeous! We look forward to celebrating many anniversaries and special memories with them—"

"Thank you for the beautiful crystal vase! Jordan will have to bring me plenty of beautiful flowers over the next fifty years. He's just planted a magnificent rose garden—"

"Thank you for your donation to the Mt. Hood rescue team. Without them, we wouldn't have been able to bring Jordan home—"

"Thank you for understanding about the canceled reception. I completely understand that you have to keep my deposit—"

"Thank you for thinking of me at this most difficult time. The orchid plant is lovely."

Instead of flowers, she found the postman on the other side of the door with a registered letter. She thanked him and took it inside. It was from one of the large law firms in downtown Portland and her fingertips prickled in unease. She had been worried about a lawsuit for wrongful death. People sued for anything nowadays and even though Jordan was dead, parents of the students he'd taken with him were bitter and angry. She was told they couldn't sue her because she and Jordan weren't married, but they could sue his estate.

The estate was a sore subject. She and Jordan had drawn up new wills. Only they hadn't signed them because they needed to find a notary. They had planned to do it the week between his Mt. Hood climb and the trip cave diving. Only they hadn't gotten around to it, so despite the fact they had shared everything for the last nine years, to Leslie's quiet disdain, Jordan's mother inherited everything that was Jordan's.

One of Leslie's grim tasks was boxing away all of Jordan's possessions. Well, most of Jordan's possessions. She wasn't giving his mother photos of Jordan and herself. She wasn't giving her every item of Jordan's clothing. There were a few fleece pullovers and t-shirts that held sentimental value. All the scrapbooks and photo albums she'd made for him over the years were staying with her.

Now this letter... a little more salt to add to her wounds. The letter informed her that the estate of Jordan Slater was going to require her to buy Jordan out of his share of the house she was currently living in or sell it to divide the proceeds equitably.

My goodness, what had taken Anna so long to getting around to it? She'd thought the woman would have tried to move in and take possession by now.

Leslie loved the house. She had loved it since the morning she'd seen it on realtor tour and called Jordan. It was a fixer-upper, slightly beyond their budget, but they could do what had to be done. She had no doubt, and he had gotten just as caught up in the action. They saw the potential. They saw the future—this house was a part of their happily ever after. Two days later, their offer was accepted, and Leslie started picking out paint colors.

They had redone almost everything but the kitchen. The living room, dining room, bathrooms, and all the bedrooms sparkled with a new vibrancy. A year from now, as budgets allowed, the house would be perfect. Would *have been* perfect, she corrected. Their labor of love would have been completed.

This wouldn't have been their forever home, but it would have been their first, their little-enchanted cottage that would have been where all their lifetime dreams started to take flight. They would have brought their first baby home to this house. On one of the doorframes, probably the master bedroom, there would have been lines that showed how much little Sam or Carly had grown until they had decided that they had grown out of this house.

And then, they would have had to negotiate for that door to be moved into their next house, because Leslie wouldn't have left it behind. Jordan might have argued for a New York minute, but then he'd have relented because he loved her. And he knew she was right. And deep down he was just as sentimental as she was.

And then their little family would have found their next house, the dream home. The home they would have only left 'feet first' sixty or seventy years from now. Their children would have rooms decorated with rock star posters and Barbie or My Little Pony because they wanted a boy and a girl and they would have kept having kids until they got what they wanted because their dreams always came true. And they'd have had a series of family pets, hound-style dogs that looked regal and would be beloved members of the family.

Leslie had pictured this future in her mind so clearly that anything else seemed unthinkable. She kept waiting to wake up from the worst nightmare of her life. But each day, she endured a sleepless night and woke up to discover that this—this loneliness and loss was her life.

Yes, in a year from now, the house would have been perfect, but Leslie didn't have a year. And she found, at that moment, that she no longer had a passion for the house in Royal Woodlands just off Jamieson Drive because Jordan was no longer in it. And all those sweet memories that filled every room now had a bitter edge because now this sweet little house, the place where all her dreams had come to thrive, had died.

Leslie went out to the garage and found a small temporary sign. It was the kind of sign realtors put up the day they listed a house before the professional sign erectors put in something more permanent.

With rubber mallet in hand and a whole bunch of anger to fuel her, she drove that *For Sale* sign into the front lawn like a woman possessed.

Once the sign seemed secure in the lawn and Leslie had stopped swinging the impressive hammer, she heard a car door shut behind her. Whirling around, she couldn't quite believe her eyes.

Charles leaned back against a black sports car and regarded her with folded arms and his familiar judgmental stare she'd come to expect. After their last interaction, when he'd been so kind to her, she'd thought she might have misjudged him. She'd actually questioned her childhood thoughts. But here he was, parked in front of her house, wearing sunglasses, watching her as if she were a lunatic. Well, today she was feeling a bit crazy, and she didn't care what anyone, especially Charles, thought about it. This day just got better and better. How did he know where she lived and why was he here?

The ring, she thought and felt a little nervous excitement.

"Hello Charles," she said as she tossed the hammer to the side and plastered a smile on her face. "This is a surprise."

"I hope you don't mind. I'm taking the afternoon off, and I thought I'd drop your ring by. I couldn't wait for your reaction. Is this an okay time?" he asked, looking at the sign and then at the hammer she'd tossed into a nearby shrub.

"Yes, great timing," she said, smiling so hard it hurt. She wanted her ring back. She had missed it like she missed Jordan.

"I'm sorry, I should have called. I didn't mean to interrupt if you're busy—"

"No, no, I've decided to sell the house today. Are you interested in a three-bedroom, two bath ranch with great bones?"

"Oh, I just bought a house this winter, but thank you," he answered with a tight smile probably thinking she was a nut. "Have you found another place?"

"Anyplace I never went with Jordan will work. Does that sound ridiculous?"

"No, it sounds like you need a change of scenery to get away from some of the memories."

"Something like that. Come on inside."

Once again, she looked like a mess. She had sweat on her brow and was wearing a ripped t-shirt and a pair of wrinkled shorts, but he hadn't called, so he got what he got.

"Let's go out back to the patio. Would you like some iced tea or water or something, Charles?" she asked to be polite, but she just wanted to see the ring and get him gone as soon as possible.

"Please call me Charlie. Charles was my grandfather. And no, I'm fine, thank you, I can't stay," he said as they sat at a little table on her patio and opened the small black velvet box which held her former engagement ring.

At first glance, it took her breath away.

"It's so beautiful," she said, her voice breaking. All the stones were radiant in the rose gold. She reached for the ring and held it up to the sunlight for a minute before slipping it on the third finger of her right hand. He'd sized the ring a half size larger to accommodate her dominant hand, and she was happy to see the fit was perfect. A wave of sadness reminded her of why she had to get the ring changed in the first place.

"Is it what you wanted?" he asked, his voice was soft, and she thought a tad hesitant.

She looked up from her ring meeting Charlie's eyes and found that she didn't have any words. Then she managed, "I think Jordan would be very happy about this."

"I think so, too. I didn't know him very well, but I know he was very passionate about you and this ring," Charlie said.

"I don't know what to say."

"I'm relieved that you like it," he said, and she could hear him take a deep breath. So, he'd been nervous that she'd like it? How surprising, considering how well the ring had turned out.

"What do I owe you for the time and the gold?"

He gave her a look that was part offended and part confused.

"There is no charge," he said.

"But you've spent a lot of time on it—"

"Leslie, I won't accept anything from you. I liked working with this sunstone. Please just think of us again. And someday when you want to indulge yourself, stop in and buy yourself something that makes you happy."

"Thank you, Charlie."

After a few minutes of small talk, she walked him out and shut her front door behind him. Then she sank to the hardwood floor, leaned against the wall that she and Jordan had so carefully painted a soft butter yellow, and cried.

Silver Linings Dress Auction

DRESS NUMBER SEVEN

TITLE: *Selflessness*

DESCRIPTION: Holding nothing back and loving fully, this stunning mermaid silhouette James Casper gown is appropriately named for a queen. "Alexandra" has a strapless, lace corset bodice with a sweetheart neckline. The skirt is an extra heavy silk satin gathered in a sweep to form the mermaid flair. Forgo the veil, wear a tiara, and grace the shoulders with the thinnest of silk tulle wraps. This is the dress little girls dream of when they think of their weddings.

DONATED BY: *The Aqua Lady*

$\mathscr{P}$resent $\mathscr{D}$ay

FIVE days before the Auction

Leslie let out a sigh as she finished reviewing her email. It had taken longer than it should because her mind kept going to her dresses and, of course, Jordan, the man who'd been her first everything. She couldn't help the few tears that leaked out as she thought back to that magical time that now seemed like a bittersweet dream.

She'd been so young and so in love. The thought that she wouldn't be spending the rest of her life with him wasn't even a possibility five years ago when she'd made her first trip to Aunt Trudel's. Absently, she glanced at the sunstone ring on her right hand. Now, she was thirty and had a bunch of wedding dresses and ex-fiancé's in her past. The tears came a little faster now.

She supposed to someone like Peggy, Leslie was a lonely heart who just couldn't get it right with men. Let Peggy and the rest of the world think what they wanted. Only Leslie had experienced and knew the truth of her life. Each person she had loved, not all the same way and not all for the same reasons. After Jordan, her idea of love had changed and morphed with each man.

And when she'd decided she'd wasted enough of the day on the ghosts of her past, she dried her tears and took stock. She had a lot to be proud of. She had a lot to be thankful for.

She had family who cared about her and her sweet fur baby Daisy, who filled her days with love. Not to say that a dog was a substitute for a husband, but it sure was nice to have someone greet you when you got home at night. And if the universe, or karma, or goddess from above had decided it was time for her to get a break, maybe they would give her another chance at happiness, but if not, she'd be okay. In fact, she'd be great.

She didn't ask for love because love could hurt, but happiness? Well, that could be a game changer. But she meant what she said to Suede. She wouldn't think about it. She wouldn't jinx it. Happily ever after was her dream and if she'd learned anything, it was to never give up on dreams. She could picture the house, had the dog, wanted the children born of the love she had for another, she wanted it all. Possibly, she wanted too much. Maybe with Jordan she hadn't realized that she had it all.

Her desk phone rang, and she was happy for the distraction—any distraction that didn't involve her past would be welcome at this moment. She glanced at the caller ID. It was another real estate office, good. Maybe someone had a question or wanted to make an offer on one of her listings.

"Hello, this is Leslie," she said, forcing a smile. Some realtor from her past, who gave seminars on sales success had once told her if you smiled when you answered the phone, it made you sound happier.

"Hey," a familiar voice on the other end said, and Leslie felt a twist in the pit of her stomach. Oh crap. Today was quickly going from a 'glass of wine' day to a 'bottle of wine' day. Forget the damn smile.

"Hey Jack," she said, and silently cursed herself for not recognizing his specific office number. Well, it had been a few years.

"Look, Leslie, I have an offer coming in for your listing on Vista. My assistant, Ryan, is in Mexico with his boyfriend, so I have to handle it. We might have to speak civilly to each other for once. Wouldn't that be a nice change?"

Over the last few years, they'd had transactions together. It was unavoidable. They were both successful realtors farming the same area. It was bound to happen. They had carefully avoided each other by using Jack's overworked and over-abused masochistic assistant. Real estate was tense as it was, add a scorned lover to the mix and you had dynamite.

And when it came to realtor tour, they could almost pass by each other at a listing without even flinching—almost.

And it appeared he hadn't watched the news that morning or he'd be flicking her crap. At least something was going her way today.

"Okay, which of my listings on Vista?" she asked, smiling, but this time the smile was genuine. She had two listings on Vista and the knowledge no doubt irked Jack to his core. Vista was his prime stomping ground. He considered himself the neighborhood expert. She considered him to be the neighborhood pest.

"Garibaldi," he barked.

"Oh damn, I should warn you, I have two other offers for Garibaldi that the sellers are considering. And they are both written for over full price. So, if your offer isn't," she said, hardening her tone, "I wouldn't even bother writing it up because my sellers have already told me not to bother them with anything less than what we already have on the table."

Leslie knew she shouldn't be enjoying herself this much, but she was. He was a bad dog, and he'd lied to her. She still remembers that day several years earlier with a shiver although it was a hot summer evening when everything had come to light.

"I want to reassure you, it is for over full price," Jack offered condescendingly. "In fact, it is the best offer you'll probably get for that homage to the 1970s. What a fucking pit! It should be torn down. I tried to convince my buyers to pass, but they like the view. No accounting for taste."

"Still swearing too much, I see. Whatever they are into, it's cool, send it over," Leslie said sweetly, slipping into professional mode and trying to un-see images that had been permanently burned into her retinas and haunted her memories for years. "Thank you for showing my listing." It was the least she could say.

"On its way," he said, then following a long, uncomfortable pause, he added, "I suppose the wedding dress you got for our wedding is going in that used wedding dress auction with *all* the others. You certainly do have a gift for getting engaged and collecting engagement rings and dresses. You must be your aunt's best customer."

Oh, of all the vicious and ugly things she wanted to say to him but bit back. She took a deep breath and said, "Oh, sorry, the dress I bought for our wedding was destroyed. I used it for a Halloween costume a few years back. I was the Bride of Frankenstein. I drenched it with fake blood and beat it with a whip for that 'lived in' look."

"I dodged a bullet with you, lady," he said.

"Sounds like we both dodged a bullet," she said, adding in the last minute, "Yeah, a special bullet, you know, with a cloudy emerald tip to match my used engagement ring."

She hung up on him before he had the chance to respond.

PART 2

Four Years Earlier

Chapter Four

Leslie stared at the lights of downtown Portland from the balcony of her five hundred square foot apartment at the auspiciously named complex, Uptown Cliffs. There was a slight chill in the air. The season was changing, and she was happy for it. She held a glass of overpriced Merlot, her second or maybe her third of the evening. To be honest, she'd lost count. It was just a regular Saturday night in her world or the new normal as she liked to think of it. Jordan had been gone for almost four months, and she still had a hard time knowing what to do with herself most of the time.

Over the last few weeks and months, which had been undeniably the worst of her life, she had made a very simple decision. She would never lose anything she loved again like a house to a greedy almost mother-in-law. And money, despite what people said to the contrary, could buy a certain level of happiness. It meant security.

There was one little positive in her life—her own secret. Not that anyone but a realtor would care, but there were rumors that the Uptown Cliffs would be converted into a luxury condominium project in the next couple of years. Her placement at the development had nothing to do with wanting to live in the cliff-hugging dwelling and everything to do with wanting to make money.

She'd met her new landlord accidentally at the open house for her little ranch.

"I'm just passing through, getting a wee peek at the market," the tall man, with a lovely buttery accent, had commented after touring her house. No doubt he drank whiskey and played football in his native land across the pond.

He introduced himself as Shane McPhee, a recent expat from Scotland who was taking a serious look at buying a ten-building complex that hung on a cliff, just to the west of downtown over-looking the city with a spectacular panoramic view. His plan was to convert the luxury apartments into condominiums and sell them for much more than their current monthly rent. He was lining up his investors.

"I could use a sharp mind with a head for the real estate busi-ness. You live in my apartments for a few months and then share your thoughts. Deal?"

She'd liked him and thought it was perfect timing. And, maybe when it came time to start the project, Shane might consider her for the listing realtor on site.

Her little ranch, the enchanted cottage she had shared with Jordan, had sold within a week. She could have moved into her father and Denice's small two-bedroom condo in the Pearl District, or she could have shoved bamboo under her fingernails. They con-tinued to tiptoe around her. They didn't raise their voices, didn't bring up controversial subjects. Her father had never been more sensitive to her and her feelings, even after her mother died. But now, as an adult, the overt sensitivity made her feel uncomfortable and a bit confused. If only her father had been this sensitive to her feelings when her mother died, it would have meant so much. It would have brought them closer, then and now.

There was talk of her father and Denice delaying their winter pilgrimage to Palm Springs. She couldn't have that. If she were going to break over Jordan's death, she'd have done it in June or July. Not now. Now, she only missed him with a deep, painful longing that no other person or thing could ever replace. No one else in the world needed her as Jordan had. And that sense of belonging to another, being needed by another, couldn't be replaced no matter how much time passed.

She had learned to sleep alone after sleeping with Jordan for seven years and tried to convince herself to like it. She didn't. She liked the protection of a man next to her. She had learned to make dinner for one, which bored her out of her mind. Jordan had always been the cook in their family. She could barely make a grilled cheese sandwich.

Why didn't things taste as good when you cooked them for yourself? It was a great mystery of singlehood. She'd learned to go to the movies solo. She didn't mind going to a café on a quiet afternoon with a book, but she didn't like to see happy couples around her. In fact, anything to do with love pretty much burned a little too deeply.

Sometimes an hour lasted for three. Sometimes no one knew her pain, and she was lonelier than she could have ever thought was humanly possible. Sometimes she had very dark thoughts about her mortality she didn't like to acknowledge a moment after she had them because Jordan would want her to go on living. He savored life. He wouldn't want her to waste a moment.

But she did. She gave herself permission to find her way and take a moment here or there to try to make sense of the big fall from grace her lovely life had taken.

Her evenings were spent marathon watching television series she'd never had time for when she was with Jordan. *Breaking Bad*, *Game of Thrones*, and *The Great British Baking Show* had been her best friends on many a night. TLC and the Food Network were clearly safe. Romantic comedies on Lifetime were to be avoided at all costs.

She and Jordan had lived together in college to her father's complete horror. In retrospect, thank goodness they had. It was like she'd been married to him since she was eighteen. Only they hadn't gotten the official paper soon enough. And there was something much less sympathetic about the fiancée losing the love of her life than the wife losing her husband.

Jordan used to joke about going to Las Vegas for a quickie marriage. They should have done it. If only she'd taken him up on his offer. How different her life might be now. She might have had his children, a combination of the best of both of them, with his smile and her coloring. She would never see that smile again, and the regret for what could have been never quite went away.

The Saturday after the funeral, her cousin had come over and supervised the return of all Leslie's shower and wedding gifts. And the pile of pastel and pristine white packages with joyful ribbons, which mocked her, slowly dwindled to just a few tag-less stragglers.

After three weeks, thankfully, only one or two gifts remained and could easily be hidden in the closet.

Suzie remained her one constant friend. Just as she had been at the start, she managed to never treat Leslie any differently. She should have been called Saint Suzie for her ability to listen to Leslie talk about Jordan incessantly.

"What did you think when I bought my wedding dress?" Leslie asked her one afternoon. "Did you think my marriage was doomed?"

Suzie grabbed her hands and gave them a squeeze. "I thought your marriage would be epic. Do you want to know something? Jordan really, really adored you. I used to be a little jealous. I once told Tim that I wished he looked at me the way Jordan looked at you. You know what he said? He said, 'Sweetie, that's the way I look at you in the dark, when I'm dreaming my sweetest dreams, but you just can't see it." He means well, but my honey will never be a poet."

Sitting at an outdoor table at her neighborhood Starbucks, Leslie's favorite Sunday reading spot, she was enjoying what might well be the last nice fall weekend. Well into her second peppermint tea an accented voice asked, "So, what fire is she facing?"

Leslie set down the book and looked in the direction of the voice. It was the owner of her favorite Indian restaurant. She and Jordan had dined many times at the Curry Tree, and Sunil had always been there, friendly and kind with a big, jovial smile on his face. Jordan had been convinced that Sunil had a little crush on Leslie, but she had never noticed—although she liked that Jordan had.

"It's Sunil, right?"

He stood to his full six foot four inches and crossed to where she sat. "May I?" he asked, with that big smile.

"Sure," Leslie said and indicated to the chair across from her. She wasn't sure that she felt like a conversation, but she couldn't be rude. She wanted to quietly finish her book and be left alone.

"Leslie, I had hoped to see you in my restaurant, but you haven't been in for a very long time. Is everything alright with you?"

"No, I'm sorry if you haven't heard, but my fiancé Jordan died in June. There was an accident on Mt. Hood."

Sunil shut his obsidian eyes as a tremor of pain crossed his features. "That explains a lot. I'm so very sorry for your loss. I remember hearing about it, but I did not realize that was your Mr. Jordan. I'm so very sorry."

"Thank you, Sunil. We always enjoyed going to your restaurant. It has just been hard to go in with all the memories. Indian was some of our favorite food. We had some wonderful conversations over butter chicken."

"And always with the extra raita."

"You have a good memory," Leslie said. She and Jordan always fought over the yogurt and cucumber raita until they started just ordering a double portion.

Sunil nodded, and she took in his outfit for the first time. He wore a raw silk cream shirt and maroon silk trousers with alligator loafers and a matching belt. He was an okay looking man, but the outfit was too much as was his spicy cologne, which filled the space around them like bad incense. She wished she had listened to her instincts and not come to Starbucks this afternoon. Her father had asked her to attend an open house with him, and she'd begged off. That had been a mistake.

"It is so amazing that you are here, for believe it or not, I dreamed of you last night," Sunil said as he looked skyward and shut his eyes to the warm afternoon sun.

"What?" Leslie asked, having burned her tongue on the hot tea.

"Leslie, Leslie, what I'm trying to tell you is that it was fate that we should meet up today."

"Okay," she replied wearily. How was she going to get out of this? She wondered if she could use her dad as an excuse.

"You see, I'm a very spiritual person, and I believe that I've been asked to deliver a message to you that involves the two of us."

Oh boy…

"I know, I know, you ask, who is the Sunil sitting before you? Isn't he just a restaurant owner, a businessman? Or is there something else about him? A quiet spirituality perhaps?"

"Well, you are a businessman," Leslie said apprehensively.

"No, my darling, I am so much more than this physical form and this lifetime. I've been a Hindu prince from a distant land. I've been here so many, many times before, as have you."

His voice was not only accented, but it also boomed a little with his declarations and the people around them took notice. Mommies in their yoga pants, who had gathered with their children in strollers to discuss their lives with their mutual mommy friends suddenly found the conversation at Leslie's table far more interesting.

Whether he knew it or not, Sunil now had an audience of more than just Leslie.

"Me? You think I've lived before?" Leslie asked, immediately thinking of how Jordan was sure that they had been soul mates in another lifetime.

"Yes, yes… I feel we were together, you and I, many, many times. Not sexually, not in that particular lifetime I'm thinking of today, but rather you were my seer, my confidant. Your loyalty was to me and me alone. You told me things, predicted my future, and advised me. I rewarded you with large jewels and trinkets. And the connection, you can see that connection has lasted because I dreamed of you last night and here you are. Thank you for obeying me, thank you for coming to me when I called you."

The words bounced off Leslie like BBs off a steel drum. Leslie chose not to censure her reply.

"I came when you called? Okay, what year exactly do you feel this time was that I, an independent woman, would obey you and come to you when you called?" Leslie asked, aware of snickering around her. "Because that doesn't sound like me at all and there is no chance in Hell I would obey you—or any other man for that matter."

"It was long, long ago. It was a time when men lived with many women who were their wives. I wore the silk robes with a large, golden, bejeweled sword attached to my hip. There were two large rubies at the hilt—"

Anger turned to appreciation for the absurdity of the moment. Leslie threw back her head and laughed. Trying to get control, she pounded her fists on the metal table to no avail. She laughed so hard that she knocked over her tea, which spilled all over the table. She laughed until tears slipped down her cheeks. She hadn't laughed since June before Jordan died and nothing, no matter how hard she'd tried, had changed that, until now. With Sunil sitting across from her, with his phallic golden sword with its two large rubies on the hilt, she couldn't stop.

"This is not funny!" he shouted.

"This is the funniest stuff I've heard in months. Thank you, Sunil. Thank you, for being the golden phallic bejeweled thing and please feel free to give me any gems that come your way—"

"I said that this is not funny. There is nothing funny about this. You are insulting me!"

"Um, yes, this is funny. And you're making a fool of yourself, and all these women know it," Leslie said, indicating the tables around them who were staring at Sunil as he jumped up from his chair. She made eye contact with several of the mommies and added, "I don't know him, by the way."

"How dare you!"

"How dare you think that I'd obey you? That is some seriously condescending stuff, Prince Sunil. For an enlightened guy, there is a lot you don't know, especially about women."

"You are not welcome in my restaurant ever again! If you come, I will have you thrown out."

"Okay, but only if you promise," Leslie said and kept laughing, some of the mommies joining in like backup singers.

As she mopped up the table with extra napkins and decided to meet her father at the open house after all, a nice-looking man at the next table, who she hadn't noticed until now said, "Did he really just tell you he'd known you before and had a bejeweled golden sword?"

"Yes, he did," Leslie said, smiling so hard that it hurt her face. How long had it been since she smiled? Three months? Four months?

Glancing back at the man at the table, she asked, "Don't I know you? Aren't you Jack Ward?"

"Indeed, I am, and you are?"

Leslie stepped around her table, extended her hand, and said, "I'm Leslie Westcott, Lux Properties on 21st."

"I've seen your name, and I know your dad. He is legendary. It is lovely to meet you. And I'm pretty sure this is the first time in this life or any other that we have met. Although I think I've seen you on West Side tour."

"Thank goodness," she said in mock relief. "I just couldn't handle two bejeweled princes on the same day."

He smiled and said, "You never know who you're going to meet at Starbucks, damn!"

Jack was the largest real estate producer in Portland. He was so famous that he gave seminars on how to find buyers and sellers. He just never gave them in the Portland market for fear his competitors might use his knowledge against him in his hometown. Her father had suggested she might fly to one of the cities where he gave a seminar, just to find out what all the fuss was about. Leslie couldn't care less. She didn't think real estate was a system. She thought it was about hard work and good relationships.

"Hey, thanks for entertaining all of us with that guy. Is he your boyfriend?" Jack asked.

Jack looked like a weatherman. He was good looking in a handsome nerd kind of way, with the perfect hair and smile, but at his words, she recoiled. "Sorry, really didn't mean that. I was kidding, trying to come off as funny. I mean, come on, you wouldn't get hitched up with a guy like that."

"Never and a day," Leslie said, thinking of Jordan as she stood and started gathering her things. "I've got to run. It was nice to meet you, Jack."

"Do you really have to go?" he asked. "Can't I get you a replacement tea?"

There were many things she could do, but giving these ladies around them anything more to speculate about wasn't on the agenda. And she just didn't think she could do perky conversation with Mr. Big Shot realtor. "Thanks, but I've got to go. I'm sure I'll see you at an open house or on tour sometime."

"Count on it. Let's run into each other on tour. I always tour."

"Good for you, I love touring," she lied. She hadn't been on tour since June. And now she was feeling like going home, ordering a pizza, and having a glass of Merlot. She'd think about the rest of her life tomorrow.

Chapter Five

Whoever said that laughter was the best medicine wasn't lying. The day after her encounter with the oversexed Indian restaurant owner, Leslie woke up and Jordan wasn't her first thought. He was her second, after she had again remembered and laughed at the expression on one of the yoga mom's faces as Sunil stomped away after his sex sword diatribe.

It was amazing what the change in perspective did for her. It gave her the freedom to smile, the freedom to not feel guilty for laughing the day before. It gave her the space she needed to reclaim a little part of her life which she feared she had lost forever.

On that Monday morning, she got up, took a shower, and got dressed in her favorite navy suit for the office. She styled her neglected hair and made a note to schedule a haircut.

Dressed, she stepped out on her deck and retrieved an empty wine glass.

This needed to stop. The excessive love of Merlot might take a bit of time to break, but she'd start watching it tonight. She didn't think she was an alcoholic. She thought she was lonely and wanted to dull the pain. And if she were wrong, and couldn't take care of it on her own, she'd get help.

It was all fine and good until she got in the car and heard one of Jordan's favorite love songs.

Parked in her parking spot at Uptown Cliffs, she cried in the car for fifteen minutes. She was stupid to think she could feel so much better without there being consequences. She couldn't hold up the façade for more than a day, but she had tried. And that was a start.

Pulling it together, she dried her tears and drove to her office. In the last four months she'd only been in a handful of times, basically whenever her dad started giving her grief about it. But this was her choice, her decision. It was time to rejoin the land of the living even if she could only stay for ten minutes. This was a step in moving forward to face whatever the future wanted to bring—time to face her fire.

Leslie could almost hear the gasps as she stepped through the front door of Portland Lux Properties. Several of her co-workers encircled her to give her hugs.

"Oh my god, you didn't need to return the espresso machine. The office wanted you to have that," Peggy, the receptionist, whispered in her ear.

"Yes, I did," Leslie replied. "It was very kind and thoughtful of you all, but I just couldn't keep it. It wouldn't have been right, and it would have reminded me of Jordan every time I saw it on the counter. But I won't forget everyone's generosity and kindness. Everyone has been great to me."

"Well, I hope you don't mind, but we returned it and gave the money to the trust set up for that little boy who died with Jordan." The boy who had slipped and knocked Jordan into the crevasse, Leslie thought as she tried and failed to find a peaceful expression for her face.

"I'm sure it was appreciated," Leslie managed but thought that she had too many conflicting emotions to say anything else.

Her coworkers were guardedly cautious around her, but her father was quick to give her some of his client files. It went without saying that she'd lost momentum in her career, but she knew she could bring it back. Real estate was forgiving in that way. You could turn it up or down, it just took time and dedication.

The morning flew by as she edited some of her father's boring property descriptions, rewrote his fliers, familiarized herself with files, and double-checked his listing paperwork and made notes on what was missing. It felt good to be productive. She hardly noticed when the receptionist, Peggy, placed a small box on her desk.

"What's this?" she asked.

"Some cute messenger with a bunch of cool tats just delivered it. He had a pierced eyebrow—so sexy!"

Leslie reminded herself to not ask Peggy any questions in the future. She knew better but had temporarily forgotten.

The small white box was tied with a black ribbon. Leslie had a sense that whatever was inside was possibly not meant for public consumption. Peggy stood in her office doorway, waiting.

"Thanks, Peggy," she said, but Peggy remained.

Leslie wanted to open the box, but not with an audience. She put the box to the side and appeared to concentrate on something on her computer screen.

Peggy let out a frustrated breath and left. Leslie got up and shut the door to her office. No point in letting the biggest gossip in the office in on whatever was in the box.

She pulled off the lid and felt uneasy as she started pulling away the fluffy white tissue.

A rhinestone-jeweled, brass letter opener that looked like a mini sword sat cushioned in the tissue. For a few heartbeats she wasn't sure what to make of the ornate, garish piece, but then she noticed the plain white card.

This ought to keep you safe if that creepy guy ever wants to show you his sword again. — J. W.

Leslie smiled and then she laughed. It was a great gift and sharp enough to make a point if she needed to defend herself.

"Well, well, what was in the box?" Peggy asked as Leslie refilled her coffee mug a few minutes later.

"Nothing, just a private joke with a friend," she said. Later in the afternoon, she took out an impersonal, company thank you note on stiff white paper, and wrote: *Dear Mr. Ward, Thank you for the mini sword. It should keep the reincarnated Hindu princes away. Best Regards, Leslie Westcott.* It wasn't warm, and she didn't mean for it to be. She thought about enclosing a business card but thought better of it.

She didn't know what Jack was up to, but she didn't want to encourage him in any way. Her fiancé had been gone barely five months, and she still missed him desperately. She didn't feel like engaging in any cat and mouse with some other man, especially a peacock like Jack Ward.

Proudly, Leslie went to the office the next day as well. She took a listing for her father, and when she returned, there was another box on her desk. This time it was a long florist box. She quickly picked it up and turned around, sprinting right out to her car. She was going to work from home for the rest of the day so she wouldn't have to answer any questions about what was in the box. Happily, Peggy was on break and not at the front desk when Leslie left, so she didn't have to answer any additional questions.

Once home, she finally gave into temptation and opened the box. Inside were a dozen soft peach roses. This time the card was more direct.

Saw these and thought of you. Enjoy. – J.W.

A part of her considered throwing the roses in the nearest dumpster. Jordan had been the last man to buy her flowers, and she'd wanted to keep it that way for as long as possible. This man, this person in her own profession was pursuing her. Had he not heard about Jordan? Everyone knew about Jordan. Her face, leaving the Timberline Lodge after the news of his death, had been flashed on every television station and internet news site in the Pacific Northwest.

What was she supposed to do? Thank him or send them back to him with a note telling him she wasn't interested in being pursued? She didn't need or appreciate this stress at the moment. One thing was for sure, coffee at Starbucks was off the table for Sunday afternoons from here on out.

Arranging the roses in an empty mason jar, she placed them in the center of her dining room table. She'd received several nice Waterford vases for her wedding. They'd all gone back, and now she thought she might need to buy one for herself.

These roses bothered her. She didn't want to like them. She didn't want to like the idea that a man had bought them for her. But there it was. Life is for the living. And now Jordan wasn't the last man who'd bought her flowers.

Late that night, the phone rang, and she about jumped out of her skin. It was, predictably, her stepmother. Denice had gotten into the habit of calling her every third day. Leslie didn't like to admit it but she was starting to look forward to the nightly calls. Denice was making the effort and Leslie needed all the support she could get.

"How are you?"

Leslie didn't say what she was thinking: *I didn't cry today, which is the first time in a week. Why? Well, some mystery guy sent me roses...*

"I'm okay today, I actually laughed at something. How are you?"

"Your father said you've been getting packages at work. Today they were roses. Do you have an admirer? Are they from a man?"

So, Peggy was keeping tabs on her for her father. Lovely. Denice had been the office secretary before her father had "taken the bait" and married her out of the receptionist role. It made sense that she and her replacement Peggy kept in contact. Leslie just never thought that they would stoop to gossiping about her. She had to remember, Denice was making a real effort.

"They are from Jack Ward. I ran into him when I was getting coffee at Starbucks last Sunday. It's nothing," Leslie said, trying to sound a little bored.

"I remember him from when he just was starting out. He is very successful and quite handsome. Just a second," her stepmother said, and then Leslie could hear Denice say to her father, "They are from Jack Ward."

Then she heard her father say, "He's a bit old for her. I thought he was married."

This was an incredibly ironic statement considering how much older her father was than Denice. Their twenty-year age gap meant nothing to them because Denice liked older men with money and her father obviously liked young things with small, tight bodies. Their relationship sometimes made Leslie throw up in her mouth, just a little bit. She needed to let it go, it just wasn't easy.

"No, he divorced what's her name," Denice said. "Was her name Melissa?"

"Yeah, that's right, Melissa that nice escrow officer with Old Republic Title."

Leslie wanted to suggest that they talk it out and call her back when they'd finished their conversation.

"Well, he's a Hell of a businessman," her father said in the background, "I think he's pretty ethical from what I can tell."

Denice returned to the phone, "Your father says he's very ethical, which is a very nice compliment in real estate as you know."

"I still am in love with my fiancé, so I couldn't care less," Leslie said growing beyond bored with the conversation.

"Life is short, honey. No one will judge you if you decide to move on."

She didn't want to have this discussion. Not after her father had moved on so quickly after her mother's death. He had not understood when she hadn't been able to embrace Denice from the start? It had been clear to Leslie at the time that Denice had all but erased the grief from his life, but it had done little to help Leslie. In fact, not being able to share her grief with her father had made it much worse.

She didn't want to think about dating Jack or any other man for that matter because none of them were Jordan. And damn it, she was breaking her one-day no-crying streak because now she was crying.

Chapter Six

"We just can't leave you here. Not this year," Denice complained in early November. Leslie had finally had enough. This kind stepmother act had hit a wall.

"Denice, I really appreciate your concern, but I'm completely capable of taking care of myself while you and Dad are in Palm Springs. Aunt Trudel is here, Suzie is here. We will all come down for Christmas, and you'll be back before Easter. Please, please go. I want to make referral fees on Dad's business. Come on, I want the money, so go!"

"Now honey, if it gets too bad, promise that you'll come for a visit," her dad began and then added, "We've got a guest casita ready for you anytime. Just turn the business over to Jemma, and we'll be fine."

"No, I'm working on that Uptown Cliffs deal. I've got an appointment with that Shane McPhee investor guy in early December."

"Do you want me to fly in for it?" her father asked.

"No, Dad. If I have questions, I'll call you. I've already met him, and he likes me, he likes my 'energy.' Now please, would you two pack your car and start driving?"

They looked at her skeptically.

"Please, can we try to pretend everything is normal? Can I please try to forget this horrible year?"

"And that is why you should come to the desert for a visit," Denice said, and Leslie wondered if she just wanted a contemporary for shopping and lunch when Leslie's father was golfing. Probably.

"You call anytime," Denice said. Maybe it was Leslie's imagination, but she looked, well, Denice looked *upset*.

"I promise I will call. You two just need to go!"

Leslie didn't breathe a sigh of relief until they called her from their home in Palm Springs.

Who were these people acting like worrywart parents? And where had they been all her life?

Somehow Leslie's new normal was becoming tolerable. She was sad, but there were glimmers of happiness, and she was throwing herself into her work which made the days go by faster. She was a little surprised when the boxes from J.W. had stopped, but it was for the best. She didn't want to date him or anyone for that matter. In fact, she was still trying to figure out who she was as a single person.

Leslie had gone from living with her father and Denice to living with Jordan. This was the first time in her life that she'd lived alone, and it felt odd. She really could eat tuna out of a can while leaning over the kitchen sink, and no one would judge. She could eat cake for dinner, and no one said a thing because no one shared her life.

On a rainy Friday afternoon in mid-November, when she was sitting in her office and thinking about calling Suzie to find out if she wanted to see a movie that weekend, Peggy delivered another mystery box.

This time it was different. It was a box from Sauveterre Jewelers. She felt a little rush of unease. Had Charlie sent her something? That would be completely weird. She'd meant to step into Sauveterre Jewelers and buy something as a thank you for the ring, but she hadn't.

"Well?" Peggy asked. "Aren't you going to open it?"

"Peggy, I don't know what it is, so if you don't mind, I want to open it myself and then decide to tell people or not."

"Jeez, Leslie, you're so pent up about stuff," Peggy said as she left Leslie's office.

When Leslie opened the box, the excitement turned to unease. There was one of those plain white cards from J.W. It read: *Thought this would look nice with your ring. – J.W.*

Inside was a thin rose gold bracelet set with a sunstone cabochon. She dropped the box on her desk and collected her thoughts.

Sunstones weren't common. Charlie would know about this. And if he knew and didn't tell her—

After the second ring, she heard a voice greet her with, "Good afternoon, Sauveterre Jewelers, this is Caroline, may I help you?"

"Hi Caroline, this is Leslie Westcott, may I speak with Charlie, please?" Leslie asked, feeling the anger rise inside her. He knew about the bracelet. Had he suggested it to Jack? What was this? A seriously sick joke?

"Leslie, he is just about to finish up with a client. Could he call you back in about five minutes or so?"

"You know, I'm close, I'll stop in."

"It will be good to see you," Caroline said, her voice filled with warmth Leslie didn't feel at that moment.

Leslie grabbed her coat, purse, and the box and booked to Sauveterre Jewelers six blocks away. It was raining, but she didn't care. She was wearing a camel hair coat and three-inch heels, and having a hard time finding purchase on the slick fall leaves that coated the sidewalk. She slipped and almost fell but was so upset she didn't notice.

Before she set foot in Sauveterre Jewelers, she took a moment to compose herself. She wanted to storm in, throw the bracelet at Charlie, and ask him to explain it, but she couldn't do that. It wasn't his fault. Jack had done this, and hopefully, Charlie could supply a few much-needed answers.

She stepped inside and said hello to Caroline. The other woman must have seen on her face that she was trying to hold it together and didn't waste a moment.

"Hello, Leslie," She greeted with a warm smile. "Charlie is just working on a project. Feel free to walk on back."

Charlie was leaning over his work desk as she quietly walked up and said, "Hi Charlie, do you have a moment?"

He looked up and smiled at her and said, "For you, anytime."

Charlie had a nice smile, but when he glanced at her right hand, the hand that had the sunstone ring he'd designed, and saw the bracelet still in the velvet box, the smile faltered, and his expression darkened.

"Yes, exactly," she said reading the change in his expression. "Jack Ward sent this to me. I'm assuming you designed it?"

"Look, it's none of my business, but I didn't know it was for you."

"When I opened the box and saw it, my heart almost stopped."

Charlie ran his fingers through his thick, dark hair, mussing it. "Jack came in here about two weeks ago. He was all excited about some woman he'd met. He wanted me to make her a bracelet to match her ring."

"Did he tell you it was for me?"

"No, I would have called you, warned you if I'd known. He described a reddish pink stone. I showed him a Padparadscha pink sapphire, a pink tourmaline, a Morganite, and finally, a sunstone. He said the sunstone was it."

"I'm sorry, I just can't believe he had this made for me," she said, eyeing the bracelet with disgust. "I'm sure it was expensive."

"He even had me rush it, paid double."

"Yuck," she replied, shaking her head in disgust.

"In fact, when I quoted him a price, which was purposefully high, he said, 'Sold!' as if this was a bidding war. I didn't want the project. I didn't want to remember the project I'd done for you. I didn't want the emotional baggage, after everything with Jordan, but I'm not stupid enough to turn down business either. I guess that means I have a price and he met it."

"I think I'm going to be sick."

"It is a beautiful piece, but I understand if you don't want it and if you want me to sell it for you, I can," Charlie offered.

"I'm going to give it back to him and make sure he knows that he crossed a line with me," she said pointedly.

"Is there anything I can do?" he asked. "Would you like me to return it to him for you?"

"No, thank you, but if any other jerk tries to make something for me, please warn me."

"Obviously, because of this experience, I will. He's a real ass," Charlie said, his cheeks bright red with what she now understood was anger and embarrassment for reading the signals so incorrectly.

"Why do you think he is such an ass? Is it only because of the sunstone?" she asked.

"That and I just don't like him," he said as his eyes darkened.

"He's supposedly a great realtor," Leslie said. "The top, number one in the Portland market."

"Too bad for Portland," Charlie muttered.

Leslie smiled and then laughed. "I'm sorry, I shouldn't have barged in here—"

"No, no, stop," Charlie said, holding up his hands. "Next time some stalker wants me to make something for you, I'll call you, I promise. I think you've been through enough. I didn't mean to add to your pain."

"I'm doing okay. Thank you again, Charlie for being so kind to me," Leslie replied.

"My pleasure and the next time you come in, come close to closing time and I'll buy you a drink as a further peace offering."

"Thanks," she said before she walked away with the bracelet in hand. The embarrassment of confronting him a bit unfairly hit her when she was a block away. She was going to have to apologize, again, at a later date. Next time she came in something told her she should buy him a drink. The thought made her happy.

Jack's office was in a large Victorian that had been converted to a real estate business in the Pearl District just east of her building. She found a parking spot two blocks away and marched through yet more slick fall leaves, a woman on a mission.

An elegant, open lobby was in what used to be the front parlor of the old historic home.

The receptionist looked both bored and irritated by Leslie's interruption as she stepped up to the desk.

"Hi, Leslie Westcott for Jack Ward."

"Is he expecting you?" she asked, her chewing gum showing.

"I'm sure he is," Leslie replied and watched as the woman picked up her phone.

After a few moments of hushed conversation, she told Leslie, "His assistant will be right down to escort you to his office."

"Thank you," Leslie replied curtly and sat in a nearby Queen Anne chair. She kept her camel hair coat on and noticed leaf particles clinging to the back of her silk stockings. She must look horrible after stomping around in the rain, first to Sauveterre Jewelers and now here. Her coat was probably ruined. Fall in the Pacific Northwest. Was she even wearing lipstick? She didn't think so, and she didn't care. The sooner she dealt with this, the sooner she could go home and curl up with a glass of Merlot and some cheese. That was something men just didn't understand, chicks and cheese. In her apartment, she had a cheese drawer in her fridge, and it was always filled.

"Miss Westcott?"

A man about her age in an argyle sweater vest introduced himself as Ryan and asked her to follow him up the staircase. Had she known she would be climbing stairs and marching through leaves today, she might not have worn three-inch heels. Her Stuart Weitzman pumps were probably ruined too. This day sucked.

They could hear Jack talking on his phone when they entered his office. There were three desks outside a much larger office that were obviously for Jack's staff. A life-size cutout of Jack with a crown on his head and the slogan, "Real Estate King" dominated one corner of the room. When the assistant saw her checking it out, he said, "That's a joke. Jack would never call himself that. A client in the printing business had it made as a gift for Jack."

"I'll bet," she muttered, wondering what made so many people want to buy and sell with him? He had a nice smile, which was ever present, but she didn't feel like smiling.

Eventually, the phone call ended, and Jack appeared in the open doorway.

"Leslie," he greeted, "Please come in, come in."

Today, dressed in jeans and a chambray shirt, he looked younger and well-built, and fit. So much younger, for a moment Leslie wasn't sure it was the same man she'd met at Starbucks. He motioned to two chairs by a window and asked her if she'd like a water or hot tea, which she declined.

"It's getting wintery out there, are you sure you wouldn't like something hot to drink? I make a mean Spanish Coffee."

"I'm fine, Jack, but I thought we should talk."

"I'm very glad you came by. I've been hoping to get your attention for some time now."

"Why? Do you want to hire me?"

Jack smiled at her. He had a nice smile, the kind that also made crinkles around his eyes like a sweet dog. She liked dogs, but that didn't mean she liked him.

"No, although I'm sure you would make a great addition to the team. I was hoping we might um… well, shucks. I'd like to take you out on a date. Cards on the table."

"You do know that my fiancé died in June, right?"

Jack's face lost that big smile and all of the sudden he looked very embarrassed. "I'm sorry, no, I didn't know. I'm very sorry."

"Do you remember the story about the high school teacher who took a bunch of students up to Mt. Hood and fell into a crevasse?"

"Jordan something…

"Jordan Slater, the love of my life. Do you see this ring?" she asked, holding up her right hand. "It's made from sunstones, actually from a sunstone that he found and then had cut for this ring. There used to be a diamond in the center, but his mother wanted it back. Do you know how I felt when I looked at your gift today?"

Jack put his face in his hands and said, "Oh shit, I'm a fucking idiot."

"Yeah, you are," she said and placed the bracelet with its box on the little table between them and started to get out of the chair.

"Wait, please, have I completely blown this?" he asked.

"Blown what? We're nothing. We'd have to be something to have the potential for loss."

Leslie brushed some stray leaf particles off her coat, ready to walk out on this loudmouth jerk who had found a way to poke at a raw nerve like no one else ever had. Charlie was right. This guy was an ass.

"Please don't go, not like this. Look, I made a mistake. I'm so sorry. That doesn't mean I don't want to get to know you. Please, will you give me another chance? I'm really sorry."

"Mr. Ward—"

"Call me Jack, please Leslie."

"Jack, I lost my fiancé and this afternoon this bracelet, well, it hurt me. It cut me deeply. I want to go home, cry, and try to figure out what to do to make the pain go away." She wanted to go home, drink a bunch of wine and eat a bunch of cheese, anything to bring this awful day to an end.

"I feel so bad. Please don't walk out of here, feeling like you do."

"Sadness is an old friend. I'm used to it. We've actually become good friends in the last few months."

"Leslie," he said, his tone softening, his expression a mix of embarrassment and sadness. "Please… I feel awful. Look, don't go home and feel worse because I'm going to go home and feel like an ass."

She hesitated as he continued, speaking quickly to no doubt make his plea before she could escape. "There is this little hole in the wall place that has great nachos and kind of bad margaritas. I go because I like the family and because they treat me like family. My parents are dead, and I have two ex-wives who hate my guts. I've had some dark times, not like yours, but I've known loneliness. The kind of loneliness that you feel when you're among a crowd of your friends. I've been there. I've been through the fire. There is only one remedy."

"Which is what?" she asked sarcastically.

"You drink enough of the margaritas, they don't taste so bad anymore, and my jokes get a lot funnier. I've got at least a dozen that involve golden swords with bejeweled handles and Hindu sheiks."

"Hindu princes," she corrected. There was a clumsy, puppy dog approach to Jack that seemed to be melting a bit of her anger. She didn't like him, but some of his words were strangely sincere. Maybe he possibly understood her. Maybe they could be friends. She needed more of those. People who knew her with Jordan were strangely absent or busy, quite frankly, they couldn't talk to her, not really. Not like this poor bastard was trying to do.

"What the fuck ever… prince… sheik… grossly inappropriate—"

"You swear too much," she said. "I don't swear much at all."

"Maybe you should try it. You might like it. It helps."

"Maybe you should stop saying fuck so much. I would think someone of your intelligence could find a better way to express himself."

"Oh, a challenge. I like it. I won't say that foul word again in your presence if you agree to have nachos with me."

"But, I might want tacos and beer." What was she saying? When had she decided to go with him? She didn't know, but loneliness recognizes loneliness and maybe he needed a friend.

"Aw, the kind of woman I could take tailgating to sample my favorite tacos at a University of Oregon football game," he said, smiling for the first time. "So many of the world's problems could be solved with tacos and beer. I'm buying."

"I don't think so," Leslie said trying to hold firm as his smile disappeared.

"Leslie, I'm so incredibly sorry about the bracelet—"

"I don't think I could tailgate at a U of O event because I'm an Oregon State University Alumni Beaver. Third generation. And my grandfather and great-grandfather built all the stone buildings on campus, Agriculture, Pharmacy, Bexel, Education—"

"Okay, okay, impressive. Tailgaters are voluntary, not mandatory. However, Civil War is two weeks away, and I have very good tickets. Want to go?"

"Probably not because I'm sure they are in the U of O section, but let's see how you eat your nachos. I'm not making permanent plans beyond tonight. And tonight is only penciled in. And I reserve the right to call a Lyft if you act like a jerk. I'm betting five to one on hitting the Lyft speed dial button on my cell phone before the night is up."

"I'd like to counter, but I know a good deal when I see one. Sold!" Jack proclaimed and gave her a bright smile that made her chuckle despite herself.

"Don't say 'Sold' like that again or I will call Lyft."

Leslie wasn't even sure the place he took her that night had a name. In fact, the chef probably walked by the alley one day and decided to enclose it, creating a narrow, dark enclave masquerading as a restaurant. She was someplace in the seedier part of NE

Portland, near the food scene in Alberta, but definitely off the beaten path. She thought she knew most of the streets in urban Portland, but this was way beyond her street knowledge.

She had wanted to drive herself, but Jack said she'd never find it, and he was right. They rode together in his black Porsche Panamera. Leslie wasn't a car buff per se, but she knew the Panamera went for more than she made in the last two years combined. It was an image, she knew, and it played to his rather large ego that she was sure would irritate her within the hour. He'd already irritated her, and she couldn't say why she was with him now. He had a puppy dog edge to him… it intrigued her. It felt transparent. You knew him. He was what he was.

He was Jordan's complete opposite, and she was pretty sure Jordan wouldn't have liked him, but he might suggest she be nice to him. Jordan drove a small Japanese car and had encouraged her to get a Prius, which her father had immediately dubbed, "The Pius." When she'd gone to work with her dad, he'd insisted she get a bigger car, and she had: a used, discreet black Lexus that she named "Black Beauty" to end the naming game by family members.

There was nothing discreet about the Panamera or its driver.

"What do your clients think of your car?" she asked.

"They fu—um—love it."

"Wow, you almost blew it again, you'd better watch it because you only get three strikes."

"So noted, I need to watch myself around you. I like it, you keep me in line. So, do you like my car?"

"Eh, it is a bit flashy for my taste," she said. She'd keep the obvious comparison to 'lack of sexual ability and the need to display masculinity in another way' to herself.

"Well, they love me at Porsche. I got this puppy for invoice because I send them so much business. Get the clients into a house and help them get a car to match. It's fun."

"Yeah, spending other peoples' money and getting a deal from the dealership, that's *fun*. Don't your clients think you make too much money?"

"Leslie, I love the way you talk to me. Rest assured, I sell real estate like no other agent in the city. My clients love me."

"Said every agent all the time."

"I give one hundred and ten percent to what I love, and I love real estate. I've helped in the purchase or sale of 1,630 homes. There are some days when I go through and quiz myself on the parties' names and the sale price. And you know what? I remember every single one."

"Wow, that makes you kind of old."

"I'm forty, and how old are you? Twenty-one? Please tell me you're legal."

"I turned twenty-six a few weeks ago."

"What date?"

"You don't know me well enough to tell you such a personal detail."

Leaning forward, he gave her a sincere smile, slightly different than his earlier full-wattage dazzlers, and said, "Someday, after you trust me, you will."

Maybe it was the fact that Jack didn't see her as a grief-stricken woman, or that he never knew Jordan, but that first evening she spent with Jack felt more normal to her than any evening had in a very long time.

Her sadness was still there, but it wasn't right in front of her eyes casting its dark haze over everything around her. She laughed at Jack's very bad, very suggestive jokes about Sunil's golden sword.

The nachos tasted fabulous, and the margaritas were strong, but thankfully, neither one of them drank too many as to say anything too stupid or become too sad.

Jack told her that he had lost his parents young. From that, she could tell that he never felt like he quite belonged. She understood what it was like to lose a parent when you were young.

"What happened to your wives?" she asked.

"You ask the hard questions."

"You know my story, but I don't know yours, and since we're just talking, I figure you've nothing to lose."

He looked at her seriously, and said, "Are you kidding me? I've got everything to lose. If I tell you something you don't like, you'll run like a scared rabbit."

"Hardly, nothing scares me anymore. More likely, I'll just speed dial Lyft and calmly walk away because I find you to be an inferior human."

"Meow-ouch! You have some steel in those bones. I like it. I simply married the wrong women. Once the joy of marriage wore off, there was nothing there. Love did not endure."

"The sex wore out," she concluded.

"Yeah, pretty much that and the money. I respect women who want to have careers. Careers being only Mrs. Jack Ward are not inspiring."

Talking to Jack was easy. Much easier than she wanted it to be. She almost felt that by having fun with another man she was cheating on Jordan. It was to be expected, but if someone had said she would feel that way because of Jack, she'd have balked.

At the end of the evening, she glanced at her watch and was surprised to see it was past eleven. It had been months since she'd been out this late. It had been longer since she'd laughed spontaneously other than with Sunil, and Jack had made her laugh. Her cheeks hurt from smiling at his real estate tales. She'd missed laughing, really missed how it made her feel.

As Jack stopped next to her parked car, he asked, "So, can we do this again, like tomorrow night?"

Shaking her head, Leslie said, "No, Jack."

"Is it me?"

"It's not you, it is me," she said and tried not to smile as she said it. "I'm not ready to date, let alone a guy like you."

"Look, I get that you're still hurting over your fiancé. But Leslie, didn't we have a good conversation? Wasn't it fun? Did you laugh?"

"I did laugh, and it was fun," she admitted finding it hard to say the words aloud.

"Then, why don't we try to have fun again, another time. Just casual, no worries."

"I need to think about it, the holidays are coming up, and I just don't know."

"Basic question, again: Did you have fun tonight?"

Regretfully, she answered, "Yes."

"You like Italian?"

"Of course. Who doesn't like Italian?"

"How about some gelato sometime next week? I'll have some new sword jokes for you."

"Fine," she replied as she opened the car door. As he attempted to open his door and run around to help her out, she said, "No. I've got it."

But points for her new puppy dog friend, he didn't try to kiss her on that first night or even try to hug her. He was smart, for she would not have taken kindly to such an intimate intrusion.

Chapter Seven

On Tuesday morning, Leslie circled houses she wanted to see on the West Side realtor tour sheet. Also known as "Voyeur Day" for its strange ritual of well-dressed strangers going into other peoples' homes while they were not home, opening their closet doors, and making disparaging comments about the expensive fixtures and finishes. Tuesday realtor tour in Portland was one of the best perks of being a realtor.

Chatter at the weekly company meeting always went something like this:

Do you have a buyer for that $2 million home? Who cares? I want to see inside!

The listing realtor is catering the open. And she always caters from Elephant's Deli. I just hope it isn't the chicken curry salad, again. Would it kill her to try the chicken poppy seed salad?

Did you hear the harpist in the entryway of that hideously overpriced monstrosity? Yeah, she always has a harpist at her opens, didn't you know? She also gets fruit tarts from La Provence.

Leslie was good at going into the new listings on tour and being able to tell exactly what was making the occupants leave. Half the closet empty with only the wife's clothing? The husband cheated, moved out, and they are getting a divorce, or someone just died.

Husband's clothes in one closet, wife's in another bedroom at the other end of the house. Another divorce in the making, but at least they are civil, probably for the kids.

Smells like a nursing home or a house that was decorated in the 1970s and still has its Formica and pastel toilets? Downsizing Mom and Dad to a nursing home, or someone just died.

Vacant house first time on tour? Buyers got transferred quickly, or somebody just died.

Two sets of same sex clothing, different sizes, and different styles? Gay couple.

On a more positive note: a baby crib in a small bedroom in a two-bedroom condo? A growing family.

Leslie hadn't been on a realtor tour to visit the new-on-market houses since Jordan died, but she thought she was ready to handle it. That intimate snapshot into other, small worlds, some happy, some sad... What did it say about her new place in this world? What would realtors say if they toured her little apartment at Uptown Cliffs?

Single lady for sure.

Oh look, she has a large supply of tuna in the cupboard and cheese in the fridge, definitely single and alone.

Big white garment bag in the closet, bet the wedding fell through...

Lots of romance novels by the bed, no love life, huh?

Wow, bet there is a story there...

Leslie used to tour with her dad, but with him out of town, she had to either go it alone or be subjected to some of the other realtor groups who looked at houses in the Portland Heights all the way down to the expensive waterfront on Lake Oswego. She was independent and controlling enough to know that kind of tour wouldn't be to her liking. She'd have to go it alone. Thankfully, she was getting used to the alone routine.

When Leslie glanced out the window of her office and saw Jack's Panamera parking at the curb, she wasn't happy to admit that her stomach did a little flutter. She'd been thinking about Jack, but she convinced herself it was only because he was a distraction from painful memories of Jordan. Her mind, her body, her emotions needed a break if only for a few moments at a time. And Jack, well, he was comic relief and gave her a respite from her grief. And that damn puppy dog face had a way of endearing itself, but not to her heart, to whatever made her stomach flutter. She had to give him points, he was trying. And wasn't it nice to see a man try, even if he wasn't Jordan?

She had two options, neither was great. She could wait for him to come inside and create a stir of chatter with Peggy, who would also flirt with him to the point of embarrassment, or she could go outside and head him off at the pass. She grabbed her coat and handbag, better to head this off before Peggy pounced and people talked.

She left her office and stepped outside with a brisk pace as if she had somewhere important to go.

"Leslie, hey, hi, how are you?" Jack asked, running to catch up with her. This time he was in full realtor mode wearing a double-breasted navy suit and a red tie. He could have also passed for a local politician.

"Oh, Jack, hi," she replied, sounding as if he were annoying her just a little and she hadn't noticed him. In truth, he was annoying her by showing up at her office without asking.

"Hey, I was just about to go on tour and wanted to see if you'd like to carpool, you know, save on the old fossil fuels."

"Jack, I'm so busy today, I don't want to have a big, long tour. And I doubt we would want to look at the same places, so—"

"I only like to tour houses that cater with Elephant's Deli, or if Rosemary Jackson has a listing, I know there will be cheesecake. And that lady knows how to make a mean cheesecake," he said with a boyish grin, and she found herself smiling back. Damn, he would tour like she did!

She let out a sigh as if she had to think about it, and said, "Okay, but I must be back by noon, not one minute later."

"Scout's honor."

Leslie just shook her head. If he'd been a boy scout, they'd tossed him out for teaching the others to play Craps or something even seedier.

When Leslie toured with her father, it was always a race to see as much "inventory" as possible. Touring with Jack was a completely different experience. It was fun! Jack knew everyone and had a great sense of humor.

"You know what I like to do? My guilty pleasure?" he asked as they were speeding along the Willamette River on Hwy 43 to the multi-million-dollar Dunthorpe neighborhood of Lake Oswego.

"Do I want to know? Is it going to make me want out of the car?" Leslie asked.

"It's nothing like that. I find a vacant house with a pool, and I swim in it."

"Seriously?" Leslie asked. "Isn't that against the law? Wouldn't an ethics committee have you sanctioned? Wouldn't the Real Estate Commissioner slap your hand?"

"A lot of my listings have pools, Leslie. And I sometimes just casually ask the seller, once they've gotten into a new house if it would be okay until their old house sells. I haven't been turned down yet. I mean, come on, I'm watching over their previous house for them while they move along to their new life. I'm like a non-paid caretaker."

"You're like a parasite," Leslie quipped. Jack threw back his head and laughed. "You know what I like about you?"

"Well, let's see, I'm young."

"Yeah, and you are gorgeous, but you call me on my shit. You keep me in line. I like it."

Leslie laughed, "Glad you do because I'm going to keep flicking it to you."

"Does that mean you like me a little?"

Leslie held up her hand, her thumb and forefinger barely apart.

"Sold! I'll take what I can get," he said, gently taking her hand in his and kissing her fingertips.

It caught her off-guard, but she didn't dislike it. And at noon, she told him that she didn't need to be back too soon. They had lunch at a hole-in-the-wall Korean barbecue restaurant where the noodles were pulled by hand. Like the Mexican restaurant, it was eclectic. This time the restaurant was in a small alleyway in Beaverton that shared its bathroom with the hair salon next door. Again, it had been a place she didn't know existed. And when he dropped her off back at her office, she let him kiss her on the cheek.

And that was the day that everything changed for Leslie. Jack became her partner in crime. They started spending more time together, and although Leslie still missed Jordan terribly, some of the hurt didn't sting as fiercely.

Jack made her feel like she was living again. He was always happy and funny. He didn't take himself seriously, and he gave Leslie crap anytime she got too quiet or too serious. He brought her laughter back.

Christmas was in Palm Springs with her father and Denice. Aunt Trudel, her husband Uncle Jerry, and Suzie and Timothy were also present. She realized she missed Jack. Maybe it was because she was the only person without a partner. But maybe she was starting to like Jack a little bit. The realization was hard to accept, but he'd managed to get past some of her defenses. It had taken him a long time, but she knew the precise moment things had changed. He'd plied her with home cooked food and too much wine. She'd caved, enjoyed the attention, felt alive again—and ended up in his bed.

"Here's my question, does it bother him that everyone colors his teeth black on all those bus benches he has around town?" Suzie asked as they lay by the pool.

"I asked him about that," Leslie said. "He said it draws even more attention to him. I'll give him that, he's a marketer. He doesn't take himself too seriously, and he has a great sense of humor."

"I see," Suzie replied and then looked around to make sure they were alone. Then she whispered, "How is it sleeping with an old guy?"

"He is only fourteen years older than me. He just turned forty. It's nothing. Not like my dad and Denice. They are a generation apart."

"Technically, he could be your daddy. In some backwater towns in America, people get married at fourteen."

"Oh, shut up!"

"Does he make you call him the realtor King in bed?"

"No, no, no. He is very gentlemanly, but I've only had sex with him twice after lots of wine and laughter. It was strange, you know, being with someone else. But it also made me feel like I was alive, and it was enjoyable, not mind numbing."

"I didn't want to ask you, but I have to, since you are kind of hinting at it."

"Make it stop, what do you want to know?" Leslie asked with exasperation.

"How does he rank to Jordan? I'm sorry to ask, but I just want to know that he makes you happy. Does he rock your world? I know Jordan did and I want anyone you are with to make you happy in that way."

Leslie turned to Suzie, slipped off her sunglasses, felt the tears prick in the corners of her eyes as she said, "I'm a little confused about all that, and I don't know what to do."

"Oh honey, what is it?" Suzie asked, as she grabbed Leslie's hand and gave it a reassuring squeeze.

"It is just that the couple times we've ended up in bed, it is so pedestrian. When Jordan and I made love, we made love. I mean, one time, we fell off the bed, and I barely noticed. With Jack, it is just straight forward. I'd notice if I fell off the bed. Heck, I spotted a cobweb in the corner. Then I worried about where the spider was. It totally took me off my game.

"I know that I don't give myself to him like I did with Jordan. Sometimes with Jordan, I lost track of time and didn't know where I was. I was so caught up I felt like we had transcended to a different time and place, but with Jack, I just feel like I'm taking care of business. Like I'm getting a massage or having a pedicure. It's fine, my body does its thing, but I know where I am, all the time. It's like a gym workout. I need it. But we are only just getting to the physical side of the relationship. There is no emotional heart bond of souls, know what I'm saying?"

"Yes, unfortunately," Suzie said. "That is so hard."

"Most of the time, but he is older so there is that," Leslie said, making an intentional joke to lighten the conversation.

Suzie started laughing, and Leslie joined in. When they finally got control of themselves, Suzie asked, "Do you like him?"

"Yes, I do."

"Well, then maybe the bang-bang will get better," Suzie said, reminding Leslie of their childhood euphemism for sex.

"That's what I keep telling myself. And my body, jeez she is a needful thing. Bad bang-bang is better than no bang-bang at all. And I miss the bang-bang I had with Jordan. I want a man to make me feel like that again. That was real. Maybe it will get better in time?"

"Eh, just have some fun, I guess? You've had a very hard, horrible year. I think you should do what makes you happy, just don't marry him."

"Oh, Hell no."

On Valentine's Day, Leslie rolled up the sleeve of her red silk blouse and smiled at the little vampire who was going to take a pint of her A- blood. She didn't know how Suzie had talked her into a blood drive on Valentine's Day, but she had. Trudel's Wedding Boutique was famous for her Valentine's Day blood drive, which up until now Leslie had successfully avoided, faking a cold, planning trips out of town, or just being too busy to make it in. No such luck this year.

Leslie was terrified of needles, she didn't like the thought of having a sharp piece of metal shoved under her skin, but she couldn't refuse her cousin. And after all Suzie had done for her over the last eight months, the least she could do was to give a pint of her precious bodily fluids.

After Leslie had finished, the world spun a bit, but she ignored it. She had a lot to do today, and Jack had told her he had a surprise for her. She didn't know how she felt about that, but he was trying hard to pursue her, and she did kind of like the break in the boredom of her life.

"Now, be careful, drink your juice, eat a cookie before you leave," the vampire had warned.

There was also an instruction sheet on what to do after giving blood, which she'd read later. She needed to get to the office and write up an addendum on a current negotiation before Jack arrived to take her to lunch, which he told her was the beginning of her Valentine's Day surprise.

As she drove to work and ate a second frosted sugar cookie that Suzie had given her after the bloodletting, she remembered not to drink too much wine on her date with Jack, part two of her surprise. Not only would she be a cheap drunk, but she might also end up with a massive hangover. She wondered if he'd take advantage of her, maybe ravage her a bit.

"Yeah right," she said aloud, thinking that the more adventurous "bang-bang" would need to be addressed soon. It wasn't all passion and steam when she and Jordan had started having sex, but it had gotten there quickly. She just didn't know what to say to a man about his lack of sexual prowess in the bedroom. Or was it her? She needed more passion from him but didn't know how to ask for it. With Jordan she didn't need to ask. He knew what to do. The very thought of her dead fiancé on Valentine's Day had her mopping up tears before they fell onto her silk blouse. Jordan had known how to chase her and catch her. Their love life had always been fun and spirited. *Comfortable* would never have been a word to describe their passion.

Her emotions bounced to all extremes, happiness, guilt, disappointment, and sadness. If an emotion had a name, she felt it. And at the moment, she felt lightheaded and nauseous, the bright sun making it worse as was the cookie she'd just eaten. Above all, she missed Jordan with a longing she hadn't felt in months. She hadn't died with him, but sometimes it felt like she had.

"Someone got flowers today!" Peggy exclaimed in sing-song voice as Leslie entered the lobby of her office and wondered if she shouldn't have gone home instead.

"I hope it was me," Leslie replied.

"I put them on your deskkkkkkk," she sang. "Are they from Jack? Is he taking you someplace special tonight?"

"Thanks, I don't know yet, we are keeping the mystery alive," Leslie said flatly, hoping to stop the saccharine noise. "Jack is coming by in few to take me to lunch. Would you send him back to my office?" She wanted to add, please do not flirt with him or stick your chest out so that he can look at your cleavage, okay?

"Okey-dokie! He is just sooooooooooo handsome! He must be taking you someplace special. You must have had a hint? OMG, you will have to tell me all about it!"

Yes, he was handsome, and a good guy. Leslie knew she was lucky to have him in her life. She just wished that whatever that little missing something was, be it passion or the right kind of recklessness that it would fall into place.

Leslie sat heavily at her desk and looked at the sweet box sitting on her desk blotter and felt a new wave of sadness. Inside was a bouquet in a bag, done in the French style, all reds, and purples, vibrant and familiar. Her heart twisted with the memories the flowers evoked. They were from the same florist that Jordan had used to send her flowers last Valentine's Day. Maybe it was a fantastic omen and Jordan's way of telling her that he was okay with her dating Jack. But how strange was it that Jack would choose to get her flowers from the same florist? He'd given her flowers several times, and they'd all come from Gifford & Doving on Broadway in downtown Portland.

Someone must have told Jack that she had a soft spot for bouquets in bags from Buddy's in Lake Oswego. But who would have told him that? She knew she hadn't. And was it in the best taste for him to duplicate it knowing how she felt about Jordan? And how could she tell him without coming off like a total bitch? Bottom line, she couldn't.

Reaching for the card, she wondered how much happier she would be to see Jordan's name inside instead of the man whose name she knew she would find.

The joke, as it were, was on her.

To my beautiful, gorgeous, passionate wife, thank you for making all my dreams come true. I love you now and forever, Jordan.

Leslie stood, not knowing what to do, and then she fell back into her chair and started hyperventilating. She could not breathe, black splotches appeared before her eyes, sweat covered every inch of her body, and a sudden ringing in her ears became deafening. Was this what it felt like to have a heart attack?

The last thing she heard before she passed out was Jack's voice shouting, "Leslie!"

When she came to, she was laying on the floor with a cold, wet cloth on her head. Jack was leaning over her, looking worried.

"Damn, babe, you gave us a scare," he said as he held her hand. "No more giving blood on an empty stomach."

"I didn't—"

"Don't worry, I fainted, too, the one and only time I gave blood. We'll get some food and sugar into you, and you'll be as good as new—"

"No, it's the flowers," she said as she began to cry, "They are from Jordan."

"Babe, that's impossible. You must have hit your head—"

"They are from Jordan!" she insisted. "Look at the damn card!"

An hour later, she was laying on the black leather couch in Jack's penthouse condo at the Waterfront Pearl building. The sun was bright, shining down on the Willamette River. She watched boats glide along as tears silently ran down her cheeks. She no longer cared about her silk blouse. What hadn't been drenched in her sudden panic sweat had salty tear spots all over it.

Jack was making himself useful by running down to the corner Italian deli to get lunch, which meant Leslie had a bit of time to figure out what had happened before he got back. Picking up her cell, she called Buddy's and waited for someone to pick up. She knew they were busy; it was Valentine's Day after all, but she didn't want to wait one minute longer.

"Buddy's Flowers," a harried voice answered.

"This is Leslie Westcott. You delivered a bouquet to me today at my office in NW Portland."

"Yes? Was there an issue with the quality?"

"No, but they were from Jordan Slater?"

"Yes," the person replied sounding a bit impatient.

"Can you tell me who ordered them? Jordan, who was my fiancé, has been dead for a little over eight months."

An uncomfortable silence descended on the conversation. "Miss Westcott, I don't know what to say."

"Could you please look at your records and tell me if someone is playing a joke on me?" she asked, her voice cracking a little.

"Sure, hold one minute."

Two minutes later, the woman was back on the line.

"Okay, I figured out what happened. When Mr. Slater ordered last year, we were offering a special. You would get 15 percent off both orders if you ordered for the current year and the next year at the same time. It was a very popular promotion, and Mr. Slater went ahead and placed the order a year in advance, paid for it then too."

Jordan had always been forgetful, and Leslie figured he was probably happy to have the burden of remembering to order flowers out of the way.

"I see," she said. No wonder the card from today's bouquet talked about her being a wife. If Jordan hadn't died, she would have been his wife now. She looked down at her sunstone ring and felt the pain deep within her heart.

"I'm so sorry," the voice on the other end of the phone said.

"No, no, I'm glad we got that settled. He doesn't have any more flowers ordered for me, does he?"

"No, ma'am. That's the last." Because he's gone.

"Okay, thank you." She hung up and started to sob.

That was how Jack found her a few minutes later, hugging a throw pillow to her middle, curled into a ball. Of all the surprises she'd ever had in her life, this had to be one of the best and worst. That little bouquet back at her office was the last gift she would ever receive from Jordan and that knowledge broke her heart all over again. And it was the first crack in her relationship with Jack.

In early March, Leslie and Jack drove to the beach for a weekend at his beach home in the little touristy town of Seaside. It was the first time he'd brought her to the house, and Leslie was looking forward to the change of scenery. The spring colors made everything brighter, bringing Leslie out of the sadness that had lingered for several weeks after a difficult Valentine's Day. She could tell that Jack had been frustrated by her sadness. He'd tried to hide it, but she could see his frustration. His smile wasn't as bright, and he treated her like a wounded animal, delicately.

"So baby," he said as they drove through the small beachside town, "I want this to be a do-over."

"A do over?" she asked, wondering what he meant.

"I want this to be a do-over for a horrible Valentine's Day. That was a below the belt gut punch you took. I know it has taken some time for you to recover, and I have to admit, this is selfish, but I felt cheated for you and me. That was supposed to be our day."

Leslie could sense the jealousy he had for Jordan. Thankfully, he hadn't vocalized it. But the ghost of Jordan was there between them. A man, with an ego the size of Jack's, couldn't NOT take it personally. But what could she say? Jordan had been there first. She loved Jordan with all her heart and soul. Jack was the second pick next to a dead man. There was no way he could compete, and that made her a bit sad, but it was the reality.

"I'm sorry we didn't get to celebrate it the way you wanted," she said. It was all she could give him on the subject. "I didn't enjoy it, if that is any consolation."

"Do you think we can have that do-over? Are you okay with it?"

She wanted to say, "No, Valentine's is forever ruined for me. I hate it. If Valentine's Day fell off the calendar forever, I'd be cool with that. Isn't it just a Hallmark holiday for suckers?"

"I'm very okay with that," she lied and slapped a smile on her face. She was good at the fake smile. She'd even learned to make it look convincing. Most of the time.

"Good, baby, I promise to make it special."

For not the first time, she wondered if he had called all of his girlfriends "babe" or "baby." It made her feel like she wasn't special. Sure, Jordan had nicknames for her, but they felt different, more sincere.

They had dinner at a casual little restaurant by the beach, which had a wonderful view of the ocean, which Leslie loved. This was another thing about Jack that she loved, and she tried to remind herself she was being unfair earlier. He always found a unique and out of the way place for them to share a meal, and they were usually delicious. He wasn't all about "being seen" at the fanciest and hippest places in town.

Would she have enjoyed a special dinner out at a fancy restaurant once in a while? Sure, but aside from his flashy car and big penthouse, Jack, she was finding, was a bit frugal. She could appreciate frugal, but she didn't like cheap.

Tonight was no exception.

It seemed like everyone in the place knew Jack. Apparently, he defined the word "regular" here. People stopped by their table to say hello, and Jake made a point to introduce Leslie to everyone.

"I never got to give you your Valentine's Day gift," Jack said as they watched the sunset over the Pacific.

"I ruined the mood by fainting and then crying uncontrollably," she said and took a deep sip of the champagne he insisted they order.

"Understandable," he said.

"I don't think we are getting a green flash tonight," she observed. "There is a low fog bank coming in."

"That's too bad. Here, you'd better open this before we lose the romantic light," he said and reached into his pocket and produced a little wrapped box, which he sat on the table in front of her. It was as if someone dimmed the lights, Leslie could feel people all around them suddenly grow quiet and turn towards them expectantly to watch what was unfolding. She could feel their eyes on her as she picked up the box.

Leslie hoped the box contained earrings. Please, please let it be earrings.

"Jack, you didn't need to—"

"Yes, Leslie, I've been thinking about this moment since I met you," he said, slipping out of his chair and onto the carpet of undefined color, which had seen better days. Now other diners were whistling and encouraging Jack.

"Close the deal buddy!"

"Go, Jack, go!"

"Sold! Sold! Sold!"

"Way to trump a sunset, man!"

"You brighten my life. You are there for me. I can't wait to see you. I can't wait to be with you. I know we haven't known each other for very long, but I love you, baby. Let's keep the music going. I want to marry you."

Leslie could feel her heart beating in her chest. She unwrapped the package and found a black velvet box inside. Had the world just stopped spinning? Leslie's past year and every moment before that flashed through her mind. As she tried to rapidly sort through the memories she realized that being with Jack had taken away a massive amount of her sadness.

Of course, some days were worse than others, but on the whole she was better. She told herself that Valentine's Day had just been a glitch. Everyone's first love felt like the sweetest love. But she wasn't seventeen anymore. Now she could be reasonable. Jack was good to her. He loved her. He would always be there for her. She could certainly do worse. He'd been married before, but, he'd explained why it hadn't worked, and she believed him. So the sex wasn't earth shattering, it was still enjoyable, pleasant even. And there was no doubt it would get better with time. Sex had gotten better with Jordan over the years, from fabulous to incredible.

Leslie brought herself back to the present as Jack took the box from her hand, opened it to show her a large emerald ring as the patrons of the restaurant were now clapping and chanting, "*Say yes! Say yes! Say yes!*"

This was actually happening. Jack had arranged a coup. He had totally duped her and these people that knew them and were cheering for them, they were all totally in on it. She couldn't believe she had been so unprepared.

He slipped the cool metal over the ring finger of her left hand. Deja vu rolled over her. It was such a different feeling than what she'd felt when Jordan had presented her with the sunstone and diamond ring in their little enchanted cottage. Leslie told herself to stop—no moment could ever be as perfect as that first proposal had been.

"Oh my," she said, looking at the large emerald that was far too large for her finger. She couldn't help but think, "Was this thing real?"

"*Say yes! Say yes! Say yes!*"

"Well?" Jack asked.

Everyone was waiting for her answer, the excitement like a dense fog overshadowing everything. Leslie found it hard to breathe.

"*Say yes! Say yes! Say yes!*"

Without even willing herself to do it Leslie found herself saying "yes." It was only then, as the cries turned to applause that Leslie stopped to think to herself, "Oh hell, I'm engaged again."

As she awoke the next morning Leslie couldn't remember much after the drive back to Portland. Only hearing the soundtrack of her fellow patrons shouting, "*Say yes! Say yes! Say yes!*"

It still felt entirely surreal.

"You know," Jack said, picking up her hand as he drove and examining the large emerald ring, "It looks loose. I thought the jeweler knew your size."

"The jeweler?" she asked feeling a bit car sick.

"Sauveterre Jewelers. I know they did your other engagement ring, so I had that guy match it to the size of your first engagement ring," he said, pointing to her sunstone.

So, Charlie had designed this ring and he'd made it the wrong size? Talk about odd coincidences. Leslie suddenly felt a moment of embarrassment thinking of Charlie and Jack deep in conversation about her preferences. Knowing her taste the way he had seemed to when it came to the sunstone pieces, she couldn't believe that Charlie wouldn't have suggested a simpler design.

Could he have been trying to sabotage Jack? He had mentioned not liking him when she first returned the bracelet. No. That couldn't be the case. She had to be reading too much into things. Still, she was surprised he allowed all the diamonds and filigree to distract from the ginormous emerald. That thing really was impressive, even if not something she would have perhaps picked for herself.

"So, lay it on me, babe," he said smiling with his puppy dog grin. "How are you feeling this morning?"

Last night Leslie had laid awake for hours tossing and turning. As thoughts flew through her mind she realized there were a lot of things she and Jack had never talked about. Leslie took a deep breath. It was now or never.

"There are things I want in the future that we haven't discussed. I don't know if we are on the same page. Frankly, I'm a little scared that we haven't talked about these things. I'm nervous that we should have discussed this before I accepted your proposal."

"Don't be nervous. Babe, let's talk. We've always been able to talk, and we've always been honest with each other, right?"

"Okay, here it goes. I want a house someday with grass and a dog, a big hound-like dog. So, you will have to move out of your condo in the Pearl and sell all your leather furniture because I want to decorate in the French country style with some antiques I got from my mother that are in storage." Leslie had no idea why she had started with this. As she said it, it all sounded so trivial and selfish. But still, Leslie felt like these things were important, and she needed some security before going any further.

When Leslie's father had married Denice they had quickly moved and gotten rid of everything. Thankfully, Leslie had been able to save her mother's favorite pieces and her father had paid for a storage unit to hold everything until she had a home of her own.

Jack paused, taking it all in. "Could that wait a few years, until we maybe travel a bit?"

She'd always wanted to travel. "Yes, that would be fine. But I want my house, my dog, and I want babies before you turn for-ty-five. And then, once we are done with the babies, I want you to have a vasectomy." Leslie blurted out in one deep breath. Okay, so maybe it was the same plan she'd had with Jordan. It didn't mean it wasn't the plan she still wanted.

"Jeez, okay babe, you've given this some thought. We'll knock out a couple of kids in a few years, cool?"

"And the vasectomy?"

"Is that a deal breaker?"

"Non-negotiable."

"And if I agree?"

"I agree to marry you, well, I already did, but I'll feel more excited about it because we've talked it out."

"Okay, I agree to get snipped."

"Okay," she said, feeling calmer for the moment.

"Hey, here's an idea, let's pop on a plane and head for Vegas tomorrow," he suggested. "We'll get a suite at the Bellagio and get married next to the big fountain by an Elvis impersonator. Now that would be different for both of us."

"What's your hurry?" she asked, appalled by the suggestion.

"I'm a closer, babe. That is something you should know about me. When I got a hot deal on the table, I close it. I don't like things hanging out there."

"Well, cool your jets. This isn't a business deal, it is a wedding," Leslie said. "My Aunt Trudel, and my family, well, they'd kill you if you drug me to Vegas."

"Okay, okay, we will do the big dog and pony. Hell, I'll even pay for the damn thing. You just plan it, baby, anything you want. How about June?"

"How about November?" she countered. She didn't want another summer wedding. She didn't want anything to remind her of what could have been with Jordan. And she certainly couldn't have a wedding so close to what was supposed to be her wedding date a year earlier.

It didn't occur to her until much later that she hadn't mentioned the word "love" anywhere in her proposal negotiation. If she couldn't have the fairytale with the man of her dreams at least she could have most of her dreams come true with a man she liked. She liked Jack and eventually that would turn to love. She could hope.

Chapter Eight

Call it embarrassing having to plan a second wedding months after what should have been a first, but Leslie couldn't conjure up quite the same enthusiasm she'd once had. Her family and friends latched on the upcoming nuptials like Titanic passengers clinging to lifeboats. She'd been saved, and they were all rejoicing. *Hallelujah!* The bride whose fiancé died a couple of weeks before their wedding was getting a second chance at happiness!

Did anyone care that Jack had been married twice before?

Hey, at least he knew how to commit… Things are so much different these days. Marriage isn't what it used to be.

Did it bother them that he was over ten years older?

Leslie was mature well beyond her years. Surely, men her own age bored her… Besides, Jack was so handsome!

Did they question if she was in love, as in love as she'd been with Jordan?

Let's not bring up hard topics. Jordan was her first love; nothing compares to that… Jack wants to share his life with her. He's successful, and she likes him. Their feelings will grow into a deep, passionate love over time. Isn't that enough?

Leslie jiggled the large emerald ring on her finger and heard it fall on her desk. Picking it up, she examined the diamonds surrounding the center stone. It was flashy, so flashy she felt a little self-conscious wearing it. And her hand was clumsier with the heavy imbalance of the ring, and she had to compensate her movements.

Over the last several weeks, the more Leslie had inspected the emerald on her hand, the more obsessed she'd become with the stone itself. It was gorgeous, but there was something about it, a bit of a cloud to it, an impurity that she didn't quite believe was up to the Sauveterre or Charlie's standards. Something about the ring just didn't sit right with her. It didn't help that Jack kept reminding her how valuable the damn thing was. He had been on her since the first night about getting in and getting it resized.

"Do you know how much that rock is worth? I've seriously got it insured for forty thousand, but I'd prefer not to explain to my insurance agent how you lost it because it didn't fit your petite little finger, babe."

She did not want to have to see Charlie about getting the ring resized. He'd called Jack an ass. And despite what he'd said to the contrary, she was still a little mad at him for the bracelet incident that fall. He'd kind of set Jack up. He had to know the bracelet was for her. Really, how many sunstone rings were out there? But if she went anyplace else than Sauveterre Jewelers, Jack would be upset. And maybe she could figure out what game Charlie was playing.

The trip to the jewelers would have to wait another day though. For now, she had more important things to do, such as another trip to Aunt Trudel's.

This second visit to Aunt Trudel's brought back a memory from just over a year ago, when the happiness was so genuine it clouded the room like a lovely, sweet perfume. This time the happiness seemed a little forced or just plain missing. This time they had a job to do, and they were focused.

"Oh darling, we are so happy for you," Aunt Trudel said as they made their way to the VIP upholstered couch on Saturday morning. Suzie stood next to her mother with a large, forced grin that looked like it had to hurt.

When she'd told Suzie she was marrying Jack, Suzie wasn't just shocked, she was floored. "Are you sure about this, cuz?"

No, she wasn't sure about anything, but she was in too deep, had taken this too far. She wasn't especially rash or ridiculous. Jack did love her. They would have a fabulous life. It wasn't the life she'd have had with Jordan, but that life wasn't possible. And when you looked at all Jack offered and who he was as a person, this alternative was pretty good.

Her father had bowed out of the wedding dress shopping trip citing the need to shut down the Palm Springs house for the season, but he had called Trudel with his credit card, and he said there was no budget. Denice had wanted to come, but Leslie had told her to stay in Palm Springs and enjoy her last few days in the warmth. Aunt Trudel didn't have her assistant ask about beverages this time. She just appeared with an ice bucket, a champagne bottle, and three glasses.

As a young employee, Leslie had never seen Aunt Trudel have a glass of champagne with a client, but she supposed everyone needed a little liquid courage today.

"Now sweetie," Aunt Trudel began, "What would your handsome young man like to see you walk down the aisle in?"

"Mom, he's like forty," Suzie said and then apologized, "Sorry Les. You know I love you, but he is a man, not a young man."

Her fabulous James Casper gown was never mentioned. Leslie knew that for several months last summer it had spent time in what they used to call "cold" storage where wedding dresses were sent to die on the hanger when something tragic happened. She'd finally gotten up the courage to rescue the dress and bring it home where it now resided like a cocooned corpse in her closet.

"Jack is a big personality. He told me he'd like to see me sparkle, which sounds like a bit of a glitz gown," Leslie said. "Something to go with the ring."

"I do love emeralds," Aunt Trudel said as she admired Leslie's ring. "I don't think in my thirty-year history of helping brides that I've seen one this large."

"And that one could choke a horse, it looks like it is at least ten carats," Suzie said as she held Leslie's hand and turned it over. "Les, my god, you've got tape on it!"

"I know," Leslie said with an exasperated expression. "I've been busy. I'm planning to take it next to get it sized."

"How long have you been engaged? A month? And you haven't taken care of that yet?" Suzie gave Leslie a long, hard look.

"I've been busy," Leslie repeated.

"We should see if we can go in today before we have lunch," Suzie said, and this time Leslie chose to ignore her.

"How about a corseted bodice?" Aunt Trudel suggested.

"A bejeweled corseted bodice," Suzie corrected.

"I think I like the look of that one," Leslie said, pointing to a dress on a mannequin.

"You've always had excellent taste. That is a new Caroline Benson. We just got it in last week. Let me take it down for you."

Leslie thought that Jack would love it. It was a sleeveless v-neck with open sides down to the waist. It was a trumpet silhouette with a long train. There was a lace overlay with crystals along the edge of the v and embellishing the lace flowers. It was a woman's dress, not a young blushing bride. It was also a bit revealing in a sexy, naughty way.

Leslie couldn't believe how well the Caroline fit especially considering it was a size too small. Over the last few months, Leslie had lost weight without trying.

Aunt Trudel added all the extras, the earrings, the bracelets, and the veil. The ladies stepped back. It looked fine on her. In fact, the dress looked damn good and Leslie knew it. She looked like a bride, a sexy bride maybe, but a bride nonetheless. Neither Aunt Trudel nor Suzie could come up with anything to say. And with that, for Leslie, the decision was made. It looked fine on her.

"Okay, I say we take it," Leslie said.

Trudel and Suzie talked at once.

"*Your first dress?*"

"*No darling, we are just getting started.*"

And the last from Suzie, "No, I need to see the sparkle in your eyes as well as your dress."

Nine dresses, two hours, and a second bottle of champagne later, Leslie asked to be placed back in the Caroline Benson dress. This time she mustered up a convincing smile, but Suzie shook her head.

"Don't you like me in the dress?"

"I like you in the dress. You look beautiful. I just want to see you look as happy as you did…" Suzie said, pausing, coming up blank, not wanting to name that which should not be named.

"Suz, it isn't going to happen. You don't have to say it, nothing will make me ever feel like that again," she said, gently touching one of the flower details. "I'm okay with that. I do like this dress, and as long as everyone doesn't think my butt looks too big or my breasts are spilling out, I want this dress."

An hour later, it was done. She had bought the dress with her father's credit card. It should arrive in five months, just in time for a fall wedding. The veil and shoes were in the trunk of her Lexus, and she and Suzie were headed off to a late lunch to soak up some of the alcohol they had managed to consume before 2 p.m.

"Can I just ask you something?" Suzie asked as they cautiously made their way through downtown Portland.

"Okay," Leslie said, trying to get her mind straight.

"Are you happy? Do you love Jack? I mean, the way you loved Jordan."

Leslie took a deep breath. Maybe it was the healing she had done, or maybe it was because it was Suzie or maybe it was the champagne, regardless, she found herself being more honest than she had been able to be in a long time.

"He isn't Jordan, so I'm not going to love him like I loved Jordan. It is an impossibility. But when I'm with him, it doesn't hurt so much. He doesn't make me cry. We laugh and he makes me smile. And I like him. My heart is involved, but there is still a shadow of Jordan. I don't think that shadow will ever fully go away. But, with Jack, I'll have years of laughter and that counts for something."

"Are you sure you want to marry him?"

"I wouldn't be going through all of this if I didn't."

"Okay, okay, I just want you to be happy. I've read about rebound relationships. I just don't want this to be a rebound."

"Anyone I'm with is a rebound, Suz. Jack makes me happy. And this is probably the closest I can get in this lifetime. There are a lot worse things than a man who makes you laugh. I'm not going to find another Jordan, but I found a Jack and he is special just in a different way."

"Oh Leslie, you break my heart sometimes."

"It will be okay." But in her heart, Leslie wasn't quite sure.

"Let's drop your ring off at Sauveterre's before lunch. Maybe they can get it done today."

Leslie took a deep breath. She did not want to do this today, but it seemed unavoidable, so she gave in.

They found a parking space directly in front of Sauveterre Jewelers because sometimes the parking angels conspired with you.

Leslie let her cousin go first into the shop. Caroline knew Suzie because her engagement ring had come from Sauveterre Jewelers as well. They greeted each other like long-lost friends.

Charlie was with a customer. He was bent over a table with a couple, looking at several rings. Someone else was getting engaged.

Charlie looked different somehow. Leslie hadn't seen him since October, and there was something about him that had changed. He looked older perhaps. Deeply involved as he was in his conversation, he didn't seem to notice her as she started looking around the store, one display case catching her eye. There were five rings in total, each more magnificent than the other.

The stones were beautiful and unusual, like nothing she'd ever seen.

"Ah, you found Charlie's new creations," Caroline observed as she and Suzie joined Leslie in front of the case.

"Charlie did these?" she asked. "They are gorgeous."

"Yes, he wanted to design a signature line of rings unlike any others on the market. His father is very traditional and prefers the classic diamond pieces, but he believes in Charlie and told him to start designing. These are very rare stones, about as far from a traditional diamond or ruby as you can get. Charlie spent weeks working with dealers around the world to get exactly what he wanted."

Leslie would have traded her cloudy emerald for any of them in a heartbeat. And she bet some of them were less expensive than the emerald.

"He has sold seven so far. He started with a dozen. He literally can't make them fast enough for the orders he's getting. And the stones, well, they aren't easy to find."

"What is that one in the corner?" Leslie asked. She couldn't exactly tell what color the large center stone was—it appeared to be yellow, green, or pink depending on which way you looked at it. On either side of the stone was a magnificent triangular shaped diamond. The ring was stunning.

"That center stone is a two and a half carat Zultanite. It is mined in Turkey and very rare. Did you notice how it changes colors?"

"Yes, it is gorgeous," Suzie said. "What a beautiful ring."

"And that one below it, what's that?" Leslie asked.

"That's Alexandrite from Madagascar."

"It is red and then green, I love it!"

"I'm not surprised. It reminds me of your sunstone," Charlie said from somewhere behind her.

She hadn't heard him walk up and couldn't remember what she'd been talking about. Slowly, she turned and found him watching her. She could almost hear his unspoken words, *You're marrying Jack? Seriously, did you forget the bracelet incident? How can you marry that ass?"*

To Leslie's surprise, Suzie hugged Charlie with a familiarity that caught her off guard. Suzie noticed her look and reminded her that her ring had not only come from Sauveterre, but that Charlie had designed it, a detail Leslie hadn't known. She managed, "Hello, nice to see you."

"Chuck," Suzie said, "Will you please fix Leslie's ring before she loses it?"

"I'd be happy to take a look," he said, smiling first at Suzie and then at Leslie.

"These rings," Leslie said as she looked at the case, "Well, they are beautiful."

"Here, let me show you up close." He walked to the other side of the case and unlocked it. Then he placed the tray on top of the display case and pulled out the large ring with the amazing Zultanite. "Go ahead, try something on."

She didn't want to remove the sunstone ring on her right hand, so she pulled off the emerald and set it on the glass. She slipped on the Zultanite and smiled. It looked amazing on her hand. It was only a quarter of the size of the emerald, but it made up for it in sparkle.

Suzie asked Caroline, "I was wondering, do you have any large, gray pearl earrings? I need something a bit larger to go with the gray pearl necklace Tim gave me for our first anniversary."

"Great timing! I just finished some beautiful earrings. Let me show you…" Suzie and Caroline faded off to a different area of the store as Leslie continued to be mesmerized by the Zultanite.

"Try on the Alexandrite," Charlie said as he examined her emerald ring and shook his head. Then he added, "I'm sorry about what I said about your fiancé, Jack. It is obvious that you are very happy. And that is all I want for you."

"Thank you. And thank you for everything you've done for me. I love my ring." She met his deep brown eyes and shook her head. "And don't ever tell Jack, but it is my favorite piece of jewelry next to my heart," she said, touching the heart shaped diamond at her neck, "The emerald is taking third place."

"Good," he murmured, and then he smiled. He looked pleased as she slipped on the different rings and complimented him. Maybe they had reached a tentative détente.

"Can I ask you a question? Maybe a question I don't want anyone to know?" She asked.

"Sure," he said, his eyes narrowing ever so slightly.

"The emerald looks a little cloudy to me. Is it supposed to look like that? Or is it dirty?"

"It's a very large emerald," he explained. "If it were smaller, you'd expect it to be clear. But with that size, it isn't easy to get a clear stone."

"Jack said it is insured for forty-thousand dollars. Is it worth that?"

"I gave him an estimate of twenty-five, so that isn't far off, but if I were buying it I wouldn't give him a penny over ten grand for the stone."

Jack hadn't exactly been honest. It bothered her.

"Okay, thanks for telling me," she said, feeling that dull ache begin in her stomach. For not the first time Leslie couldn't help but wish Jack had taken her with him to pick out the ring. Just something simpler, something less gaudy, something more suited to who she was as a person.

She tried on each of the rings from the case, thinking that any of them would have made her happier than the one she was stuck with. "What motivated you to design these? Where did you get the idea?"

"My father likes traditional stones," he said pointing towards his dad James in the back who Leslie immediately recognized. Aside from having gray hair, he hadn't changed a bit.

"My dad's a traditional guy, he still thinks engagement rings should be made of diamonds, but I wanted to mix it up a bit, I wanted something that felt a bit more authentic to the Portland scene—natural and unusual, but still very beautiful.

"I have more demand than supply. These two rings," he said, pointing to a Morganite and a smaller Zultanite, "Are already spoken for. That only leaves me with three exotic stones to display. I have six more in design, and a long wait list for more of the Alexandrite, which is obscenely expensive and very hard to find. It has been a successful idea. Kind of like a treasure hunt. And most importantly, I've enjoyed every minute of it. This is my passion. I am having so much fun making people so incredibly happy. I've enjoyed every minute of it."

James looked up from the ring he was working on, breaking Leslie and Charlie's moment, and winked at Leslie. She winked back. Then he said, "Even an old man can learn from a young buck."

"You taught him everything he knows, Mr. Sauveterre," Leslie said.

He smiled broadly and went back to work.

Leslie turned back to Charlie and asked, "So if you are only interested in the lesser-known stones, what made you go back to an emerald for my ring? Or did your dad do this one instead?"

Charlie looked uncomfortable and stumbled over his words, "It just seemed like the right fit."

She watched him, saw the flicker in his eyes, he was lying to her.

Then he turned his attention back to her ring, taking his time dismantling the tape she'd placed on the band.

"Charlie, what? Is there something that you aren't telling me?" Leslie asked as her stomach took a palpable dip. She knew this was the beginning of something she wasn't going to like.

"Well, this probably wouldn't have been my first choice for a stone, I've always thought this emerald was a bit cloudy," Charles said as he shrugged his shoulders. "But you can't deny it is magnificent for its size alone."

"Always?" Leslie asked. "What do you mean, always?"

"I don't know, Leslie. Since I first saw it I guess."

Leslie felt the blood pumping in her veins. He was holding something back, and it wasn't fair to her.

"And how long ago was that?" she asked, trying to remember to smile.

"What?"

"Charlie, when did you first see this emerald?"

Charlie stalled. When he saw Leslie wasn't going to give up he muttered, "I don't recall."

"You of all people don't recall when you first saw a large stone like this emerald?"

Looking more uncomfortable by the minute Charlie said, "Do you know how many stones I see in a day?"

"Bullshit, Charlie. I don't believe you. You don't see stones like that emerald every day. Tell me what you know. Why are you obviously hiding something from me? Tell me about my damn ring, I deserve to know. We have history, you owe me. I would think you would want me to know."

"Leslie, my information is confidential. It shouldn't matter who owned the ring previously. It should only matter that you have it now."

"I get it. Your loyalty is to Jack, always to the man who paid you for the ring. Forget that it might matter to me. Forget that I could be making life decisions based on this. No, you keep the information to yourself. It's just *fine*," she said, narrowing her eyes like an angry cat.

"Leslie—"

"Oh please, don't trouble yourself. It is clear you're not interested in your customer's happiness, you're only interested in making a buck, or maybe it's just in making a name for yourself. Who cares if I've known you since we were six years old? I'm not the one handing over the cash so I'm not important."

"Why, after what I've done for you, would you say that?" he asked, appearing to be upset.

"Does it hurt to hear the truth?"

At that Charlie came alive. "That's enough, I've had all I can take—get back here so I can talk to you," he said, circling the display case and grabbing her hand. He pulled her towards the back of the store, past the workspace where his father glanced up and smiled at her as they passed by to a back doorway.

"Where are you taking me?"

"Out of earshot," he whispered.

Once in the private office area of the store he let go of her hand and turned and looked at her, his brown eyes smoldering like warm, melted chocolate.

"Alright, I think I've had enough of this bullshit."

She'd never heard strait-laced Charles sound so mad. Leslie couldn't help but notice how beguiling his eyes were as they flashed out of anger before remembering that this man was keeping a secret from her.

"You want the truth? Fine. Your fiancé, who is a complete ass, bought that emerald four years ago for his *then* wife. He asked me to polish the ring a couple of weeks ago because he was giving it to his new fiancé. When he made the request I was shocked, not to mention disgusted. I didn't realize you were that serious and I hoped it wasn't for you, but regardless, I did my job. I tried to persuade him to get a new engagement piece but when it became clear he was set on using his old ring I obliged. What choice did I have? As we were finalizing the details on the rings refurbishment he mentioned it was for you. I couldn't believe it," Charlie exhaled. "How could you? What are you thinking? Have you lost your mind?"

"He gave me a used ring," Leslie said. For the first time she understood what Jack must have felt like sharing her with the memory of Jordan for the past year because now all she could think about was Jack's ex-wife. The woman was as real to her as if she were right there beside them as they held her ring.

"He is a complete idiot," Charlie said. "I'm sorry that I don't like him but I'm even more sorry that you're marrying him. Now that I've told you what I know I would appreciate it if you didn't tell him it came from me. Jack knows a lot of people and he could really ruin my reputation around town. I'm in a position where people expect me to keep their secrets."

Then, as if he thought better of it, he said, "Frankly, I don't care. Tell him that I told you. I don't care if I lose him as a client. I don't like him. Having him give you a used ring is completely disrespectful. I just can't believe you are marrying him."

Leslie thought about the ramifications of what Charlie was saying as he changed his mind. She was starting to wonder if there wasn't even more history between Jack and Charlie that he wasn't mentioning. "Do you not like him for some reason besides the ring?"

"Yes."

"What is it?" she asked.

"None of your damned business," he said, as he opened the door back to the main showroom and ushered her through, putting a clear end to the conversation.

Chapter Nine

The ring was ready after lunch. Unsure of how to proceed, Leslie figured it best to act as if nothing had happened and at least give Charlie some business for his honesty. It had taken every ounce of Leslie's willpower not to tell Suzie everything Charlie had told her while Suzie was selecting gray pearls. The girls grabbed a sandwich around the corner as the ring was getting a final polish, as if it could fix the cloud hanging not only over her ring, but now her relationship. She needed to have a conversation with Jack, the sooner, the better.

Now that the previously owned ring fit, she didn't want it anywhere near her hand. It had been another woman's ring. A ring the woman had worn when she and Jack had made love and promised to be together for the rest of their lives. The very thought of such intimacy made Leslie sick to her stomach.

She couldn't tell anyone. It was one of those awful secrets that could destroy happiness. Heck, if Suzie found out, if Trudel found out, they'd kill Jack. Or worse.

One thing she did know, she and Jack were about to have their first fight, and it was going to be epic.

Later that night, after she had stewed all afternoon about Jack's dishonesty, she sat across from him at the new Indian restaurant he'd found.

"Damn, could this butter chicken be any better?" he asked.

The food wasn't half as good as Sunil's restaurant, but it would have to do since Leslie was still banned for life.

"Eh," she said, her fork drawing designs in the thick tomato cream sauce, "It's not my favorite."

"Baby don't tell me that. You know we can't go there, and I don't want to punch that guy for saying lewd things to my girl."

"Speaking of lewd things," Leslie said, slipping the emerald off her finger and placing the ring loudly on the table next to Jack's plate, "You should give this ring back to Melissa because I don't accept second-hand engagement rings. And I'm more than a little shocked that you'd think I would."

Jack choked on the food in his mouth and Leslie just leaned back in her seat, folded her arms, and watched. Served him right for being such an idiot.

"But… but," he managed, "It's a very beautiful ring. I couldn't just stick it away. It should be seen and enjoyed by someone special."

"You are a cheap son of a bitch, you know that?" Leslie asked, feeling furious in a way she hadn't felt since Jordan's funeral. Was he really going to try to act like this was acceptable? "How *dare* you give me a used ring? Seriously, I'm not like your damn Porsche. You don't get a kickback for selling me on a used ring."

"Leslie—"

"Don't you dare try to defend yourself. I feel cheap. Like you think I don't deserve any better. Well, newsflash for you, I do. I can't believe you."

"Come on, baby… don't be mad. I don't want you mad. I wanted you to have something beautiful. And to me, that emerald is the most beautiful ring I've ever seen." Jack appeared to be sincere in his explanation which was even more unbelievable to Leslie.

"Well, newsflash, I'm mad and I'm getting angrier by the moment," she said as she leaned close and whispered, "And you want to know something else, that emerald may be big, but it is not that beautiful. It's cloudy, and I know it certainly isn't worth forty grand the way you keep insisting. But even if it were, it signifies time you spent married to another woman and I'll never put it on my finger again."

"I'm so sorry, I really didn't think about it that way, not until you pointed it out to me, baby. We'll make it better," he said and then corrected himself, "I'll make this right."

"Damn right you will," she said. As they finished their meal Leslie couldn't help wondering if after this conversation she would ever be able to eat Indian food anywhere again. Much like this meal, her new engagement ring brought her very little joy.

The next morning Jack and Leslie didn't speak as they walked down the sidewalk to Sauveterre Jewelers. Jack opened the door for her, and she stepped in ahead of him, immediately drawing Charlie's attention, his head snapping up so quickly from the project he was working on she wondered if he got whiplash. She saw him smirk and figured he'd guessed what had happened.

Leslie hadn't told Jack that Charlie had outed the identity of the previous owner. She lied and said a friend of Melissa's had recognized the ring, which had been completely mortifying. And it was never, ever going to happen again. Jack was still smarting. He complained that he didn't understand why it bothered her so much, but he hadn't argued when she said it needed to be replaced as soon as possible.

And when all else failed, she went to speaking in real estate terms, a language she knew from the vasectomy conversation that he would understand. "This is a non-negotiable deal-breaker. If you don't make this right, I'm back on the market."

Charlie came from behind the front counter trying his best to look surprised to see them. He extended his hand to Jack and put on a smile, "What can I do for you today, are you in to take a look at our fine wedding bands?"

Leslie wanted to punch him. Charlie knew exactly why they were there. His fake politeness toward Jack only added to her anger. As professional as he was attempting to be this was still damn embarrassing for her—Charlie knew she was marrying a cheap-skate. She glared at Jack, deciding that he was currently a softer and much more deserving target of her fury.

"Leslie wants a different engagement ring. This one," Jack said pointing down to her hand, "Just doesn't fit her personality."

"And it belonged to his previous wife," Leslie said.

Charlie, she noticed, tried to hide a smug smile but he was a little too late with the cover up. He offered politely, "I'd be more than happy to show you an assortment from the case, or we can design something special for you."

Leslie turned away from the men and started to meander from case to case looking at all the beautiful rings. In reality, she knew where she would eventually end up. She stopped at the case of exotic designs, Charlie's beautiful and rare Zultanite and Alexandrite rings. Just looking at them, her heart raced with joy. They were something Jordan would have loved—

What is she thinking? She's picking out an engagement ring for another man. Regardless, she loved these rings, and knew that there wasn't another woman in the world who would have anything like them. After her fiasco wearing the literal exact same ring as Jack's ex-wife that sounded really appealing.

Charlie and Jack had come up behind her as she pointed to her favorite and asked, "May I please see that one?"

An hour later, Leslie felt bittersweet as she looked down at the Zultanite and diamond ring on her left hand. The two and a half carat Zultanite and diamond ring was not only gorgeous, but it also complimented the sunstone ring she wore on her right. Now she had two rings with stones that changed colors. Jack almost had a mini stroke when Charlie had exchanged the emerald for the Zultanite for an additional twenty grand.

"Do you like it, baby?" Jack asked stiffly.

"Yes, yes I do," she replied and never said another thing about the emerald engagement ring. Still, hours later as Leslie lay awake in bed thinking about her gorgeous new ring all she could think about was that old cloudy emerald and Jack thinking that she was just like all his wives before—and suddenly the widening crack in their relationship was starting to feel a little more like the Grand Canyon.

Later that week when Jack was showing property to a couple who had flown in from Texas looking to relocate, Leslie invited Suzie over to her apartment for a girls' night.

"That is awesome, but I loved the emerald," Suzie said as she admired Leslie's new engagement ring.

"Yeah, but it had a big crack in it. And it was only going to get worse the longer I wore it on my hand. I just felt it was bad karma. Besides, it didn't go with the sunstone." The crack was symbolic, but Suzie didn't need to know that.

Suzie looked surprised at that but had no reason to doubt Leslie. "You are one lucky girl, you know that? You've found love twice. I am so relieved to see you happy."

"Jack takes the pain of Jordan away," Leslie said knowing it was what Suzie wanted to hear, but still, she couldn't help but think that she didn't feel all that lucky. Her second fiancé had shown a flaw she had yet to forgive. And she wasn't altogether sure that she could. Although he'd apologized to Leslie several times, she just couldn't quite forget about it.

Suzie and Leslie moved out onto her balcony taking their glasses of wine with them. "Suz, can I be honest with you?"

"Of course," Suzie said, looking caught off guard, "you know you can always tell me what's on your mind. Remember, we are in the circle of trust."

"Thank you. The thing is that I feel like I've changed. And I can't help but think about Jordan and wonder if he would like the woman I've become over the last few months since he been gone. I'm not just bitter, I'm jaded. I feel like I've aged ten years in the last one, and my optimism has all but disappeared. I no longer make decisions based on emotions. It's like I'm a machine, only thinking about what's a good business decision. Did I lose my softness, my compassion, myself when I lost Jordan?"

Suzie paused, then said, "You've gone through a tragedy, give yourself a break, anyone who has lived through what you have is going to come out different on the other side."

"I'm just not the same person that I was, and I'm not sure that is a good thing."

"You're the strongest person I know," Suzie said as they sat on her deck and watched the sunset reflected against the glass-fronted skyscrapers of downtown Portland.

"Thank you," she said and meant it. Leslie had earned her strength through pain, and she was proud of it.

"So, when do you move in with Jack?" Suzie asked trying to change the subject to something more light-hearted.

"I have an open-ended lease here. And Shane, he's the developer, well, he has some continuing issue with the partnership agreement with the other investors, so he isn't ready to move on the conversion just yet. He'd hoped to start selling these as condos this summer. Now, it will probably be next spring. They need to be upgraded, so it's all just a mess."

"At least you are doing well without this business," Suzie said.

"I am. Business with Dad is booming. We bring different but complementary skills to the table. It's really working for us. Jack wants to make me a partner and have us work as a team, but I like being at a different company and having my own thing, you know?"

"Sure, I get that. Besides, you're a different kind of realtor than Jack is, you are higher end," Suzie said.

"Thank you," Leslie said and not for the first time wondered if Jack's way of doing business could hurt her own reputation. "Listen, I need to let you in on a little secret that I haven't shared with anyone including Denice and Dad. Jack doesn't know, and he won't be happy about it."

"Are you pregnant?" Suzie asked, using a smile that Leslie had come to think of as her cousin's 'fake' smile.

"No. In fact, I want to postpone the wedding until next spring."

"What?" The shock on her cousin's face could have been hilarious if what Leslie wasn't proposing was so serious.

"I just don't think I know Jack the way I need to know him to marry him. I'm not ready to make a lifetime commitment to him."

"Oh boy, that is a bit of a surprise but I'm glad you're being careful and thinking it through."

"Yeah, well, once bitten, twice shy. I had no doubts with Jordan. I loved him. I knew he loved me and that I was his world. I knew, without a doubt, that any adversity or issues that came up, we would work through them. I never worried. Jordan was my foundation. Jack, well, I'm just a little scared that Jack likes me like he likes his Porsche. I feel like if I just give things a few months I'll have a better picture of what the long-term big picture looks like."

"When are you going to tell him about the wedding?" Suzie asked.

"In a couple of weeks, when I'm ready."

"You seem okay with this," Suzie said. "I don't know what to say, but please listen to your heart. If you are not feeling it, don't do it."

"I've got to figure it out. And I think with time, I will. Now let's talk logistics, will the dress transition into spring?"

"The dress will look stunning. Wow, and speaking of stunning, it is just such a gorgeous night."

"I will miss this view," Leslie said. "That is, if I move in with Jack as planned."

"I'm crossing my fingers for you, cousin."

"Thank you," Leslie said feeling better for the first time in days. It was as if letting Suzie in on her secret somehow lessened the burn in the pit of her stomach that she couldn't quiet.

"This weather reminds me of sitting by the pool at your dad's house in Palm Springs."

"That was fun," Leslie replied remembering how she felt that day. "Hey, do you want to get out of here? Maybe go for a swim?"

"Gee, last time I looked, I didn't see a pool here, but what did you have in mind?" Suzie asked.

"Jack has this vacant listing in Dunthorpe. It has an amazing pool in the backyard, and I know from personal experience that it is heated."

"Are you suggesting that we go swimming in somebody else's pool?"

"Yes," Leslie said. "I need a distraction. Are you in?"

Suzie looked scandalized but recovered quickly. "Sure, let's go! Tim would never be so spontaneous. Leslie this is reason number 2098 I love you, you keep me on my toes." Leslie laughed as they drove towards Dunthorpe with the sunroof open in the Lexus with the music blaring.

"I can't believe how balmy it is out tonight," Suzie said as they drove.

"I know. I hope it stays like this all the way through to summer."

"So, do the people who own this house know that you regularly swim in the pool at their vacant house?!"

"Yeah, Jack asked them if it was okay when they moved out. And they didn't care. They live in New Jersey now so it's not like they're going to come home."

"But, the house is for sale, what if a realtor shows it?"

"At seven on a Saturday night? Highly unlikely, but we will take the key out of the lockbox just to be on the safe side."

They wound through several, tree lined, narrow lanes that sheltered large mansions behind gates until they came to the private driveway they were looking for. As they came around a bend in the drive, they saw several cars, one being a black Porsche Panamera with the license place 'SOLD.'

"Is that Jack's car?"

"Yes," Leslie said and shut off her headlights.

"He's showing this property?" Suzie asked.

"Not unless it is in Camas, Washington," Leslie said, biting back yet another betrayal.

"But—"

"Yeah, something isn't right. And I intend on finding out what it is."

"What do you want to do?" Suzie asked. "Do you want to call him?"

"Absolutely not," Leslie said as everything felt increasingly wrong with the situation. Something told her that she needed to see what was going on and that she wouldn't like it.

They parked the car in the driveway, blocking the only way in or out, and Leslie put her keys in her jean's pocket.

"Let's leave the towels and everything in the car. We can always come back for them."

"Sure," Suzie said as they got out and headed for the house. But it was the music that pulled them away from the front door.

"Do you hear music?" Suzie asked.

"It's Debussy, one of Jack's favorites," Leslie said. What she didn't say was that Jack liked to make love to Debussy. "It's coming from around back by the pool."

"Leslie, maybe we shouldn't do this."

"He's my fiancé. We shouldn't have any secrets from each other," she said with a sarcastic edge as she picked up her pace.

They rounded the corner to the patio and paused by the side of the house in the shadows, looking toward the pool which was illuminated.

Leslie's brain tried to process what she was seeing as a little missing puzzle piece of unease started falling into alignment, answering questions she never in a million years would have thought to ask. It was so much worse than she had ever imagined.

Jack was mostly nude, standing close to the edge of the pool. He was wearing something that looked like a black leather garter belt connected with chains that ran up to a collar around his neck. His erect penis was visible in the cutout section of his crotch-wear.

Two women, who were similarly dressed in black leather bras and panties, and black masks, were taking turns whipping him with long apparatuses that looked like dusters with black licorice strips.

"Hey, watch it! Remember, don't leave marks, Candy!" he complained.

"Oh holy shit," Suzie whispered next to her.

Leslie looked over the scene, careful not to miss anything. A box of condoms scattered on the ground along with several other 'toys.' A bottle of empty Beefeater vodka stood on the travertine edge of the hot tub. Subway sandwich wrappers littered the fine brickwork on the patio, and she could smell marijuana still lingering in the air.

"Beefeater, how ironic," she whispered to herself more than to Suzie.

It was way past time to interrupt this little party.

Leslie stepped out of the shadows and at the top of her lungs, yelled, "JACK! What the Hell is going on here?"

Everything stopped.

Jack muttered, "Oh fuck," tripped on the chains wrapped around his body, and belly flopped loudly into the pool.

"Is he wearing a dog collar?" Suzie asked as she followed Leslie toward the women with their whips.

"Uh-huh."

"Here, you might need this," Suzie said, handing Leslie a can of pepper spray from her purse.

Jack's playmates realized the party was over and started gathering their toys, uninterested, as Jack floundered in the water.

"You might as well take a seat," Leslie said addressing the ladies for the first time, "I've blocked the driveway, and I'm going to need some answers before anyone leaves."

"Look, lady, we just do what he asks. We're not hurting him," the first woman, Candy said, pulling off her mask. "He likes to be whipped. We do it to him every couple of months."

"You must be his fiancé," the second woman surmised, "You know, he really loves you. You can tell by the way he talks about you."

Leslie had to remind herself to shut her mouth as she stared.

Jack lumbered up the pool steps and grabbed a large terrycloth towel, apparently feeling self-conscious.

"Don't feel the need to cover up on my account. No way will I ever forget what I just saw. It's burned into my retinas forever," Suzie quipped. Leslie wanted the bricks to part and the ground to break open and swallow her alive. She'd never been more humiliated in her life.

"Jack, Bethany and I are going to get out of here if this is going to get crazy," Candy said.

Like it wasn't already crazy?

Jack walked toward her, his voice pleading, "Leslie, baby—"

"What does he pay you to beat him?" Leslie asked Bethany who had correctly guessed that he was her fiancé.

"It depends. Usually $2,000 for the night, but the sex is always extra," the woman answered.

"Of course," Leslie said as Jack tried to interrupt, and Suzie told him to shut up. "Did you hear that Suzie; the sex is always extra?"

"I heard, I heard. Nice dog collar, Jack."

"You use condoms sometimes when you have sex with Jack?" Leslie asked.

"All the time, Jack is very much a germ-a-phobic!" Candy replied, and both girls started to giggle.

Leslie turned to Jack and ordered, "Pay them so they can leave."

Jack's hands were shaking as he found his wallet and counted out the money for the girls.

"Hey Suzie, would you move my car so the ladies can leave?" Leslie asked, handing Suzie the keys to her car, her eyes never leaving Jack. "I want to speak to Jack for a moment. And here, take the pepper spray, I don't trust myself with it."

The women didn't need to be told twice. They fled like wounded gazelles.

When they were alone, Jack pled his case, "Leslie, baby, this has nothing to do with you. It is my thing."

The music was still on, so Leslie kicked the boom box into the pool to make it stop. Then, as Jack advanced, she heard the rattle and realized he was still wearing chains.

"What Jack? This obviously wasn't your first time with the S & M Barbies."

"I'm sorry, I fucked up. I should have told you that I occasionally like to play."

"*Play*? Whips? Sex? Leather? Dog collars?" Then she sniffed the air and added, "Pot? Jeez, what kind of fresh Hell is this?"

"It's nothing, babe. My therapist says it's completely normal if no one gets hurt. It is my stress reliever when I get too wrapped up in my business. You know how hard I work, baby. I'm getting ready for another seminar in Vegas, we are getting married. I have a lot of stress in my life. Everyone needs a break occasionally. It isn't like I'm an alcoholic."

"News flash, Jack. I got hurt. Just now. I'm hurt, and I'm really, really angry. What I'd like to do to you right now, would leave marks."

"Would you be into this? Is this something you might be willing to do?" Jack asked, a glimmer of hope in his puppy-dog eyes.

"No, I would not be into this bullshit. And, let me guess, Melissa didn't like the way you wanted to play either?"

"I love you like I never loved her, or my first wife. We can make this work, don't you see? I just need you to be understanding every now and then. You can even watch if you want."

"You are wearing a dog collar, Jack. You had sex with prostitutes. I'm just not that understanding! And I really, really do not want to watch."

"It isn't that unusual. And it isn't like the sex meant anything. I paid for it."

Leslie took a deep breath. Jordan would have kicked her butt for being so stupid as to have planned to spend her life with this sick bastard.

She exploded, her voice like that of a screeching cat going to war. "That's it! I am done! Done with you! Done with your car and your branding and your bullshit! And I'm done with used rings and being called babe or baby which isn't at all an endearment. My name is Leslie, and I'm done with finding my fiancé getting whipped with a fucking leather whatever the Hell that thing is!"

"It is just a whip. Lots of people enjoy them—"

"I never want to see, speak, or hear from you again. We are over, done, finished, that is all!"

She pulled the Zultanite ring off her left hand and considered tossing it in the swimming pool, but then the words of the S & M Barbie rang in her ears: *Usually $2,000 for the night, but the sex is always extra...*

She slipped the ring back on her finger. "Hey Jack, I'm keeping the ring. I hope *that* hurts!"

"Leslie, be reasonable—"

Ignoring him, she turned and calmly walked toward the front of the house and almost ran into Suzie.

"I've never heard you swear like that, I've never heard your voice sound like that," Suzie commented as they made their way to the car.

"I've never been that disappointed in a human being in my life."

"Okay, okay, we'll get out of here, and we will go try to figure out what we just saw because I know my retinas are still burning."

Leslie stopped and turned to Suzie, asking, "Did I just see my fiancé, Jack Ward, the biggest realtor in Portland, dressed in leather and chains, getting whipped by a couple of women dressed as dominatrixes?"

"Yes, you did."

"I'm not just having a bad dream?" Leslie asked as she laid on the couch in her living room, one hand holding an ice pack to her throbbing head and a glass of red wine in the other. Suzie sat in a chair opposite her, shaking her head and grimacing.

"Nope, sister. I saw it too. Ick."

"Well shit, I knew he was hiding something, but I thought it was the ring, this was beyond my imagination."

"I wouldn't have guessed this bullshit in a million years," Suzie said and added, "Are you okay? You look like you might be going into shock."

"No, I'm not okay, but I'm not going into shock."

Suddenly Leslie had the most random thought.

"I have another wedding dress on order with your mother," Leslie complained. "Everyone is going to have to find out."

"No one will know. You're going to tell everyone that he cheated. That will be enough. I got your back, honey. We found him with someone, that's all you need to say."

"We found him in an S & M orgy."

"Well kind of," Suzie agreed.

"I think I am going to be single for a while now," Leslie said, feeling the emotional crash start to overtake her. There was only so much heartache the heart could take.

"I can't say that I blame you."

"Hey, did I tell you he gave me a used engagement ring?"

Charlie was with someone when she entered Sauveterre Jewelers two weeks later, but Leslie felt his eyes on her. His mother and father were with other customers, so Leslie tried to look busy by browsing the cases. Charlie had added some new inventory to the rare engagement ring case, but nothing that was as beautiful or extraordinary as her Zultanite.

Several minutes later, he stepped up beside her and asked, "See anything you like?"

"Yes, but not as much as my former engagement ring."

"Former?" he asked, a little smile breaking out before he contained it, but she noticed.

"You were right about Jack, but I kept the ring. I love the ring. Not as much as the sunstone, but I definitely wasn't giving it back. But now what do I do with it? My right hand is taken."

Charlie paused for a moment taking this bombshell news in. After several seconds he broke into a smile and responded with an honesty that Leslie could appreciate now, more than ever.

"This news makes me very happy," he said.

"Because you thought he was an ass," she whispered.

"Yeah, that's one reason. Come on," he said, leading her to a small table. He grabbed a tablet and pencil along the way. "Let's brainstorm some ideas for the Zultanite, get it out of the ring and make it yours."

A half hour later, Leslie left Sauveterre Jewelers, smiling for the first time since breaking her engagement with Jack. Charlie had suggested a bracelet in rose gold to compliment the sunstone, not too unlike the bracelet that had started her relationship with Jack. But it would be wider, more of a small cuff than a dangle bracelet.

Jack had called her several times in the last two weeks, trying to get her to "understand," but when he realized it wouldn't work, he started asking for the ring back. She explained to him that he'd have to take legal action to get it back and that Suzie would testify to what she saw. A court case like this would surely make all the news stations salivate. Needless to say, the matter was dropped. As Jack became more firmly a part of her past Leslie felt herself returning to the woman she was before she was with *Jack Ward, the Real Estate King of Portland*. While happy to be moving on, she knew that working in the same profession their paths would surely cross at some point or another. At least she would be wearing nice jewelry when it happened.

Silver Linings Dress Auction

DRESS NUMBER THIRTEEN

TITLE: *Fidelity*

DESCRIPTION: This naughty nude and blush-ivory Caroline Benson fig-ure-hugging gown is called "Can You Blush?" with a cathedral length train. A mermaid with a plunging neckline and natural waist, this lace gown hides nothing and reveals every curve of the figure with elegant crystal details and cutaway peek-a-boo side panels that reveals the blushing bride's skin.

DONATED BY: *The Aqua Lady*

Present Day

FOUR days before the Auction

As Leslie negotiated directly with Jack on the Vista property, she was very proud of herself for sending the counter offers back and forth without any snarky comments. This was new, this was maturity. She thought of several clever quips, of course, especially after he tried to get the sellers to pay more than their fair share of closing costs and attempted to get them to remove all the carpet and refinish the hardwood floors.

This was his form of real estate blackmail. It was a cute little trick he'd told her about when they were engaged. She hadn't liked it then as it wasn't how she did business, but she did make note of it. In Jack's mind if you gave the seller an overpriced offer, you could justify a few nasty last-minute contingencies right after the home inspection. A Honey-Do List from Hell.

That was Classic Jack—dirty little tricks that you would never suspect of the polished top realtor in town.

Having had been his fiancé, this side of Jack's personality had once embarrassed Leslie, but an older, wiser Leslie didn't need to make excuses for the man behind questionable business practices. And didn't that feel great? Now, he was just some bully realtor being his normal trouser snake in the grass.

She hadn't just dodged a bullet with Jack. She'd saved her future.

She'd actually considered a life with Jack that included marriage and children? She shuddered at the thought.

It was in her past. Today, what she needed to do was get a great offer on the table for her clients. They depended on her.

Her desk phone rang, and she recognized the number—Denice.

"Hey there," Leslie said. "How was your flight?"

"Fabulous," Denice said, "I love all this cool, fall air. I felt it the moment the plane landed. I think I lost at least thirty percent of my wrinkles the moment that moist air hit my skin."

"You don't have any wrinkles!" Leslie and Denice had grown closer over the last few years and it made Leslie feel good that she had finally found peace with her stepmother. She hadn't referred to her as a stepmonster for almost five years; those times were behind them now.

"You're biased, and I love you for it," Denice said warmly.

"Are you staying through the weekend?" Leslie asked, wondering if Denice was going to the Silver Linings Auction. They could sit together and watch the happenings.

"I wish, I'd love to go with you to Trudel's auction, but your father made plans for us with the Dunbars. It's their fiftieth anniversary, so I'm flying back Saturday morning after a little sales-tax-free Christmas shopping."

Leslie didn't point out that the plane flight had probably negated the lack of sales tax. She knew that Denice liked any excuse to pop back up to Portland. She didn't want to take too much credit, but she knew that Denice liked to spend time with her. It was a new realization and it felt good to admit it, especially because of the animosity that once existed.

"I can't wait to see you," Leslie said. And she meant it. She wanted Denice's opinion about the auction.

"We have an appointment to get our nails done tomorrow morning and dinner at Mingo the night before I leave. Does that still work for you? Would you like to go shopping after we finish our nails? Maybe get a new dress for Trudel's auction?"

"Let's play it by ear. I'm definitely up for the nails and dinner, but the negotiation on one of my listings is having some issues."

"I'm glad we are spending a little time together. I know you're busy, so I'll take what I can get."

"The thing is I really don't think I'm in a good mood to go dress shopping," Leslie said. Besides, thanks to Suede's serious makeover she had several dresses that would work for Saturday night.

"Would you like a spa day?"

"No, thank you, Denice, I just had my hair done and work really is crazy."

"Leslie, hon, are you okay?"

"I'm just trying to figure out what to do about my wedding dresses. Suzie and Aunt Trudel want me to put all of them in the show, and there was a news broadcast on Monday. It was embarrassing."

"I heard Trudel mentioned you."

"She called me out."

"Trudel gets flustered and says things she doesn't mean. Bless her heart, she loves you."

"She is cunning like an alley cat."

"In a sweet way," Denice said, and they both laughed. "Listen, they are your dresses. I want you to do whatever is best for you. Don't feel pressured to put them in the auction unless it would feel good to do it. Clean slate."

"But they were so expensive, and Dad spent so much—"

"Nonsense. Talk to your father if it will make you feel better. He won't care one way or the other what you do with those dresses. You're his daughter after all, and he just wants you to be happy. We all want you to be happy."

Leslie's throat felt thick with unspoken words. She made an excuse to get off the phone before she made a fool of herself and started to do something really crazy, like burst into tears. She hadn't had a mother in over twelve years, and Denice was actually stepping up and offering the love she had so desperately missed. At the end of the day, she didn't have the man she loved, but she had the love and support she'd always craved.

PART 3

Three Years Earlier

The Maggie St. Clair

Chapter Ten

Leslie wasn't in a mood to be fixed. She was in the mood to put as much distance between herself and the last few years of her life as possible, but well-meaning Denice had other plans. For a wedding shower gift when she'd been about to marry Jordan, Denice had given Leslie a gift certificate for a full day of spa treatment. The gift had gone unused, and Denice was insisting now was the time to use it and she wasn't taking no for an answer.

Denice went to the gym every day. There were also frequent visits to the salon, the tanning bed, you name it. She took personal care and treatment to a higher level. She was practically on a first name basis with every sought-after trainer, laser, waxing, and makeup professional in Portland and Palm Springs.

"Are you sure you don't want a facial?" Denice asked as they sat side by side getting pedicures at the White Lily Day Spa.

"Denice, we've been here for like five hours. I've had a massage, my hair is cut and styled, I've had a manicure, and I'm getting a pedicure. I think that is enough for one day but thank you. You've already been so kind to make today happen," Leslie said, vowing not to get used to this gateway pampering. Pretty soon, she would be looking at small, non-existent wrinkles and want to have them neutralized with Botox. Then what? Tanning? Waxing?

"It's a good start, honey. And I've selfishly enjoyed every minute of it. By the way, I've made us a reservation at The Heathman for afternoon tea. We'll just make it after our polish dries."

Leslie wanted to say no, but damn it if Denice wasn't being super kind to her. She hated to admit it, but she was sort of starting to like it. What she didn't like was that she was starting to enjoy Denice's company as well.

"Do you have an outfit for the Fourth of July party? We could swing by Mario's after tea and pick something up, my treat," Denice offered.

"I've got a dress," Leslie said, "You've got to stop spoiling me."

"I'm enjoying this day so much. I just wish we could do this kind of thing more often."

And Leslie realized she kind of did, too. Did this make her disloyal to her mother's memory? Something told her that her mother would be glad that someone cared enough to offer her a little much needed pampering. And if her mother couldn't be there and Trudel was too busy, maybe she should be open to Denice.

Leslie brought her mother's cheese enchiladas to her father and Denice's rooftop garden Fourth of July party at their condominium in the fashionable Pearl District. She knew the old family dish was one of her father's favorite recipes and that Denice refused to make it for him because of all the "fat, cheesy goodness" that it contained. Leslie suspected Denice's lack of enthusiasm around the dish also had a lot to do with the fact it was something that represented his past before Denice. The sideways glance Denice gave her when she recognized what Leslie had brought confirmed Leslie's suspicion, but Denice hid it well behind her smile and warm hug.

"I'm so glad you brought those for your father. You know that I can't make them for him, not with my diet. I'm so glad you can give him a treat now and then," Denice said looking especially festive in a sleeveless St. John red sheath dress and lots of gold bangles which made about as much noise as the kids on the street below with their fireworks. She was walking on impossibly high, bright-red, pencil-heel sling-backs that had to be four inches tall.

"You look beautiful," Leslie said, and she meant the words.

"Well, aren't you a sweetheart," Denice said and gave her a hug.

It had been thirteen months since she'd broken it off with Jack, and two years since Jordan had died. She hadn't felt like dating in months. In fact, she'd thrown herself into her business, and worked as many hours as she could. When she wasn't working, she read Nora Roberts' entire catalog of books, and she learned to cook because it was something she had always wanted to do. When she'd been young, she had always imagined her mother would teach her—and then her mother got sick, and they had run out of time.

Leslie had a lot of tender, bittersweet memories going through her mother's recipe box and seeing her mother's notes on the little lined cards with little yellow daisies in the corner for things like the cheese enchiladas.

She could make risotto and cook shish kebobs just as well if not better than Jordan used to. He would be horrified to know that she could make the perfect medium rare filet mignon thanks to one of her mother's daisy cards. *Five minutes side one, four minutes side two, turn ninety degrees and three minutes on side one, two minutes side two, a final minute on side one, and Voila!*

When she mastered savory cooking, she'd bought a Kitchen Aid mixer—a big red one that dominated the kitchen in her apartment—and started baking some of the desserts she remembered from childhood like coconut cake with meringue buttercream icing or carrot cake with thirty-seven ingredients. She took special desserts for her office on Wednesdays, "just because."

She bought Mary Berry's baking book on cakes and considered trying to bake every recipe in the book. And she'd learned to make elaborate flowers out of icing. Violets with delicate yellow and orange centers and heart-shaped leaves were her favorite designs.

Leslie started going to the gym daily. She needed it, because the more she baked, the more she ate, and the tighter her clothing felt. But she also went to the gym for other reasons. When she rode the machines—"Seabiscuit," the elliptical and "Buttercup," the rowing machine—she thought of Jordan and how much she missed him and how much he taught her about love. And sometimes, when she was in a particularly bad mood, she thought of Jack and how much he taught her about deceit.

Today, Leslie compared her simple seersucker dress of blue and white stripes with a small red lobster design to Denice's elegance and shrugged. Maybe she should have let Denice buy her something from Mario's, but it was the Fourth of July for goodness sake. They were there to eat fattening food and drink margaritas until the fireworks at the waterfront began. Hopefully, they'd also be able to see the fireworks to the north from Fort Vancouver.

"You made your mother's enchiladas," Leslie's father whispered as he handed her a margarita and gave her a hug.

"Hi, Dad," she said as she hugged her father back. "I thought the pan would add a downhome vibe to all those catered entrees. I thought this was a semi-potluck. Seriously, don't people cook anymore? Isn't food love?"

"Your food is love. Thank you again. I think I might have to take a big chunk out of that pan and put it in the fridge before Denice starts complaining about my cholesterol."

"Be careful, that's where I put the cake that is decorated like an American flag with strawberries for the stripes and blueberries for the stars."

"That is fantastic," her father said with a smile.

"I just couldn't stop myself, and I was waiting to hear if the Johnson house on 25th would record in time for the weekend. It did by the way," she said as a guest she didn't know greeted her father and pulled him into a conversation.

"Congratulations, that deal was a bearcat," he said, and a moment later, she was looking at his back and he was engaged in another conversation. This reminded her of most of the social events she'd ever attended with her father or mother for that matter. They were always the most popular people in the room, leaving her to observe from the fringe. Little about that scenario had changed.

A shadow blocked out the sun and then it spoke to her. "So, a little birdie told me that you're the one who made the enchiladas."

Leslie put her hand up to shade her eyes. A man she didn't know was smiling down at her.

"Guilty," she said. "They go well with margaritas."

He leaned conspiratorially close and whispered, "They are the best damn thing on that whole table."

"I think you overplayed your hand. Denice has jalapeno poppers on the end. They are serious decadence."

"I'm Mitch," the man said, extending a hand and adding a smile. "I don't like spicy things, so I must repeat that your enchiladas are the best thing on that table."

"I'm Leslie, and that was my mother's recipe, so thank you for the compliment."

Mitch was a neighbor and lived in the condo a few doors down from her father and Denice. He was a coffee executive who owned a company called Hot Lava. She'd had their coffee. In fact, they served it in her office.

"I'm partial to Molten Heat," she said, thinking he had to be in his early forties.

"You like strong coffee," he said with a wink.

"Why settle for less?" she asked and took a sip of her margarita.

When the lights went out and the fireworks began, Mitch made his apologies and stepped away for a phone call. Leslie felt his gaze on her throughout the rest of the evening, but he didn't get too close again.

As she helped Denice carry platters from the roof back to their condo, she said, "I had a nice conversation with your neighbor, Mitch."

"He's very nice," Denice said, "but you wouldn't believe the messy divorce he's in the middle of."

"Yeah, I figured there was something wrong with him," Leslie said more to end the conversation than to encourage more girly banter with her stepmonster.

Three days later, Denice called while Leslie was at her desk eating a salad from Elephant's.

"Hey, hi there," Leslie said warmly, "I'm eating a kale salad."

"Good for you!" Denice exclaimed. "Maybe you could share with your father how much you enjoy kale."

Leslie had known her salad choice would make Denice happy. Super foods were one of Denice's favorite topics. Leslie thought the salad needed cheese and a lot more dressing, but she kept that observation to herself.

"He wouldn't believe it coming from me. I'm his cheese enchilada enabler."

"He loves it when you make that. By the way, did you have a good time at our party?"

"Yes, thank you, you and Dad throw a mean party. Well, more you than Dad," Leslie said thinking that she'd never in her life be able to host perfect parties like Denice.

They shared a laugh about her father and then Denice asked, "I remember you mentioned meeting Mitch at the party?"

"Hot Lava, I remember," Leslie replied.

"I ran into him in the hall and he asked about you."

"The guy going through a bitter divorce?" Leslie asked.

"Yes, very bitter," Denice said, sounding as if she disapproved which was surprising to Leslie.

"He isn't just thinking about it, he's really doing it, right? The divorce, I mean."

"Yes, he is really getting divorced. He said they are settling this week. I've heard the fighting when his wife shows up to drop off their child, a little girl named Roma. The mother is always an hour or two late, which is no doubt purposeful. The daughter is a handful, but Mitch appears to be a nice enough guy. His company is very successful, although I don't personally care for their coffee. It's too strong and I always have to water it down," Denice observed.

"What did he say about me?"

"He said wants your number. I just… this is hard for me, Leslie."

"What? You don't like him?"

"I don't want to come off the wrong way. I don't like to interfere in your life. I figure if you want my opinion, you'll ask," Denice said.

Leslie wondered how many times Denice had bit her tongue in the past. Time to change that.

"I want your opinion."

Denice sighed, then spoke, "I've enjoyed my conversations with Mitch, you know when we run into him in the hallway or have invited a few of the neighbors over for a drink on the terrace, but I think it is too soon after his marriage failing for him to be dating. I just don't think he is the man for you. But if you can separate your heart from your brain and just have fun with him, I don't want to stand in the way of you having a good time. I want you to get out and enjoy yourself."

"And?" Leslie asked. "Come on, Denice, don't hold back. I want to hear your thoughts, and I know you have more to say."

Denice sighed again, and there was a pause as she considered her words. "Recently divorced men, they sometimes judge other women for what their wives did to them in the marriage. They almost punish them for their issues with their wives. The men have to burn through a rebound relationship or two before they are decent humans and ready for love again. Maybe Mitch won't be that way, but I just want to warn you because I think you've been hurt enough. Do you understand?"

Leslie understood more than she wanted to. Jack had exhibited some repeat patterns based on his ex-wives, but his dishonesty had been his downfall. Leslie wondered if this was how Denice felt about Leslie's father. Denice was the first and only woman he'd dated after her mother died.

"Thank you for that," Leslie said. "I appreciate it."

"Well, I'll give him your number, but be careful with him. And don't take any crap from him. Promise me."

"Thank you for the warning, and for looking out for me. I appreciate it." And Leslie realized that she was not only growing to like Denice, but to appreciate her words of wisdom as well.

Chapter Eleven

When Mitch called Leslie that same day Leslie wondered if she'd made a mistake. She liked her simple life of selling houses and baking like some sort of single domesticated female. Yeah, it was a little boring, but she wasn't sure she wanted the weight on her shoulders of a potential new man just lurking in the shadows.

Denice's words had sunk in, and she was reluctant to go out with him, but finally agreed to dinner.

They met at a big, airy Italian restaurant that felt like it had been lifted out of Tuscany and transported to Portland. It was named Serratto, which ironically meant intense in Italian. Mitch wanted to pick her up, but Leslie thought it was best to meet him at the restaurant. She wanted the freedom to escape if she had to.

"I have to say, I was a bit surprised you agreed to go out with me," Mitch said as their Barbera was delivered to the table and they'd each had a sip of the dry, red wine.

"Why?" she asked, genuinely curious. The guy was good looking and rich. Insecurity was a surprise. Maybe his divorce was affecting his ego.

"You're younger and you know I'm not quite divorced, but I'm working on it. In fact, it should be finalized this week. All of that can be a turn-off."

"It is, but I'm not looking for anything serious, and you are kind of cute. I'm not stupid. I don't want to wonder if I missed an opportunity."

"You're very honest, aren't you?"

"Why wouldn't I be? I have nothing to hide."

"So, what do you think when you see me?"

"That based on your circumstances, I doubt you want to jump into anything too fast or too serious, but you met me and like me, you're curious. Curiosity doesn't mean we are a couple, just meeting a new friend. It takes some of the pressure off."

"Is this how dating works now? No one wants any strings, but you can't help the curiosity, so you go out?" he asked, smiling. He had a nice smile and cold blue eyes that made Leslie a bit self-conscious.

"Not exactly, I just think that people don't want to get too deep too soon," Leslie said and then added, "Especially if they have loved and lost. They are optimistically cautious, but not jaded."

"Is that the way it is for you?"

"I want the fairytale, I always have, but I'm a realist. I take it easy. I start slow. I just want to have fun and get to know someone before I get too deep, because in reality it takes a long time to get to know someone, not months, but years, really. Besides, it might not turn out how I used to envision it, where we get married, and we have children and a picket fence. They might have been married before, they might already have children, or be older. So, I stay open to new opportunities, new ways of looking at my dream. But that doesn't mean jumping into something. Give it time. Years."

"Come on, you know someone after spending a few months together. It doesn't take *years*."

"Nope, it takes years," she said and took another sip of her wine.

Leslie thought of the many years she'd known Jordan. Up until the day he died, she was learning new things about him. Thankfully for her, she liked each new discovery. The same couldn't be said of Jack. She was sure he had some rather dark surprises that she never discovered.

She wondered if Mitch was getting a divorce because he'd discovered some secrets that he didn't like. She wasn't going to ask him. It wasn't any of her business. Not yet, anyway.

"Go ahead, ask me," he said, ignoring her contradiction.

"Ask you what?" Leslie asked, as she bit into her pappardelle pasta with braised wild boar.

"About why I got divorced, how many kids I have, if I now hate women… Take your pick."

Leslie paused to finish her glass of wine and said, "I don't care. Well, if you beat your wife or cheated on her, I'd care about that, but really, I don't care about the domestic details of your failed marriage."

"But don't you want to hear—"

Leslie held up her hand. "Look, I can be your date or your therapist, not both. However, if you want to spill your guts to me about all the intimate details of your life with your wife, I charge three hundred dollars an hour because I'm worth it. But really, I do not care."

"You're really evolved, you know that?" He looked at her as if she were a red rose in a bouquet of white blossoms.

She gave a little knowing nod as she took another bite of pasta. He didn't get out much. She could relate.

Despite a few rocky moments where he wanted to share too much information, they had a nice time. Leslie learned a lot about the coffee business and how Mitch had built his company. She liked his drive, his desire to come clean about any question she asked. However, she stayed true to her word and avoided subjects that would sour the evening.

He suggested they enjoy the warm weather and take a stroll. She liked the idea, thinking the evening was feeling a bit more romantic than she'd imagined. They walked along 21st Avenue and then up to 23rd where they waited in line at Salt & Straw for black pepper strawberry balsamic ice cream.

Luck was on their side, and a little wrought iron café table opened up in front of the ice cream shop. They enjoyed their dessert and watched people walk by.

"You know what I like?" he asked.

"This crazy good ice cream?"

"Yes, but also, I like a woman who eats ice cream."

"I'll ride my elliptical machine tomorrow, so no guilt," she replied.

"I don't trust people who don't eat ice cream or cheese."

"I love cheese," he said, smiling at her. "For our second date, let's go get fondue at the Melting Pot, what do you say?"

"I say, yes," Leslie said with a smile, realizing that she'd just agreed to a second date.

As he walked her back to her car, he asked, "Okay, I just need to know, how can you not care?"

"About your past?" she asked.

"Yes," he said.

"If I know all the ugly, petty details, it will jade my opinion of you. Isn't it better for all the mystery to unfold and you to tell me slowly over time? Don't you want me to see if I like you at the moment instead of judging you on your past?"

His smile had a little hard edge that she found both curious and sexy, as he said, "I like you, Leslie Westcott."

The next weekend, she and Mitch went to the Melting Pot where they ate cheese and then chocolate fondue.

And this time, she let him pick her up at her apartment at Uptown.

"Your view is better than mine," he said as he stood on her deck and had a glass of wine after dinner.

"Yeah, but you own your place. This is just a rental." In fact, she knew the Uptown Cliffs had financing and partner issues up the ying-yang which had delayed the condo conversion indefinitely.

At the end of the evening, Leslie let Mitch kiss her, and she found that it wasn't only enjoyable, but it helped her to get past Jack. Now he was no longer the last man she'd kissed. And on some level, that mattered to her. He wasn't slick. She had a feeling that with Mitch what you saw was what you got. Wasn't that a nice change? Was she curious about his divorce? Yes, in fact she knew she'd have to ask him about it if they kept seeing each other.

Mitch was attentive. He called her every day that he didn't have his daughter. He tried to explain to her that he wouldn't be able to call the second weekend into their relationship during his Friday afternoon call.

"I just don't want to have to explain you to my daughter Roma, not yet."

"Okay, I actually think that is a wise decision," Leslie said, looking down at a deal on her desk that was going to require more than a little finessing to close.

"Someday soon, I will, but right now—"

"That's fine, wait until there is something to tell," Leslie said, wondering how many addendum items she'd need to make this deal fly. Another damn bearcat.

"Because of the divorce, which is final by the way, she feels very displaced, and I don't want her to worry."

"Mitch, it's fine, I'm not worried or upset. When things calm down, call me, and we'll go out again. Okay?"

"Wow, you are so incredible."

"No, like you, I have a busy life." And if time and experience had taught her anything, she could break it off. If they were meant to be, they would be, it was as simple as that.

A week later, they went to Five Spice in Lake Oswego, where the beautiful people had expensive Asian-fusion seafood in a pretty restaurant.

"I need to tell you about Roma. I have one, beautiful daughter who is the center of my universe. She's six, and she is amazing. She is the little love of my life," Mitch volunteered. "She now comes first in all things in my life. I haven't missed one event at her school. When it is my week, I take her to school and pick her up. Then we spend the rest of the day together. She has a nanny for when I'm working in the summer, but the nanny brings her down to my office, and we have lunch together. It's great fun. That's why I really couldn't see you last weekend. I just didn't want to disrupt Roma."

See? This was why Leslie didn't want to know the details of Mitch's life yet because now she felt the brush of a red flag in her mind. What? Did she want him to say his significant other came first, then his kid, who was his flesh and blood? It was a bad question to contemplate because there was no right answer. He was a devoted father, that wasn't a bad thing. If she pursued this relationship, she needed to understand she wasn't first with Mitch. How did she feel about that?

"Roma sounds like a lucky girl to be so close to her Daddy," Leslie said and took a deep pull on her glass of wine.

"So, Leslie, I just have to ask, why are you single? Ever been married? Kids?"

For some reason she didn't feel like she knew him well enough to tell him all about the dead fiancé. And the "Why are you single?" question was always a landmine. What should she say? "Because the love of my life died and then I had a relationship with a twice-divorced guy who gave me a used ring and liked S & M Barbies to beat him up?"

Leslie took a deep breath and said, "I've had a couple of relationships that didn't work out. Now, I'm just enjoying myself. I'm not looking for anything serious. I'm just looking to meet new friends for new adventures. Then we'll see where it goes from there."

But when he took her home that night, she could sense that something was on his mind. He kissed her at the door of her apartment and slowly made his way back to his car. She knew he was trying to make a decision.

She was, too. She liked him, but she didn't need him, not in the way she'd needed Jordan. She'd tried to convince herself that slow and steady won the race, but it hadn't with Jack. Maybe he was going to tell her what she was starting to suspect, this, whatever this was, lacked passion.

"You know something?" he asked as he opened his car door and looked back at her.

"What?" she asked, thinking she did not want to sleep with him and would turn him down if he tried to get there with her.

"I'm falling in love with you."

What? Was he drunk? Or just stupid?

Whatever she was expecting, it wasn't this, and she didn't like the suddenness. It was too soon to make such declarations, and it held no weight with her. He didn't know her. He didn't know her flaws or the parts of her that made her unique from everyone else in the world.

She raised a hand and wiggled a finger at him. "Ha ha, now don't ruin it," she warned. "You know that it is too soon for that kind of talk."

"Fine, spoilsport, I'll see you Saturday night, but I am falling in love with you."

Chapter Twelve

Leslie went through the sales racks of close-out dresses at Aunt Trudel's like a woman on a mission.

"The Black and White Diabetes Ball is a really big deal," Suzie said as she pulled dresses in Leslie's size. "I've been helping people with dresses for the last six months."

"I know, which is why I'm here looking for a dress. Please only pull the dresses—"

"That don't look like wedding dresses, yeah I know," Suzie said shaking her head. "He could have given you more notice."

"We only started dating three weeks ago."

"So," Suzie whispered, "Is Mr. Hot Lava, hot in the bang-bang department?"

"What?" Leslie asked, looking disgusted. "I told you, we've only been dating for three weeks, and he has a daughter. It's complicated." She didn't tell Suzie that he'd told her that he was falling in love with her. She wasn't having sex with him. Something told her he would read too much into it, not that sex wasn't serious, but with him it would really mean the world, and she wasn't ready to give him her world.

"That's too bad," Suzie said.

"Just because you and Tim did the bang-bang on the first day, you little slut, doesn't mean that I should."

"All I'm saying is if the passion is there, the bang-bang takes over. It isn't even a choice, it is power. It takes you over, your body, your soul—"

"I found it!" Aunt Trudel announced coming from the back room with a short, shift style dress in white silk crepe.

"Way to go! That Maggie St. Clair is perfect. Great choice, Mom," Suzie announced, changing her tone so quickly, Leslie had to laugh.

"Are those crystals?" Leslie said, giving the dress a double take.

"It doesn't look like a wedding dress, which makes it perfect," Aunt Trudel announced.

"And you've got the legs for it, kid," Suzie said. "And I love the real quartz crystal drops."

"You look so gorgeous," Mitch gushed as they danced at the Black and White Diabetes Ball the following Saturday evening.

"Thank you," Leslie said, admiring how handsome Mitch looked in a tux.

And Leslie had to admit, she liked the dress Trudel found for her. It was a halter that was weighed down by the crystals dangling from the hem. It was a lousy wedding dress, but quite a spectacular cocktail dress, the crystals sparkling like diamonds.

"You know," Mitch said as they danced. "I've had a change of thought on something. I want to run it by you and see if you agree."

"Okay," Leslie said, feeling suspicious just from his tone. The "falling in love with you" comment was still doing a number on her.

"I want you to meet Roma, the sooner the better."

"But don't you think it is too soon?" A few days earlier he hadn't called her for three days because Roma was with him. Now he wanted to throw them together? This did not make any logical sense.

"I've spent a lot of time thinking about this. I think you'd be a great role model for Roma. She needs a positive female in her life, unlike her mother."

"You don't think her mother is a good influence on her?" Leslie asked.

"I don't like her life choices," he said, but he didn't elaborate which made Leslie nervous.

"I really, really think it is too soon to meet your daughter."

"I talk about you to her, and she is curious. She is asking about you. We would keep it casual, grab a casual lunch, maybe a picnic. We can see how well you two hit it off. I feel very sure that this is going to be a great experience for both of you. Children, especially little girls are wonderful. And Roma, well, she is totally adorable, like a precious little doll. I know you'll love her."

"I don't doubt that. She sounds like a very sweet little girl. You know that I'd like to meet Roma. She is your daughter, of course I want to meet her, but could you do me a favor? Let's wait until September, okay? That way we'll have been dating a couple of months. I will feel like I'm really a part of your life."

Mitch looked defeated but finally agreed.

Leslie relaxed. She'd been able to put off the inevitable for two months.

The third Saturday in September, Mitch arranged for Leslie to meet Roma. And this time, there was no way out of it. The relationship had been progressing, but she still hadn't slept with Mitch and he didn't seem to mind, which bothered her on a completely different level. What was wrong with her? She didn't want to be pressured, but she didn't want the guy to be able to keep his hands off her. Mitch respected her, maybe too much.

The warm fall afternoon would prove perfect for a picnic or an outdoor restaurant, but Leslie suggested neither. This was Mitch's call. She trusted him to plan the afternoon. And she was just a bit curious to see what he'd come up with.

As she dressed for the lunch date, Leslie considered her wardrobe selection for longer than she usually did for a date. She'd never met someone's daughter before, and she tried to remember to just be cool. Denice had been pretty cool and okay at their first meeting, not that Leslie had been exactly welcoming. She settled on a pair of jeans, a heather colored cashmere sweater set, and a pair of black loafers that matched her handbag.

When Mitch knocked on her door a few minutes later, she was ready. She opened the door to see Mitch and his little daughter, Roma, cowering in fear against Mitch's leg.

"Hi there," Leslie said and carefully bent down to Roma's level. "You must be Roma, I'm Leslie. Your dad has told me all about you but he didn't tell me how pretty you are."

"Daddy! I don't like her," Roma screamed as she clung to her father, trying to climb him to the point he bent down and picked her up. In her father's arms, you could see the resemblance, dark hair and cold blue eyes. She was the apple of her father's eye.

"It's okay, sweetheart," he said, cradling his daughter to his chest. "Maybe it would be best if you came out here, Leslie. Roma gets overwhelmed meeting strangers."

"Sure, sure," Leslie said. "I understand." But she didn't. The kid, if she wasn't mistaken, knew exactly what she was doing and the affect it would have on everyone.

"You look mean!" the little girl said, scrunching up her face.

"Roma," Mitch cautioned, "Be nice."

"I'm really not," Leslie said in her kindest voice. "I'm just a little nervous to meet you."

"I don't want to go out to lunch with *her*! Daddy, can we leave now?"

Leslie considered admitting defeat and telling Mitch that she thought it wasn't a good time, but he acted as if Roma's reaction to her was perfectly normal.

That first few minutes of interaction was pretty much how the rest of the day went.

Roma demanded that she ride in the front seat of her father's car and that Leslie ride in the back seat. To Leslie's surprise, Mitch obeyed his daughter without a second thought. They ended up at Harborside, a restaurant along the Willamette River. Leslie thought they might go to a more kid-friendly restaurant, but Mitch informed her that Roma had adult tastes.

"Roma isn't a typical child with a child's palate. She demands a more sophisticated menu."

Of course, she does, Leslie thought. She was six going on twenty-six.

After they had parked, Mitch took Roma's hand and seemed to remember that Leslie was along for the ride. He gave her an apologetic look when Roma said, "Leslie, you stand over here." It happened to be on the other side of Roma. Leslie wondered if maybe the little girl wanted to hold her hand. She held her hand out, and Roma regarded it as if it were a snake.

Leslie pulled back and walked beside Roma and Mitch until the sidewalk narrowed and then she was forced to follow behind.

Leslie tried to remind herself that Roma was a child whose parents had divorced. Of course, she was going to be guarded and make sure that Leslie knew her place. But what Leslie hadn't bet on was that everywhere they went, and everything they did, Roma would be considered first as the woman in Mitch's life.

"Daddy, you sit by me," Roma ordered as the hostess showed them to their booth. The child then turned to Leslie and pointed at that opposite side of the booth. "You sit over there."

Leslie tried to put her best foot forward, but she had to admit that it wasn't going well.

"What are you going to have, Roma?" Leslie asked, hoping to engage the child in a conversation.

"I don't eat off the children's menu," she replied.

"No, you are too sophisticated for a children's menu," Leslie agreed. "I'm thinking of the parmesan encrusted sol."

"It's fantastic here," Mitch said, as he smiled at Leslie reassuringly.

"What are you going to have?" she asked Mitch.

"I love the lobster cobb—"

"Daddy, I want my Shirley Temple."

Leslie looked at Roma, who was giving her dad the evil eye of an angry child.

"And I want a glass of wine," Leslie said under her breath.

"I'll get one for you just as soon as the waiter arrives," he said to Roma, "Now, do you know what else you want?"

Leslie watched the interaction carefully. Mitch deferred to the little girl as if she were an adult with adult privileges.

The Child, as Leslie came to think of Roma, ate an order of popcorn shrimp, fried calamari, and drank several Shirley Temples before demanding a hot fudge sundae. Leslie tried not to think of the lack of nutritional value of all the fried food and sugar. As The Child ate, she made sure to interrupt her father anytime he asked Leslie a question or engaged her in conversation.

The Child was a lot smarter and much more cunning than her father had given her credit for. She was effectively sabotaging her father's relationship and had to be one of the most spoiled, awful children Leslie had ever met. And more than anything, The Child was a game changer.

When Mitch got a work phone call and excused himself for a moment while Roma was eating her sundae, the little girl looked at Leslie and said, "I don't like you."

"That's not a very nice thing to say to someone, Roma. You don't know me."

The little girl never blinked, didn't get at all distracted from her ice cream. "It's the truth. Daddy says it is important to tell the truth, no matter what."

"Well, your father has taught you well," Leslie said.

"I'm going to tell Daddy that I don't like you."

"Okay, that's fair. I do make your dad happy, and I can keep doing that when you are with your mother."

"I don't like you," Roma replied.

Leslie had to laugh. The kid was a brat and jealous of her father's love life. Someday, kid, she thought, you'll need a lot of therapy to work through your daddy issues.

Leslie appeared at Trudel's Wedding Boutique with an orchid plant and lemon cake with lemon curd filling and lemon buttercream frosting.

Suzie was helping someone try on four-inch high, bejeweled stilettos that made Leslie nervous for the bride.

She took the cake container and the flowers back into the private lounge where the consultants hung out during their breaks.

Suzie popped her head around the corner of the doorframe like a meerkat emerging from the darkness.

"Happy birthday!" Leslie exclaimed. They were going to go out to dinner that night, but Leslie knew that Suzie liked to eat cake and she didn't like to share it with her husband, nor did she want to have him scrutinize how much she ate.

"Thank you, thank you, thank you! Is it what I think it is?" Suzie asked as she hugged Leslie and then jumped up and down like a little kid.

"Trifecta lemon, lemon on lemon on lemon," Leslie said. "And the curd, if I do say so myself, is the bomb!"

"Ménage a la lemon!" Suzie beamed.

Aunt Trudel and two of her associates appeared. They stuck a candle in the cake and sang "Happy Birthday" to Suzie. After everyone had some cake and went back to the floor, Suzie and Leslie lingered.

"Damn, that's some good cake," Suzie said. "Thank goodness you're no longer hiding this talent."

Leslie laughed and said, "Well, thank you for appreciating it. I think if I made a cake for Mitch's kid, she'd throw it at me."

"No positive movement on The Child front, huh?"

"Nope and I have to tell you, after having to accept a stepmother like Denice, I guess I respect The Child for having an opinion. I wasn't nice to Denice, but I don't think I was vicious either. I was just kind of like 'whatever.' I knew I wasn't going to change it, so I accepted it."

"You hung out here. And, your mother was dead, Roma's is alive. Different story. This kid sounds like a brat."

"Would I be an awful person for telling Mitch that I think his kid is a spoiled brat?"

"I can't believe you've denied yourself all this time."

"It's my guilt over Denice. But I have to say, our relationship might be the best it's ever been."

"I'm glad," Suzie said. "You know, despite her size two body, and perfect perky boobs, she is a nice lady. Uncle George could have done worse, but I could've kicked him in the shins for how he introduced her to the family and how it hurt you at the time."

"Thank you for that," Leslie said and gave her cousin a hug.

"You know what would make life a lot easier?" Mitch asked as they walked through downtown Portland on their way to Huber's for a Spanish Coffee. They'd had dinner atop the Nines Hotel where he told her all about his new coffee deal he'd closed that day.

"What?" Leslie asked, walking with him and thinking that he was a very kind man. Her relationship with him was entering their sixth month, and she liked the ease of it, although she knew in her heart it was doomed. No matter how many times she'd encountered Roma over the last few months, the result was always the same.

"I don't like you."

There had been three more get-togethers like that first lunch at Harborside and the results were always the same.

Roma would wait until she had Leslie to herself and then she'd say, *"I don't like you."* Or the ever popular, *"I hate you."*

"What if I didn't have to be away from you for seven days while I have Roma?" he asked. "Especially in the next month or so when I start having her with me full time."

"Full time? I'm sorry, what did you just say?" she asked trying not to sound terrified at the thought of having to spend more time with the six-year-old who hated her guts. She was just getting used to the idea of a relationship with Mitch. They'd only been having sex for a month. They wouldn't be having it tonight. Nothing like a good conversation about Roma to ice their passion to frigid temperatures.

"Her mother is thinking of taking a job in Seattle near the man she cheated on me with and I'm thinking of going for full custody."

"Wow," Leslie said, knowing that he didn't have a good relationship with his ex. Despite her free pass that she had offered about not wanting or needing to know anything about his divorce, he'd told her all about his ex-wife's affair and how he'd found out. He told her about calling his ex-wife a lot of names he now regretted. Leslie told him he was apologizing to the wrong woman.

"Her lawyer was an idiot, so I'll win. No problem there."

"Doesn't your ex-wife want to be close to her daughter?"

"She's more interested in the grunge band lead singer who is five years her junior. Wait until he pisses her off and suggests she go to the gym to work on her cottage cheese thighs, then you wait and see how fast that relationship fades. Roma needs a mother, not some grunge groupie who no longer wears a bra. She needs a positive role model. Roma needs someone like you."

The lovely dinner she'd just eaten was giving her indigestion, her personal gut thermometer of doom. She'd never heard him speak this way about anyone especially not his ex-wife.

She wasn't sure what kind of a mother she'd be but having been a daughter of a father who remarried, she did know a thing or two about how it felt to meet the new woman in your father's life. She felt incredibly sorry for the little girl whose life had been seriously messed with in the last few months.

"Thank you, that is a very kind compliment. Just so I'm clear on the details. You're going to be taking Roma on, full time?"

"Yes, and I think it is time that you and Roma worked on your relationship."

What was there to work on? The Child hated her.

"She has had to deal with a lot of change in her young life."

"And that is where you can help her. Be there for her."

"But she doesn't like me, Mitch. She *really* doesn't like me."

"Maybe you need to try a little harder. We are in a relationship that is important to me."

"I agree this is an important relationship. But if Roma doesn't like me, Roma doesn't like me. I've been in her position, only I was older. It takes years for the trust to be established. I'm only just now starting to appreciate my stepmother."

"She'll get used to you. My god, Leslie, we've been making love for several months. Do you think I'd do that lightly?" he asked as the harshness in his voice sounded a little more concentrated. They'd only been having sex for a month, but she didn't correct him. And she really didn't like him mentioning sex in the same statement with his daughter. She wanted to tell him to separate out their relationship and his relationship with his daughter.

They'd only been doing the bang-bang for a month, and it wasn't a lot better than the bang-bang she'd had with Jack. And it wasn't close to the mind-blowing bang-bang she'd had with Jordan.

She had hopes it would get better, but again the pressure of trying to make it better had almost gotten to the point she was having anxiety at the thought of sex. That couldn't be good.

"No, I don't have sex lightly either. I think we waited until we knew each other a bit, which is very good."

"You know you drive me crazy," he said as he opened the door to Huber's for her, but she detected a slow burning frustration in his words that wasn't at all good.

They were seated at a small marble-topped table in the bar. The black and white checkered floor held too much of her attention. He wasn't done. She could feel it in her bones that he wanted to have a serious discussion.

He circled back to his earlier words. "What if there was a reason?"

Leslie felt her little house of cards momentarily wobble and fall. "What do you mean?"

The waiter arrived with their tableside order and made the big production Huber's was known for, the making of the Spanish Coffees. Leslie watched as the waiter sprinkled sugar which sparked as it caught the flame burning away in the special glass cups.

She had visions of the fire burning her lips as she tried to consume the drink. That would be all she needed to make this evening complete.

The waiter bowed after depositing the flaming drinks on their small table and then he was gone.

"I'm a very direct person. But I think I need to make my point very clear," Mitch said as he pulled a black velvet box from his pocket and opened it.

Every muscle in Leslie's body tensed as she looked at the large, sparkling solitaire in the Tiffany velvet box.

Déjà vu!

It was Jack and the restaurant proposal at the beach all over again. She wanted to scream, "NO!" before anyone in the restaurant started screaming, *"Say yes! Say yes! Say yes!"*

She stared at the Tiffany box and out of the blue her mind flashed to Charlie. He hadn't gotten this business, and she felt a little bad for him.

But then, she didn't want to have to explain a third fiancé in as many years to the family jeweler.

What was wrong with her? Why was Charlie popping into her head now of all times?

Others in the dark, moody light of Huber's quieted as they observed the drama playing out at Leslie and Mitch's table.

"Well, what do you think?" Mitch asked, beaming with joy. He'd been telling her he loved her since their fourth date, she just hadn't taken him seriously. She thought it had become a game with them. But she guessed that for him it wasn't such a game… Not really.

"What is that?" she asked, thinking she shouldn't have accepted the diamond tennis bracelet from Tiffany's for Christmas a month earlier. He said at the time, it was nothing because he was loaded. He just wanted her to have something sparkly at the holidays. Oh, it was something. It had been the gateway jewelry to this engagement ring.

"You said we wouldn't know each other for years."

"I did," she said.

"Well, we just crossed over to a New Year. I've known you for years."

"You've only been divorced for four months, Mitch. Don't you want to regroup? I mean maybe you shouldn't get married for a year or so?" Would he have proposed to any woman who was the first he'd dated after his divorce?

"I didn't get to where I'm at by letting good opportunities pass me by. I want to pour some concrete in these fence posts and make it solid. I want to have a wife to come home to each night. I want a good mother for my daughter—"

His words became like a Peanuts Television Special after he mentioned his daughter. All the adults' words blurred. *Wahhh… wahhh… wahhh….*

She could hear Roma's little menacing voice saying, *"I hate you!"*

But Roma's father had decided they'd get along famously and that was it. She was suddenly thankful to her father for his attempts to get her to know Denice before he married her, futile attempts as they were at the time.

People were watching them. They wanted to share a romantic engagement story with their friends at work on Monday morning. Well, that wasn't the story they'd be sharing. She would not be publicly bullied into an engagement, not again.

Leslie willed her mind to snap into place to help her find words that would work in this very delicate situation. She was kidding herself. They didn't write etiquette books for this kind of circumstance.

For the most part, they'd been having fun. Why did it have to change?

"You want a wife to come home to, I respect your desire for a partner, but Mitch, it is a little soon for me," Leslie said, feeling again that she was in the right place at the wrong time. If he'd met another woman at the Fourth of July party, she might be here with him now.

"What's it going to take?" Mitch asked. "We've dated for months. It isn't like we are seeing other people. I brought you into my daughter's life. I made you a part of it."

"And she hates me," Leslie repeated and then she repeated herself again to make sure he heard her, "Roma hates me, Mitch. That child absolutely can't stand me. You need to understand that her feelings are very confused right now and who could blame her? Her life has been turned upside down."

"Not going to make it easy, huh? You're going to embarrass me in front of all these people."

"You made the decision to do this in a public way. I'd have told you not to do it because I'm not ready," Leslie warned. "And I bet this wouldn't make Roma happy either."

"You're turning me down?" Mitch asked looking at her as if she'd crawled out of a crack in the floor and he wanted to step on her.

"You're upset because I am not following your relationship timetable. I'm sorry. I like you, Mitch, but the timing is a little off for me. I'd need to know that Roma was okay with it. It might be a different answer in three months or six months, but it all depends on her—"

"You know," he interrupted, raising a finger and pointing at her, "Women like you don't know a good thing when it is sitting right in front of them. Do you know how many women flirt with me on a daily basis? I ignore them because of you. Do you think they all have boyfriends who buy them diamond tennis bracelets or wine and dine them every Saturday night?"

He grabbed the ring box off the table and snapped it shut. It disappeared back into his pocket as he continued, his smiling face now a mask of anger, "You never talk about your past. I've asked Denice and she won't tell me. I bet you're one of those women who really likes to torture men. You act superior, but really, when it gets down to it, you're just a tease, look how long it took me to get in your bed? I could go to the bar in this restaurant and end up sleeping with one of the women I picked up there tonight. They would be real, not some kind of cock tease who strings a man along."

The contents from the tall ice water they'd been served upon arriving hit his face and effectively shut him up.

Leslie couldn't believe she'd done it. One moment she was holding so tightly to the Spanish Coffee it was burning her hand, so she switched to holding the pint glass filled with the ice water. Lucky for Mitch it was ice water because when he'd called her a cock tease, her reaction had been severe, unforgiving, and completely unplanned. If she'd had her hand on the hot coffee he'd have been burned.

Standing, she grabbed her handbag, pulled several twenties from her wallet and tossed them on the table as Mitch dabbed at his face with napkins and called her far worse than a cock tease for ruining his Armani suit.

It did take years to really know someone.

She paused for a moment, thought of several parting remarks, then flashed on Jordan and decided Mitch wasn't worth it. Then she remembered the bracelet. She undid the clasp and dropped it into his Spanish Coffee.

"What do you think you are doing?" he yelled as he looked from her to the Spanish Coffee.

"Breaking up with you," she said her voice calm and clear. "No one says things like that to me and ever gets to spend another moment in my presence again. Get some therapy to process your divorce, Mitch. You need it, and Roma deserves a father who is healthy and understanding. Thanks for letting me get to see the real you. It only took years."

Later, after she'd hired a Lyft to take her home from a hotel several blocks away from the restaurant, she called her father's house in Palm Springs. After a few, cursory comments with him, she asked to speak to Denice.

"Leslie? Is everything okay?" Denice asked.

"I just wanted to thank you for warning me. You were right. Mitch isn't ready for me. He is still mad at his ex-wife."

"I'm sorry," Denice offered. "You deserve to be treated better than that."

"Thank you," Leslie said. Then she added, "Thank you for warning me."

"Leslie, how could I not? You're my family. If I'd ever given birth to a daughter, I'd want her to be like you," Denice offered, a kind, warm tone filling her voice.

"I'm sorry I didn't embrace you when you married Dad," Leslie admitted, fighting back a few tears. "I was still missing my mother so much that it was killing me."

"I know. I knew it was a hard time for you. I just wanted to be there if you ever needed me. And you were a good kid. I liked you from the start. I'm proud of you, really proud of you."

"Thank you, Denice. Thank you for making Dad happy and being there for me."

"Anytime," Denice said. "Now, you take good care of yourself. I'm looking forward to seeing you in a couple of months."

"Oh damn, you're his neighbor."

"In two months, he'll be dating someone without a brain, and you'll be thankful it isn't you."

"New prey for Roma."

"Exactly."

Silver Linings Dress Auction

DRESS NUMBER EIGHTEEN

TITLE: *Communication*

DESCRIPTION: Communication, through the ages, has been the cornerstone of any good relationship. This ivory Maggie St. Clair silk crepe modified halter dress with a rock crystal accent hem sends a flirty message that not all wedding dresses need to hide your legs.

DONATED BY: *The Aqua Lady*

Present Day

THREE days before the Auction

Leslie decided that it was time to disconnect from anything electronic. Since the news segment of the Silver Linings Dress Auction had broadcast two days before, she had been unable to go out without someone saying something to her about being a "forever bride," or the even more humbling, "five-time-loser bride." Her personal favorite had been when she was getting her nails done with Denice, and someone had commented that she was "the chick who couldn't commit."

Denice had given the other woman a cutting look and then gently patted Leslie's hand as she said, "Jealousy is so ugly on some people. Remember what your father said and smile. You're very loved."

Leslie's father had called the night before and suggested that if she wanted to put her dresses in the auction that she should.

His words were still echoing in her mind, "Maybe it is time you had a fresh start. Get rid of those old rags. What good are they doing taking up space in your closet? Heck, when you meet the right man I'll buy you whatever dress you want. And this time, I'm making sure that Trudel gives us the family discount. Heck, you don't even need to buy from Trudel if you don't want to."

Her father had become a softie. News of her mentioned on the morning news had reached him in Palm Springs.

Seriously, hadn't she heard that local television viewership was on the decline? Unfortunately for her, the story had been placed on the station's website and received the most hits for the day. Slow. Damn. News. Day. Just her damn luck!

Eventually, Aunt Trudel had called, the apology mixed in somewhere with her ecstatic joy over all the coverage the auction was getting. They'd sold out of the tickets and had enough interest to add wedding dresses that didn't make "the cut" for the live bidding to the silent auction. She was so excited about the money they'd be raising for Rachel's House that she was beside herself. After all, Trudel had volunteered at Rachel's for the last twenty-five years. *Didn't Leslie want to be a big part of it? Her dresses would go a long way to helping a lot of women who weren't as fortunate, whose love stories had been not just sad, or tragic, but in some cases frightening.* And then Trudel added, *"There for the grace of God go we…"*

Leslie was done with today. She was going to go home, order a pizza or something delivered and then she was working from home for the rest of the day. Or maybe she and Daisy would cuddle on the couch with a good Nora Roberts book. She didn't want to think about the wedding dresses. She didn't want to think about the auction. She didn't want to feel guilty about the women in the shelter, but she did.

Leslie's last errand before the big, personal disconnect was to pick up Daisy from the Pearl Pet Spa. She hadn't wanted to keep the appointment, but the princess's nails needed a buff to keep them smooth and short.

Daisy was lounging behind the lobby in a cordoned-off area on an oversized satin pillow like a regal, Hungarian canine princess-in-waiting. When Daisy saw Leslie, she didn't immediately get up but wagged her tail like a propeller against the purple satin. The queen didn't like to be disturbed. Daisy was a pretentious dog, and Leslie wouldn't have it any other way.

Miss Kitty, the proprietor, greeted her and said, "Daisy is all pretty for you!"

Considering that Daisy was a short-haired dog who only needed a bath and a Dremel pedicure, she didn't think that Miss Kitty had much to do on Daisy to make her look fabulous.

"Thank you," Leslie said, and gave a low whistle. Daisy jumped up from the pillow and did a full body wiggle toward the gate that separated the back area from the lobby.

"Oh my gosh! I just put it together! You're the bride with all the fiancés! I read the article online this morning. I can't believe you're Daisy's Mommy and that you're one of our clients."

"No fiancés, just a few dresses," Leslie corrected with a quick smile and a dismissive wave with her credit card.

"So, you're giving away all your wedding dresses? Like five or six?" the woman asked becoming more excited.

Leslie smiled her best *I'm going to smile to make this conversation end as quickly as possible* smile.

"Well, I haven't quite decided how many I'll put in. But at least I know they are going to a good cause."

"Sounds like a good cause, but aren't you the lucky one to be engaged so many times."

"I don't think I'd use the word lucky," Leslie said, but couldn't think of the appropriate word, so she said, "I'm in sales. I'm good at closing deals. An engagement is just an agreement to a marriage contract if you think about it. Was Daisy good today?"

"I'll say! Maybe you should give a seminar on closing the deal with men, I'd go! Heck, I'd even pay money. Maybe we could go to lunch sometime, and you could advise me."

"Oh, I'm no expert, that is pretty obvious," Leslie said and bent down to double-check that Daisy's leash was secured.

"I bet I could get a group of my girlfriends together and we could do a mini-seminar—"

"Wait for my book to come out," Leslie said with a hint of sarcasm that she wasn't sure the groomer caught. All she wanted was for the conversation to end.

"Oh, fabulous! Will you tell me when it is published?"

"Sure, but it is going to be a while," Leslie said. She would never openly discuss her past to strangers.

Leslie took Daisy out to the car and helped her into the back seat harness that kept her from jumping into Leslie's lap while they were driving. The dog's nails glittered. They had used sparkle polish on her again.

"Oh Daisy, they gave you hooker nails, again," Leslie said, as she started the car and drove home.

Suzie called her on the way, and Leslie used Bluetooth to answer. "Hey, you free for lunch at Pastini? Or we could go to Serratto? Your choice."

"I'm avoiding public spaces after my recent celebrity. Your mother…"

Suzie laughed and said, "I'm sorry, but you can't control crazy, and my mother is a bit crazy. You know that. Let me make it up to you. I'll bring lunch to your house. What do you want for lunch? I'm afraid I'm all out of mini lobster rolls, but I might be able to whip up a Cosmo from your liquor cabinet."

"Remind me to never share any date details with you again," Leslie said, thinking the private joke between them hurt a little. She'd never be able to eat lobster again. "I've got Daisy in the car, and we are headed home from the groomer."

"Well, then it is a good thing that I'm right in front of Yum Bowl. I'll meet you at your house."

"Okay, but—"

"I know, I know, no 'demon herb' cilantro in your bowl."

"Thank you and feel free to let yourself inside. The house is a mess, but I'm planning on cleaning it Saturday night when my dance card is empty."

"Touché, and oh no, you don't. You'll be at the auction with some of your dresses going bye-bye along with their bad-ass karma. And you'll be smiling when they go away because you'll be thinking about all the money they are bringing in to help other women, who married the wrong men."

Leslie sometimes thought that Suzie could read her mind, but she could almost read Suzie's. Suzie was hoping to leave Leslie's house with a carload of dresses. Not going to happen.

She wondered if Suede had a hand in this too. It would be just like him to have an ulterior motive and gang up with Suzie. She could almost hear him saying, *Are those dresses a part of your future? No. They represent your past, a past that should be forgotten. Move on. Move on now.*

Suzie was already waiting inside, setting the kitchen table for lunch when Leslie and Daisy arrived home.

PART 4

Two Years Earlier

Chapter Thirteen

Leslie sat across from Shane McPhee and waited. She was better at this game than he was, and she wasn't about to be outsmarted by some dude with a great accent. Why did the man have to be sexy too? It had been a year since her ice water breakup with Mitch, and she hadn't been on a date since. But this was business, remember that. Just business. She wanted the Uptown Cliffs condo conversion.

Shane, with his thick, unruly mahogany hair with golden highlights, was built like a well-muscled bull. He looked like he could toss her over his shoulder and carry her off to some highland field and ravage her. Damn it if the idea didn't appeal to her. She hated this kind of complication. Hadn't the last few years of her life taught her anything? Getting all messed up over some guy could only lead to pain, but it had been a while since she'd felt such instant attraction to anyone. Maybe it was his great, toothy grin. And his voice, she couldn't ignore it. She was a sucker for accents and the fact he sounded like smooth whiskey sipped by the dram in some quaint little Scottish town warmed her from the inside out. Damn complication. Why did she wonder what kind of lover he would be? Damn it!

"I find you a wee bit over my budget, which isn't acceptable," he said, smiling at her as if he were bargaining over something trivial like a felt hat at a street fair in his native Scotland. "I'd have some explaining to do to my partners if I made this deal."

"Do you want the best realtor, or do you want a bargain agent with sloppy paperwork and no work ethic?" she asked, as she folded her arms and took a stance across from him.

"I want to make some money for myself and my investors. Don't you think we deserve to break even? With your commission, I'd starve and be living on the streets and my partners would never do business with me again. I wouldn't even be able to afford a trip back to my homeland to visit me mum and da."

Maybe she should recommend her ex-fiancé. Maybe Shane and Jack could hang out by a pool together and get whipped by some dominant Barbie women. Shane McPhee was probably into that kind of thing. At least, he looked like he knew how to please a woman, repeatedly.

"Mr. McPhee, you can get quality, you can get it fast, or you can get it cheap. Pick two of the three because with what you're proposing to pay me, that's all you'll get from anyone."

"You know something, luv, you're a bit of a hard-nosed businessman wearing a tight skirt."

That did it for Leslie. She could fantasize all day long, but she didn't like machismo for the sheer ignorance of it. She stood, adjusted her black suit jacket, and grabbed her briefcase. Too much was too much, and life was too short for this hot Scotsman and his big ego. Let some other realtor deal with him. She was going to go back to the office and forget she'd ever heard of Uptown Cliffs. It was time to slam the door on this deal and move on. The whole thing had been a cluster, plagued with construction delays and lender issues. Time to stick a fork in it—she was done. Shane McPhee could stew in his own juices for all she cared.

There were days when she could forget about the last few years of her life. Thankfully, she'd figured it out before she'd said, "I do." As for Mitch, well, he was just an unpleasant blip in the radar.

She had a new bottom line that had come from experiencing men like Jack and Shane. It was simple and easy to remember should someone's charm and good looks try to get the better of her ever again: She Did Not Take Shit From Any Man.

"Miss Westcott," Shane called after her.

"What? Did you want to cry a little more about how the big, bad American businesswoman was too tough for you to deal with?" she asked, looking at him over her shoulder, her hand on the doorknob of the condo that would become the sales center for Uptown Cliffs.

"I was just having a wee bit of fun with you," he said with big smile. "I like your spunk, now come back here and let's talk this out, maybe have a wee nip of something to solidify our business agreement. I'll need a little liquid courage to face my business partners with the deal you've charmed me into making."

"I don't walk back to the table for less than 3.25 percent on every sale, whether I'm the selling agent or not. This is non-negotiable, do you understand me?"

He smiled then, a cockeyed smile that reminded her of a riverboat gambler. "You're a complicated, difficult woman, an Ice Princess. That is just the kind I like."

"I'm no one's princess. You ever call me that again, I'll walk out of here and you can just enjoy the view of my backside."

"You've got a nice wee bum," he said and winked at her.

They ended up at the Ram's Head Pub just down the street from her office to share a pint and celebrate their new business relationship. She tried not to think of how much she'd enjoy it if it were a date. And if she was truthful, it felt like one, but he'd agitated her and she was unlikely to forgive him, screw the accent.

"Why Portland?" she asked.

"I like America. I've got the money and a green card. It seemed natural to try me luck at a bit of the real estate."

"So, you just bought into Uptown Cliffs?"

"My investors and I thought it had some good bones."

"Who are your investors? Are they Americans?"

"Yes, darlin', they are mainly from the east coast. I'm the only foreigner. I met Richard Cantwell at a real estate investment seminar in New York a few years back. When I found the Uptown Cliffs, I remembered the man and gave him a call. He flew out with a couple of his investment friends, and we decided to partner on the deal. We all voted on it, and it was unanimous. I was the one who volunteered to stay in Portland and get the deal off of the ground.

It wasn't like I had a wife and kids, so it was easy for me. And I wanted to see a bit of the Pacific Northwest."

He was a good-looking man, and she suspected there was a long list of broken hearts in his wake. She didn't want to add her name to the list despite how much attraction she felt for him.

"What will you do after Uptown Cliffs?"

"It's at least a two-year project, so once I finish, I'll see how much money we've made and then I'll decide if I can stay in the country. My new mates, Richard and alike, might want me to scope out another project, which I'd be happy to do. So far, this country has been good to me. I mean, look at you, when would a man like me get to spend time with a gorgeous American beauty such as yourself?"

She knew he was flirting and thought he was pretty good at it, but she knew better. He was a bit rusty and corny. This kind of approach didn't usually work with her. It might have a few years ago, but not the newer, tougher Leslie. Although she could admit the bum comment was still circling in her mind.

He smiled then with a wolfish grin that said he knew exactly what he was doing. He was a predator. All the rusty, corny crap was his 'aw shucks' approach.

Well, it wasn't working on her. Not at all. Okay, maybe a little bit.

She could ignore his broad shoulders and muscled arms. She could ignore his green eyes. Heck, they were probably contacts anyway.

She just smiled at him and shook her head as if she had heard it all before. He wasn't going to negotiate with her by playing to her supposed feminine vulnerabilities.

"Does that work with women?"

"What, luv?"

"The humble foreigner approach. Do American women fall for the accent?"

"I don't know, darlin', you tell me."

"Call me Leslie, not darlin', please."

"Les," he said aloud and then smiled. "Rhymes with Lock Ness."

"Leslie," she corrected.

"Naw, it will always be Les to me."

"What about family?" she asked, ignoring his grin.

"Me Mum and Da? Well, they are proprietors in Scotland, near Edinburgh."

"Proprietors?"

"They have a tartan shop, the family business that supports my two, slightly lazy brothers."

"So, you wear a tartan now and then?"

"And wouldn't you like to know what I wear under it?" he asked with a deep laugh.

As it was a Friday night, the Ram's Head was quickly filling with patrons and tables were becoming scarce. And the conversation was taking on a decidedly sexual edge. Another whiskey or two and she'd stop just wondering what his lips might feel like on hers. She might let those big hands run over the curves of her body. And if she got really schnockered, she might just ask him to throw her over his shoulder and carry her off.

She was screwed. So much for everything she'd learned over the years, she was blushing at the thought of this man making love to her. She tried to remember her anger from earlier, but it wasn't easy.

It was time to take defensive measures while she still could. "Well, as fun as this has been, Shane, I've got to be heading out."

"Are you having a date this evening?" he asked, smiling at her a bit lasciviously. He had a slight gap between his two front teeth. It only added character to his smile.

"No, but I have had two shots of whiskey and a pint of beer. I need to get some dinner and sober up on the couch in my office before I head back to my apartment at Uptown."

"Why didn't you say so? I'm starving myself," he said and flagged the waitress to their table for menus.

A half hour later, they were each eating large cheeseburgers and had a huge basket of twice-cooked French fries between them.

"You see," Shane said, pointing to his burger, "this is why I love America."

"Cheeseburgers?"

"Yeah, this is the life, a pint, a cheeseburger, and a pretty lady to share the evening."

"I once toyed with being a vegetarian."

"You're breaking my heart. When was this blasphemy?"

"When I was with my fiancé, Jordan."

"You're married?" Shane asked, concern etching into his face.

"My fiancé died a few years ago." Leslie was surprised at how easy these words came now.

"I'm sorry for your loss," he offered and then said, "But honestly, I'm not sorry that you are without a man in your life."

Before she could respond, a familiar face appeared at the entrance of the Ram's Head. Charlie descended the steps with a small dark-haired woman, who was playfully punching his arm as she laughed at something he'd said. Leslie had never seen Charlie outside of the jewelry store and was surprised to see him in jeans and black V-neck sweater. He looked like a brooding artist or angry model. Damn it, he looked good.

"What is it?" Shane asked. "You've got a strange look on your face."

"That man," she said as she gave a short courtesy wave at Charlie. "He's my family's jeweler."

"Have him join us. We've got the room."

"What?" she asked turning her attention back to Shane. "No, let's not."

But at that moment, Charlie waved back at her and smiled broadly as if they were long lost friends. She couldn't believe it. Not only did he have a fantastic smile when he chose to use it, but he was also now directing it at her. He was also proving to be as unpredictable to read as they came.

Shane waved Charlie and his companion over and shouted, "Join us!"

Charlie waved back and mouthed, "Thank you!"

Charlie sat next to Leslie and a girl he introduced as Crystal, sat next to Shane.

The waitress appeared, and they all ordered a round of drinks.

"Thank you for taking pity on us. This place is jam-packed tonight," Charlie said.

Leslie felt the need to explain that she wasn't on a date. Why this was important or bothered her, she didn't know, but she didn't want Charlie to think she changed boyfriends or fiancés like shoes. "Well, we've been taking up this table for a couple of hours. Shane is the developer on Uptown Cliffs. We have been hammering out a marketing plan for the condominiums."

"It's freakin' beautiful property," Shane said, describing Uptown Cliffs. "It's going to be the best views, the best location, and the best of everything. And with Les and me selling the sheet out of it from day one we be making a killing on it."

Leslie's black and tan arrived, and she noticed that Charlie's girlfriend had ordered a black and tan as well. They clinked their glasses together, and Leslie turned her attention to the other woman.

"Crystal, how long have you and Charlie been seeing each other?" Leslie asked as the men spoke in detail about the Uptown Cliffs.

"We're not together. We're friends from school. We hang out now and then when we are both free," she said with a wink that bothered Leslie.

Charlie had a fuck buddy? She'd pictured him with a sophisticated woman. After all, he was a handsome guy, with chiseled features, big brown eyes, and long eyelashes.

Charlie gave her a sideways glance as his conversation continued with Shane. He raised an eyebrow, his hand cupping his chin in contemplation as his thumb rested on his lower lip. What was he thinking? It bothered her.

"That's damn cool, mate! I love the idea. Tell Les. She'll get a kick out of it."

"Huh, what?" Leslie asked, knowing she'd missed something as Crystal had been telling her that she was getting a doctorate in women's studies.

"I was telling Shane about my new line of jewelry," Charlie said. "It is made entirely out of aquamarine and diamonds. I need someone with very Scandinavian coloring to model it for me. Leslie, wearing that black suit, well, my mind is racing with the possibilities, the ad layout, the look I want. What do you think, Crystal?"

"She'd be hot," Crystal said with no malice or jealousy, and Leslie did a double take. "You should totally have her model."

What just happened?

"Can you see her in icy blue? She'd look angelic draped in aqua. Leslie, you'd be the perfect model for my new designs."

"Hard to tell now that she is blushing a wee bit, but I see what you mean," Shane said. "Just this afternoon I called her an Ice Princess, and she took offense. See luv? I was right. Charlie thinks you're an Ice Princess too."

"Ice Princess?" Charlie asked, appearing to roll the title around in his mind. "I love it. May I use that, Shane?"

"Sure," Shane said good-naturedly. "It fits her to a tee."

"Excuse me," Leslie said. "I'm not an Ice Princess. An Ice Princess infers a frigid ice maiden. I'm neither frigid nor a maiden."

"Wow, you go sister. I like her," Crystal chimed in and pointed at Charlie. "She put you in your place. Nice, healthy boundaries. I wish more women knew how to talk to pushy men."

"She is so cool she burns," Shane chimed in.

"Gee thanks, but I'm not cut out to be a model or an Ice Princess," Leslie said. "So, okay moving on, how are those rare gemstone engagement rings selling, Charlie?"

Everyone ignored her.

"You are beautiful, darlin'," Shane said, a new twinkle in his eye that told her he just might want to toss her over his shoulder and have his way with her in some Highland meadow sooner than later. This was a new, interesting development.

"Guys, you've got to respect her wishes. She'd be a bitchin' model, but if she says no way, it's no way. Leave her alone. If she doesn't want to do it, she doesn't want to do it. No means no," Crystal warned.

"Sheet, Les, think of how much promotion it would add for us at Uptown? Charlie, you make our girl here your model, and I get to do a joint marketing campaign with you. Maybe something like all the people who tour through on our grand opening weekend are entered to win a piece of the jewelry and get to meet the model. Meet *The Aqua Goddess*. Or some bullsheet like that. What do you say?"

"I like it. More bang for the whole promotion. I tell you what, I'll donate some earrings or a pendant to your drawing, but only if Leslie agrees to be my model for a photo shoot."

"Done," Shane said.

"Hey, wait a minute," Leslie said. "No one makes this kind of decision for me."

"Three percent, darlin'," Shane reminded her.

"Not enough, darlin'," she countered.

"Fine, fine, let's make it 3.25, but you must agree to be Chuck's model. Agreed?" he asked, extending his hand across the table.

"I want it in writing," Leslie said, ignoring the outstretched hand.

"Allow me to sweeten the offer. Maybe you'll see something at the shoot that you like and we can make a deal," Charlie offered vaguely.

"Ah Chuck, aren't you the sweet talker, show them something sparkly," Shane said. "And yes, little Les, I'll put our deal in writing."

"Thank you," Leslie said and glared at Charlie who just smiled back at her. "As for you, I'll do it. But no billboards with my face on them, you understand?"

Charlie held up his hand, "Okay, no billboards with your face on them, but your neck and hands, well, they aren't up for negotiation."

"Whoa," Crystal said, holding up her hand. "She didn't say yes. Listen, Leslie, from one sister to another, put it in writing, and specify which body parts you will show. I've had some friends get screwed on that," Crystal warned, suddenly Leslie's advocate. Leslie had to admit, she liked Charlie's um... buddy.

"Leslie, please think about it. I've been looking for a model for two months. You have to understand the aqua," Charlie explained. "Aquamarine is a tricky stone. It doesn't photograph well with a lot of backgrounds, but on a skin tone like yours, well, it would be stunning. When I saw you tonight, it all came together."

"He even asked me if I knew any blondes who'd do it. Can you image me stepping into my Feminism class and asking someone if they'd like to model jewelry? Those who wear bras would strip them off and beat me with them," Crystal said with a laugh.

The visual imagery seemed to take them all away from the topic for a moment. Charlie was the first to break the silence.

"I didn't think of Leslie until we were sitting here, but now I see how perfect she'd be," Charlie said as he studied Leslie. It made her blush a few shades darker. What was going on behind those long eyelashes of his?

"I'm not a model," Leslie whispered, looking at him and giving her head a little shake.

"It doesn't matter, you'll be fantastic," he said.

Leslie couldn't look at Charlie, so she glanced at Shane who gave her one of his sidelong glances that made her blush further. If anything, she was picking up on the fact that he liked her. It felt kind of fun, exciting almost. She wondered how the evening might have played out if Charlie and Crystal weren't with them.

"You'd better pay her, you cheap son of a bitch," Crystal said, pointing at Charlie.

"Don't worry, Crystal, I'm a businessman. I'll pay her. I want to sell things. Leslie has what I need," Charlie said as Leslie whispered to Shane, "You owe me so much more than 3.25 percent for this."

"We'll come up with something to please you, lass."

"You'd better," Leslie said and surprised herself by winking at Shane. What was she doing? Two hours ago, she was negotiating with her boss, and now he'd pimped her out to be a model, exposing her peaches and cream skin, and she was winking at him, giving him what, encouragement? Maybe she was letting the cocktails get the better of her. She was going to have to leave her car downtown and take a Lyft home, probably the sooner, the better.

A long hour later, Leslie, who had sobered up considerably, made a beeline for her car. The conversation had turned to tamer subjects, but finally, Crystal and Charlie had made their goodbyes, Crystal hugging Leslie and telling her how proud she was of her boundaries with men.

"Wait up, lass," Shane called, but Leslie kept walking. She wanted to go home, slip into her jammies, watch a movie, and eat chocolate. But she couldn't do that because it might break out her skin and she understood that sometime in the last couple of hours she'd become a model.

"My gawd, you book with the step, doncha?"

Leslie stopped, turned, and said to Shane, "I didn't enjoy that."

"Sure, you did," he said dismissively.

"You committed me to be a model. Are you crazy?"

"I'm shrewd like a cat."

"Goodnight, Shane."

"Have a drink with me."

"I just did and see what happened? I'm going home."

Shane put his arms around her and pulled her to him. She supposed she could have resisted, but her body thought otherwise.

"I like you a little mad, I'll be damned if I don't want to tame you, a little," Shane said, and then he kissed her. Maybe it was her anger at Shane, or maybe she was still in denial about her new job as a model, she didn't know, and she didn't care. Something was making her kiss Shane back. And she found to her surprise that she liked it. A lot.

Chapter Fourteen

"I'll go with you," Shane said as he ran his hand over Leslie's lace covered behind. She was standing in her closet, picking out an outfit to wear to the aquamarine photo shoot.

"No, I'm doing this alone," she said and slapped his hand away. This love-and-hate was part of their relationship, but lately it was more love than hate. Come here, go away, was only come here. It was passionate in a way none of her relationships since Jordan had been and she loved it. Shane never made her wonder, she knew what he wanted, and what he wanted was her. It was carnal and raw, she loved it in a way she hadn't loved any of her other relationships. Not only did it feel good, it was fun.

"But I got you into it, now I want to see it all come to life. See you draped in precious jewels…"

"I think you've seen enough," she said, watching him stride around with a towel wrapped around his waist. The man had a magnificent body and was not at all self-conscious. She knew that if she wanted to have him, right now, right here on the floor of her closet, he'd be a willing participant. He was just a bit feral. Like a dog that liked to hump things. Thankfully, Leslie was in the mood to be humped. They'd been in a sex induced haze for several weeks and the sex had yet to wear out. But Leslie wasn't fooled.

Sometimes she wondered if that was all their relationship was, a physical thing. But Shane listened to her and followed her business advice, so that was something. Although, when it came to the photo shoot, there was nothing she could do to persuade him to forget it.

He just kept reminding her, "3.25 percent."

He'd made it too lucrative for her to walk away, damn him! Where was that Crystal chick when she needed her?

She'd thought that perhaps Charlie had forgotten about the photo shoot when she didn't hear from him for several weeks. Then, right when she thought she'd gotten out of it, he'd called and asked her how her schedule looked for the following week. Since their evening at Ram's Head, she and Shane hadn't spent much time apart. In fact, he was all but living in her apartment at Uptown Cliffs.

And despite her tough talk and best intentions not to get involved with a man again and lose control of her emotions, she liked having Shane in her bed. Sleeping next to a man was something she had missed since Jordan's death. Shane came the closest to filling that void. Their relationship had started on physical lust but it had evolved into something else. They were falling into something that just might have the potential to endure.

"Come on, luv," he said, his hand trying to cup her bra clad breast, but she sidestepped him.

"I'd love to kiss you, feel you touch me, but I need to be pristine. I just spent the morning at the spa getting buffed and rubbed, so until after the shoot, don't touch the merchandise," she quipped.

"You know if he knows you're wearing these little undies, he might want to photograph you in them alone."

She'd chosen a pair of ice blue silk panties and the matching bra. They had reminded her of aquamarine when she'd bought them. And she'd had her nails manicured and polished with a very light natural polish that Charlie had delivered to her office the week before. Hair and makeup were going to be done onsite.

"Well, considering you all but pimped me out to Charlie, I suppose that is his prerogative."

"Oh, come on! You don't mind, do you?" he asked, sounding concerned. "I mean, it isn't everyone who can be a model."

"I'm just doing it this once, for you and for Charlie. Okay?"

"I'm sorry, luv. If you don't want to do it, I'll call Charlie myself."

"I'm doing it because I don't welsh on promises. And if it helps us sell more condos, that would be wonderful." And she secretly wanted to be a model. She'd always thought Charlie didn't approve of her, but maybe her mother had been right. Maybe all those years ago he had liked her. After all, here she was, about to be his model. It messed with her head, and she wanted to go and experience the whole thing, make sure it wasn't some odd dream.

"Whoa, you sounded a bit Scottish there. We are always blaming the Welsh."

Leslie slipped into her jeans and a powder blue cashmere sweater set.

"Goodbye," she said and dodged a kiss which made him laugh.

"Until later," he said with a wink.

"Later," she agreed.

Leslie went to the address Charlie had given her and did a double take. She was staring a warehouse that had been targeted for conversion to lofts. She'd initially thought the shoot would take place at Sauveterre Jewelers.

"Hey, Leslie! Up here!"

Looking up, she saw Charlie hanging out of a window above her, waving and smiling that dazzling smile he hid from the world most of the time.

"Wait there and I'll come down to meet you."

A rickety freight elevator, which had Leslie holding her breath, took them to the top floor of the warehouse.

Charlie, who was usually in a suit or button-down shirt and tan trousers, wore jeans and a leather jacket.

"Are you sure we are in the right place? This setting seems more appropriate for some teenage horror movie."

"Trust me, you are in the right place, and Miguel is one of the best photographers on the west coast. And just so you know, I have two security men here. With the jewelry and the questionable location, I thought it was a good idea."

"It was a good idea," she agreed as the elevator stopped, and they stepped out into a loft that was an artist's studio.

"Leslie, this is Miguel. Miguel, this is one of my favorite clients who has graciously agreed to be my aquamarine model."

Miguel was a thin, tough-looking Hispanic man with a bunch of tattoos and an angry scowl. If she was walking down the street and he was coming from the opposite direction, she'd arm her pepper spray.

Charlie then introduced her to two other men who were going to do her hair and makeup and the security staff who stood beefily by, looking too large for their bodies and too big for their tight clothing.

An hour and a half later, Leslie was in a silk robe that had no doubt been worn by countless other "models." It was hanging off her shoulders precariously because they had air brushed and powdered her skin with something that sparkled effervescently. She sat in a chair, trying to stay perfectly still as to not mess up her makeup or her tousled hair.

"Look, Miguel, I want her draped in the silk sheet," Charlie said to the photographer as he adjusted the lighting around the large cushion Leslie was about to lounge on. "It should look like she just woke up after a night of passion where she forgot to remove her jewelry."

"The jewelry would leave marks," Leslie muttered as she waited for Charlie to finish directing the shoot.

It was hard not to watch Charlie. He was wearing tight jeans and a gray t-shirt with a pair of pointy black Gucci loafers. She wouldn't have guessed the semi-nerd boy who'd always stared at her when he was a kid would've grown into this man. Who would've guessed he had such a good body? He was an artist. She hadn't thought of him as someone who went to the gym. Maybe this was Crystal's influence.

Charlie's wavy, dark chocolate hair was styled, not the usually absent-minded professor look she had come to expect from him.

To distract herself from staring at Charlie, she took in the loft. It was full of strange and unusual props. In one corner was an inflatable whale with the label "Moby Dick," in the other, a cut out of the Golden Gate Bridge, leaning up against the Statue of Liberty. It was also about ten degrees too cold. Large windows were open to the street three flights below, and it was raining—a warm, May rain that was not all that unusual for Portland, but murder on the spring roses.

How had Leslie let herself get talked into this? *Oh right.* She'd wanted to do it. As much as she wanted to blame everyone around her, she had been secretly thrilled at the prospect of getting draped in cool gemstones. The thought of the aquamarine touching her skin, all those beautiful cool crystals made her very happy. Possibly, she was a bit of a voyeur. Not like Jack and not like people who tattooed their faces, but there was something almost naughty about being photographed while you were half naked and draped in jewels. It was almost, well, erotic.

Would she have done it a few years ago? No. She'd come a long way to feeling comfortable and confident in her own skin. Contemplating different futures with different men had done a lot to help her know for sure what she didn't want. She was a bit more selfish with herself and giving herself permission to be okay with that.

She *knew* she looked good. She *knew* her skin was flawless. And she understood why it had been important to Charlie. That he had seen that perfection in her and he wanted to use her as his canvas to showcase his art. If anything, it was a homage to her mother who had gifted her with this coloring and genes.

And that is the reason that although she felt incredibly sexy, she also felt shy. Shy around Charlie.

What was wrong with her? Charlie had seen her at her most vulnerable when she had just lost Jordan. And then he'd called her second fiancé an ass. And now, she was getting ready to shed her clothes in front of him for a photo shoot.

The thought of him layering cool jewelry on her skin made her tremble.

"I want to run something by you," Charlie said as he approached her with a large box in his hands and the man who'd styled her hair.

She looked to the box and back to Charlie. What was this? Did he have lingerie in the box he was going to ask her to model? Would she say no? Doubtful.

He opened the lid and pulled out three different masks that looked like they had come directly from Carnival in Venice. One was the exact color of aquamarine. It was decorated with rhinestone butterflies in aqua and clear crystal. One had tall, aqua feathers and streamers of aqua silk ribbon. The final was a silver mask with sprays of aqua glitter around the eyes, aqua feathers that were mounted with a large aqua stone in the center. "I know you are a little concerned about being recognized. This should take care of that."

"Is that a real aqua?" Leslie asked looking at the big stone in the center of the headpiece.

"Yep, I had to glue it in position, don't tell anyone I used super-glue," he said with a wink.

She couldn't decide which mask she liked best, and the consensus was that she looked equally good in all of the masks, so they decided to use all three.

"Okay, I think we are ready. Hey Leslie, why don't you get on the cushion and wrap the sheet around yourself," Charlie suggested. "Just be careful of the makeup. Here, let me help you."

The makeup artist had asked her to apply large bandages to cover her nipples and bring a modicum of modesty to the shoot. She felt ridiculous with her glittery shoulders and her band-aided boobies, but thankfully she'd been able to do it in the small dressing room, and now she was maneuvering the robe off her body and the sheet on in such a way as to keep herself covered. And she still had her jeans on, which reminded her they were only creating an illusion of nudity, not the real thing.

Charlie bent next to her and helped with the satin sheet and also made sure the first mask with the butterflies was in perfect position. He was close enough she could smell his cologne, something that was deliciously cedar laden and smelled intoxicatingly good.

The cushion she reclined on had been covered with a white silk sheet and placed on a white screen which had been unrolled and covered a large chunk of the floor and backdrop. The only color in this entire photo would be her and the gems as they were only shooting her from the top up.

"Hey doll," Miguel called to her, once they'd arranged her under the satin sheet, "I can see the edge of your band-aid, rip it off, okay?"

"Not okay. Charlie," she warned.

"Miguel, once the jewelry is on her you won't see anything," Charlie said, "The band-aids stay."

"Doesn't matter how much jewelry you put on her, the band-aids ruins the line of her breasts. See for yourself."

Leslie watched Charlie through her mask as he looked through the viewfinder of the camera on the tripod and shrugged. "Yeah, okay she needs to lose those band-aids, they show up. But, I don't want to see any nipple in the ads, got it?"

"Charlie, what kind of photo shoot is this?" Leslie asked and then added, "No one sees my breasts. I'm starting to feel more than a little uncomfortable."

"Don't worry, Leslie. I'm not going to let anyone see any other part of you that would cause embarrassment. I'm focusing on your face, neck, shoulders, arms, and hands, okay? Just take a deep breath and get ready to be draped in aquamarine. Remember, you're a mysterious woman who has just awakened from the Carnival and thankfully you still have your mask and all your jewelry. Maybe you spent the night with the mask on. Maybe your lover has escaped out the balcony, or maybe he is still asleep next to you… Heck, maybe he is out getting you a cappuccino and some flowers."

She complained, "As if—"

"Humor me," he said with a smile. "The right man would bring you cappuccino and flowers."

He called to one of the large, burly men who had been lurking in a corner. The man lumbered over, placing a titanium briefcase next to Charlie, who put on cotton gloves, opened the case, and started unloading black velvet boxes.

"We'll start with three of these," he said as he held three strands of round aquamarines. They were all of different lengths, and gorgeous, sparkling madly as they caught in the photographer's lights.

"I think I want them to cascade down your neck like a waterfall. What do you think?" Charlie asked.

"Wow," she said as she sat up and let him place the cool, sparkling necklaces around her neck careful not to disturb the mask.

"Earrings next. What do you think of these?" he asked holding up two aquamarine teardrops and diamond earrings. "We need something big that can be seen with the mask."

She smiled and held out her hand.

"Here, I'll put them in," he said. "That way they won't get finger-prints on them. By the way, I need you to take off your sunstone ring."

Leslie didn't take off her sunstone for anyone. It was on her hand all of the time. She had left the heart pendant in her safe at home but she hadn't even thought of the ring because she never took it off. Her frown must have given her away for Charlie held out his hand and said, "I'll take good care of it. I promise." He then took off his glove and slipped the sunstone on his left pinkie.

"Thank you," she said. "Don't forget to give it back to me."

"I won't," he said and leaned toward her. She got another whiff of his cologne, and this time she could detect the sandalwood as well as the cedar, something very masculine and woodsy. She considered asking him what it was so that she could buy some for Shane. But she bit back the words before they left her mouth. She was thinking of buying the cologne for Shane so he could smell like Charlie? She needed him to get out of her space with his tight t-shirt and great smell. He was doing funny things to her head.

Leslie sat ramrod still as Charlie gently put the earrings on her ears. She felt his warm, soft fingers linger on her earlobes turning the cool earring to the perfect angle. She trembled again and hoped he hadn't noticed. Then he turned back to the case. "Now for some bracelets and rings," he said and started sorting through his inventory.

"What are those?" she asked, pointing to what was in his hand as she tried to make small talk to calm down.

He held up a pair of thick aquamarine cuffs. "You like these?"

"Yes, they are beautiful."

In the end, they draped her in over a million dollars of aqua-marine and diamonds. Miguel started playing some sexy jazz and taking his photos. Leslie relented about the band-aids and eventu-ally tossed them off, along with her jeans. They arranged her body and played with the silk sheet to perfect every ripple and curl of fabric. Charlie stood next to the photographer and smiled at her. Despite her natural modesty, when she looked at Charlie, warmth spread throughout her body, and she posed for him. Anything he wanted, anything he asked for, he got. And when she met his soft gaze and focused on his eyes, they got the shots Charlie wanted.

"Wow man, you're going to sell a lot of this stuff," the photographer said to Charlie.

"It is all her," Charlie replied.

"Hardly, Charlie," she rasped with a rough sexiness that surprised her and drew both men's attention. "The jewelry is stunning."

"No babe, you made the jewelry freakin' sexy. I'm ready to buy this ice if it means I'd get to drape it on a babe like you," Miguel said with a lustful gaze.

At last, Charlie said, "I think we are finished. I couldn't be any more pleased. Thank you, all of you, for your help today." He called out everyone in the room and had a personal word of thanks for each person. Then he held out a hand to Leslie to help her up as she held the silk sheet against her chest.

"Most of all," he whispered, "I couldn't have done it without you, my beautiful model." Then he smiled at her in a way that made her heart hitch and her cheeks flush in all the wrong ways for a woman in love with another man.

Before she could reply, her stomach growled loudly in protest. She hadn't eaten in hours. Wish she had thought to power eat some crackers at the very least.

"Excuse me," she said, embarrassed. "I was too nervous to eat this morning."

Charlie leaned close, his t-shirt brushing her bare shoulder as he whispered, "And I got too absorbed in the shoot to think of a lunch break. I'm sorry. Let's see what we can do about that."

"It was my fault... I'm fine, don't worry about me," she said as she scurried off to the dressing room. Seriously, she decided she must have a little crush on Charlie. It was so stupid—Shane had bent her like a pretzel the night before, and she'd enjoyed it. She was falling in love with Shane, but she fleetingly wondered if Charlie ever bent women like pretzels and pushed the thought away, far away...

"Hey, Leslie," Charlie said from the other side of her curtain dressing room a few moments later.

"Um, yes?" she asked as she hastily slipped into her aqua sweater. She hoped he wasn't going to ask her for more photos, she was exhausted.

"Do you know what is right around the corner?" he asked.

Leslie had no clue. They were on Thurman Street. She never ventured this far down into Northwest. It was too close to Yeon Streets and the shipyards. Heck, some of the streets weren't even paved but were still the original old brick.

"St. Honoré."

The French Bakery. *The Boulangerie.*

"Oh," she said in exclamation as she pulled back the curtain and pointed at Charlie. "They have these little donut hole like things that they sell by the bag."

Charlie nodded, "With sugar crystals on them. You dunk them in coffee."

"I didn't think I'd like them the first time I had them, but they are—"

"Amazing," he said and smiled, his face lighting up. "Come on, let's go!"

A light rain was falling as they made their goodbyes and shared an umbrella that Charlie provided.

"Okay," Charlie said as they walked. "So, we are in agreement. We are getting some coffee and those pastry things."

"Yes," she nodded and grabbed Charlie's arm good-naturedly to avoid the now more torrential rain.

Over coffee, pastries, and two orders of quiche, they discussed the shoot.

"I felt so luxurious, wearing your creations. I didn't think modeling jewelry would be so, um, so—"

"Passionate? Erotic?" he asked as he took a sip of coffee, his eyes narrowing, watching her over the rim of the cup.

"Yes," she admitted, a little too quickly, thinking that if she didn't have Shane at home, she'd seriously consider leaning across the table and kissing this handsome male. She only hoped he couldn't read her thoughts, or she would have a very large mess on her hands. But sometimes in life you had to get dirty.

Shane. She had Shane at home. But somehow Charlie had stepped out from the darkness, and she was really looking at him for the first time. She could look, but she couldn't touch, not Charlie. Not now, not ever.

"I almost forgot," he said, holding up his left hand.

Her ring. She'd almost forgotten her ring!

Charlie slid her sunstone ring off his little finger, gently picked up her right hand, and slid it on the third finger. "Back where it belongs."

Was Charlie Sauveterre flirting with her?

She had to physically restrain herself from curling her fingers around his hand after he slipped the warm gold over her knuckle.

"So, I know you've had a chance to wear emeralds, zultanite, and sunstones, but do you have any feelings for aquamarine?" he asked, looking at her so seriously that she found it hard to meet his eyes.

She smiled and exhaled, "You know my history. I will always have a special place for sunstones in my heart, but I think aqua might be my favorite stone of all time."

"Good. Because once these photos hit, well, I think this is just the beginning."

"I hope it works out for you. Your designs are so beautiful."

"Thank you. Just wait, you're going to be known as The Aqua Lady. This isn't any longer just about me. The photos, they're fabulous. You were fabulous."

"Charlie, stop it. I'm blushing."

"Promise me you won't model for anyone else. I have a feeling you're going to get offers, and I don't blame you for taking them, but let me have a chance to match them first, okay?"

"No one is going to want me to model, but you."

"You have no idea how beautiful you are, do you?"

"Charlie, I don't know what to say. I thought you didn't like me when we were kids."

"Well, there you are mistaken. I liked you, a lot."

The pastry was like glue in her throat as the meaning of his words hit home. "I…"

"Timing. You're with Shane and I like him for you. I'm really jealous of him, but he's a nice guy, so let's remember that we are friends and get past any awkwardness."

"Okay," she managed, smiled, then added, "Friends."

Charlie walked her back to her car, and she hugged him good-bye. The hug lasted several moments longer than it should have, but eventually she got in her car. Charlie smiled sadly in the rain, holding the umbrella with one hand, and waving with the other as she drove away.

Watching him from her rearview mirror, she whispered, "Another place and time, Mr. Sauveterre, but damn if today wasn't a blast."

Two months later, images of a masked Leslie draped in aquamarine jewelry were everywhere in Portland. She couldn't walk down the street, open a magazine, or surf the internet and not see an image of herself draped in blue ice. Despite the mask covering at least half of her face, she was surprised to see that her eyes exactly matched the color of the aquamarine.

Had she known that Charlie was going to spend so much on an advertising campaign, she might have had second thoughts. She might have demanded royalties.

"Darling, we need to talk about the grand opening next week," Shane said as they sat across from each other, having dinner on the east side at Pok Pok. The condo project at Uptown was ready to go live. It had finally come to fruition and many realtors were chomping at the bit to get their clients in to reserve the most desirable units.

Shane loved the magazine ads and wanted to have several of her photos blown up and framed. The term "The Aqua Lady" has been used in all the ads and was now the favorite buzz phrase associated with the campaign. No one but Shane, Charlie, and the crew from the shoot knew the real identity of the model and Leslie liked it that way. She wasn't sure she wanted to be outed as the model at the condo grand opening, but there wasn't much she could do about it at this point. Charlie had been good to his word and provided an aquamarine pendant for their drawing at the grand opening. The lure of winning the pendant would draw realtors and buyers alike to their event. Would it sell condos? Buzz was buzz. Charlie was selling jewelry, and they'd sell condos with a twisty promotion that was fresh and new—much different than the standard Starbucks card.

"The sales packets are ready," she said. "The signage is in the sales center. We got the ads placed. And I've got three agents from my office signed up to give tours and hold the opens. You've got the trust account set up at the bank for reservations. I think everything is covered."

"It is covered beautifully, luv. But there is something else. We need to have your signage up promoting a special appearance by the Ice Princess."

"'The Aqua Lady,'" Leslie corrected and then buried her face in her hands. "Can't we just make it go away?"

"Charlie said the signage would be ready on Wednesday. There will just be a few tasteful photos announcing the pendant giveaway."

Leslie put down her chopsticks and folded her arms. "Shane, wouldn't you agree that we are trying to sell condos?"

"Of course, darlin'," he said, "But what gets a wife more excited than touring a property when she knows there might be a something more in it for her? The women will love this promotion. And for some lucky husband, she will be forever grateful."

"I hate these kinds of gimmicks."

"It is different, unusual, fun. You'll get used to it. By the way, I have a little something for you." He reached into his jacket pocket and produced a black velvet box which he set before her. She knew the box well. How many times had she been faced with mysterious black velvet boxes from Sauveterre Jewelers? She just hoped it wasn't an engagement ring.

"What's this?" she asked.

"A little something to say thank you for all you've done on the project. And this seemed especially fitting."

She opened the box and found a pair of rather large aquamarine studs, not unlike a pair she had modeled for Charlie.

"Wow. They are beautiful."

"It seemed a shame that you didn't have a memento from the shoot. Now, every time you wear them, they will remind you that you were a beautiful model for a day. Besides, they match your eyes."

Their first reservation on Uptown Cliffs was placed on July 15th. By late September, the furor over The Aqua Lady campaign had died down and the project was pacing more quickly than anticipated. As soon as they had seventy percent of the reservations needed, and had finished the upgrades, they would be able to start placing properties into escrow and start closing deals.

Shane was a natural-born salesman. He was always on site, right alongside Leslie, showing the property as if it were his pride and joy. She found she enjoyed working with him more and more each day. They were a good team and he told her often how much he enjoyed spending time with her. They liked the same movies, the same food, and wanted to travel to the same places. They thought of life in the same way. He made it easy to like him. She could see a future with his kind, gentle ways that complemented hers. He would be a good father—she could see it and she liked that she could.

She liked the idea of this kind of life. Getting up and spending the day with Shane, conducting business and then going home together and discussing their day. It was something she'd hoped for with Jack but was always out of reach. She hadn't altogether trusted Jack, because he didn't like to do business the way she did. Shane was more like her.

The week they were open for reservations, Leslie put Uptown Cliffs on the West Side realtor tour. Once they had a certain number of reservations, they'd close the sales and people would move in. The threshold they wanted was 80% in the first year. It was a large undertaking, but she knew they could do it.

Most of her office came through on tour, and even Jack made an appearance, but he pretended she was a piece of furniture and ignored her, so there weren't any awkward moments.

She and Shane had the best summer she had had since Jordan had proposed to her.

One night when they were barbecuing on the deck of her apartment, he asked, "Would you like to go to Scotland sometime and meet my mum and my da?"

He'd met her family, and they liked him, especially Suzie.

Leslie took a sip of her wine, felt a little thrill, and said, "I'd love to meet your family."

"This operation should be winding down by late spring, early summer. Let's say we sneak away to see the folks."

"That sounds lovely. Have you given any thought to what you want to do after Uptown Cliffs sells out?"

"Yes, my little lass, I have."

She wondered if he was about to break her heart. It was a serious possibility. A man like Shane was always looking for the next deal, and it could be something that had nothing to do with her, in another city, state, or country. It wasn't all up to him, but also his business partners who she had only met through conference calls.

If he left her, she'd get over it. That was the thing about loss, once it became standard operating procedure in your life, you came to expect it.

"Good," she said, trying not to sound anxious. Nothing she said would stop him from his plans anyway.

"I thought we should be scouting out our next deal. We make quite a team. And I think my partners trust me enough to support something that we would find."

It was better than she expected, much better. "I agree," she said and touched her wine glass to his Guinness.

"You know darlin', this partnership agreement with you being my realtor is fine, but I'd like to see what we could do about making things a bit more legal."

"The documents we signed are pretty legal," Leslie said, as he pulled two salmon filets off the grill and put them on the clean plate she'd brought to him.

"I don't think we'll need a barrister for what I have in mind."

She didn't understand what he was getting at, but she followed him inside and waited.

"You see, luv, where I come from, this kind of partnership is sealed with a ring."

He set the salmon platter on the dining room table and dropped before her on bended knee.

"Leslie Marie Westcott, I love you something awful. Will you marry me, luv?"

Shane smiled up at her and waited for her reply.

She had her wine glass in one hand and his Guinness in the other. And for just a moment, she was stunned. He saw the problem and took the glasses away from her, placed them on the table, and resumed his position.

"Well, do you love me too?" he asked, worry lines crinkling along his eyes.

"I do," Leslie said, having a hard time finding her voice. It wasn't the way she'd loved Jordan, but it was love. The kind of mature love that comes with time and experience.

"What do you think?"

She smiled and said, "I think it would be a wild ride and a great adventure."

"And?" he asked.

"How could I say no? I can't wait."

"Are you be telling me yes?"

"Yes!" she said, and he sprung up and grabbed her. The next minute he was swinging her around like a wild top.

"Stop, stop! You're making me dizzy!"

When he finally set her down, he said, "Excuse me, darlin', I was just so excited that you said yes."

"Did you think I'd say no?"

"Well, you can never be too sure about these things."

He kissed her then, and they held each other tight as their dinner grew cold.

"I'm such a daft fool," he said.

"Why? What?" Leslie said as he let her go. Had he made a mistake? Was he already having second thoughts?

"Don't you be going anywhere!"

He returned a moment later and said, "I can't believe I forgot the ring."

Leslie could see it sparkling before she even knew what it was. She must have looked excited because he said, "Now, I'm nervous. If you don't like it, it won't be easy to return. I have a friend in the diamond industry in New York. He got it for you."

He took her hand in his and gently placed the diamond ring on the third finger of her left hand.

The ring was a perfect fit. A large emerald-shaped diamond, with channel-set diamonds on either side, forming the band. It was simple, traditional, and gorgeous.

"It's beautiful."

"Beauty for my beauty."

Leslie called Suzie first.

"Are you sitting down?"

"Oh my god, you're marrying the Scotsman!"

Leslie laughed and said, "I am!"

"I think we've told you before, but Tim and I like him. He is so fun and so good for you, you kind of glow when you are around him."

"I think so, too. Or maybe it is the good bang-bang."

"Lord have mercy, good bang-bang! Oh damn, he isn't taking you back to Scotland with him, is he?"

"We are going for a vacation next summer. We want to live here in Portland, but there is talk of maybe making our summer vacation a June wedding in Scotland. His parents are older and can't travel. How do you feel about being my matron of honor across the pond?"

"My mother will have a cow! That is her busy time. Are you sure you don't want a long engagement? Maybe get married next fall in Portland."

"It is a long engagement. June is eight months away."

"Listen, most people take a full year. Think about it."

Leslie had. She had wanted to wait a good year, but Shane was a bit insistent about his parents. And at least she'd known Shane for a couple of years. They had only been acquaintances at first, but they had spent almost every day together for the last nine months. It was right. It was real. She was finally going to be a bride.

"I have. It is just so easy with Shane. I want it all to be easy— easy dress, easy wedding, great party, and a fabulous honeymoon."

"When can you come in to try on gowns?" Suzie asked.

Chapter Fifteen

Aunt Trudel looked at Leslie with a bit of skepticism. And for the first time, as she entered Trudel's Wedding Boutique, Leslie felt a little… well… judged. And it didn't feel good. "Are you sure you don't want to change one of your other dresses? Maybe add a sparkle around the bust or add a belt?"

"Trudel," Denice said her tone exasperated. "Those other dresses are unlucky. You told me that yourself. This is a new groom. She needs a new dress."

Denice had insisted that she be there when Leslie tried on dresses. Leslie was happy to have her. Their relationship was becoming a surprisingly good friendship. After Mitch, they'd gotten closer. They were too close in age to have a "mother-daughter" style bond, but Leslie tried to think of her as another aunt. It was digestible. And, at the moment, she was happy to have her on her side against Aunt Trudel, who was being difficult.

Leslie looked at Suzie, who just rolled her eyes.

"I don't know if I fully believe that, but it's just that I hate to see you buy yet another dress when you have two beautiful dresses in your closet at home."

"Mom, this is unlike you," Suzie chimed in. "Just because Leslie has been here before doesn't mean she doesn't get the full experience again. Remember, Leela or Leila what's her name? She's been a repeat client five times. We always encourage her to get a new dress that reflects the new relationship. And every time she comes in, we treat her like it is the first time."

"Leila, not Leela. It's just that the spring line isn't half as pretty as the one when you bought the Caroline Benson." But Leslie thought that Aunt Trudel was starting to feel guilty about spending family money. She always had looked for opportunities to rib her brother, Leslie's father, including using a different realtor when she bought her new house fifteen years earlier because he'd complained that she'd overcooked something at Thanksgiving dinner.

"Well, I am a bit superstitious. I don't think I can wear that dress again. In fact, I know I can't. And honestly, I don't think it is appropriate for the wedding Shane and I are planning. We are getting married on some cliff in Scotland. And this time, I'm paying for the dress."

"Leslie, for heaven's sake," Denice complained. "Your father and I can afford to get you another dress. In fact, we talked about it before I flew up here, and he told me to tell you that he insists and I'm in complete agreement with him. We are buying you the dress."

"Oh Denice, that is a very kind offer, but you and Dad paid for other dresses and look how that turned out?"

"This isn't a negotiation," Denice protested with a good-natured smile.

"Okay, okay... You can buy me a dress."

"Thank you," Denice said, looking coquettish.

"But look, let's be practical. I need a dress that is simple and easy to pack, nothing frothy or filled with ruffles. And you all need to make sure your passports are valid and ready to go for our wedding. We are trying for June, but it could be July. I think it sounds like it is shaping up to be a pretty cool party."

"Leslie, I wouldn't miss your wedding for anything, but neither month is better for us, it is the height of our season," Aunt Trudel explained. "I just don't know if we can get away."

Leslie glanced at Suzie who nodded and gave a wink.

"I'll be there, no matter what," Suzie said, under her breath.

"As will we," Denice said. "I can't wait to see Scotland."

"Thank you. Look, I know Scotland isn't convenient for a lot of people. Maybe we could have a second ceremony here. I've been talking to Shane about it, and he seems open to the idea so maybe later in the summer or early September we will have another ceremony."

"With a big reception," Denice, ever the party planner, added.

"If you want to plan it, I won't stand in your way," Leslie said as Denice clapped happily.

"That is the wise thing to do. You can't expect everyone to travel to Scotland. And so many people want to see you have your fairytale wedding," Trudel said. She didn't add what everyone was thinking, FINALLY! Leslie was *finally* closing the deal and walking down the aisle. She'd FINALLY snared herself a husband!

"The thought of another big wedding is daunting. I'm looking forward to something simple, so whatever we do, back here or in Scotland, it must be simple," she said, pointedly looking at Denice who nodded in agreement.

No one mentioned her first wedding dress as if it had gone to a place where sad dresses went to hide along with their promise of happiness.

"We can do a simple dress for Scotland, but seriously, cousin, think of a dress like the Caroline Benson for your wedding here," Suzie added. "I mean this is Shane's first wedding too, right?"

"Yes, it is the first for both of us," she said, smiling and feeling that happiness that had been eluding her since she set foot in Aunt Trudel's.

"So maybe you try on something frothy for the Hell of it," Suzie said.

"Show me something simple for the Scotland wedding first please."

An assistant, who looked very excited, crashed their conversation and asked if they'd like a beverage. Aunt Trudel, who had yet to smile convincingly, cut her off with barely a glance, "Please bring the champagne in a bucket with four glasses and check back in a half hour because we *will* need another bottle."

Wedding dress shopping was overrated. Leslie hadn't felt that way as a teenager, but the older she got, the more she understood that just like getting the brakes fixed on your car or the grass mowed, getting a wedding dress was something that had to be done.

Exactly ninety-three minutes, and a second bottle of champagne later, Leslie and her whole family were in the middle of a large disagreement.

"It is perfect," Leslie said as she turned each way and looked at her silhouette in the big mirror.

"You cannot be serious, Leslie. It is a cotton dress," Aunt Trudel said.

"How many two-thousand-dollar cotton dresses do you own?" Leslie asked as she touched the delicate flower cutouts on the dress and thought that she might not even need a special garment bag. She could just fold it up and pack it in checked luggage bound for Scotland. Heck, she could even take it in her carry-on.

"Come on, you like it, don't you, Suzie?" she asked.

"I hate it," Suzie said.

"You just aren't being practical," Leslie complained. "It has to fly to Scotland. Look at the label. It's a Brian Jones. It's a designer dress."

"Oh, it is a designer," Aunt Trudel said as if it pained her to admit. "He is known for his textures, and you can see on this dress that the flowers are laser cut with the small tulle overskirt."

"Yeah, that comes off, right? I don't want the tulle skirt," Leslie said.

Suzie protested, "It is the only thing that makes this look like a wedding dress."

Leslie looked at Suzie and said, "It's white, it goes past my knee. I could almost wear Wellingtons with it. It is perfect for a Highland wedding. I'll take it."

"Without the tulle, it looks like a lace doily," Suzie said.

"I agree," Denice said, breaking her usual 'let's all get along' protocol and speaking up. "Leslie, do you want to get married in a doily? I mean it is your wedding day, but that dress is... well... it is very breezy and thin. Hold out for better, hon."

Leslie thought of the cold mountain air of Scotland. The fact that she would be standing on a grassy, mossy cliff, probably during a rainstorm, and said, "You make a good point, Denice. Suz, do you have any matching jackets? Maybe something that might be a tad rain proof?"

"I hope you're kidding," Suzie said.

"Tell no one where you got this dress," Aunt Trudel said as she looked up from making notes in her little black book.

"I appreciate the input from all of you, but it's so perfect that I'm going to take it."

"Hey, darlin'," Shane said as he entered the sales office of Uptown Cliffs and gave her a quick kiss on a Thursday afternoon a week after she had ordered her wedding dress and angered every female relative in her family.

"Hello yourself," she said and sank into his arms for a hug.

"How was today?"

"By my count, we are one reservation away from phase two and opening up escrow. With the holidays coming, the traffic should start to slow down in a few weeks, but we've done really well."

"Then what's making you sad, lass?" he asked, reading her disappointment without her having to say a word.

"My family is still mad at me over my practical dress selection."

"They will get over it. As a Scotsman, I value your practicality. If we had to travel to Scotland with a big, ruffled cupcake, I'd be thinking twice about introducing you to my family."

"No, you wouldn't," she said, punching him lightly on the shoulder.

"No, I wouldn't," he agreed, kissing her. "Come on, let's close up early and go celebrate."

"Our engagement?"

"No, silly, we've been celebrating that all over the place. I'm talking about our sales, my little buttercup."

"Shane, oh, I wish I could, but I can't. I don't have any other realtors scheduled to staff the office, and I still have a bunch of stuff to do. And besides, we haven't made it to the magic number, yet. I don't want to jinx it."

"But, by the time I get back on Saturday, you will have passed the magic number, and I'll have missed it."

"Saturday? You're going somewhere?" she asked with a chuckle.

"Didn't I tell you?" he asked, bumping his forehead with a fist. "I can't believe I forgot. I'm so daft sometimes."

"What is it?" she asked, thinking this was different.

"James, you know James from our conference calls, he is passing through Seattle on his way to Japan tomorrow. I'm meeting him at the airport to show him what we've done with Uptown Cliffs. He'd love to meet you. I was going to ask you to go with me—"

"I don't want to be away when we are so close to making our sales goal and selling out of the first phase of the project."

"I know. I wish I could take you, and I'm not keen on being away myself."

"So, you're going up tomorrow?" she asked.

"Yeah, I thought I'd leave early tomorrow morning," he announced, then paused to check something on his cell phone. "He gets in at ten and then his plane leaves for Tokyo at five. That gives us time for him to get through customs, see a bit of Seattle, discuss Uptown, and get back on the plane. After that, I'll drive back."

"You said you were gone until Saturday," Leslie said.

"I was a little nervous about doing the entire drive in a day, but then I saw you and remembered what I have to come back to. Now I don't want to stay until Saturday. I want to cuddle up next to your warm body tomorrow night."

"I think you should stay over. That is a lot of driving for one day, especially a Friday, which is really awful traffic. I'd worry about you."

"Yeah, okay, you are probably right, especially if James and I get a pint or two."

"Especially if you have cocktails, I want you to be careful and be safe. Stay the night and come home early Saturday."

"Yes, my luv, but only because you're asking me to."

The next morning, he called her when he made it to SeaTac airport. "Is there anything you want from Seattle, my luv?"

"Nope, just come home safe and sound."

"I'll see you tomorrow, love you, my little Les."

"Love you, too," she said and hung up.

Because Shane was out of town, she called Suzie, and they ended up having dinner at a little Italian restaurant in the Pearl.

"Is the family ever going to get over my choice of wedding dresses?"

Suzie shook her head. "Nope. Besides, you didn't have any fun picking it out."

"It's just a dress."

"Stop it. It isn't just a dress. We used to dream of our wedding dresses, and I don't remember seeing you get excited by anything like this when we were kids."

"That was before I was on my third one."

Suzie picked up Leslie's left hand and examined the ring. "At least you got a nice ring this time. And don't tell me you didn't feel a little thrill when he slipped this on your hand."

"I did."

"Look, I know you've had the worst luck with fiancés, but Shane is a sweet guy. I like him, Tim likes him. Your dad likes him. Denice looks like she wants to climb him like a tree. My parents like him."

"You are preaching to my choir, Sister Suzie. I like him so much that I'm going to marry him," Leslie said. "Don't hit me, but I could see having children with him."

Suzie looked thoughtful. "I see that, too."

Everyone thought he was down to earth and a good guy. It made Leslie feel happy, but mainly she liked the fact that he loved her. And she knew her life with him would be fun and passionate. They would have a wonderful time.

"So, look, you need a dress that reflects your joy. The cotton dress is on order. You're getting it, but why not come down to the store tomorrow and just the two of us will look for another dress. No one needs to know. Mom is off at the beach with Dad. Denice is back in Palm Springs. We'll have fun like we used to when we were kids."

Leslie felt the hint of happiness that had been missing from the appointment.

"Well—"

"Just say yes."

"Okay, what time do you want me there?"

"Anytime you want. I want you to scour the racks like you used to when you were a teenager. Try on anything you like. We will get you back your wedding dress mojo, I promise."

"I'd like to come in early before Shane gets back from Seattle."
"I'll open early for you since you're family."
"Eightish? I'll bring bagels."
"I'll have the champagne chilling for mimosas."

Chapter Sixteen

"Leslie, Leslie! Help me! Please—"

Jordan was falling away from her, and she was reaching for him. But the closer Leslie got to the edge of the ice, the faster he fell. His eyes grew wide, registering the unspoken terror as he realized he was slipping away. Their fingers just touched but didn't hold as he fell away from her. His red down jacket with the ridiculous matching hat that she'd knit for him—

Leslie sat up in bed grasping at her chest. She couldn't breathe, the air locked in her lungs, refusing to move. She was alone in the darkness of her apartment at Uptown Cliffs. There was a glow from the living room of the city lights below, but they no longer mesmerized her like they once had.

Her brain tried to catch up to her body as she breathed in large gulps of air. Jordan was dead. She had lost the love of her life, and now she was engaged to Shane. But it wasn't quite the same.

As she slept that night, by herself for the first time in months, she had several bad dreams. The first was Jordan telling her that he would always love her and then the whopper that had awakened her, Jordan falling into a crevasse.

Glancing at the clock, she saw that it was a little after two in the morning. She hadn't had a dream about Jordan in almost a year. She was glad that Shane wasn't there to witness her panic. He would have insisted that she talk through it and tell him what had bothered her. She didn't feel like talking about this. Jordan was hers alone.

She looked down at her sunstone ring and placed it against her heart, brushing the heart shaped diamond pendant. Jordan would have liked Shane and Shane would have thought Jordan was a right good mate. Who knew? Maybe Jordan had sent him to her. She knew Jordan wouldn't want her to be alone. He'd want her to be happy.

But something had her unsettled.

Despite her best efforts, she couldn't get back to sleep. She sat in her living room with her laptop and bought some books on Amazon, caught up with friends' lives on Facebook—yet she still felt like something was off. She'd felt it before. A gut reaction she couldn't explain. Only two other times it had happened, and there had been serious ramifications for her life. When she hadn't wanted Jordan to go in the cave before their wedding, and he had gone hiking and never come back. And then there was her sudden desire to go swimming, which led her to finding Jack being a bad dog. She hadn't wanted to swim since she'd found Jack by the pool getting whipped by the S & M Barbies.

What was it? What was keeping her up now? Was Shane in trouble? Had he decided to come home tonight and had an accident?

She had installed the 'Find a Phone' app on Shane's phone months earlier when he'd checked his phone, left it on, and then gone to take a shower. She shouldn't have done it. She should have trusted him, but it was at the beginning of their relationship, and she wasn't as trusting with men as she'd once been—not after Jack.

He'd been looking at an email, which turned out to be completely innocent, but placing an app tracker on the phone hadn't been.

But at this moment, she was damn glad she had. It was ridiculous. She knew what she would find. Shane was staying at the airport Hyatt by SeaTac. Yet, she still picked up her phone and decided to find his phone.

Glancing at the screen, she didn't understand what she was seeing. Shane wasn't in Seattle. He was in Florida. Obviously, the app was malfunctioning. Maybe she should call Shane. And say, what? *"Hey, Shane, I don't trust you or any other man completely, so I'm checking up on you and funny thing, it shows you're in Florida. Oh, didn't I tell you? I put spyware on your phone. You're cool with that, right?"*

Leslie felt nervously for her sunstone ring. It was securely on her right hand. She went to Shane's side of the closet and started going through every pocket of every jacket, shirt, and pant he had.

Why was she doing this? Why had she started this hunt? Shane would be home tomorrow, and she would be feeling very guilty the moment he asked her how she'd spent her time while he was away. There was nothing in his clothes pockets. Not even a lucky penny. She had given him the combination to her safe to store his passport and other valuables. When had he last used it? Had she ever seen him placing things inside? He said he'd put things in it, but had he?

Kneeling before the safe, she spun the dial and pulled open the door. Inside, her belongings, including her passport and jewelry were still there, which gave her an odd sense of relief. But every item that Shane had supposedly placed inside it was gone. In their place was a note addressed to her in Shane's handwriting.

Oh shit.

It hadn't been there earlier. She'd pulled out her aquamarine earrings several days before. No, this note had been left in the last couple of days.

Carefully, she held the envelope and knew without a doubt that she wouldn't like what was inside. It would turn her life upside down. It would hurt. And for a moment, she didn't want to see inside. She didn't want to know. If she never opened it, she would never know and could be the woman with the sexy Scottish fiancé. She could be the once sad bride, now happily planning her wedding to a man who truly loved her.

But it wasn't in her nature to slowly pull the band-aid off of a wound. She preferred to be hit between the eyes and deal with the consequences later. When she was done, she was done. The feeling of completion was already covering her like a web before she even pulled the letter from the envelope.

My Darling Leslie,

By now you have probably guessed that I'm not coming back. I've played my last hand in Portland and must leave. I never meant to hurt you. And I know you won't believe this, but I loved you. I still love you. You're a kind, tender, passionate woman. Just the kind of woman I'd always hoped to marry. I can't tell you how deeply sorry I am that I pulled you into this, but I couldn't help myself.

You see, luv, I have a bit of a gambling habit. I stayed away from it for a while, but old habits are hard to let go of. My mates are a bunch of mostly good guys, but they tell me they are done with me and tired of extending credit. It was suggested that I should leave before any harm comes to me. In fact, my darling, if anyone comes asking, it might be best if you get a case of amnesia. I wouldn't want them to take out their anger on you.

If I thought you'd walk away from everything and join me for the future adventure, I'd have taken a chance and told you my plans. But that isn't who you are. It broke my heart to leave you on Thursday morning, but as you might have guessed, I didn't go to Seattle. I went much further away so as to put some distance between myself and my mates.

You've probably been to the bank by now and seen what I was up to. I needed a bit of traveling money although I'm sure it will upset my former partners.

I'm sure life is going to be hard for you for a while. I'm sorry for that. Who knows? Someday, I might pop out of the shadows and see if you can forgive me. We could have a wonderful life.

I love you, my darling.

— Shane

Leslie dropped the letter and ran for the bathroom. It was all she could do to make it to the toilet before she vomited. After she'd emptied her stomach, she took a long, hot shower, the water burning a little as it washed the feel of his hands from her skin.

She dressed quickly and thought about calling the police, but she had to be sure. All the money in the client account at the bank couldn't be missing. He couldn't have taken it. But a quick trip to the office and an automated telephone teller told her all she needed to know.

"Last transaction, a withdrawal for $647,500 was made today at ten-fifteen a.m..."

Two hours later Leslie was sitting across from a compact woman by the name of Detective Bonnie Anderson at the Portland Police Station, who appeared to have no sympathy for Leslie's situation; undoubtedly that of a stupid penis-whipped woman taken in by a con man. This woman had no idea the price Leslie was paying at this moment. Leslie was doing what she knew was right, but it cost her. She was being a smart businesswoman and putting her head before her heart, her business before her emotions. And no matter which body part she'd chosen to follow at this moment, it was going to hurt like Hell regardless.

"So, you were in business with this guy, but you never checked him out?"

"His partners obviously checked him out. They had enough money to buy Uptown Cliffs. I didn't question it because all the paperwork provided by the title company appeared correct. I was hired as the selling agent, nothing more. I'm not obligated to 'check him out.'"

"So, Mr. McPhee told you he was the owner, and you just believed him?"

"No, he told me he was one of the partners. Every property profile trio that I pulled from the title company had the company name of his partners," Leslie defended. "The only thing I personally checked out was that he had a valid id for the notary. Why would I suspect that he would steal from the escrow account he set up? And by the way, what are you doing to try to get the money back for my client? He's a thief and I want to prosecute. Actually, I think it will be his partners who need to prosecute."

"What is a trio?" the detective asked ignoring her questions.

"It is a copy of the plat map, the property description, and the last deed recorded."

"Well," the detective said, "they are probably correct."

Leslie took a deep breath and said, "I have about seventy investors I'm going to have to call tomorrow to explain that their client trust account was robbed."

"Would it surprise you to know that from what we can figure out so far, there is a real Shane McPhee, and he lives in Australia?"

Leslie felt the pit of her stomach touch the floor and bounce up to hit her in the chin. She felt sick. "Then who was the man I knew?"

"We aren't sure, but we suspect he has done this before. We are pulling some photos for you to look at."

Leslie didn't feel like she was being listened to. She'd already provided photos from her cell phone. Couldn't they match them?

"He had business partners. I need to call them. We had telephone conferences and emails. They had to have documents signed—"

"Yes, I've talked to two of them already this morning. They appear to be legitimate businesspeople whose only mistake was getting involved with Shane. I'm not saying you were the only one fooled, Ms. Westcott. We just don't know the whole story yet, but there is a lot of money missing."

"Yes, that is why I came to see you. I realized he stole a bunch of money. I just don't understand how he did it," Leslie said, frustrated by the cat and mouse game Detective Anderson was playing with her. "Did he just walk into the bank, and they gave him a check? Did he have the account transferred?"

"Yes, that we do know, the funds were electronically transferred. Do you have any idea where he would have transferred them to? Did he mention a foreign location he'd like to travel to? Possibly someplace warm in the Bahamas or the Caribbean?"

Leslie went over her story four more times, explaining about how she'd met Shane and all they had done with the Uptown Cliffs.

Then they had her identifying mug shots of Shane. In the photos, he looked like a criminal, who she wouldn't let take care of her goldfish if she had a goldfish. Heck, she wouldn't have even opened the door to him if he had knocked. He looked dangerous, and she felt a tremor of fear. It could have ended so much worse for her. A little voice inside her head told her that she got off very, very lucky. She wondered just how long it had taken him to polish himself enough to pass for Shane McPhee and how many other women had seen something good in the bad man.

"What's his real name?" she asked Detective Anderson.

"You're going to love this. Rodney Leach. He's wanted in Lexington for a little scam with racehorses. He was telling you the truth that he does have a gambling problem. But in this case, he is wanted for suspicious animal death."

"He killed racehorses?" Leslie asked, horrified.

"Well, someone who calls himself Ian Keller is suspected of it. Oh, and of course, he had a fiancé. He left her three days before their wedding. He's a cute guy, but is he especially charming or something? Didn't his past ever make you nervous? Did you have any inkling that something was off?"

Leslie was such a fool. She'd trusted the most untrustworthy person she'd ever met. She'd let him into her bed and into her heart. She wanted another shower. She wanted to make an appointment with her doctor and get screened for every venereal disease known to man. And for once, she was happy for her allergy to birth control pills. She'd made Shane or whatever his name was wear condoms. He hadn't complained too much. Maybe he didn't want to leave any of his DNA behind. That thought almost had her laughing out loud until she flashed on every little intimate thing she'd shared with this criminal. He'd played her for a fool, all the while seducing her into a blissful, sexual haze, using her body like his own personal playground. Well, that part had been fun. Someday, she hoped it would only be a cringe-worthy memory.

As she sat in the police station, having allowed a search warrant on her apartment, another horrible thought crossed her mind. What if this affected her real estate license? What if this made her get suspended?

She hadn't handled the money. She was an independent contractor who was contracted to facilitate the sale of the properties. Had she done her complete due diligence?

Shane was gone.

Their engagement was a scam.

Everything was based on a lie.

He'd never loved her, because this feeling, *this betrayal*, wasn't love. She probably had a lot in common with the other fiancé.

She couldn't even call anyone because they were looking at her phone. She needed to tell someone. Not her father, not Denice, and not Suzie. This was business first and foremost. She needed to call Jemma, her managing broker.

On shaky feet, she walked to a desk where a woman was typing on a computer. "Excuse me, could I borrow a phone?"

The woman looked annoyed, but pointed to an empty desk and said, "Help yourself."

For a moment, she couldn't remember Jemma's phone number. She took a deep breath. Visions of her wedding dress swam before her eyes. Why had he proposed? Had he wanted to hurt her? She felt a surge of anger, and that was all it took. She dialed Jemma's cell and got her on the second ring.

"Good morning, this is Jemma Kellogg," the silver-haired fifty-something answered with a slight Southern accent she'd been trying to drop for thirty years. She sounded like she was happy and had all the time in the world for a lovely morning chat.

"Jemma, it's Leslie, I'm in the middle of a huge mess and I need your help."

"Why Leslie, what is wrong? Are you hurt—"

"Shane isn't the Shane McPhee that is a partner in Uptown Cliffs. The real Shane is in Australia. The Shane I knew that you knew—he left yesterday, told me he was in Seattle, but he's in Florida. He cleaned out the client escrow account at the bank. And he left me a note in my safe. I think he's a con artist. He claimed he was a gambler and that his friends were threatening him, but I think it is all a lie. His name is actually Rodney Leach."

There was a long silence. Then, "Does my caller ID say you are calling me from the police station?"

"Yes, I reported it all."

"Say nothing. Let Suede do all the talking from here on out."

Suede was Samuel Winston Drake one of the best-looking men that Leslie had ever seen. He was also Jemma's personal real estate attorney, and the attorney of record for Portland Lux Properties.

"They are searching my apartment. They took my phone."

"Suede will be there within the hour. Don't answer another question. Tell them your lawyer needs to be there if they ask you anything."

"You think I need to lawyer up?" Leslie asked.

"Oh honey, you needed to do that before you called the police. Suede will just have to clean up this mess, bless his heart."

As Leslie waited in the hard wooden chair for the return of Detective Anderson, or Suede, or the end of time, she glanced down at her hand and saw the ring. Pulling it off of her finger, she tossed it in her purse like a used stick of chewing gum. Heck, maybe she could sell it and help pay back the clients' deposits which were now probably paying for Fake Shane's luxury cabana somewhere in the Florida Keys.

She counted out the reservations in her mind like she had every day since she'd been a part of this project seeing the happy clients, watching as they picked out their condos and wrote checks to secure the reservation. Ten buildings with ten units a building—with seventy reserved. The reservation deposits were anywhere from seven to fifteen thousand a unit. It wasn't a lot in total, but it wasn't bad for a few months' work. And it wasn't like Shane had paid her anything yet. She wouldn't get paid until the close of escrow. She'd spent about half her time in the sales office, but she hadn't neglected her other clients.

At the thought of all those clients, all the people she'd have to call and explain what had happened...she contemplated going to the ladies' room and throwing up again.

Before she had a chance, an impeccably dressed man in a navy suit arrived at the police station. If she were drawing his entrance in cartoon fashion, there would be billowing swirls of wind all around him because he created a stir. Every female in the building stopped what they were doing to bask in the glow that was Samuel Winston Drake.

Turning to her before she had a chance to speak, he stuck out his hand and said, "Leslie, so nice to see you again. I'm here to help."

"I've never been so thankful to see anyone in my life." And at those words, Leslie burst into tears and realized what a true and awful mess her life had become.

"Hey, hey, none of that," Suede said, sitting next to her and putting a comforting arm around her. "We need to get you out of here. Your life has been messed with, and this place is depressing the Hell out of me, and I only just arrived."

Detective Anderson stood before them and folded her arms.

"Yo Bon, how are you doing," Suede said with a sexy voice that had the effect of butter on warm biscuits.

The tiny detective shook her head and said, "Oh great, Suede is here. I should tell all the ladies to avert their eyes so as not to get hypnotized by your glow."

"What are you doing to help my client?" he asked, showing a bit of steel.

"We have a few more questions for Ms. Westcott."

"No, I think we are done here. Ms. Westcott just discovered that her fiancé lied to her and turned her life inside out. She needs to go home and get her locks changed."

"Some of her fiancé's partners would like a chance to talk to her as well."

"We can't wait to meet them and let them know how everything was going up until yesterday. Thankfully, Ms. Westcott brought it to your attention even before the bank discovered the embezzlement. What are you doing to catch him? Is the FBI in Florida working on the case? From what I can tell, the alleged Mr. McPhee was probably a fairly good impersonator if even his business partners couldn't figure it out."

"And you expect me to believe that your client didn't know anything?"

"She brought the information to you. She let you search her apartment. You have her cell phone, which we are going to need back along with a list of anything that you took from the apartment. In my book, that is full transparency. She is a dream witness. You should be thanking her."

"Suede—"

"Come on, Leslie. Let me take you home. Hopefully, Bonnie's Neanderthals didn't break anything in your apartment when they were searching for the con man that tried to ruin your life."

"We aren't done with Ms. Westcott—"

"You're done for today," Suede replied. "If you need her, you call me," he added and handed her his card.

When they got to the parking lot, Leslie said, "My car is just over there."

"Give me your keys. I'll have your car delivered to your apartment. You're riding with me." And a moment later, he was on the phone making arrangements for her car.

Suede held the door of a big black BMW for her, and then got in on his side and started the engine.

"Am I going to lose my real estate license?"

"Did you co-sign on the bank account?"

"No, that isn't ethical."

"Good. Then you get to keep your license. Now, we have to keep you and Jemma from getting sued."

She knew his office was downtown, but when he got on the freeway and headed north, she didn't know what to think.

"My apartment is in Uptown. Where are we headed?" she asked. "Are we making a run for Canada? Am I in much worse trouble than I thought?"

"No," he said with a chuckle. "I'm taking you to Salty's on the Columbia River. I feel like crab cakes for breakfast, and I bet you haven't eaten for hours."

"I don't know if I'm hungry."

"Sure, you are. And if you only want dessert and alcohol, I won't tell a soul."

"I look terrible," Leslie said, indicating her unruly hair and disheveled appearance.

Suede gave her a critical eye, "You're a natural beauty. You look better than 99% of the women who spend hours getting ready. But if you must smooth, there is a brush in the glove box. Don't do anything else. You're perfect."

This day couldn't get any stranger, Leslie thought. She didn't believe his words, but oh how she wanted to.

The valet took Suede's car, and he handed the man a twenty and said, "Park it nice, Octavio, okay?"

He was extremely polite, and took Leslie's arm as he walked her into Salty's. The hostess knew him, and they soon had a very nice booth that had a view of the boats passing by on the Columbia River, which separated Oregon and Washington.

Now that she was away from the police station, her world destroyed, she felt tired and sad. Despite what she'd told Suede, she was also hungry.

He suggested she try the Maine Lobster Eggs Benedict.

"We're on the wrong coast for Maine Lobster, and I just don't know if I could."

"They fly in the lobsters fresh every day," he added.

"I shouldn't. I was sick this morning."

"Are you pregnant?" he asked, looking concerned.

"No, definitely not," she said, thinking he looked like a youngish Jon Hamm right down to the cleft in his chin. Not a bad person to look like, given a choice.

He asked her practically a hundred questions over brunch. He had a deep voice and a direct way of speaking, probably the lawyer in him. She didn't mind. She liked his honesty, and it was a refreshing change after all she had been through in the last few hours. And she hoped that something she would tell him would bring some clarity to the situation which made no sense.

"Okay, seriously, what is going to happen to me?" she asked. "Will the partners come after me for the money? Am I, in any way, responsible?"

"Several things could happen. First, you could get personally sued, but I'll fight that, and no jury is going to convict a woman who lost her fiancé the way you lost this guy. Second, Jemma could get sued because technically you represent her company, thanks to Oregon real estate law. Thankfully, she has errors and omissions insurance that will cover the loss. It will cover my fee as well. However, as a licensed realtor, you are responsible for a personal deductible of ten thousand dollars, which is the worst-case scenario, but worth some preparedness."

"I'll write you a check today if it gets me out of this mess."

"Let's wait and see how he got the money out of the bank. He could have done it one of several ways, said he needed it for construction deposits, for example. I bet we will discover that is what he did. I have a call into the Real Estate Commissioner, who is a friend. We will see if we can get ahead of this."

"What am I going to do?"

"You will show your grief. You will be the heroine whose hero left her at the altar, the girl who never saw it coming," he said matter-of-factly.

"I didn't see it coming," she emphasized.

"And, be prepared because he will contact you again," Suede said as he pulled the straw from his iced tea, placed it gently on his bread plate, and then drank from the glass like an adult.

Leslie gritted her teeth. She hated Shane. Hated him for what he'd done to her. Hated him for the farce, the lie, incriminating her in this mess—and she still had to tell her family and friends, not to mention her clients who might never forgive her.

"Why do you say that?" she asked, glancing down at her plate where chunks of succulent lobster sat untouched. She usually loved lobster, but not today. "He left me. He lied to me."

"The note, it's a tease. He is challenging you to be his partner in crime, his bad girl. He knows you aren't there yet. But you didn't have to go to the police. There was a small part of him who believed you loved him enough to let him get away with it."

"That's nuts. I had to go to the police," she said, shaking her head.

"Because you are an honest, law-abiding citizen who upholds the oath you gave when you became a realtor."

"So, why would he ever contact me again?"

"To see if he had seduced you enough that you would throw it all away for him."

She knew how it looked from the outside. She didn't have a house. She was a lonely heart looking for her fairy tale. She didn't have much of a life now that Shane was gone. She got it. She was an easy mark, an easy pathetic mark for a con man. But this wasn't who she was, not anymore. Since Jordan's death, she'd become a tough businesswoman. There was no way Shane was going to break her. She'd survived much worse. She'd survive this. And she'd get even.

"I'd like to help throw him in jail. I want to turn the key in the lock."

"Let's protect you first then we can go after him."

"I don't care what it costs," she said, already thinking about her accounts. Suede already had her check the balances to make sure Shane hadn't stolen from her. Shane hadn't touched them, but they were going to get new accounts set up to be on the safe side. She'd need every cent in them if she were about to get sued. "Actually, I should ask you your fee—

"This falls under your errors and omissions insurance. You're covered. I'm yours."

She couldn't take the richness of the Eggs Benedict, but he insisted she have dessert, some ridiculous four-layer chocolate cake.

"I can't," she said.

"You need the sugar. You've been through a shock," he said, pulling out an iPad she didn't realize he had carried into the restaurant. "Now, eat it while we come up with a list of what we know and what we need to find out."

Chapter Seventeen

"I think you should stay at my house for a few weeks."

Leslie turned to Suede who was driving toward downtown after their brunch. She must not have heard him correctly.

"I'm sorry, what did you just say?"

"One, Fake Shane's partners, who may or may not want to ever speak to you again: it is unlikely they will want you to reside in a unit on their property until they know if you were involved. Also, I don't like that Fake Shane still has keys to your apartment. I need to get you out of there today."

"I could go to my father and stepmother's condo." They were in the desert, and she could have the place to herself. In fact, her father had all but retired. She'd almost completely taken over his business.

"It is also a place he knows about and would know to look for you there if he didn't find you at Uptown."

"There is that. I could go to my Aunt's house. You don't need to trouble yourself."

"Has he been to her house?"

"Yes and to my cousin's. Do you think he is that dangerous? Should I hire bodyguards?"

"I just don't know about the level of danger. It is better to err on the side of caution, but bodyguards aren't trained as well as you think, and they are expensive. I have a proposition for you. I have a huge house in Alameda, three thousand square feet. You'll have your own space. My roommate moved out last month, and my dog is depressed. We could use the company. Ginger especially."

"You need company for your dog?"

"Look, I know this is a little strange, but Ginger is pregnant, and she is acting very moody."

"Ginger is the dog?" Leslie asked.

"Yes."

"You want me to move in to your house for your pregnant dog? So she has another woman in the house?" Leslie asked, not understanding.

"Yes, is that an odd request? She is a very emotional animal, moody. And she has been depressed since Bridgette moved out."

"The roommate?"

"Yes," he said. Leslie thought that Bridgette probably just wasn't a 'roommate.'

And that is how Leslie's life did another hundred-and-eighty-degree turn in twelve hours or less.

The police had taken all of her electronics. Thankfully, she had her business laptop locked in the trunk of her car.

"They will probably ask for it," Suede warned. "You will need to go out and buy another one. Copy anything important onto the new computer. We will want to have a close look and make sure that Fake Shane didn't conduct any business on your computer."

"What about my iPad? The police already have it."

"What do you do on it?"

"I play games like Monopoly and Hidden Treasure."

"Business?"

"Never. In fact, I don't know if Shane even knows I have it. I haven't been on it in weeks."

"We will see through discovery if they find anything if we go to trial. Now, we need to get you packed up and out of Uptown Cliffs today."

The thought of packing was overwhelming. She'd have to call Suzie and Aunt Trudel. There was no way she could pack everything on her own.

"I'll go to U-Haul and get some boxes," she said. "Then, I'll need to start calling friends and family. What a mess. I'll have to explain it all, and the questions are going to kill me. Thank you, Shane. Thank you for being a complete asshole. If you were here now, I'd kick your Scottish ass back to Scotland. Bastard—"

"That's the spirit. That is the way I want you to act. You are pissed off, but you are also sad, devastated."

"Of course, I'm pissed off!"

"Good, let the anger feed your resilience. Now, no need to worry about finding friends to help you move, I've made the arrangements. It is all coming to you."

She'd never met a more full-service lawyer, and she had to ask him why.

"Mr. Drake—"

"My friends all call me Suede."

"Okay, Suede, why are doing all this for me? You don't even know me."

His answer was to the point and honest, again. "Do you have any idea how much money I've made because of Jemma over the last ten years?"

"Lots?" Leslie asked as she looked around her apartment like a stranger might look around someone else's living room.

"When she told me to take special care of you, well, that means you get treated like my sister would get treated."

"You have a sister?" Leslie asked.

"One, she is a criminal defense attorney."

"Have you ever had to take care of her?"

"No, she kicks my ass. Now, back to the list. Who has the utilities?"

"Everything was paid for except cable."

"We'll get that disconnected today. We need you to have your mail forwarded to your office—no, scratch that, my house. I have a tamper resistant mailbox."

The knock on her apartment door made her jump, but Suede didn't even flinch. He opened the door to three very large Samoan moving men who smiled at the sight of Suede. They all looked like they were related to The Rock.

"Hey, guys, right on time. Thanks for getting here so fast," he said, greeting each of them with a handshake. Then he turned to Leslie, "Her fiancé is the enemy. Leslie do you have a photo of Shane?" She grabbed a framed photo from one of the end tables and handed it to Suede. It was of the two of them at the beach that summer. Up until this morning, it had been her favorite of Shane. She remembered that weekend as one of the most romantic she'd ever had.

"Now guys, this is the asshole. Protect her from him. We will be calling the police if he shows up so they can take him into custody."

"I don't think he will—"

Suede turned back to her, "Better safe than sorry. If we have a plan, there will be no surprises."

Resistance was futile. Suede was not only good looking, but he was authoritative and in full take-charge mode. She felt cared for and protected. It had been a long time.

Boxes were getting built in her living room like an assembly line in a corrugated orchestra. Muscles were bulging. The men were serious and moved with the grace of boxers dancing around the ring.

"How can I help?" she asked Suede, who called to a man named Rangi and asked, "What direction do you need?"

"Are we taking everything?" Rangi asked.

"No, I want to leave Fake Shane's things behind."

"You make a pile anywhere that feels good to you," Rangi said, "And we'll ignore it. Or maybe we will burn it later for kicks," he added with a smile.

His smile was infectious, and she smiled back, a small kindness recognized in an otherwise bleak day.

Inside the bedroom, she decided on the spot to leave the bed and bedding behind.

She'd never sleep in those sheets or that bed again. She thought of how it had been when she originally bought those sheets with Jordan. She'd loved that pattern, that duvet cover. It had been for her marital bed. And it had fallen short. And maybe she'd committed the ultimate sin by sharing it with not just one man, but several. Another horrible ending she hadn't predicted.

There would be time to mourn over the past later. She didn't have the luxury now.

Her antique dresser in the bedroom held two drawers of Fake Shane's tighty whities and t-shirts. She dumped them on the bed. Then she went to the closet and added more of Shane's clothes to the pile. Just yesterday, she might have buried her face in his robe and basked in the fact that it smelled a little like him, lemon and soap, fresh and clean. Today, it was hard to touch anything of Fake Shane's without protective latex gloves. She felt dirty.

As she was scouring the rest of her bedroom for anything that reminded her of Shane, she heard the unmistakable sound of her cousin, sounding flustered, introducing herself to Suede in the living room.

Leslie sighed, shut her eyes, and stomped her foot. It just got better and better. That is how Suzie and Suede found her, stomping her foot like a toddler and talking to herself, mainly in curse words.

"Les, what in the heck is going on? Are you okay?"

Leslie opened her eyes and looked at Suzie, who had come right from Trudel's still dressed in a black dress and pearls.

"What are you doing here?" Leslie asked.

"I've been trying to call you. I thought you were coming by this morning. I was worried, really worried."

"I'm so sorry, I forgot to call you," she said, hitting her forehead with her fist, "I was going to pick out yet another dress today, wasn't I? Shit. Shit. Shit."

"Leslie, what is going on?" Suzie asked her tone so serious that Leslie almost burst out laughing.

Oh, you know me, Suz, I just burned through another fiancé.

"Seriously, are you okay? You're scaring me. Where is Shane?"

Leslie put her hands up and said, "That is the million-dollar question. Where is Shane? Everything will be fine, so Suede tells me. But I need your help to see if I can cancel another wedding dress."

"No, damn it! No! What happened?"

"Yes, oh shit, yes."

She spent the next few minutes explaining to Suzie just how her day had gone and cried all over again. Suede appeared at her side with a box of tissues. At that point, she wondered what he couldn't do. It was easier than listing all of his talents.

Considering it had taken her almost a week to decide where to hang her pictures in the apartment when she'd moved in, the fact that Suede's movers had her packed and out of her apartment in less than two hours was shocking.

"I think," Suzie whispered as they stood on the sidewalk near the moving van, "that you should stay with me. That is the rational, smart thing to do. But Leslie, I'm telling you, don't listen to me. You need to move into Suede's house. Oh my god, is he good looking or what? He looks like Jon Hamm from Mad Men. That granite jaw and the great smile, it is unbelievable. They could be twins separated at birth. OH. MY. GOD! He is so hot. Just have him help you through this hard time. Did you pack your lingerie? You didn't throw it away, did you? I can get some from the shop and have it delivered to you tonight."

"Need I remind you that my fiancé, who is a master at real estate fraud, just left me and stole almost a million dollars? Do you think there will not be a backlash?" Leslie asked. "Suede said I won't lose my license, but I just can't believe him."

"No, you won't. Jon Hamm out there would never let that happen," Suzie murmured as they watched the movers who ran up and down the four short flights of stairs like large, well-muscled ants moving the contents of an anthill.

"He is not Jon Hamm the actor. He is Suede. His name is Suede."

"I just bet it is," Suzie said. "He is so smooth."

"Samuel Winston Drake."

"That's so cute. You know the movers are all hot too. It's like the song, 'It's Raining Men,' hallelujah!"

"I hate to go bursting your bubble, but Jemma and I always speculated that he might be gay."

Suzie made a dismissive sound and said, "No way. My gaydar is very sophisticated. He's straight as a big, bold arrow."

"If you say so, dirty girl. By the way, would you mind telling my father, Denice, and your mother?" Leslie asked, snapping Suzie back to the present. "Because that is how I'm going to spend my evening."

"I'm sorry. But just so we are clear, if Fake Shane shows up and you want help hiding his body after you go ape shit crazy and kill him, I'm here for you. I even keep latex gloves in the trunk of my car at all times. I never know what 'projects' my mother might have for me at any given time."

"Thanks. Good to know that you can help me hide bodies of ex-fiancés."

"Of course, we're family."

"You know, I've bought three wedding dresses and one cocktail dress from you. I figure that should get me some above and beyond kind of service."

"Yep, I'm here for you," Suzie said, but even as she uttered the words, she walked to where Suede had just ended a call and asked him for his address so she could visit Leslie and the pregnant dog.

Suede had one of the Samoans follow them back to Suede's house in Alameda with Leslie's car. She no longer had a say in the matter, Suede had made the decision and for once, she was letting a man guide her.

She had always loved Alameda and Suede's house didn't disappoint. It was a large Portland Craftsman with a brick façade, but what she liked about it most of all, Fake Shane had no idea where it was.

They were greeted at the door by a girl named Krista, who Suede explained was his fall intern and Ginger's babysitter.

"She loves dogs, so I am supplementing her intern's wages with a little dog sitting," he explained after he made the introductions.

Krista, who didn't question her boss moving another woman into his home, especially a woman who looked something akin to road-kill, announced, "Ginger is napping, but she had fun today. We played in the backyard until I thought she'd had enough. Then we watched a movie and had snuggles in the den."

Suede thanked her and then showed Leslie to a guestroom on the first floor that was right off the kitchen.

"I hope you don't mind, it is the maid's quarters, but it has its own bath, sitting room, and easy access to the kitchen. I thought you might enjoy the added privacy, but feel free to have run of the house," he said, and then added, "Mi casa es su casa."

The maid's quarters were larger than her entire apartment and better decorated in shades of midnight and cream.

"I think this will do, it's an incredibly gorgeous space," Leslie said, and then asked, "Seriously, are you sure about this? You could rent this out to an intern like Krista and make money. I could rent an apartment."

"No way. I want you right here. I'm happy to have you. Now, while I look around for some dinner, why don't you unpack and settle in? Can I get you a cocktail? A little something to take the edge off?"

"I'll have what you're having, but the idea of another shower is very appealing," she said, not wanting to impose any further.

"I make a mean dirty martini." Of course, he did.

Suede with his Jon Hamm / Don Draper directness was hard to resist, and she wasn't feeling especially powerful in light of the horrific day she'd had.

"Gin or vodka?"

"Your choice, I have Absolut, Grey Goose, Belvedere, or Tanqueray, Tanqueray Ten, Bombay Sapphire, or Beefeater if you like a rawer experience."

She shuddered a little at the mention of Beefeater and the memory of another ex-fiancé. "How about Grey Goose?"

"My favorite, too," he replied with a lop-sided grin.

He went off to make the drinks, and she fell back onto the bed, her mind having a hard time coming to grips with all that had happened. Shane wasn't coming back. It was likely she'd never see him again, or if she did, she might be testifying against him in court. She looked forward to that day.

All the plans she had made, the life she had envisioned. It was all gone. Not that this was an unfamiliar feeling for her to experience. In fact, it was bad when the worst scenario possible was the one that was familiar and in some odd way comforting. It was as if the universe had said, "See? This is what happens when you believe in happily ever after. You don't get that. Other people do. You see it all the time, but when you try, the only thing you do is slap Fate, and she slaps you back like a little bitch."

Leslie was used to picking up after the bottom fell out. How pathetic was that?

But she was learning.

When she'd fallen in love with Shane, she'd held a part of herself back. A little part that meant he didn't get her whole heart. Jordan still had a rather large piece of it and probably always would. Jack had tried to prove his worthiness, although, in retrospect, he hadn't tried that hard. And he had failed miserably. Mitch hadn't even realized she was a person. He'd tried to force her into a mold he'd created. All in all, Shane hadn't broken her like Jordan. Only with Jordan had it been real.

The cell phone, on the bed beside her, buzzed like an annoying bumble bee. Suede had worked his magic on the tough red-haired detective and gotten the phone back for her.

Whoever was calling, she didn't want to talk. Suzie had no doubt blabbed to her mother Trudel, who had no doubt called her brother and broken the news that Leslie's third engagement was off. She just hoped it wasn't the detective, Bonnie Anderson. Bonnie was intent on trying to break Leslie down, which wasn't going to happen. She appeared convinced that no woman could be that stupid. Leslie had been, okay? No need to rub it in.

The phone buzzed again, and this time she made the mistake of glancing at the number. New York. It had to be one of the partners.

"Hello?" she answered after the third ring.

"So, you didn't go with him, huh?"

"No, I found a note this morning, and I went to the police station," Leslie said, recognizing the voice, but not sure which of the partners it belonged to, so she waited for a clue.

"Where was it?"

"In my safe where his passport had been. Thankfully, he didn't steal any of my jewelry."

"I didn't think you'd go with him. I didn't think *you* were a criminal."

"Look, I know I'm speaking to one of the partners. I recognize the voice, but I'm having a hard time matching up the name. I've had a terrible, humiliating day. So, who is this?" she finally asked.

"Richard Cantwell, I'm sorry, Leslie, I should have introduced myself when you answered. I know this hasn't been easy on you."

He was the big partner, the money man, the man that Shane had always wanted to impress.

"Hello, Mr. Cantwell," she said. He was also the hard ass.

"What did his note say?"

"It mentions that he has a gambling problem and that he was threatened and had to leave town."

"Nice story. He made three withdrawals yesterday and had construction invoices for each one."

"We've only received our first invoice from the remodelers. It came yesterday," Leslie said. "I know because he mentioned that he'd have to draw his first check on the account."

"Well, let me tell you what I have: building materials, Copeland Lumber, painting supplies, Miller Paint, and finally roof replacement, Washington County Roofing. Have any of those vendors been around?"

"No. In fact, I've never heard of Washington County Roofing. I don't think they exist."

"Where are you now? Are you near the office?" he asked.

"No, I've vacated out of Uptown. I'm staying with a friend. I figured the partners probably didn't want me to stay after what happened. And I didn't feel safe there. Not anymore."

"I can't speak for all of them, but I liked and trusted you more than Shane. Now, you could surprise me and disappear tomorrow, but I'm seldom wrong about people."

"Thank you, Mr. Cantwell. If I had any idea Shane would be capable of such a thing, I would have told you. This kind of deceit, well, it is foreign to me."

"I'm flying out to Portland tomorrow afternoon. Let's say we meet and go over things."

He'd asked it as a question, almost—but it was an order.

"I have to check with my attorney. He is very protective of me at this time. We don't want any of Shane's actions to affect me any more than they already have."

"Bring him, I don't care. But I'm curious, why do you think you need a lawyer?"

"I'm worried about my real estate license. I don't want to be the scapegoat for all of this."

"That's fair. We will talk it all out when I get there."

Leslie disconnected and contemplated calling her father and Denice in the desert. They would be so disappointed. They liked Shane. She could just hear her father's words when he met him, "He's such a great guy! I like him."

In fact, she was pretty sure her father would question if she hadn't made a mistake.

Are you sure? Have you called the hospitals? Maybe it was all a misunderstanding..."

Almost a million dollars wasn't a misunderstanding.

Falling back into the plush pillows, she felt tired and sad. She wanted to cry, but she didn't have any tears left.

Something soft, warm, and a little wet nudged at her hand. A nose.

Opening her eyes with a start, she found soft amber eyes looking back at her.

"Hello," she said to the copper-colored dog. She had forgotten the dog's name, but she could see that she was pregnant.

The dog put one paw on the duvet and batted at Leslie.

"Do you need some attention?" The dog's fur felt like velvet.

"I don't know about you, but I could use a hug," Leslie said as the second paw made it to the duvet. Leslie reached out and touched each paw.

"If I didn't know any better, I'd think you wanted to join me," Leslie said, and the dog jumped up onto the bed and settled in next to her. "Hey, I don't know if you are supposed to be up here."

"Ginger! Where did you waddle off too?" Suede called.

The dog raised her head, looked at Leslie as if to say, "Seriously?" And put her head down on Leslie's shoulder with a sigh.

"I should've known," Suede said as he entered Leslie's bedroom carrying an ornate tray with a martini and a plate of small hors d'oeuvres.

Leslie heard Ginger's tail wagging against the duvet fabric in a swish-swish of rebellion.

"I'm sorry, is this not okay?" Leslie asked.

"Let me put it to you this way, there is no way I can keep her off the furniture, so, I accept what I cannot change. Besides, I know better than to argue with a pregnant female, human or otherwise."

"Do you mind if I ask how you ended up with a pregnant dog? You don't seem to be the kind of guy who is a typical dog breeder. Not that I know any dog breeders. I don't mean to offend."

"You're not offending. It is curious. You see, I went to Europe a few weeks ago with a friend. I found a Vizsla kennel to board Ginger because I wanted her to be with her own kind and the owner went crazy over her. Thought she was the perfect specimen of Vizsla. Unfortunately, Ginger accidently got bred to the resident stud dog."

"Accidentally?"

"Yeah, things that go bump in the night, you know? I highly doubt it was an accident."

"She wasn't fixed?"

"I was planning to have her tubes tied. They do that now so as not to mess up the dog's hormones. I was researching it, but I didn't know she was fertile when I took her to the Vizsla kennel."

"So your dog got knocked up by some stud muffin."

"Yes."

"Are you going to keep any of the puppies?"

"Probably not. My life is hectic. I can barely handle one, energetic Vizsla. Why? Would you like one?"

Leslie had spent her recent life trying to find happiness. She had been dating since she was sixteen and never lived in her own home. And that was something she'd decided she wanted, her own house. She wasn't sure she could do it without a little help. A dog might be exactly what she needed. She'd always wanted one, but her parents hadn't wanted that kind of responsibility.

"Yes," she said, giving Ginger a pet. "I want a little girl and I'm going to name her Daisy." She'd always thought if she had a little girl, she'd name her Daisy. At the rate she was going it was safer to name a dog Daisy than wait for a kid.

Chapter Eighteen

Suede hadn't wanted her to take the meeting with the partners, but he decided it would be good to clear the air.

They chose Suede's impressive office on Broadway Street, which looked down on Portland's Pioneer Square with Nordstrom just across the street.

Richard Cantwell brought two of his partners, Bobbie Firenze and Julian d'Ambrosio.

After Leslie told her side of the story, the partners, who she likened to extras in a Godfather movie and seemed a little too large for the spacious conference room—relaxed and looked a little less confrontational than they'd been when they'd first met Suede and Leslie.

"Shane McPhee should be hiding," Bobbie Firenze said.

"He'll turn up, and when he does, we will get the money out of him, and a little something extra for hurting you," Julian d'Ambrosio commented with a wink.

Leslie felt Suede stir next to her, but whatever he was going to say, he had stopped before the words exited his lips.

Leslie took the engagement ring Shane had given her out of her blazer pocket and placed it on the table. "I'm getting my engagement ring appraised, and then I'll give you the money I get from the sale of it."

"Leslie!" Suede exclaimed.

"Really, Ms. Westcott, that is unnecessary," Richard Cantwell said.

"This kind gesture after all my client has endured is a surprise to me, gentlemen, and I will advise her to reconsider—especially considering she hasn't been paid any commission on the sale of any units," Suede said, placing his hand on top of Leslie's as if to pull the ring back from where it rested on the table.

"No, I don't want it. I can't even look at it. If it helps you with the retrieval of some of the money lost, I'll feel better about it." She also had the aquamarine earrings that Shane had given her. She wasn't sure what to do with them and therefore didn't want to commit to any plans for them.

"Aside from Shane's embezzlement, this project is going well. Now, if we can just find a way to get our money back, we would be back on track," Mr. Cantwell concluded.

"You have seventy-six clients who want to purchase units," Leslie said. "If they don't bail after all of this, the sales can be completed."

"The FBI, Real Estate Commissioner, and the Police are involved," Mr. d'Ambrosio said. "We have a mess."

"It is not my place to advise you, I know you all have attorneys," Suede said.

"Go ahead," Mr. Cantwell suggested spreading his hands before him in invitation. "We're just having a friendly conversation."

"Get in front of it," Suede said and then leaned back in his chair as if he were waiting for a waiter to appear with his martini.

"Explain," Bobbie Firenze ordered.

"I can't advise you, but let's say we are talking as friends, who are having a nice lunch."

"Sure. In fact, after this conversation, I'll even buy us a nice lunch."

Suede looked at Leslie and then looked at the partners. "Have you seen, *It's a Wonderful Life?*" They all nodded as Leslie worried about the direction this conversation was going. She only hoped Suede could bring it home.

"Good, then this will be a familiar concept to execute. Be Jimmy Stewart. I'd bring as much attention to what happened as possible. Full transparency. Make it hard for this Shane thief to hide. You reassure the reservation holders. Replace the money with your own. Reassure, reassure, reassure. Then, you go on the defensive. Find him. Make him pay for your investment and what he did to Leslie's heart. This man is cruel, and he needs to be caught and held accountable."

"Be Jimmy Stewart?" Leslie asked as they got in Suede's car after the meeting and lunch. "And what happened to 'I can't advise you'?"

"I wanted them to hear every word I said. They won't sue you. I could be surprised, but I think they feel sorry for what happened to you too. I like the ring thing. That was a nice touch."

"I am selling the ring."

"Good. If you write them a check, put 'paid in full' on the memo line."

"Do you ever stop plotting?" she asked.

"No," Suede said, as he smoothed back his already smooth hair in the rearview mirror.

Humbling, that is how Leslie would have to describe the moment she pulled open the door to Sauveterre Jewelers and knew she had to step inside and face the music with Charlie. She could have gone to another jeweler, but despite her embarrassment and unease, Sauveterre Jewelers was family to her. Besides after "The Aqua Lady" photo shoot, she felt that she and Charlie had turned a corner and were friends. Put their crazy chemistry on the back burner. Friends helped when you were in a bind. She was in a bind. And Charlie's Aqua Lady jewelry campaign association to the embezzlement might be an issue for him.

Charlie hadn't liked Jack. That was obvious. But she thought he had liked Shane. This was going to be a difficult conversation, no matter how either of them felt about Shane. And for reasons she couldn't explain, she felt like a failure. And she didn't want Charlie to feel that way about her, to be disappointed in her.

What? Did she want his respect? Why did she care what Charlie thought about her? She didn't know, but it was important that Charlie knew that she was okay. She didn't want his sympathy or his empathy. She wanted to do business with him, conclude it, and move on with her life.

Sure, Shane was another failure on her part, a very public failure that had played out in the newspapers and online in pivotal fashion over the last few days. The partners had taken Suede's advice. The day after their meeting they'd scheduled a press conference and shared their experience with the world. And then they had reassured everyone that the money had been replaced, but that still didn't mean they didn't want Shane's head mounted above one of their fireplaces. And suspecting the connections the men had, Leslie wouldn't be surprised if the safari for Shane's head was well under way.

It seemed to Leslie that her love life had forever played out in the media. First, Jordan's death, being so public and appearing in the papers, and now Shane, combining both a public scandal and a surprising character flaw. It was all too much. The desire to pack her car and drive away was overwhelming. But the timing wasn't right. If she fled town with a packed car, the partners would think she was involved with Shane. Suede would kill her. Ginger had had her puppies several days earlier and the only human allowed anywhere near them was Leslie. Poor Suede had been relegated to puppy laundry and poop patrol.

In three weeks, she'd fly down to Palm Springs and see her family for Christmas. She needed the break, but there were the next few weeks to deal with, and it all began with this awful little chore at Sauveterre Jewelry.

Charlie greeted her with a sad smile, and that told her all she needed to know. He knew, and he felt sorry for her. Hell, everyone in Portland did.

"Good morning. How is my favorite model?" he asked, with kindness on his face that made her want to cry. Damn him for knowing the perfect thing to say!

"Hey, Charlie," she said. "I've been better, and I'm sure you know why."

"Yes, I'm sure it hasn't been a walk on a warm, tropical beach," he said managing to sound sincere. Some people hadn't been as generous but then Charlie wasn't like most people. Gone was the tight black t-shirt and jeans he'd worn to the photo shoot. She was a little disappointed to see he was back to his businessman's uniform of the conservative blue button-down shirt and khaki pants. He'd get more clients, females anyway, with the t-shirt and jeans. She didn't think he'd appreciate her observation, however.

"Doesn't that sound great right about now? A warm, tropical beach?" she asked, shaking her head.

"I could be packed in an hour. We could be in Hawaii in a few hours drinking Mai Tais on the beach."

"Don't tempt me. I wouldn't even need to pack. I'd buy a bikini and some suntan lotion from some beachside vendor. We could go directly to the airport from here," she said, thinking it sounded like a lovely idea.

"Say the word and we'll go," he said his smile turning wolfish.

She smiled, she couldn't help it, but just shook her head. Then his smile faded, and he asked, "Okay, how are you, really?"

"I'm not great, but I'll survive."

"I'm very surprised that he did what he did," Charlie said. "I thought he was a good guy. Heck, there is a part of me that even liked him."

"The bottom line is that he knew he was going to do it from day one. He planned the whole thing. And I, stupidly, didn't see him coming."

"I find that hard to believe. I could tell how much he liked you when I saw you at the Ram's Head."

"Thank you. I feel so incredibly stupid."

"You're not stupid, Leslie, far from it."

"Thank you, but I think the jury still might be out. How is Crystal?" she asked, wondering if he was about to tell her that he was engaged or married. Someone deserved to be happy, even if she couldn't see him exactly with feminist Crystal for the rest of his life.

"She's just an old friend. I haven't seen her in probably six months. I think she is in Central America, maybe Africa... I can't keep up with her," he replied vaguely, and she sensed she shouldn't ask any more questions.

She decided on a more neutral topic asking, "How did the whole aquamarine promotion do? Okay, I'm guessing? Hopefully what happened with the client trust account didn't cause you any scandal."

"Not at all. It was one of the best ideas we've ever come up with. I can't believe how many people decided they couldn't live without aquamarine. I've had to make it my top priority. I have you to thank for it, Leslie. I'll never forget how you helped me."

"No, it didn't have anything to do with me, the jewelry is beautiful. And, I have to admit, it was kind of fun being a model for a day."

"Maybe we can work together again. I'd like that, but I'm getting a different photographer. Miguel has called me twice asking for your number."

"As if I don't have enough drama in my life," Leslie said.

"Don't worry, I would never give your number to a man who wanted to pursue you."

"Good, thank you." At least someone was looking out for her.

"I see you are wearing the earrings, do you like them?"

"I love them, but I need to sell them, so it is killing me. I've been upset for the last week, once I knew what I had to do."

"What?" he asked, looking like he couldn't believe she'd ever sell one of his treasures. She couldn't believe she would either. "Can you please tell me why? Satisfy my curiosity?"

"Well, Shane gave them to me. I'm here today to get my engagement ring and the earrings appraised so I can sell them to help make restitution for what he did. I can't keep them knowing he probably bought them with stolen money. It's such a mess, but I have to do what I can—"

"Wait. He told you he bought the aquamarine earrings?" Charlie asked, holding up his hand in protest as he shifted his weight from foot to foot, looking agitated.

"Yes, he bought them to remind me of what it was like to be a model for a day, for being The Aqua Lady. On no, he didn't buy them from your store? Oh, that is disgusting! They came in a box from your store—"

"The earrings were a gift, a thank you," Charlie said, his eyes narrowing as he pointed at himself and then at her. "They were from me to you. He didn't buy them. I gave them to him when he came in for your photos. I wanted to thank you for modeling for me. I thought it was the least I could do."

"You gave these to me?" she gasped, as her hands went up to touch the large studs in her ears.

"I knew I should have called you myself," he muttered looking like he wanted to punch something.

"You made them?" Leslie asked.

"Yes. I made them for you. They are set in platinum. He didn't tell you any of this?" Charlie asked, his voice no longer reserved and sophisticated, but angry and loud in the quiet space.

"No, I'm so sorry, I didn't know. I would have thanked you for them. Didn't it surprise you when I didn't?"

"I didn't know what to think," he replied.

"I love them! It would have broken my heart to give them back or sell them, but I would have. And I would've thanked you if I'd known. I'd have written a note and probably stopped by in person to deliver it."

"Well," Charlie said, his nostrils flaring. She thought he looked like he was barely containing himself. His cool reserve seemed close to crumbling. "You didn't know. And now you don't have to sell them. In fact, I won't allow you to sell them. They are yours and have absolutely nothing to do with Shane. He was just the delivery boy. What a bastard."

She smiled and let out a breath. She could keep the aquamarines. It was the only good thing that had happened to her in the last two weeks.

"I'm so relieved! Thank you, Charlie. I love them. Are you sure you want to give them to me? They must be very valuable."

"You are valuable. You made the campaign, Leslie. I have you to thank. It is the least I can do. I don't think you know what you did for me, being a model. It helped my career, established my reputation, brought it to a whole other level. In fact, Mom and Dad will be holding down the store for a few weeks as I go on a buying trip looking for aqua in Brazil and then Madagascar."

"I had no idea how big this aqua campaign has become. I'm happy for you, Charlie. And now I don't have to think about Shane when I wear the earrings. I can think of you off on your adventures."

"They look great on you. In fact, take them off, and I'll clean them. That way we get off any of his remaining fingerprints and I'll give you a new box."

Feeling shy, she looked down and smiled. They were hers. And they were no longer tainted with Shane's energy.

This next part wouldn't be as difficult now because she got to keep what she really loved.

After he cleaned her earrings and made a big production of getting her a new box, she reached into her pocket and pulled out the diamond engagement ring. "Can you appraise this for me? It was Shane's engagement ring, which I noticed he didn't buy from you. But I still need to know what it is worth to sell it or pawn it."

"Sure, I think that sounds like a great idea. Items associated with the wrong people feel like the person is almost touching you and that doesn't feel good," Charlie said as he turned the ring this way and that, checking it out. He was correct about objects holding energy. She loved the bracelet he'd designed from Jack's Zultanite ring, but it was hard to wear because although she wanted to think of Charlie designing jewelry with exotic stones, instead she remembered Jack and his dog collar every time she put it on.

Leslie thought of all the times Shane had touched her. She only wished she could feel somehow clean again. There was only so much a shower and soap could do.

"I suspect Shane used money that didn't belong to him to buy it. I'm going to sell it and give the money to his remaining business partners who are on the hook for almost a million dollars. And it isn't like I can wear it and look at it with loving thoughts. I hate this ring."

Charlie shook his head and sighed. "You've got a good reason, and it isn't just because Shane gave it to you."

"What? Why?" she asked.

"For starters, this ring doesn't look like you."

"You don't think so?"

"No, too flashy in the wrong way, yet the diamond in the middle—"

He put on a pair of magnifying glasses and adjusted a large light over the ring. Then he let out a hiss of air as he murmured a nasty curse, so out of context, it made Leslie step back.

"What?" she asked.

"It's fake."

"What?" Leslie asked, not sure she had heard him. "What do you mean?"

"I'm looking at the way the light is refracting through the stone. It isn't a real diamond. There are no small imperfections. The stone is too clean, too perfect, like a manmade cubic zirconia. Let me be completely sure, although I wouldn't touch this stone with what I already suspect."

He turned and looked in the general direction of his father, "Hey Dad, do you have a moment for a consultation?"

"Sure," his father said, and greeted Leslie with a smile not unlike his son's, "Hello Miss Leslie Westcott, pretty as ever, I see."

Leslie blushed and smiled as she thanked him, but she couldn't take her eyes off the ring in Charlie's hand as he passed it to his father.

James hit the center stone with a light instrument and went into a long explanation of what should or should not be happening. Leslie tuned him out after about five seconds. Charlie met her eyes and shook his head as his father continued to explain.

Shane had given her a fake ring. If she had even the slightest doubt, it had now been justified. Shane had been planning on ditching her for months. It wasn't a last-minute plan or something that he had to do because of some gambling issue. He'd played her from the start. Did he need to take it this far? Had he needed to give her a ring?

"Are all the diamonds fake?" she asked flatly. "Even the ones on the side?"

"The baguettes aren't passing the test either," Charlie said. I'm so sorry, Leslie."

"Why am I just not surprised? I mean is there anything else he could have done to me?"

"Don't say that. It could have been worse, you could have married him. You could have had children with him, and then he might have left you. That would have been much worse, especially if he'd taken the children. He could have hurt you, physically. A man that cold could have done much worse. I don't even want to think about it," he said, running a hand through his curly hair and then shutting his eyes as if he were picturing her injured or worse.

"Sounds like this fiancé was a bum," James said as he turned and began his way back to his workbench, but not before adding, "Glad you kicked him to the curb."

"Thank you, Mr. Sauveterre," Leslie said and then turned to Charlie, "You're right. If we'd married, and had children, that would have been much worse. I'd have had to kill him. Heck, I still might."

"If you do, we never had this conversation. I won't recall it. But seriously, for your safety, if he contacts you, or suddenly shows up, call the police. Always have your cell phone on you."

Was he worried about her? It was as sweet as it was surprising. Well, he certainly didn't want to lose a good client, and she was a good client. She always came to him for her jewelry.

"I'm taking precautions. And you're a good man, Charlie, thank you for caring," she said, smiling for the first time. She didn't know him that well, but she knew he'd never do anything so cruel to a girlfriend. He was a kind-hearted soul. She needed to pick someone like him next time.

"There is a bit of good news. The ring is set in 14-karat gold."

"Oh, goody-goody. How much?"

"Probably worth about eight hundred to a grand, give or take."

"Great."

"There are stores that specialize in costume jewelry. They could sell it for you. I can't touch it. If I could, I would," he said sounding almost disappointed.

"Thanks Charlie. I appreciate it. And thank you for the earrings. I'm very thankful that I don't have to give them back."

"My pleasure. And for what it is worth, I'm sorry."

Silver Linings Dress Auction

DRESS NUMBER TWENTY-TWO

TITLE: *Trust*

DESCRIPTION: Simple, basic, and honest in its understated elegance, this Brian Jones dress captures the designer from Texas at his perfection. Known for his fanciful design tactics, you will delight in the detail of this elegant lace gown. And, if you look closely, you will see that the delicate buttercup flowers are laser cut. The small, detachable tulle overskirt adds that extra hint of feminine whimsy.

DONATED BY: *The Aqua Lady*

Present Day

TWO days before the Auction

As Leslie predicted, Suzie had tried to get her hot paws on the wedding dresses after their Yum Bowl lunch the day before, but Leslie wasn't in the mood to open that Pandora's box—aka her guest room closet.

"It's just that we need to print the programs and I'm not sure which of your dresses to include."

"How about none of them?" Leslie suggested.

"I just can't believe you feel that way."

"Today, I do."

"Look, why don't I let you sleep on it?"

"You mean you want to come back tomorrow?" Leslie said with a groan.

"I can ask Milan to push the printers to the limits, he knows everyone so it shouldn't be a problem. If the printer we have lined up can't do it, he'll know someone that can. I can give you a day to think it over."

"Why are you being such a pest about this?" Leslie asked.

"I want the Germaine! And the Casper's! They will make the show," Suzie said. "Please! I'll walk your pretentious dog, I'll wash your car, or I'll mow your lawn—"

"I need to sleep on it."

As promised, Suzie had let Leslie sleep on it. But she'd shown up the next afternoon ready for action and holding a bottle of champagne in one hand and a box of pastries from La Provence in the other.

Leslie was no longer in the mood to fight her. They ended up in her guest bedroom, the one with the infamous closet that held an assortment of wedding dresses wrapped in garment bags and hanging from their necks like white corpses on hangman's nooses.

"I cannot believe you didn't have these sealed in boxes like all good brides should."

Leslie rolled her eyes. "You wanted me to have them sealed? For what? So someday a daughter I may or may not have would suddenly say, 'Mommy, I want to wear the dress you bought for the man you didn't marry, you know the one that had the dog collar, no wait, I want to wear the one Aunt Suzie called a doily...'"

"They turn yellow if they aren't preserved. You know that. And that dress is a doily. It would look gaudy even on a plain table in an empty room with white walls. It should be the first to go into the auction."

"And you say you are in wedding dress sales?" Leslie asked, sarcastically.

"Now look, by your very reaction you don't care about them. Why have them in your closet collecting dust and emitting bad mojo? In fact," Suzie said, sniffing the air, "It even smells a little morgy in here, like dead engagements."

"'Morgy'?" Leslie asked.

"You know, old, dead, the past... Like a bad retirement home from the '70's. Something not right with this," Suzie said indicating the dresses in the closet.

"Fine, let's get them out and have a look, but just for you, and realize this, I haven't made any decisions yet," Leslie said as she started laying garment bags out on the bed.

She would have preferred to do this exercise on any day but today, but Suzie was already unzipping and looking at the different gowns that represented Leslie's torrid past. As each dress was uncovered, she felt a different pang of sadness for each one.

"This one," Suzie said, looking down at the Paris Germaine gown, "is my favorite."

"Mine too," Leslie said. "In fact, I don't think I ever tried it on."

"How could you have never tried it on?"

"If you'll remember, a lot was going on the day I got that dress. I just didn't think about it because I was in shock. I shouldn't even have that dress in my closet. It shouldn't count. In fact, it might not even fit me."

"You were thinking about *him*. It will fit. It is ironically your perfect size for wedding dresses. I'm putting it to the side."

"Could we not talk about *him*, please? He hasn't called, I don't know where he is, I thought your purpose today was to take all my dresses away? Didn't you specifically call out the Germaine yesterday?"

"The Germaine is special for several reasons."

"Name them," Leslie said, thinking this would be good to hear.

"It is by far the most expensive of all your gowns. You didn't buy it. And it doesn't represent any of your fiancés. You won it, so it has a clean record. I mean, come on, the day you got it was a pretty good day. It is probably the only one in the group I'd let you keep, if you tried it on."

"Moving on," Leslie said, not wanting to think about the day she got the Germaine as she looked at the plain cotton buttercup doily dress that no one else liked.

"I never knew what you saw in that dress," Suzie said, pointing to it as if it were roadkill. "I know it is a Brian Jones, but none of us liked it on you."

"Again, I'll tell you. Ease of packing."

"That should have been a sign that Shane wasn't the right one," Suzie said as she zipped the Brian Jones back in its bag. "I'll just take this out to the car, unless you protest."

"No," Leslie whined, "Take the doily dress away."

"Yay, this is a positive start! I wonder if anyone will bid on it? My bet is no."

"Hey!"

That left five dresses: the two James Casper's, the Paris Germaine, the Caroline Benson, and the Maggie St. Clair, which shouldn't count because she'd worn it to a black and white ball with Mitch and it wasn't like it was a "traditional" wedding dress. It was more of a cocktail dress. She touched the lacy edge on the plunging neckline of the Caroline Benson and felt beyond thankful that she'd never worn it walking down an aisle to marry Jack.

Despite what she'd told him on the phone, she'd never hurt this dress by turning it into a Halloween costume. It was a sexy dress, by far the sexiest she'd ever had. For a moment, she'd thought of keeping it. She could almost hear all her female relatives shrieking in displeasure if she chose to wear it at her next wedding, if there was a next wedding. It was more the idea of looking sexy for her groom that appealed to her. And as she thought of it, she could easily picture the groom, which was completely ridiculous. She needed to get a grip. He wasn't hers to keep.

Suzie stepped back into the guest room and said, "The Caroline Benson. I loved that one. You looked naked in it with the nude underdress. My mother was secretly a bit horrified by that choice, which is why I loved it."

"I know, that is why I loved it too," Leslie said, touching one of the sequins and remembering how revealing the dress had been.

They talked about the detailing, looked at some of the little touches that made that gown unique. "Okay, time to let this one go. And this one," she said, grabbing the second James Casper.

"He has really good taste, you know? Picking out this dress for you," Suzie said.

"I know. That would have been such a mess."

"When a groom sees the bride in the dress before the wedding, it is as good as jinxed."

"If I had ten bucks for every time I heard Aunt Strudel Trudel say that over the years, I'd be able to afford a handsome man servant to carry these dresses out to your car."

"What a nice idea! But, you have to agree, it all turned out for the best. I mean you couldn't have predicted it would turn out so well for everyone but the bride. Sorry about that. You got hosed."

"I got saved. I didn't get married for the wrong reason and thumb my nose at love. And, in this case, I'm okay with it because we kept what was important, the friendship. And he is a very good friend and dog god/grandfather."

"Are you sure about both of these?" Suzie asked, obviously sensing Leslie's growing hesitation. "You know, despite all my hard-love talk, you don't have to let them all go. We will have another one of these auctions next spring. I just thought you might want a clean slate and get rid of all this bad karma smelling up the place."

"Oh good, I did have a choice. After the interview, it sounded like I didn't have a say in the matter."

"I'm sorry about that," Suzie said.

"No, you're not," Leslie said with a chuckle, "You're a little like Aunt Trudel. You get excited and you mean well, so I forgive you for now. Aunt Trouble is still in the doghouse."

"She'll feel worse next week after she thinks about how it all unfolded."

"It's all fine, we're family," Leslie said and gave a little shake of her head as she zipped the Caroline Benson back into its garment bag.

"I can't look at the Caroline Benson without thinking of Jack getting beaten by girls in black leather, so I guess I have to let go of it. That isn't an image I want to have in my head. And as for the second James Casper, I bought it off the rack and only was excited about if for a few hours. I mean it had to be one of the shortest engagements in the history of engagements." Leslie let out a sigh and said, "Go ahead, take those out to the car, please."

Suzie made another run to the car, leaving Leslie with her first wedding dress, her favorite James Casper, the dress that had held so much love and promise for a future with Jordan and the two others that held odd sentimental value.

The James Casper had been hanging in her closet for almost five long and lonely years. Nothing had ever felt as precious to her as the moment she had tried it on in front of her father, stepmother, aunt, and cousin. Then she had pictured Jordan at the end of the aisle waiting for her, seeing her in the dress for the first time.

When Suzie returned to the bedroom, she found Leslie sitting next to her first wedding dress, crying.

PART 5

One Year Earlier

The Second James Casper

Chapter Nineteen

Could anyone have a bad time at Christmas when the temperature was in the low eighties and everyone was drinking margaritas by the pool in Palm Springs?

Yes, Leslie could.

She lay by the pool, covered with an umbrella to avoid getting her pale skin scorched in the sun, her nose stuck in the newest Nora Roberts novel. Thankfully, Nora was always there for her at times of distress. And after only three days at her father and stepmother's home, she wanted to toss herself over a cliff—so it was time for Nora.

Her family had discussed Shane repeatedly like a bunch of gossipy women, egged on by Aunt Trudel. Only Denice and Suzie hadn't engaged. The rest of them had quizzed her and dissected the relationship as you might cut up a raw chicken for a barbecue. They drank their margaritas and theorized until she thought she might grab a butter knife from her bread plate at dinner and slice her wrists.

Were all their lives so boring that her story was the main event?

Apparently so.

Was she the unofficial entertainment for the holidays?

Yes.

"Hey," Suzie said, taking the chaise lounge next to Leslie.

Leslie glanced over the top of her book. Suzie had rolled her eyes so many times in the last few days that she must be dizzy. Denice told them she didn't like negative conversation and Suzie had defended Leslie and told them all to "lay off."

"How are you doing?"

"Peachy," Leslie said and then added, "I'm thinking of going home early. Maybe I'll rent a car and drive if I can't get a flight. Or hitchhike with a serial killer."

"Take me with you," Suzie said.

"No, I'm leaving you with that asshole you call a husband." Leslie was still pissed that Tim had jumped into the mockery last night after one too many mojitos.

"He won't say another thing to you. I cut him off. No bang-bang for three weeks. If he says anything today, I'm taking it to six. Here, have a little more of mama's little helper," she said and topped off Leslie's drink. "Denice and Mom want to go shopping for shoes. You interested?"

"No."

"Shoes," Suzie repeated. "Stuart Weitzman. Chanel. They have all the boutiques here, and Denice said she wants to buy away your depression. Get up! This is an opportunity to stock your closet."

"All I want to do is sit here and read my book. And I want to drink as many of these margaritas as I can. Tonight, I want to be so drunk that I can ignore every word they say to me or I want to call the airlines and book a ticket home. At least back in Portland I have friendly faces and snouts waiting for me."

"To Suede and his puppy children," Suzie said with a hint of laughter. "Damn, I wished you'd brought him. He's just so hot. Yum."

"He's my lawyer and my roommate. That is it."

"Have you ever looked at him? If I were you, I'd be taking all my frustration over Shane out on Suede. I think he'd like it. Most men would."

"As I told you earlier, I'm pretty convinced Suede is gay. He's never openly discussed it with me, but he has 'friends' he hangs out with that I've never met. And I've walked around him in skimpy things. No reaction. He's inert, which is fine by me."

"Have you thought of jumping him and just seeing what happens?"

"Yeah, 'cause my life isn't messy enough? No, I haven't thought of that! I'm not interested. He just gives off a vibe that is more gossipy girlfriend than hot, sexy male."

"I think I'm really worried about you," Suzie said.

"Join the club," Leslie said and flipped over on her stomach, shut her eyes, and adjusted her straw hat so that she was hiding her face. "I think I'm worried about me too."

"How could a week in Palm Springs be terrible?" Suede asked after picking her up from the airport on New Year's Eve.

"If you ever meet my father, my aunt, and all of my jerk-off male relatives you will understand just how terrible it could be. Aside from Suzie and my wicked-stepmother-turned-fairy-godmother, Denice, they are a pack of jackals. Thanks again for picking me up at the airport," Leslie said, and took a deep pull on her champagne. It was New Year's Eve after all.

"Not a problem. My ancient grandfather is no party, so I think I understand."

Suede never talked about his family, so she considered this a large admission, but when he offered nothing else, she changed the subject.

"Do you think I'm truly out of the woods on Uptown?"

Suede pondered her question as they sat by the fireplace in his large home and drank champagne from exquisite crystal flutes.

Samuel Winston Drake was a very kind man. He'd taken her into his home like a long-lost sister. In the last few weeks, they'd developed a nice friendship, and when she'd made noises about finding other accommodations, he'd quickly told her that he liked having her around and hoped she would consider staying on as his roommate. She'd decided it wasn't a bad idea but had demanded that he take a rent payment from her. It hadn't been easy for him to accept, but finally, he had, and Leslie was officially his tenant.

He was a good-looking man, by far one of the best-looking men she'd ever met in a slick, model-hardened way. But something, some little something about him was tender and kind to the core. It made him feel like a long-lost friend. Thankfully, attraction didn't mess up the friendship, and for once she was happy to have a man around that didn't light up all her circuits.

His once-pregnant dog, Ginger, lay on the ottoman between them. The dog loved Leslie, and she loved the dog. She'd never lived with a dog before and now couldn't imagine how she'd ever managed without one. It was like having a real live stuffed animal in the house. Of course, they drooled and ruined the grass, but they were so loving that they made up for any of the bother of their upkeep. And in the last two months, she'd seen the full gamut of dog care. The puppies had all come and gone with the exception of one, Daisy. Neither Leslie or Suede could bear to let the runt of the litter go, and before long, Daisy had become Leslie's dog, who she now held in her lap.

"You didn't do anything wrong," he said with his deep, warm voice. "You acted in good faith. I don't know if I would have recommended that you continue with the project because I'm not sure that continuing to work for these gentlemen is a good idea. But they want you to stay. And the Real Estate Commissioner hasn't even questioned your involvement."

"Yet," she said.

"I don't think he will. We had a very cordial conversation, and after our chat I thought he felt very bad for you."

"Add him to the list," Leslie said, thinking of her family who had been trying to deal with Shane's betrayal for the whole time she was in California for Christmas.

"You know that isn't who you are."

"What do you mean?" she asked.

"Leslie Marie Westcott isn't a victim."

"Not by choice, but 'victim' keeps circling me like a vulture. I thought I'd done so well. I'd put together the Uptown Cliffs deal, had moved on after Jordan, Jack, and Mitch, thrown myself into my work and now this?"

"Seriously," he said, turning his cool eyes to her. "You're built of tougher stuff than this one blip in your past. All of those complications are just life."

"I don't know, sometimes I think this is what my life is meant to be. Coming close but never quite making it," she said, feeling all the weakness take hold.

"You know I'm telling the truth."

"I feel like a loser."

"You feel like someone who hasn't gotten all the good things in life that they deserve. I would say this to you, things have happened, there is no denying that. But you are still here. You are a survivor. What do you want in your life?"

"Oh, come on! What does anyone want? I want to be happy."

"That is kumbaya bullshit. You control your happiness, not those around you. What do you want life to give you back?"

"I think when Jordan died, and Jack lied, Mitch was just a dick, and Shane embezzled—they did affect me, they changed me, hardened me. I couldn't control that. I'd like to control my happiness," she said as she snuggled against Daisy, who had fallen asleep in her lap.

"You can and you will. All that stuff is now in the past, Leslie. It gave you armor to defeat anything that tries to hurt you again. You're a gorgeous, vivacious, powerful woman. The world is yours for the taking. Being happy is great. Why not be rich, too? Get a big house? A new car?"

"Material things," she replied.

"Security. Money will go a long way to buying you a kind of happiness you have never had before. Happiness that can't be taken away from you. When Shane stole from you, did you feel vulnerable?"

"Of course," she said. "I felt robbed, violated. I still do. And really pissed off, don't forget that."

"How about when Jordan's mother took your house away from you, how did you feel then?"

"I felt like my world had been rocked and then I'd been kicked when I was at my lowest point, but I'll never let that happen again."

"No, you won't, because now it is time for you to protect yourself. Buy your own diamond rings and make sure to get matching earrings. Be responsible for your financial security. You lived in an apartment when I met you. What is a realtor doing living in an apartment? Does that sound right to you? It shouldn't. And I doubt it sounds right to your clients, either."

"See? I told you being your roommate was a bad idea," she said, secretly sad they were having this conversation. She liked living with Suede, but maybe he didn't feel the same way. Maybe he was trying to tell her it was time for her to move on. Maybe it was his New Year's resolution to fix her and move her along.

"Not now, for shit's sake, stop being so sensitive. You are living in a house with me. But someday, you will get a house, your own house... Someday, not now," he said shaking his head. "I'm very happy having you here. I enjoy your company and having you around. Are you happy living here, seeing my ugly mug every day?"

"Um, you are hardly ugly, you handsome devil. Yes, I am happy living here."

"Then we put your house plans on hold for the future, but nothing soon because I don't want you to leave. But you could start buying investment property. Get in the game. Do it. So, what beyond the normal bullshit do you want in your life?"

"You'd make a good motivational speaker."

"Stop trying to avoid the question. Make a list. Start now."

When Suede got fired up, he was strikingly handsome. She felt like an ash covered troll, trying to break free from her cursed past as she sat curled in the chair with her little sleeping puppy.

Suede was good. *"It's all in the way you sell it."*

Didn't matter, it was working on some part or her.

"I got a dog, isn't that a positive step?" she asked.

"Yes, she brings out your tender, maternal side. Now, what else?"

She wanted to laugh but kept it in. He was serious, and she wanted to hear what else he had to say.

"Someday, when you are tired of me, I want to make enough money to buy a great house, not just a house, but something with a story or character."

"Won't happen, I won't get tired of you, but work on the Uptown Cliffs deal, and you'll have more than enough money for the house with a story and a new car. A bigger, more loaded Lexus."

"I want to walk into my closet and get lost in all the clothes. I want to buy a pair of expensive shoes or a purse and not worry about it. Not feel guilty the moment after I do it. And I want girly things that will make me feel like a high-end realtor. I want to walk into a place like Sauveterre Jewelers and buy a piece of jewelry to celebrate a successful business transaction."

"Sounds like we need to go shopping," Suede said.

She did not doubt that he would have exquisite taste. She used to like to go shopping with her mother, missed those very happy times. Shopping with Denice wasn't bad. They were finding their way to making it a fun adventure. Maybe shopping with a man who knew what made women look good would be a good idea.

"That could be fun, letting you dress me with a man's sense of what looks good on a woman."

He looked at her and smiled, then he said, "I want you to get a large black garbage bag out of the kitchen. And as you go through your wardrobe, place anything in the bag that reminds you of something bad. It could be Shane or Jack or even Mitch. Maybe it was the dress you wore to Jordan's funeral. Anything that makes you feel anything but happy goes into the bag. Thank the outfit for its service and send it on its way."

"I don't have the largest wardrobe now."

"That is about to change. We are going shopping day after tomorrow."

She liked the way this New Year was starting off.

"I've tried to add a few pieces here and there, but I don't tend to shop unless it is for wedding dresses. And I have a few of those."

"And how many wedding dresses exactly do you have?"

She smiled and took a sip of champagne as the fire crackled. "A few."

"Toss them."

"No, they are safely shrouded. I'm not touching those. Some of the other stuff, well, I could be open to it, but not those."

"Baby steps."

"Like the condo project. It is a damned if you do, damned if you don't kind of thing."

"I think cleaning out your closet will go a long way to getting your confidence back. And I'll be there to watch over everything. Don't worry, I won't let you throw out anything great," Suede said. The remaining partners at Uptown liked him and offered him a retainer which he refused. He belonged to Leslie.

"I should tell you, I have offered to reduce my commission from 3.25 to 2.9 percent to help out the partners."

Suede scoffed and sat up straighter in his chair. "That is $32,500 per million sold. Why in Hell would you do something like that?"

"I talked to Jemma. My commission should be close to $29,000 per million. Considering the project will come in at over $50M, I'll still clear $1.4 or $1.5 million. That buys a lot of security, and shoes, and purses, etc."

"Kaboom," he said and bumped his glass to hers. "But, I'll be speaking to the partners, because you are not reducing your commission."

"But—"

"No, Leslie Walcott is worth paying for, especially after all she has done to save their asses."

"Wow."

"Remind me the next time you decide to get engaged that you need an ironclad pre-nup."

"Yeah, lesson learned."

Ginger moaned, and they both turned their attention to her.

"Easy girl," Suede said and continued petting her.

Chapter Twenty

Leslie came home from Uptown Cliffs in mid-March to find that Suede was not alone. At the sight of the red-headed detective sitting at the kitchen bar, she felt her heart skip a beat. They were drinking martinis as Suede cooked dinner, so she didn't think she was about to get arrested, but it was still disturbing.

"Hey Les, you remember Bon, don't you?" Suede said by way of introduction and then opened the freezer to pull out a pitcher of martinis and a chilled glass.

"Yes, hello Detective Anderson, to what do I owe the pleasure?" she asked as she petted Ginger and Daisy who'd rushed in to greet her.

"I stopped by after my shift to share a bit of news and Suede invited me to stay for dinner," she said. "Have you heard from your ex-fiancé in the last few weeks?"

Leslie was immediately put on guard. This wasn't the way she wanted to be greeted upon returning home from work.

"I haven't spoken to him since he told me he was off to see his friend in Seattle. If he'd tried to communicate, I'd have told Suede, who I'm sure would have told you."

"I'm sure," Bonnie said with a doubtful tone as she sipped her martini. Leslie wasn't as delicate. She took a large swallow of her drink, grimaced, and wondered again if it was time to find her own home. She didn't like coming home to Detective Anderson.

"Tell her the news, Bon," Suede said as he used a large knife to hack up something that resembled a cauliflower, only it was purple.

"We've had Rodney in custody in Florida since last Tuesday."

Eight days earlier. Nice of Detective Anderson to let them know so quickly.

"How did you catch him?" Leslie asked, hoping they'd found the money.

"He was romancing a woman in Palm Beach, and she grew suspicious. She saw through his disguise. She called the cops, and they recognized his photograph."

Another woman. Ouch. Well, good for her, she had better con radar than Leslie.

"Great. Did they find the money?" Leslie asked.

"Not yet."

"Will I get to testify against him?"

"Kentucky wanted him for the horses first. He was extradited there and has plead out."

"What happens now?"

"He goes to prison and when he is released he will be shipped to Portland where he will face the charges we have waiting."

"So, I don't get to testify against him?"

"Not for a few years."

That didn't seem quite right.

Leslie wondered what would happen if her partners found out he was in Kentucky. She'd have to call them later.

She thought she'd be happier knowing he'd gotten caught. In the end, Shane was just another issue to deal with and if she couldn't testify and help to get him put away for longer, she didn't feel as good as she could about the entire situation.

After Bonnie left and Leslie was sure the other woman was laughing in her car about how stupid Leslie had been to get close to Shane in the first place, Suede said, "Enough."

"What?" she asked.

"You're mad and justifiably so, but remember living well is the best revenge. He will be in a prison cell for years. Be happy they caught him and move on. You don't care about him, that isn't who you are."

Suede was in his motivational speech mode, but sometimes he made a lot of sense.

She nodded and said, "He's rotting in a jail cell. That's the bottom line."

"Precisely."

Leslie felt at peace as she came home in mid-May, Daisy next to her in the car. They'd had a very good day at Uptown. The first wave of new owners had moved into their new condominiums. It was a day so long in coming that Leslie had to remind herself to breathe.

At Suede's she parked in the garage and Daisy got excited at the thought of playing with Ginger. Leslie wondered how it would be when she moved out someday. Daisy would probably go through withdrawals, and they'd have to schedule play dates. That would be good for Leslie too, as she'd miss Suede.

In some ways, she thought she was closer to him than she'd been to Shane or Jack or certainly Mitch. He'd helped her through what was one of the darkest times of her life. In the seven months she'd been living in his house, he'd never had a date or even acted smitten. He was clearly a workaholic and spent long hours at the office, but she couldn't figure out his other vices. He had his dog and his house, but nothing else seemed to matter to him. Yet, if there was a business affair or dinner when he needed a date, he always asked her to go, and she had a wonderful time. Several times, people commented on what a striking couple they made, and she had followed Suede's lead, thanking them but never correcting them.

She wondered if there was another part of Suede, a part he didn't share with her. She was a little disappointed that he hadn't talked to her about what she assumed was his alternate lifestyle, but she had to respect that it wasn't her business. He was a great friend and a wonderful shopping companion. In fact, her style had dramatically improved in the last couple of months under Suede's watchful eye.

He was cooking when she opened the door from the garage and entered the kitchen.

"Hello!" he called as Daisy charged ahead of her in search of her mother.

"Hello, yourself," she said and stepped into the kitchen inhaling the scent of something wonderful. "Something smells great."

"We are having my special pasta," he said. "How about a glass of Prosecco to celebrate today?"

"To what do I owe this special occasion?" she asked.

"Didn't you have your first owners move in today?"

"Yes, I did!" she exclaimed, and did a little dance in the kitchen. The man listened to every word she said. He cared. He thought about her and tried to do nice things for her. He was, quite frankly, perfect. If only they were attracted to each other.

"And how was your day?" she asked.

"I had to defend a crooked realtor in Clatsop County."

"The one who was caught having sex with the prostitute?"

"Running a business out of a vacant house," Suede corrected.

"Or you could call it what it was, a brothel. Is he only going to lose his license?" she asked.

"The district attorney filed a slew of charges against him today, the idiot." They talked about the case as Suede finished preparing the dinner. Leslie fed Ginger and Daisy succumbing to a barrage of licks and fevered tail wagging.

They sat out on the back terrace looking at the downtown view.

"You can almost see Uptown Cliffs from here," she said.

"And no matter what your thoughts, Leslie, we wouldn't have met if it wasn't for Uptown."

"You were so kind to me, Suede. I don't know what I would have done without you."

"It was my pleasure."

"You're a good friend and I appreciate you."

She was thinking it was about time for her and Daisy to find a place of their own. She was about to have enough money in her account from the closings at Uptown to buy any house she wanted within reason. She just didn't know how to break the news to Suede.

"I really respect you and our friendship, Leslie, and I've been meaning to ask you something. It is actually more of a proposition for you…"

Leslie had the distinct impression that her housing conversation was going to have to wait. What kind of proposition could he possibly have for her?

"Wouldn't you agree that we have a good time with each other?"

"I would," she said, not liking the direction this was going at all.

"Wouldn't you agree that we cohabitate well?"

"Um, yes," she said, as Daisy put one paw on her leg and then another. Before Suede could ask his next question, Daisy had climbed onto her lap, all puppy kisses and long limbs.

"Do you remember I told you about my grandfather being difficult?"

"I remember," she said. But he hadn't elaborated. He'd just said his grandfather was antiquated and liked to make his life miserable. Leslie had learned not to question people when they made powerful statements like that. It usually served her well to sit back and wait to hear what they had to say. However, in that instance, Suede had remained silent.

"They have put a little hitch in his will, which he informed me of last summer. It has been on my mind for months with no solution in sight. Then I met you."

"And this is part of the proposition?"

"My grandfather had a stroke yesterday."

"Suede! Oh my god, why didn't you tell me? Is he okay? What can I do?"

He reached over and touched her hand. "He's resting in Seattle. My parents are up there. I'm going up this weekend to see him. He's okay, but he's also ninety-three. He's lived a good life."

"I'm sorry, but I just don't understand. How can I help? I'll definitely take care of things here, pet sit, but what else can I do?"

"Would you consider marrying me?"

Leslie walked Daisy and Ginger in the neighborhood early the next morning after a night with no sleep. At one point during the walk, she was pretty sure she was lost. She hadn't been paying attention to where she was going. Even Ginger would look over her shoulder and give Leslie a look of confusion as to the route they were taking. And despite the fact that Daisy was only still technically a puppy, even she slowed down to accommodate her human mommy's irregular behavior.

Leslie couldn't stop thinking about it. Last night, her platonic, best male friend had asked her to marry him. Even as the memory came back to her, she had to take a seat on a low brick wall in front of someone's house and try to regulate her breathing.

The conversation came back to her in a wave, and she almost pinched herself to remember that it hadn't been a dream.

"Why? What?" she asked.

"I'm sorry, that isn't the way I wanted to do this," he had explained.

"Come on, Suede. You can't be serious."

But the look on his face was serious. Then she'd asked a very stupid question. "Are you telling me that you are in love with me?"

"I do love you, Leslie."

"But let's be clear, you aren't in love with me," she said, knowing it was true. "What brought this on? Does it have something to do with your grandfather?"

"It has more to do with his will. And the little hitch he added last summer," he said, and then seemed to hesitate.

"I'm listening, Suede. Tell me all of it."

"My grandfather is worth a lot of money. Life-changing amounts of money, millions of dollars."

"Lucky you," Leslie said and refilled her glass. A sleeping puppy and champagne just might not be enough to get her through this conversation.

"Not really. The hitch my grandfather added was that I must be married to inherit."

"Son of a bitch," Leslie said.

"Exactly. It isn't that I'm opposed to marriage. It is just that I haven't found anyone that I want to spend my life with. And then I met you, and we get along so well, I wondered if you might be willing to do me this very personal, very extreme favor. Nothing would have to change. We could go along exactly as we are now."

"Marriage as a favor? A life changing event. I don't know how I feel about that."

"I've thought it all out. I haven't come to this conclusion lightly. I just will ask that you hear me out. And if you decide that it isn't something that you want to do, no hard feelings. It just seems that we are both at a point in our lives where a partnership of this kind might be a really positive thing."

"Go on."

"First, we like each other, which is half the battle in any relationship. We get along. We haven't fought over one thing since you moved in. I would take care of you and make sure that you would want for nothing. I make a lot of money, Leslie. There isn't anything that I couldn't give you.

"And if, after I inherit the money, you haven't grown to like me more or even to fall in love with me, we can divorce. In fact, I think it goes without saying that we would probably be one of the nicest divorced couples out there."

What went without saying was that Leslie was going to need a lot more alcohol to get through this conversation.

"When you think about it, it is companionship that matters most in this life. I will be there for you for the highs and the lows. You will be able to count on me. We can have a wonderful life. We can travel, get more dogs—"

"What about children?" she asked.

"I like children."

"Do you want to have any of your own?"

"Yes," he said, but she wasn't convinced.

"Suede, I've lived in this house for what, seven months? You've seen me in my nightie, you could have made a move on me at any time, yet you haven't. Aren't we dancing around a bigger issue here?"

"What are you saying, Leslie?"

"I'm saying that I think you are gay. If you were going to make a move, you'd have done it by now."

"Maybe I respect women more than that. Maybe I wanted to get to know you before developing the physical side of our relationship. Assuming that I'm gay is kind of a low blow, Leslie."

His words made her feel bad, so bad that when they'd called it a night, they were both upset.

Ginger and Daisy both whined in boredom, so Leslie stood, rubbed her behind to remove the dirt of the brick wall she'd been sitting on, and continued her walk.

Suede was in a bind. His grandfather wasn't getting any healthier and the thought that he could die any day was a bit of problem. Suede needed to get married to inherit, and he wanted to marry her. In fact, he wanted to go pick out an engagement ring today.

She returned from her walk with the dogs and found Suede in the kitchen making his divine French toast. She'd promised him the night before that she'd sleep on it, but sleep hadn't come. She thought if Suede really knew her, he'd have followed her into her bedroom and proven to her that he was attracted to her. But she didn't think she could do it. If Suede tried to kiss her, she wasn't sure she could let him.

"Good morning," she said as she entered the kitchen and got water for Daisy and Ginger.

"Good morning," he said, and she could tell immediately that something was wrong.

"What is it?" she asked.

"My mother just called. My grandfather died last night."

"Oh Suede, I'm so sorry," she said, crossing the kitchen and wrapping her arms around him in a friendly hug. "Are you okay?"

"No, I'm not," he said, holding her tightly. She could feel his warm tears as they dripped down his cheeks.

"I don't mean to sound callus but is it too late for you to get married to inherit the money?" she asked.

"No, if I get married in the next couple of weeks, I'll inherit."

"That's crazy."

"That was my grandfather. I don't think he was in his right mind when he added that to his will, but I'll be damned if I let him win after he's dead. We feared him for years. He tried to control each and every one of us in his own way. I can't let this be his legacy to me."

"Is there another way?"

"I can't think of one. Leslie, damn it, you're my only hope. I'm so sorry, but please consider it. I'll give you some of the money—"

"No, I don't want any of the money, and I think that was a very horrible thing for your grandfather to do to you."

"You have no idea how cruel he can be. He didn't just put a condition on me. My sister had to have children. She never wanted to have children. I know she did it only to satisfy my grandfather. My mother had to promise to give ten percent of her inheritance to the NRA. She has been anti-gun and anti-hunting her whole life. The whole thing is crazy."

"So, can't you get out of it?"

"He was deemed of sound mind by the lawyer who drew up the will. His final, last battle of control—and guess what, he won."

"You're a good friend, Suede. You know, you're one of the few people in my life that I'd do anything for. I used to think I'd do it with no questions asked, but I guess I can't say that. You know my past. You know my darkest secrets. You know my pain. I've been entirely transparent with you over the last seven months we've been together. Hell, I haven't even tried to hide it. I can't think of another person in my life who has seen me this vulnerable or has helped me through my heartache, my embarrassment. It's been you, all in and there for me for the last seven months. But if you think that after all you've done for me, that I'm going to just strap on a pair of blinders and dive headfirst into a relationship without knowing what I'm getting into... Well, that's an insult to you and everything you've taught me.

"Maybe the Leslie from a few years ago who let her fiancé climb a mountain two weeks before her wedding would be ready to say I do without reservation, but that isn't the woman I am today. You should be proud of the part you played in this, and I will be forever grateful, but I have to know that I am going in with all the cards on the table. I need you to be honest with me."

Chapter Twenty-One

Leslie had to admit when they got to Sauveterre Jewelers later that day and discovered that Charlie was away on a buying trip, she was relieved. She didn't need him to see her with Suede. Why, specifically, this bothered her, she didn't know, but Charlie being out of town just made it easier. Before they entered the store, Suede pulled her aside and said, "Leslie, do you know what this means to me?"

"I have an idea," she said, still not believing that she had agreed to marry him.

Caroline helped them find an engagement ring. Leslie tried to get caught up in the other woman's enthusiasm, but it just didn't quite feel right. This was going so fast, so recklessly, she just had to remember that she was doing it for Suede. Doing something that was right for someone else. And with her eyes wide open.

She had laid it on the line, she told Suede what he meant to her and all he had done for her. She told him how much she'd grown as a person with his encouragement and support. Then it was his turn to tell her how he felt about her. It was that absolute transparency and love he showed her with his words, even if they were words of love of a friend that made her know she could go through with this. She could marry Samuel Winston Drake, even if it were for reasons she couldn't quite have dreamed up, even after everything she had been through.

"Leslie, what kind of ring would you like? I'll buy you whatever tickles your fancy. And don't worry about the price, we don't have a budget," he said, winking at Mrs. Sauveterre.

"Well, isn't that refreshing? Most grooms pick something out that is wrong for the bride and then she is in the awkward position of not liking her ring. What would you like, dear? I remember you always fancied the more exotic stones. An aquamarine would, of course, look lovely on you."

"Oh no," Leslie protested. Aquamarine was sacred to her. No way could she have it be a part of this. "I don't want an aqua for an engagement ring. Probably a diamond, don't you think, Suede?"

"Sure, but let's make it a good one, a big one."

But Leslie found a more sedate band of diamonds.

"How about that?"

"What?" Suede asked. "That little ring?"

"It isn't little."

"It might be a good wedding ring, but it isn't an engagement ring."

"Sure, it is," Leslie said.

"You have excellent taste, Leslie. You always have. The band has five half-carat Asscher cut stones, channel set."

"Oh, Asscher cut," she said. She knew one thing about Asschers, they were a very expensive cut.

"I don't like that the diamonds don't go all the way around, like an eternity band," he complained.

She looked at Suede. He wanted her to have an eternity band? That was crazy. This wasn't a love match. This was a friend helping a friend.

"Suede, that is a lovely ring."

"Humor me, let's look at solitaires, big solitaires," he said and moved to another case.

Charlie's father joined them at one of the cases. Leslie made the introductions, feeling like a fraud. Suede and James quickly got into a conversation about stones and Suede tried to talk her into a crazy expensive three carat diamond solitaire that fit the third finger of her left hand perfectly. Did she love it as much as the sunstone on her right hand? Not by a long shot, but it was a beautiful ring. It sparkled brilliantly, but it wasn't backed with love.

They left Sauveterre's an hour after they arrived with the three-carat ring on her finger.

"Now to your Aunt Trudel's."

Leslie felt a little sick. Her family would be shocked, again. Less than eight months earlier, she'd been engaged to a different man, and here she was again, engaged.

"I should do that one alone," she commented. "I haven't even told my family, and I have a closet full of dresses."

"We are doing this the right way. If you are questioned by a lawyer someday, I want you to be able to answer that you were swept away. By the way, we fly to Vegas tonight at eight, so you'll need to get a dress you can take with you. I've got Krista lined up to take care of Ginger and Daisy."

"Seriously, I have four wedding dresses in storage."

"Are any of them family heirlooms? Your mother, grandmother, wore them?"

"No—"

"Then we are going to Trudel's. We want a paper trail and a record."

Leslie thought this was yet another red flag. Then she thought of how Suede had helped her through the mess with Uptown Cliffs. She thought of all the money she was making on the commissions. Was a quickie marriage too big a price to pay for a friend in a bind? It wasn't like there was another man in her life who would object.

Leslie slapped a big smile on her face as they crossed the threshold into Aunt Trudel's Wedding Boutique without an appointment. They had a word for clients who just showed up and expected to be waited on: *Inconsiderate.*

Suzie was the first to see them. There was a hint of surprise which she tried to cover, but Leslie caught it.

"Leslie and Suede, to what do I owe the pleasure?"

Suede picked up Leslie's left hand and flashed her ring.

Suzie's mouth fell open as her lips formed an "o" followed by a quick, "Holy sh—"

"We're eloping. Shh… it's a secret!" Suede said, sounding almost giddy. It was a very playful tone Leslie hadn't heard from him before, and she didn't know if she could get used to it.

Suzie turned her attention to Leslie, pointed to the ring and said, "Seriously? You didn't tell me any of this? I mean, when did things ratchet up? You bitch. How could you not tell me? Ah, damn it! I love you!"

"I love you too, but I need another dress because he doesn't want me to wear any of the… um… others. And we can't tell my father. And I need to walk out of the store with it today. Where is Aunt Trudel?" It was a lot to get out in a few brief statements, and Leslie felt winded when she finished.

"She took the day off, so you're lucky," Suzie said, and then turned to Suede, "First things first. You're not staying. I don't like grooms pouring their fear of commitment energy all over my dresses. This is going to be a flurry of white as we try to make this work, so get out."

"I'm not scared at all. I'm very excited to be marrying Leslie. I'm staying. I want to help her pick out a dress, and then I'm paying for it. Besides," he said, pouring on his charm, "Think of me as your errand boy. I'll help with whatever you need."

"That's bad luck," Leslie and Suzie almost said in unison.

But when he wouldn't be persuaded to leave Suzie put him to work. "Start looking through that rack. Pull three dresses at a time. No puffy skirts." Leslie and Suede started looking through the racks for a dress that would fit Leslie as Suzie started muttering to herself, "Mom hates it when I sell a floor sample, but sometimes you've got to do what you've got to do. And you're family."

Another bride, who was working with one of Suzie's consultants, kept eyeing Suede and then engaged him in conversation, "So you are flying off to Vegas, how romantic!"

Suede politely complimented the woman on the dress she was modeling.

Leslie contemplated asking Suzie if she wanted to come along and be the matron of honor, but she just couldn't. "Leslie, why don't you come on back to the stockroom and help me for a moment?" Suzie asked, and Leslie could see her anger just starting to bubble under the surface.

"How mad are you?" Leslie asked, as they stepped into the back storeroom for what she knew would be an unpleasant conversation.

"I don't know if I've ever been angrier at anyone in my life than I am at you right now. What the Hell is going on?" Suzie whispered.

"We realized that we love each other," Leslie said. It wasn't a lie. She did love Suede, but she wasn't in love with him.

"All this time, you have kept this secret from me? I'm the one who has been there for you through how many relationships?" Suzie said, her voice cracking with emotion. "You are like a sister to me, and you keep this, this whole thing from me? How could you?"

Leslie felt horrible, but she'd made a promise to Suede. There couldn't be any hint of fraud. "I'm sorry," she said, "Please, damn it, Suzie, don't cry!"

"What do you expect me to do? We've been through everything together, and you do this? I feel like you betrayed my trust. We don't have secrets."

"I'm sorry, I didn't mean to hurt you. It just kind of happened."

"Bullshit."

"Come on, this isn't that unusual. Think of my past. Think of all I've gone through. Each time I do it the supposed right way, look how it turns out?"

"I don't like this, and damn it, I won't be party to it," Suzie said, as she stepped back onto the sales floor and yelled, "Chelsea! Where are you? I need you to take over for me."

Leslie felt a lump forming in her throat. She had three wedding dresses in her hands and nowhere to put them so she could give into the tears that were threatening.

Chelsea, one of the younger associates, appeared and freed Leslie of the dresses in her arms. "It's okay," she said reassuringly. "Suzie will forgive you. She's got a migraine, and she's been barking all morning. I think it is totally romantic that you're eloping. Come on, I've got a dressing room all set up for you."

Suede was waiting for them with a pile of dresses he'd selected.

"Suede, half of these aren't my size. I will have to go up one or two sizes to fit into a wedding dress. And we aren't paying five thousand for a dress I'm going to wear once," she said looking at one of the price tags.

"Stop looking at the price and go try it on," he softly ordered. "With your figure, it should look fabulous on you." She wondered how he could sound so relaxed. He almost seemed to be getting happier with each new errand they ran. It was probably relief that he was finding someone to marry in time to inherit and have the final victory against his tyrannical grandfather.

Leslie heard her cell phone ringing from her purse but ignored it. Chelsea helped her into Suede's first choice, an old friend—a James Casper that was a simple white satin ball gown.

"Wow-za, that's sexy," Chelsea whispered as she stepped back.

They tried on eight dresses for him, but Suede kept going back to the first one, the James Casper.

"You like this one?" Leslie said.

"Um… yes," he said, smiling wolfishly.

"It fits you like a glove," Chelsea said and then gave Suede instructions on how to get her in and out of it as a seamstress that Leslie had known for years appeared and made a couple of quick alterations on the spot.

Leslie felt no joy. Suzie was the tip of the iceberg.

This wedding betrayal was going to go over with the family like a lead balloon. For years to come, they'd be talking about her wedding betrayal. It might be an improvement over their constant rehashing of Jordan, Jack, Mitch, and Shane. Heck, it would be a nice change.

As Suede and Chelsea went off to wrap up the dress and settle the account, Leslie's cell rang again. It was a number she didn't recognize. Maybe someone interested in Uptown Cliffs.

"Leslie dear, is that you?" a kind voice on the other end of the line asked.

"Yes, who is this?" Leslie asked.

"It's Caroline, Caroline Sauveterre."

"Hi, is there a problem with the ring?"

"Leslie, I'm sorry for bothering you, but I can't stop myself from asking you this."

"What is it?" Leslie asked, but she had a feeling she knew. Caroline Sauveterre saw hundreds of happy brides each year.

"I just have to ask you, are you happy about this wedding?"

"Didn't I look happy?" she asked.

"No, you didn't. I was a very good friend of your mother's, so I'm butting in where I shouldn't. I've loved James for thirty-five years of delirious happiness. I've watched you grow up from a little girl, and I've seen you happy. You weren't happy today."

"It's just complicated and we are rushing—"

"Love is quite simple, dear. It doesn't need to be explained. Think about what I said. And if you need to talk, call or come by."

"I'm a little confused," Leslie admitted and realized in that moment how much she missed her mother.

"Why don't you come back in? We will have a nice chat and a cup of tea."

Suede was not very happy to be taking her to her office, but he understood that she had to arrange coverage and he had a few things to wrap up at his office as well. As soon as his car was out of sight, she turned and walked the six blocks to Sauveterre Jewelers.

Chapter Twenty-Two

Leslie sat in the VIP area with Caroline at Sauveterre Jewelers, drinking tea and eating homemade chocolate chip cookies, as she told her the whole story about Suede and the wedding. She shouldn't be telling this woman, but she couldn't stop herself and something about her reminded Leslie of her mother in a way that Trudel and Denice just didn't.

As she took a Lyft home, she remembered the most poignant thing that Caroline had said to her, "I love my husband more each day. Sometimes, the feelings I have for him are consuming. That is the kind of love I want for my son. That is the kind of love I want for you. If you marry Sam Drake, I guarantee you will regret your decision. You will have officially given up on love, and all of us hopeless romantics who believe in true love will be a little sadder for it."

In that moment, something inside of Leslie broke and she imploded. She thought of the love she had for Jordan and how she had lost him. She had always thought she would love again—that another great love was waiting somewhere out there for her. To settle for a half truth when it came to love was the ultimate betrayal to herself, and to the love that was just beyond her reach.

She was vaguely aware of Caroline hugging her and giving her tissues.

"I've just been through so much. I can't keep doing this to myself," she managed to say.

"Nothing worth having comes easily," she announced as she wiped away Leslie's tears. "When you fall in love again, it will be the greatest gift you've ever received. You won't miss it, I promise."

Leslie glanced down at her left hand where the engagement ring had rested for approximately three and a half hours, possibly the shortest engagement in history. But after listening to Caroline's words, Leslie felt no regrets when she slipped the ring from her finger and handed it back to the other woman.

Caroline gave Leslie one last motherly hug and said, "My dear, I know I will see you another time when you've found true love again. That will be a happy day, and we won't need to force our smiles. We'll be shedding happy tears. I can't wait to see it."

As the hired car passed over the Burnside Bridge, Leslie got a text from Suede.

Are you almost done at the office?

She replied: *I'm taking a Lyft home. See you there.*

What she didn't say was: WE NEED TO TALK.

The dog babysitter was just settling in when Leslie arrived at Suede's house. She reached into her wallet and pulled out a few large bills and handed them to the girl. "There has been a change of plans. We won't need you after all. But I want to pay you for your willingness to come on short notice."

The girl left with a smile on her face. Leslie was glad that some-one was having a good day. She wasn't—and it was only going to get worse.

Leslie made herself a martini. She could have one. Only one. After she said what she needed to say to Suede, he might not want her and Daisy staying at his house. That was fine. Suzie would take her in. Heck, she might even be happy about it.

Suede found her in the living room, staring out the back window at the backyard, flanked by Ginger and Daisy. They picked up on her unease and came right by her side.

"Hey there," Suede said, a big smile on his face when he entered the room.

"Hi," she said and took a sip of her martini.

"Are you all packed?" he asked, with an edge of surprise in his voice.

"No, actually, I'm not. We need to talk."

His face fell as she had predicted it would. Now came the hard part.

"What brought this on?"

"Sam," she said, using his real name. She preferred it to Suede. Always had. "Can we sit down for a minute?"

"Have you changed your mind?" he said, sounding a little panicked.

"I can't go through with this," she said as placed her drink on a coaster on the corner of the glass-topped coffee table. "Up until a few hours ago, I thought I could, but the truth is that I need to be with someone who adores me, all of me. And if we're married, and the physicality won't happen, then I will have officially given up on love. I can't give up on the one thing that is most important to me in this world. Can you understand?"

He put his head in his hands and rubbed his face until it was red. "You don't want to even give it a try?"

"It wouldn't be right for either of us," she said, as kindly as she could.

"You think I'm gay, is that it?" he said, defensively.

"I don't know, and I don't really care. I just know how I feel. I love you, but I'll never be in love with you," she said, as the dogs settled in next to her on the couch. Her hands absently pet each of them.

"I've had sex with women."

One thing that Leslie knew beyond a doubt, you couldn't convert a gay man into being straight. She felt sorry for the women he'd had sex with. And she was very thankful she hadn't been one of them.

Suede, you shouldn't have to control your sexuality. And quite frankly, no thank you. I care about you, but I want you to live an authentic life. I don't want to sleep with you."

"I like women," he argued.

"But you have sex with men too, don't you?" she asked.

He looked crestfallen, so she tried another tact.

"I had a talk about love with someone. You know—true, consuming love. It is what we both deserve. Suede, marrying me will not make you happy. It won't make me happy. Oh damn, this is why your grandfather did this to you. He knew, didn't he?"

Suede didn't answer. He just took her drink from the coffee table and downed it.

"There has got to be a way to fight it, Suede. Something you can do that doesn't involve marrying me. Wait—if you have to get married, gay marriage is legal in this state. There is a subject we've avoided despite all our deep conversations over the last twenty-four hours. So, I'm going to ask. Do you have a special someone? A boyfriend—"

"Leslie, for Christ's sake, shut up."

Leslie stood and walked back to the window. "I won't shut up. Not now. Not after we've gone this far. I returned the ring this afternoon. And if you give me the dress, I'll see what we can do. Aunt Trudel usually won't accept returned dresses that have been altered. And I know what the seamstress did today would be considered alterations that were not refundable. And Daisy and I can stay with Suzie for a while—

"I don't care about the damn dress. And I don't want you to leave. You're my best friend."

"Then talk to me," she implored.

"I've thought of coming out," he told her over the course of the next few hours.

"You should," she said. "You have a lot to offer. You could be sharing it with someone. Come on, Sam. Is there a special someone?"

"You won't believe me if I told you."

"Who is it?"

"I told him this morning about our elopement, and he is really mad at me. I think he might be jealous."

"I think I like him already. A name please."

"Milan Sutton."

"The wedding planner? He is a close friend of Suzie and Aunt Trudel's."

"I know," he said. "I've been terrified that he might call them and tell them that I'm a fraud. He threatened to do so this morning."

"How long has this been going on?"

"Nine months."

"That is a good chunk of time. Is it serious?" she asked.

"Enough that he was pretty upset when he found out about our wedding."

"He is jealous."

"Yes."

"Do you love him?" she asked.

He nodded and said, "Yes."

"I'm happy for you! Invite him over. I'd like to meet him," she said.

"What?"

"Invite him over. Marry him, Suede. From what you've told me about the will, it didn't specify that you had to marry a woman. Propose to Milan."

Suede stood and left the room in a hurry.

He reappeared a moment later with a sheaf of papers in his hand. "You're right. It doesn't say I have to marry a woman, just that I have to be married."

"Can I be your best woman or your maiden of honor?" But he didn't hear her, he was talking to someone on his cell phone. No doubt, it was Milan. And that is how Leslie ended up being the best woman in the wedding of her best friend, who happened to be her gay ex-fiancé.

Leslie had only seen Aunt Trudel angry on a couple of occasions, such as when a client with bright red lipstick lip printed a dress right in the center of the bodice and ruined it. She'd also yelled at Suzie and Leslie for refusing to help a client who had asked to try on wedding gowns—it had turned out the client was a woman despite her mustache and very prominent voice box. Leslie learned a valuable lesson that day, love is love, no matter what form it takes.

So, when Leslie arrived at Trudel's Wedding Boutique two days after the "big reveal" with Suede and a garment bag in hand, it wasn't a surprise when she got the cold shoulder from her normally warm aunt.

"Let's see your hand," Aunt Trudel said by way of greeting.

Leslie held up her empty left hand.

"What is all this about?" she asked, pointing to the empty finger.

"I gave the ring back two days ago."

"Well, you didn't have it altered did you?"

"No ma'am, it fit perfectly, unlike the dress."

"Leslie, what were you thinking? You almost gave me a heart attack when I found out. My beloved niece buying off the rack and needing a quickly purchased gown like some knocked up high school junior a month after prom. You are becoming that crazy relative that everyone talks about and wonders if the crazy might be hereditary, or god-forbid, rub off on another family member."

"Aunt Trudel, I didn't realize your love was so conditional. I didn't realize I was such a bother to you. I'm so sorry my life inconveniences you!" Leslie said, not that surprised, but still hurt by the other woman's words.

Suzie stuck her head out from a dressing room curtain and gave Leslie a dirty look. Leslie couldn't remember a time when both Trudel and Suzie were mad at her. This was bad. And she had no excuse, she'd chosen Suede over Suzie.

"Leslie, we are just tired of seeing you hurt, tired of the Merry-Go-Round that is your love life," Suzie said.

"And I'm not taking it back," Aunt Trudel added, raising her chin in defiance. "So, that is your dress. You can look at it and remember what happens when you make rash decisions like deciding to get married and excluding your family. Really Leslie, that hurt me deeply, I can only wonder how your poor father and Denice took the news."

"You didn't tell them, did you?" Leslie asked.

"No, I left a voicemail for your father."

"Great. Look, I'm sorry. I was trying to help a friend who was there for me. I thought I was doing the right thing, but I realized I wasn't. And thankfully, I realized before it was too late, so if I have to keep this dress as a reminder of the time I tried to help out a friend and turned my entire family against me, so be it."

Suzie appeared with a pair of pinking shears in her hand and a pencil behind her ear. "Look, I'm still royally pissed at you—"

"Really Suzie, not on the floor," Aunt Trudel scolded.

"Mother, for shitsake," Suzie said, using the sharp end of the pinking shears to point at Leslie. "The only customer in the store is Leslie." Then she directed her question to her cousin, "As I was saying, what changed your mind?"

"Caroline Sauveterre. We sat down and had a cup of tea after I left here the other day."

"So, if I'd put some fucking Lipton in a cup and handed it to you, you would have changed your mind?"

"Suzie!" Aunt Trudel reprimanded. "May I remind you that you're a lady? I didn't raise you to be crude—"

"She told me about her love story. About how passionately she loves her husband. And she told me if I married Suede, she knew I'd be giving up on love. And you know what? She was right," Leslie said as she dabbed at her eyes.

Leslie drove to work hoping not to be late for her weekly office meeting and called her father on the way. She tried to let go of the long conversation she'd had with Aunt Trudel and Suzie. They'd reached a mild peace, but there was still damage that needed to be repaired.

The phone rang and then she heard her father pick up with a gruff, "Hello?"

"Hey, Dad—"

Click.

And with that abrupt sound assaulting her ear she had another name to add to her list of people disappointed in her.

Silver Linings Dress Auction

DRESS NUMBER TWENTY-THREE

TITLE: *Partnership*

DESCRIPTION: Every girl needs to feel like a princess waiting for her prince charming. And in this James Casper rose inspired ball gown made from 100% silk satin and 100% silk organza you'll make a grand entrance on your wedding day. The floor-sweeping stiff silk satin is bolstered by yards of ethereal organza. Fanning out at the front of the skirt is a cluster of magnificent silk organza roses in the palest pink peeking from elegant deep folds in the front of the ball gown. The sheer-sweetheart neckline will frame even the slightest blush in timeless elegance.

DONATED BY: *The Aqua Lady*

Present Day

TWO days before the Auction

Suzie gently pushed the James Casper to the side and sat next to Leslie, who was dabbing at the tears running down her cheeks, as she said, "I'm sorry. This is just getting to me today."

"I know, honey, and it isn't like you haven't run the gamut," Suzie said, giving Leslie a hug.

Leslie looked down at the dress she'd picked out to marry Jordan. If he'd lived, what would her life be like now? They'd probably have children. She wouldn't have Daisy or the house she now had, but she wouldn't know what she'd missed. As it was, she could only think of what she'd probably missed, children that would have looked like her and Jordan. *Happiness. Joy. Love.*

"You don't need to let this one go," Suzie said. "I've got a pile of dresses in my car. Did you know the news stations have even been calling asking specifically to see your dresses?"

Leslie regarded her cousin with a raised eyebrow. "I'm begging you, media silence, please. This story has got to die. Make sure Aunt Trudel knows that as well. I'm working from home this afternoon because I need to get away from the calls and the attention."

"I'm sorry, cuz. Had I known there would have been so much interest I wouldn't have let Mom do the interview. She didn't mean to mention your name, she just got nervous. You know how she gets when she is flustered."

Leslie knew her aunt didn't have a mean bone in her body, but sometimes she didn't use her common sense or her filter. "I know she loves me," Leslie said.

"She'd do anything for you, so would I."

"Okay, then please ignore their requests to see my dresses."

"Media silence, I promise. By the way, I've been thinking about how we should mention them on the program to give you a layer of anonymity."

"And?"

"How do you like 'The Aqua Lady'?"

"Suzie, that would create a frenzy."

"It will. The perfect kind of frenzy," she said. "Think of the one person who will really notice."

PART 6

Three Months Earlier

Chapter Twenty-Three

"Three inches to the left," Suede said.

"I think it is fine," Milan argued.

Leslie just shook her head as she watched her former fiancé and his new husband hang the pictures in her new house. Suzie stepped out of the kitchen and shook her head as she unwrapped another wine glass from packing paper.

"You'd think it was the most important thing they'd done in the last five years."

"I try not to judge," Leslie said as she joined Suzie in the kitchen. "And considering the duration of their marriage, it might be the most important thing that they've ever done."

Suzie stepped closer and whispered, "So, Milan just married him, with only a day of notice?"

"Suede says it is love, but in the gay world, that happens often and quickly, but seriously, who am I to judge?"

"You dodged a bullet."

"And I've got another designer wedding dress in my closet to show for it. Consider that a hard lesson learned."

"My mom refuses to budge. I'd have let you return the dress," Suzie said.

"Eh, after you've got a dress or two, or four, what's another? And listen, I *really* am sorry. Do you forgive me?"

"Well, here's the thing. You're as close to a sister as I'm ever going to get and you're my best friend. You know where all my bodies are buried, so I've got to find a way to forgive you," Suzie said, as she placed a wine glass in the dishwasher.

"Thank you," she said, giving Suzie a hug. "You know what Suede told me about the dress? He said it was a small price to pay for happiness and not to pay him back."

"So, now that I know the back story. Just how much money did Suede get from his grandfather anyway?"

"Oh, that? You don't want to know, but it is a large number with seven zeros next to it. You need to be nicer to Suede and Milan."

Leslie watched as Suzie's mouth fell open in shock. Had she really only thought Leslie would marry someone for anything less than serious money?

"You never told me the amount."

"You were so upset I was doing what I was doing, I didn't want to make it any worse."

"No wonder he wasn't worried about the price of the dress."

"Nope, he even offered to buy the ring back so I could have it as a *memento*."

"Did you do it?"

"Of course not!"

Suede stuck his head into the kitchen, "Hey, could you ladies stop talking about me and come tell me what you think of how we've arranged your living room?"

Leslie smiled and said, "I can't wait."

She'd given Suede and Milan free reign to arrange and decorate her new house. Suede and Milan had decided to go into business together, and they were going to be wedding planners, maybe even throw in a little home décor on the side, which Leslie had discovered was one of Suede's passions. And couples using their services also got a discount on legal advice and pre-nups if they wanted them.

Milan, a man equally as nice looking as Suede, had decided that Leslie's karma was bottled up and congested. He'd recognized her from The Aqua Lady campaign and said he'd had a dream about her walking along a beach picking up aquamarines of all different shades of blue and green, the sizes of seashells. It had inspired him. Consequently, her new, three-bedroom cottage was done in themes of the beach complete with white-washed walls and plantation shutters. Milan had found a way to integrate her mother's French country pieces and the strange thing was that it all came together rather beautifully.

A lot of her old furniture from college and from her house with Jordan hadn't made the cut. With each day that passed, she felt better about letting go of the old things. Once the commission checks had started arriving in her bank account from Uptown Cliffs, Suede had taken her on more and more shopping trips. Now she did have a closet that was the envy of her colleagues and women everywhere. She had a bunch of expensive handbags, shoes, and clothing to match. Jordan would probably be horrified at the money spent on such luxuries, but she'd decided to stop apologizing for her success.

Leslie was happy that Suede had found his way. He'd been her lifesaver, and she felt like she'd in some way leveled the playing field by helping him to come out of the closet. It warmed her heart to see her friend happy.

Leslie and Daisy had the best fall Leslie could recall in years. Daisy had graduated from two different obedience classes and was proving to be the sweetest dog Leslie had ever met. Whatever drama her life had thrown at her, it was finally over. The Uptown Cliffs were almost finished. Suede and Milan were even consulting with Suzie, and there was some talk of joint ventures with Trudel's Wedding Boutique. Weirder things had happened, but she thought this was odd enough.

"Finally, this place is habitable," Milan said, holding out his arms to encompass the completed living room.

"You guys know what you're doing," Leslie said, "I love it."

Leslie didn't just decorate the inside of her house, that fall she planted several hundred daffodil and tulip bulbs in her yard, while Daisy frolicked in the damp grass ensuring a bath was in her future. As Leslie bathed Daisy and then toweled her off, she felt her sunstone ring snag the terry cloth. She looked at the ring, worried about what she might find and with good reason. One of the prongs on the center stone was sticking out at an odd angle. Thankfully, she hadn't lost the stone although she wondered when and where she had done the damage that had led to the current problem.

She'd been looking for an excuse to go to Sauveterre Jewelers. She needed to take Caroline some flowers and thank her for the motherly heart-to heart talk. She felt a little guilty that she hadn't given Denice an opportunity to have that talk, but they were getting closer and she was grateful for that.

And she could see Charlie about her ring. She could admit that when it came to Charlie, she was still battling thoughts like that awkward six-year-old little girl. It was stupid to keep reflecting on something so beyond reason. Obviously, if he'd thought she'd grown into an ogre, he wouldn't have had her model for him. Besides, he'd called her beautiful and didn't that just trump all her childhood fears?

Maybe her mother had known best. She liked to think of Charlie having had a little crush on her while she was growing up. She wondered how he felt now. After all the times she'd darkened his door, had his feelings ever gone to the 'what if'? Ironically, in the last few months, Leslie's mind had gone there. When she thought of Charlie, a warm feeling spread along her skin. That feeling told her more than mere words ever could. There was something there. There was something about Charlie.

She smiled at the memory of the aquamarine shoot. For one, glorious day, she'd been an actual jewelry model, Charlie's model. And in that one day he had made her feel treasured and special… The way no man other than Jordan ever had.

The next morning, she took care with her makeup and hair. Could she admit that she was dressing up for Charlie? Yes. But she was also a businesswoman and had a meeting with a new client that afternoon. Still, her new black suit complete with Christian Louboutin black patent heels probably weren't necessary for a quick stop-in for jewelry repair, but she wanted Charlie to notice.

He'd seen her be the upset, angry, disappointed, swindled, and heartbroken fiancé. Maybe today he could just see her as the secure woman she believed herself to be. She was single, and she was okay with it.

Then what did she think would happen? Did she want him to ask her out? She pondered the question as she put on her lipstick, looking at her expression in the mirror as a little voice inside her head whispered, "Yes."

She wanted, no, she *needed* to get her ring fixed. Period. All this other, strange speculation was ridiculous.

Leslie stopped at the flower market near her office and picked up an assortment of roses that she thought looked elegant. She second-guessed her choice along the way. Maybe she should take Caroline orchids. It was the thought that counted. She had an agenda. She needed to deliver the flowers, talk to Caroline Sauveterre, and then find Charlie so that he could fix her ring and see her looking good—

Stop, stop, stop it!

As she stepped into Sauveterre Jewelers, she was greeted by Caroline, who crossed to her and gave her a big hug.

"These are for you," Leslie said, handing her the roses. "They really don't adequately measure up to what you did for me last spring, but I wanted to tell you how thankful I am that we had that heart-to-heart conversation. It helped me more than I can say."

"I'm so glad," Caroline said, then glancing at the roses, she said, "And these, these are beautiful. James always brings me roses because he knows they are my favorites. How are you doing?"

"I'm good, I'm not dating anyone, but I'm happy." Now, why had she said that? Did she hope Caroline would tell Charlie? She doubted the other woman would consider her a good catch for her son, not after the drama the Sauveterre family had witnessed over the years.

"And I got a new house for my dog and myself—and I just had it decorated. The Uptown Cliffs have been closing, new people moving in daily. Everything is smooth sailing."

"I'm proud of you," Caroline Sauveterre said. "You've really got your life together. Your mother would be proud. You know we were in Junior League together. It wasn't the coolest thing to do, but your mother always made it so fun because she was happy. She loved you and your father, and I was the one to sell them the heart shaped diamond you now wear around your neck."

"I knew she always came here but I didn't know about the Junior League. I remember the bridge games she used to have with the

Junior Leaguers once a month. I used to help her set up the tables with red velvet tablecloths and See's chocolate in crystal bowls. I still miss her," Leslie whispered as she touched the diamond and blinked back some tears.

"I know, honey. You've got a lot of people who care about you, I'm one of them. You come see me anytime. Now, how can we help today?"

"Sometime in the last few days I damaged my ring, and I was hoping that Charlie could help me get it fixed."

"Oh, I wish he were here," Caroline said, a frown crossing her face. "You know there has been quite a buzz about his aquamarine collection. He has actually been spending a lot of time with a couple of venture capitalists who would like to partner with him to take the operation to a higher level."

"Wow, all from his aqua designs?" Leslie asked, hoping to hide her disappointment.

"Yes, it is amazing. I don't have to tell you how proud we are as parents."

"I'm proud, and I'm just a client."

"No, you're The Aqua Lady, and you had a hand in all of this," his mother said and added, "You will always be special to Charlie and to us."

Special, she thought, but probably not in the best way...

James joined his wife and Leslie. "Hello to our pretty aqua lady, what brings you into the store today?"

Leslie held up her sunstone ring. "My ring is injured. I was hoping Charlie was here to fix it."

He gently took the ring from her fingertips, slipped on his glasses, and looked at the stone. "I'm afraid the prong is damaged, but I'm glad you brought it in when you did. You might have lost the stone. Watch." He reached down and removed the sunstone from the setting with a small tool from his pocket and Leslie felt her heart leap into her throat.

"James, I wish you wouldn't do things like that! Don't worry Leslie, he does that for effect to show you what could have happened. Your ring will be fine. Don't tease her like that," she warned her husband.

"I'm sorry, honey," he said to his wife and then kissed her on the cheek. Turning back to Leslie he said, "I remember this ring. It's special. It is one of Charlie's favorites."

"Yes," she said, watching as Caroline blushed from her husband's kiss. Charlie was lucky his parents were so happy. "It is very special to me."

"We'll take good care of it for you," James said, and Leslie noticed how his wife stepped closer to him so that their bodies were slightly touching. That was the kind of love she had with Jordan. She wondered if she could have it again someday.

Chapter Twenty-Four

"I'd like to make a toast to my dear friend, Leslie. If I'd married you, I wouldn't know what true love is," Suede said as he clinked his wine glass to hers and Milan's. Leslie had invited them over to discuss plans for them taking care of Daisy while she went out of town for a bit of a working vacation with Suzie.

"I'd like to make a toast to the most pathetic toast in the history of the world. My goodness am I truly that pathetic?" she asked, as she raised her wine glass.

They all spoke at once trying to convince her she was anything but, but Leslie felt sad.

"It will happen," Suede said using his convincing tone. "Your partner is out there."

"And he will be worthy," Milan added.

"One thing is for sure," Suede said, "You hid your cooking talent while you were living at my house. If I'd known you could cook like this, I'd have never let you leave."

Leslie had prepared chicken breasts in a clay pot with a wine sauce that they described as "fantastic" and "sublime."

Since moving into her new home, she'd gone back to honing her cooking skills which had taken a brief hiatus during the Uptown Cliffs sale. To her, cooking was part love and part therapy.

When she cooked for her friends, and they liked it, it made her feel like she was taking care of them. Maybe she did have motherly instincts after all.

"Your future husband, whoever he may be, is one lucky bastard," Milan said with a wink.

"He'll be lucky for a lot of reasons," Suede added.

They had dessert, a cake Leslie had made for the occasion, in her newly decorated living room.

"You're nervous about leaving Daisy," Milan observed.

"I just need to know my dog is okay," Leslie said.

"Daisy is my favorite niece," Suede said, and added, "Look at that."

Milan sat on Leslie's new white couch with Daisy on his lap.

"I'm sure everything will be fine," Leslie said. She hadn't been on a vacation in years. New York wasn't exactly a tropical beach with drink service, but there were a lot of bars right off of Times Square where she and Suzie would be staying while they attended White Bliss, the largest bridal show in the United States.

Typically, Trudel and Suzie went, but this year, Trudel was too busy with the planning of her Silver Linings Wedding Dress Auction. Suzie convinced Leslie to join her saying she deserved a little vacation.

"Ah," Milan observed as he petted a mesmerized Daisy, "She is also nervous about facing her fears and attending a bridal show."

"I'm only doing it for Suzie because Aunt Trudel can't get away. It is one of the most ridiculous things I've ever done," Leslie quipped. "But Suzie asked and I'm not letting her down again. Not after the wedding dress fiasco."

Suede put his hands on her shoulders and said, "Remember what I said? This is just an event. It isn't personal. Put it into perspective, like buying a car or a house. Some people do it once, but most people do it many more times. Have fun at the bridal show. Let the experience put your past into perspective for you. See it for the business and the racket it is. Just don't buy any new dresses!"

"I'm not so sure this was a good idea," Leslie said as they walked around the Big Apple White Bliss Bridal Expo.

"It is exactly what the doctor ordered. It is putting weddings in perspective for you," Suzie said.

"So everyone says," Leslie replied dryly.

"Look, if you should ever decide to give up real estate and come into the other family business, you would see that weddings can be extremely lucrative. Sure, there is emotion and getting swept up in a bride's story, but to be honest, it is just a really good business—almost impervious to economic changes. Brides still want to get married and have their dream weddings and because of that emotion, we still make money. Little girls never forget their dreams of growing up to have a glorious wedding. And usually, they can guilt mommy, daddy, or grandma into totally going over their budget."

"Wow, you sound like a mortician or an accountant at tax time," Leslie said, "I think some of my jaded self has finally rubbed off on you."

"I'm just an integral part of the process," Suzie said. "Hey, let's go check out the jewelry vendors. I need to see what engagement ring styles are coming into fashion for the upcoming season."

"Oh good," Leslie said with a sarcastic edge, "Engagement rings. It isn't like I haven't seen my share of those. In fact, I think I've gone from intermediate to expert. There should be some sort of accreditation available to me."

They started at one corner of the ballroom and saw all the big names with their equally big displays. DeBeers, Tiffany & Co., Zales, Blue Nile, and Ben Bridge: they were all there.

As they walked, Suzie said, "Tell me what trends you are seeing."

"I'm seeing a lot of ornate stuff that makes me think you can hide a smaller diamond as the center stone as long as you disguise it with loops of gold and small diamonds."

"They call that Edwardian if it has a lot of ornate filigree, but if they are interesting loops around the diamonds, they are called Halos."

"I call them all gaudy, but then I'm a traditional girl."

"What else?" Suzie asked.

"I see black diamonds, and they are way too expensive considering they look like a polished piece of coal."

"They are passionate and edgy for the Goth bride who wants to be different."

"Spinning, that's really what I see," Leslie said, giving her cousin a sidelong glance as Suzie laughed.

They rounded a corner, and Leslie stopped as she met the gaze of one of the vendors. She couldn't contain her smile and realized she wasn't the only one who was surprised.

"Oh my," Suzie whispered as they stepped toward the familiar booth, "Looks like Leslie found a friend, and he looks very happy to see you."

"Well, this is a pleasant surprise," Charlie announced, coming from behind the booth, past his security guards to hug each of them.

"What are you doing here?" Leslie asked, smiling like an idiot. "I was just in your store a couple of weeks ago. I needed to get the prong fixed on my ring, and your mother said you were traveling but she didn't mention New York. I should have realized with New York being the jewelry capital of the US you'd be here. I just didn't think you'd be here for so long." She sounded like an idiot, but she couldn't seem to stop talking.

"She said you were in. I'm sorry I missed you. Let me see your hand," he said, and didn't wait for her to offer it. He picked it up and examined the ring. "Dad did a good job. I'd have had to fix it if he hadn't. What are you doing here?"

"Well, Suzie asked me to come. You remember my cousin, right?" she asked, turning to see that Suzie was long gone. "And you?"

"I have a couple of investors who want to help me expand my business. I'm trying to see how much interest we can generate. Taking this from a local operation to something more is daunting."

"I bet," she said, as several women arrived and started going crazy over his designs.

"Listen, this isn't a great place to catch up. Would you like to grab a drink later?" he asked.

"Yes," Leslie said, and watched as he handed her his card.

"My number is on the back. You want to meet in the lobby at sixish?"

"Yes," she repeated sounding like an idiot, and then Charlie smiled and told her he'd see her later. A moment later, the bridal vendors had engulfed him with questions.

She stood back in the aisle and told herself to stop smiling.

"You know," Suzie said, sideling up to her, "I finally figured out who he looks like."

"Who?" Leslie asked wondering how Suzie had disappeared and reappeared so quickly.

"The Canadian Prime Minister, that heartthrob Justin Trudeau."

"What? Justin Trudeau? You're kidding," Leslie said with a shake of her head. He was better looking than Justin Trudeau, not to say Justin Trudeau wasn't a good-looking man—

"And you're in denial. Did I hear him ask you out for a drink tonight?"

"Yes, a quick drink in the lobby, no big deal. Come on, we will be late for the lunch if we don't book it out of here."

"And then you need a nap to get your beauty sleep for your big date. And get that big smile off your face so you don't wear it out."

"Bite me," Leslie said, as they made their way to the ballroom.

As they entered the large space and started looking for a table, they were approached by a woman in a bride's maid's dress selling raffle tickets. In fact, there were ten lookalike bride's maids in the room selling tickets. And with those tickets you could get a smorgasbord of prizes from gift certificates to wedding dresses.

They each bought half a dozen tickets for twenty dollars. Suzie put them in different baskets she wanted to win. Leslie put them all in on a honeymoon trip to Fiji.

"The last thing I need is to win a large gift basket. I have so much swag as it is that I'm going to have to mail some of it home," Suzie said as they found seats, which had more swag bags waiting for them.

"You haven't even begun to realize how much swag you have," Leslie said with a smile, as she removed a split of champagne with a sample personalized label for the "Duke and Duchess of Happiness," cherry scented lip balm, wedding cake pops on sticks with cream satin bows, heart-shaped, vanilla scented candles, and a small, bottled water with an attached "hangover kit."

"What do you mean? No. No way. Your stuff, including this bag of crap, is yours."

Leslie laughed. She'd planned to dump all her swag on Suzie. None of this wedding detritus was coming home with her.

As they waited for the keynote speaker, the editor of a bridal magazine, *Happiness Ever After*, to discuss the latest trends in bridal fashion, Suzie asked, "Come on, you can admit that you've had a little fun."

"A little and I'm really wondering if they will serve us wedding cake as dessert today. I like wedding cake," Leslie said. "Because you know I haven't tried a lot of cake in my amateur career as a fiancé. Somehow, I never managed to make it to the reception in all of my wedding preparations. I could really go for some sugary buttercream."

"I love cake too, but we are in New York. I can hook you up with wedding cake any day, but there are some things we can't get at home. Let's blow the afternoon session. After the keynote let's go get macaroons at Laduree, what do you say?"

"I'm in. I love macaroons!"

"Then let's hit Saks and get you a new outfit for your date tonight—"

"Ladies and gentlemen, welcome…"

Yes, Leslie knew she was on vacation, but hearing about bridal fashion for ninety minutes was a lot for her, and she wondered if Suzie would kill her if she snuck off to check her cell phone and make sure everything was being taken care of back home. Suzie would. In fact, when she even glanced at her screen, Suzie gave her a dirty look.

"Okay, ladies! I hope you're ready!" a loud woman with a microphone warned, "It is time for the raffle!"

For the next twenty minutes they pulled tickets for the baskets. Suzie was genuinely mad when she missed out on a basket she wanted.

When they pulled for the honeymoon trip to Fiji, Leslie leaned toward Suzie and said, "If I win, I'm taking you with me."

"Go, Fiji, go!" Suzie chanted, but when they announced the winner, it wasn't even close to any of Leslie's tickets.

"Now, ladies and gentlemen, it is almost time for the grand prize!"

Leslie watched as they took all the tickets from every one of the raffles and poured them into a gigantic tumbler.

"Now, just to remind you, maybe you didn't win a gift basket or the pearl earrings. You still have a chance at the grand prize, a fifteen-thousand-dollar Paris Germaine gown!"

Leslie watched as one of the models from the fashion show re-appeared on stage wearing the very expensive Paris Germaine dress. It was the kind of dress she used to dream of as a girl. Beautiful and sleek in silk satin that just hugged the model in all the right places. It was so white it was almost silver with highlights, of all things—aquamarine. It was, quite simply, gorgeous.

"One very lucky person from our audience is going to go home, today, with this beautiful custom gown from the new spring collection."

"My luck, I'll win it. I need another gown like I need a hole in the head," Leslie whispered to Suzie.

"You've got weird karma with wedding dresses. You're tempting fate, sister. And by the way, the program says the dress is your size. You'd look beautiful in it. You don't have anything like it."

"Thanks," Leslie said. "If I won it, I would give it to you to sell."

"Can't, there is some rule against reselling it. You could donate it to that charity auction my mother is having in a couple of months."

"Okay, are you ready!?"

Suzie pulled out her tickets and arranged them in front of her.

Leslie just shook her head and smiled.

"And the number is four, seven, six, five, eight, one, and nine! That's 4765819!"

Leslie glanced down at her card and back up at the number on the screen. *Oh shit!* Suzie grabbed Leslie's arm and raised it. "Here! She's right here! She won the Paris Germaine! And it's her size!"

Times Square beckoned beyond the windows of their hotel, yet Leslie had a problem to deal with.

"Is it wrong that I find this so funny?" Suzie asked.

"I can't believe I won it," Leslie said, looking down at the large designer garment bag taking over one of the beds in their hotel room.

"Well, do you want to take it out and try it on?"

"No," Leslie said. "I want to go to Laduree and Saks and then make it back here in time to get ready for my drink."

"With Charlieeeee!" Suzie teased.

"I think I want a new outfit," Leslie said and pointed at the dress, "Other than that. You do know I have to pay taxes on it, right?"

And she was going to have to carry the enormous garment bag with a big Paris Germaine logo on it on the airplane the next day. Everyone was going to think she was flying off to exotic Portland, Oregon to get married. Life had a nasty sense of humor. Well, this dress could hang out with the other dresses in her closet, because no way in Hell was she going to wear it.

"Sorry, but it is hard to keep from laughing. Of all the women in that room, you were the least likely to need or want a dress."

Chapter Twenty-Five

Leslie wished she'd thought to bring her aquamarine earrings to New York, but they were back in her safe along with her diamond heart necklace and her Zultanite bracelet. The only jewelry she'd brought with her was her sunstone ring and a pair of small diamond earrings that Denice had bought her for Christmas years earlier. When they'd gone to Saks, Leslie found a little black cocktail halter dress with a matching wrap and paired the look with three-inch, strappy, black Stuart Weitzman sandals.

Suzie, who was getting ready to go out to dinner with some of her friends in the bridal business, said, "Normally, I'd tell you to give us a call after your drink to see if you'd like to join us, but instead I'm going to remind you that we need to leave the hotel at six tomorrow morning to make our flight home."

"I will be back bright and early, but I will take that as a compliment to mean that you like this dress."

"You look pretty damn stunning. And if I were you, I'd keep my dance card open. I think Justin will be making plans to fill it the moment he sees you. And might I add, you looked at him in a way I haven't ever seen you look at anyone. Hungrrrry... Meow."

Leslie finished applying her Chanel lipstick in the shade of 'Passion' and said, "His name is Charlie, not Justin. You are so vulgar."

"I like that your dirty mind went there too. You like him."

"Maybe a little," Leslie admitted.

Charlie was leaning against a pillar in the lobby with carefree indifference that made him look sexier if that was possible. Women walked by him, giving him longing, come hither looks, which he seemed not to notice.

Leslie's stomach gave her the butterfly flutters. It had been a long time since the sight of a man had brought this reaction and to this degree. *Jordan.* Jordan had been the last man to evoke such a reaction. Her steps faltered on the marble floor of the hotel lobby. She willed herself to keep it together. She didn't need to trip or go into a full-blown panic attack. It was Charlie. She'd known him most of her life.

But when had he become such a good-looking man? And when had her stomach decided to go all fluttery?

He'd changed into a different suit than he'd been in that afternoon. He'd traded in the gray for a navy, which he wore without a tie. His white shirt was open at the collar displaying a smattering of chest hair. Leslie was old fashioned. She liked a man with chest hair. All that manscaping that men did was a turnoff to her. She liked her men a little rugged. At the sight of his open collar and tanned skin, she had a fleeting thought to how it would feel to rub her bare skin against it, and she felt her nipples pucker.

What was wrong with her? She felt like a teenager facing her crush.

The moment Charlie saw her, a smile broke out on his face that could have stopped an object moving at the speed of sound. She was so glad she'd bought the sexy little dress Suzie had talked her into.

There was something here, something undefined, yet undeniable, and making itself known. Attraction. Chemistry. Take your pick, they were going to have a good time.

"You look lovely this evening," he said, as he offered her his arm.

"I could say the same of you," she said, as she took his arm, feeling the fabric of his suit coat brush against her bare arm, and had to remind herself to breathe.

"Why thank you," he said with a smile and added, "I was thinking that we could have drinks at the Palm Court at the Plaza. It has become a favorite of mine. Does that sound good to you?"

"I'm open to any suggestion," she said, not letting go of him when they entered the elevator. In fact, when she had to get in the cab, it was hard to let go.

Seated inside the elegant room that resembled the park just beyond the fabulous Plaza Hotel, they drank Cosmopolitans, a house specialty.

"I couldn't believe it when I saw you this morning," Charlie said, as they sipped their drinks from a private corner booth. She couldn't believe it either, but maybe they had very different reasons for being surprised.

"Why? Because a wedding show is about the last thing I need to be attending?" she asked uneasily, daring to meet his eyes.

"No," he said, shaking his head. "It's just that I've been thinking about you a lot in the last few days."

"Me? Why?" she asked, as he turned a little more toward her and their legs brushed, neither one of them moving away from the connection.

"I don't mind designing the exotic engagement rings. They are fun because they are so unusual. The profit margin is incredible, but I prefer my work with the aquamarine. You inspired me like no one else ever has, which I guess makes you my beautiful, unforgettable muse," he said, now he was the one not quite meeting her eyes.

She couldn't believe it. She was his muse. That meant that he thought about her, a lot.

The resulting blush from his words started at her cleavage and worked its way up her arms, to her shoulders and neck.

"I'm really your muse? Me?" she asked and watched as he nodded and looked embarrassed By the time the color had spread to her cheeks, she'd found her voice enough to say, "Despite what I might have said at the time, you made one of my dreams come true. I was a model for a day."

"Is there anything I could say to persuade you to consider modeling for me again sometime?"

"Just ask, I'm yours," she said, as a waiter placed elegant mini lobster rolls in front of them. She didn't remember ordering them, but Charlie just shrugged and said, "I have to get these every time I come here, they are addictive."

You are addictive, she thought. Why hadn't she been nicer to Charlie earlier? Why hadn't she seen Charlie for who he really was?

"You know, I know I mentioned it at the shoot, but I'm serious when I tell you that when I was a little kid, I thought you didn't like me. I used to beg my mother not to go to Sauveterre because I thought you'd be there and give me dirty looks," she said.

He threw back his head and laughed and then he admitted, "I was shy and awkward. And as I mentioned before, I had a very, very big crush on you. My parents tried to get me to talk to you and get over it, but I was too shy. I don't know if I ever fully grew out of it. You were the most beautiful thing I'd ever seen. For a kid, those are a lot of emotions to come to terms with."

"I'm shocked. You liked me," Leslie said, feeling confused and happy and overwhelmed all at the same time.

"I still do. Can you see why you are my muse? Why I need you to be my model? You're the ultimate for me. I never grew out of my crush."

Leslie met his eyes and then had to look away. Now she was the one who was shy and awkward.

"So, the next time I'm in Portland, I'd like to see you and get something set up," Charlie said. "I have some lovely new designs that will look beautiful on you."

"Ah, so you want me to model?"

"Yes," he said, "I want you."

Flustered, she asked, "Aren't you flying home tomorrow like the rest of us, from the bridal show?"

"No, maybe you don't know. I've got an apartment in New York."

"You... You're living in New York?" she asked.

"I have some New York partners, so we are exploring some ventures together into the exotic gems and the aquamarine. I get out to Portland maybe once a month to see my parents and make sure everything is going well. I usually need to help them with special projects, which I love doing."

But aquamarine was their special project. The thought of him working with other people, well, it bothered her. He'd moved away and no one told her. Just when she had all these feelings that were rushing through her for this man, this man who had been there all along, he was gone.

"Are you alright? You look upset," he said, his hand gently reaching out to touch hers. She gripped his fingers, not even realizing that she had.

"I'm sorry, maybe I shouldn't have told you all that about you being my muse—"

"No, I'm stunned to hear that. I... I just didn't know you'd moved away. I guess I always thought you'd be there, and I'm sad you aren't. I guess I need to get used to the idea that you're gone," she said, and wondered if she could have sounded any more stupid.

He kissed her cheek, taking her completely by surprise.

"What was that for?" she asked, her heart beating so hard she was surprised he couldn't hear it.

"That's the nicest thing you've ever said to me. I liked it," he replied, and then kissed her quickly on the lips. She stared at him and tried to think of a response.

"And what was that for?" she asked, leaning toward him, her breath coming out a little too fast.

"That was something I've wanted to do for years."

"Please, do it again," she said, and he didn't hesitate, and this time, his lips lingered, igniting a fire along her skin that she hadn't felt in a very long time.

After what turned into dinner and another round of cocktails, Charlie suggested that he show her the view from his apartment. In the cab, he held her hand, and she clung to it like it was a lifeline—not caring what it meant or what he thought. She simply didn't want to let go of him, not tonight, not ever.

Somewhere between the first and second round of cosmopolitans, Leslie Marie Westcott realized she was in love with the man who'd always been there, just beyond reach.

This was the passion that had no reason but couldn't be denied or explained with words. Every cell in her body tingled with joy at the realization that love had found her again. This moment would be forever the turning point in her mind, an awakening, a *knowing*. For the rest of her life, she would remember this moment, this instant of time that her life changed forever.

It made no sense that it could happen this fast. But she knew, just like she'd known with Jordan. She loved Charlie. And if he asked her to move to New York and live with him in his small apartment and be his model, she'd have done it as long as she could bring Daisy with her.

As they entered his apartment, the lights were off, but she could see it clearly from all the outside light. He had good taste and must be doing well because it was a lovely space.

"I'll turn on the lights in a minute or two, but I wanted you to see the view first," he said coming up behind her. It took every ounce of willpower she had not to reach back to touch him, to make sure he was there.

"This has been such an interesting day," she observed.

"Interesting good or interesting bad?"

"Definitely good," she said.

"Why?" he asked, his lips close to her ear.

"Well, seeing you, being here, and knowing that you didn't hate me all those years ago."

"I never hated you," he said, his lips brushing her ear.

"Good," she managed.

"And you won a very expensive wedding dress."

"How did you find out about that?" she asked.

"I was in the room. It's a beautiful dress. You'll look stunning in it."

"I don't know about that."

"I do," he said, and she could feel his lips curving into a smile against her neck.

She took a step back and bumped into him. He reached out to steady her, his arm encircling her waist as he kissed her neck. Tingles shot through her body. It was wonderful, but it wasn't enough. Turning in his arms, she faced him.

"If you don't kiss me soon—"

He placed a finger to her lips and warned, "If we start this now, it doesn't end here. We are starting something. And I'm not one of those other unworthy bastards—"

She silenced him with a kiss. How long had it been since she'd wanted to kiss someone this badly? She couldn't remember.

He kissed her back with a ferocity that had her surrender to him, body and soul. They half walked, half stumbled into another room where a bed quickly was beneath her and then she was pulling Charlie down for another kiss.

Leslie heard one of her new Stuart Weitzman's knock something off the wall as Charlie flung it off her foot. The second Weitzman followed hitting with a dull thud. Then Charlie was kissing her again as she pulled at his jacket and eventually ripped several of the buttons off his shirt while trying to remove it.

He had better luck with her halter dress. He carefully draped the black silk over a nearby chair as she leaned back and watched Charlie undress in the twilight.

"You're so beautiful," he murmured as he joined her on the bed. "I've wanted to touch you like this since the photo shoot."

"You and Miguel," she teased as she reached for him.

"I had to threaten him to stay away from you," Charlie said as he leaned down and kissed her breast.

"Really?" she asked, her words coming out a little breathlessly.

"You are mine," Charlie said.

"Prove it," she said as he before he captured her mouth with his.

Charlie held her from behind, his arm wrapped around her, cupping her naked breast. She purred as she turned toward him, kissing the tip of his nose, his cheek and finally, his lips.

Leslie's body felt languid and relaxed despite the fact they'd fallen off the bed once or twice. She hardly remembered, which she knew from experience long ago was a very good sign.

"I can only think of one thing that would have made the last few hours better," Charlie murmured.

"I can't think of anything," Leslie said. They'd made love with a depth and passion she thought she'd never have in her life again. His comment started to sink in, and she wondered if he hadn't enjoyed it as much as she had. They'd made love three times. She'd held nothing back, giving completely of herself.

"Next time, I want you to wear your aquamarine earrings," he whispered in her ear. "The earrings I made for you. Then I could die a happy man."

"For a moment... I... never mind," she said.

"Leslie, I've dreamed of loving you like this for years. What we just shared... It was better than any of my fantasies."

"You've had fantasies about this? Me?"

"Yes, you're my muse, remember?" he asked and kissed her.

"I'm happy, but I'm not happy to be going back to Portland without you." Please ask me to stay, she thought. Please. Don't let this be all there is.

"I wish I didn't have to fly to South America day after tomorrow."

"When will you get back to Portland?" she asked, trying to keep the neediness out of her voice, but she didn't care. She needed him. She would need him until the day she died.

"Hard to say, I'm flying to Brazil, then Madagascar for aqua, and then I go to Antwerp for diamonds and then back to New York. The itinerary is open. Sometimes these negotiations take days or weeks. When I finally make it back to New York, I'll have to spend a couple of weeks with the new stones and with any luck, then to Portland for a quick weekend trip."

She started adding up the destinations and weeks in her head. It could be months before she saw him again and then he would only be in Portland for a "quick" weekend. She wasn't a priority. If he felt about her the way she felt about him, he couldn't be away that long.

"I hope you have time to see me when you are in Portland," she said, feeling a little sad.

"Of course, I told you, this is the start of something," he said, kissing her cheek, "But the timing is difficult. Speaking of time, what time is your flight?"

"We are leaving for the airport at six," she said.

"It pains me to say that it is 4:30 and I should get you back to your hotel. No time for cappuccino and flowers."

Reality was a harsh witness when it came to love. She sighed, she was already late. "Oh damn."

"Come on, we'll take a quick shower," he said leading her into his tiny bathroom. It was hard not to touch him and be touched by him and not have it lead to another session of lovemaking, but the clock didn't stop for them.

He turned on the lights in the apartment so she could find her shoes. One of the strappy high heels had made it all the way to the living room. She picked it up and paused. Over the couch were three framed photos of her in the aquamarine from the photo shoot. They weren't the published photos from the ads, but outtakes of her smiling and laughing without the mask but wearing his jewelry. It was the only art that adorned the trendy, urban space.

"They went up before the furniture arrived," he said from the doorway to the bedroom.

She didn't know what to say. But when she turned to him and saw a sparkle of something passionate and unsaid, she replied, "I was smiling for you."

He smiled and said, "Next time we make love, I'm draping you in aqua and nothing else."

They dressed quickly as he called for an Uber and then walked down to the street. "You don't need to go with me," she said, feeling bad and missing him already. When would she see him again?

"Before five in the morning, I'm not leaving you to an Uber driver. I'm riding with you," he said.

"Good," she said and felt his arm around her, giving a little squeeze.

On the ride back to the hotel, she wanted to ask him to come home with her and meet Daisy. She wanted a lot of things but knew she had no right to ask.

"Did I tell you that I'm the mother of a fur baby?" she asked, thinking of Daisy.

Charlie chuckled low and replied, "A dog, right?"

"Yes, a sweet cat-like dog named Daisy. She's a Vizsla, but you probably don't know what that is. You aren't allergic or anything, are you?"

"No, I'm not allergic, and I know what Vizslas are. They're Hungarian and very sweet. It doesn't surprise me that you'd have one."

"You know Vizslas?"

"I've seen you walking her."

"You have?"

"Yes," he said with a chuckle. "You walk her by the store and look in the windows."

"I wave to your mother, but you're always too far in the back."

"Yeah, but I could see you."

"Really?"

"Yes," he said and kissed her hand.

"She'll like you," Leslie said.

"Is she going to demand to sleep on our bed?"

His words took her breath away. "Our bed." Maybe those were her favorite words in the English language.

She smiled, far too broadly for so early in the morning when she said, "Maybe."

He laughed and kissed her in the dark of the cab.

They arrived at the hotel, and he said to the driver, "I'll be back in a moment." He walked her into the nearly deserted lobby and pulled her close.

"Last night," he said, "was amazing."

"I thought it was too," she said knowing she sounded like a weak woman.

"Remember what I said. This is the beginning," he said and gave her a quick kiss. "Now go, before you miss your plane. I'll see you soon."

"Don't say it," Leslie warned as they drove to the airport a half hour later.

"What did you think I'd say?" Suzie said with a chuckle.

"I don't know."

"Hmmm… You do know, when I told you when we needed to leave for the airport, I was kidding. I didn't think you'd actually spend the night with Justin."

"Charlie," Leslie corrected, sounding irritated.

"How was it?"

"There isn't enough distance from it for us to discuss it yet. It is still personal, private, mine."

"It was that good of a bang-bang, huh? You've been smiling like an idiot since you did the walk of shame."

"He's in New York. He has an apartment. I finally met someone who makes me feel alive again, and he now lives in New York."

"You're so dramatic. You can see him in five hours anytime you want. It's called an airplane."

"It's called the other side of the country, and he is traveling to far off places for aqua for a few weeks. He won't be home for who knows how long."

"You'll feel better after you pop a Xanax for the flight and have a nap."

"I don't think narcotics are going to solve this one," Leslie said. And she thought: *Because I'm in love with him.*

"Wow, maybe you're in love."

"Oh, shut up!"

The wedding dresses were stacking up like bodies after a natural disaster, Leslie thought as she added the Paris Germaine to her other dresses in the closet. It hadn't been an easy trip home carrying a huge garment bag. She'd wanted to check it, and Suzie had threatened to birth a bovine at the Delta counter when she'd made the suggestion.

She fell onto the bed in her master bedroom and stared at the vaulted ceiling as Daisy snuggled in beside her. She felt nauseous and tired, like jet lag with a hint of food poisoning and a hangover mixed in. Despite the Xanax Suzie had given her for the flight, she didn't sleep. For five hours she just stared at the little screen in the seatback ahead of her. As she'd watched the little map track their progress from New York to Portland, one thought circled in her mind. With each minute, she was further away from Charlie.

She looked over at Daisy who had been a cling-on since Leslie had arrived home. "Daisy," she said, watching the dog's velvety ears perk at the sound of her name on her mommy's lips. "I'm in love."

The dog raised her head as if to say, "What are you going to do about it?"

"I have no idea."

And for the life of her, she couldn't get Charlie out of her mind. It was the most mind-blowing, passionate night that she'd had in years. And he was in New York, and she was in Portland. The universe really didn't like her.

Silver Linings Dress Auction

DRESS NUMBER FORTY-FIVE

TITLE: *Love*

DESCRIPTION: This dreamy, Paris Germaine gown features draped silk satin. It doesn't have any crystals, pearls, or lace. It is extra heavy duchess satin so white it looks silver with hints of aquamarine. It is, quite simply, stunning.

DONATED BY: *The Aqua Lady*

Present Day

TWO days before the Auction

"I feel so sorry for that girl that I was before all the dresses, before all the wrong men," Leslie said. "She had her whole, beautiful life laid out in front of her. She couldn't wait to live it and enjoy each moment. She knew pain, she'd lost her mother, and nothing would ever hurt that badly again in her life. She couldn't even fathom that lightning would strike twice. But it did, and she almost lost herself."

Suzie topped off Leslie's champagne glass. They sat on her living room floor next to Daisy while the remaining three wedding dresses held court on the couch. The yellow and white striped La Provence box lay open and empty on the floor. The fruit tarts, macaroons, and chocolate éclairs had been consumed. The wine bottle had been opened and split. They stared into the fire and were contemplating a second bottle of wine as Leslie talked about the last few years of her life. It was a way of rationalizing all that had happened. Maybe it was a way to let go of her past and finally accept her unknown future.

Daisy largely ignored them as she chewed on a rawhide bone, her glittery nails catching the firelight. Now and then she'd pause, look up at them, wag her tail, get some praise and pets, and then return to her bone.

"I wonder if I'd stopped him from that climb if it would have changed the outcome of anything," she said.

"What do you mean?" Suzie asked.

"Maybe it was Jordan's fate to die young. Maybe if he hadn't fallen in a crevasse maybe he would have died in the cave or been hit by a car right before our wedding, I don't know. But I have to try to bring some sort of logic to the situation."

"Leslie, I mean this in the best possible way when I say this: *Jordan would be proud of you.* He would want you to live the best life possible. He wouldn't want you to be sad. I think he'd be cheering you on for how you handled Jack and Mitch. He'd want to punch each and every one of them for how they treated you, and he'd have killed Shane with his bare hands. I think he'd have thanked Suede for taking care of you. And maybe, just maybe, he'd tell you it is okay to love again. And Jordan knew Charlie. They worked on your ring together and it sounds like they liked each other. Don't discount that."

Leslie wiped away a few tears, grabbed Suzie's hand, gave it a squeeze, and said, "Thank you."

As the afternoon turned to evening, they ordered the pizza Leslie had been thinking of for several days. Daisy begged for and received strips of the crust edge. And finally, Leslie knew what she wanted to do with the remaining dresses and even before she said the words, she felt the weight lifting off her.

"I think I've come to a decision," she said.

"And?"

"And it feels good. Take them all."

"Leslie, honey, are you sure? Please keep the Germaine. You love that one. It is the showstopper among all the dresses," Suzie said.

"No, I think it has to go. I'm tired of having a house full of wedding dresses."

She didn't want to tell Suzie the truth. The Germaine reminded her of the night she'd spent with Charlie. It had been two months, and he hadn't come back to Portland, or if he had, he hadn't chosen to contact her. If he felt half of what she felt for him, he couldn't have waited this long to see her. He'd made no move to see her. There have been no grand gestures, no flowers, no notes, not even a postcard. And who was to blame for that? Maybe she'd done it to herself.

It had been three weeks since his last call. He was in Myanmar or some other exotic or war-torn place, treasure hunting.

She remembered the last phone call with a painful shudder as if it had just happened.

"Hello Leslie, can you hear me?"

"Barely, where are you?" she'd asked trying to sound upbeat and happy. The truth was she felt sad and heartsick. She wanted to see him, to be with him.

"Myanmar. I got some beautiful aqua. I can't wait to get it back to New York and start designing some pieces."

"Great. When will you be home?" And by that, she'd meant Portland.

"I'm not sure. We have a couple of other leads we are working through. As soon as they pan out, we will head back." The "we" stuck out to her like a siren on a quiet night.

"Who all is with you?" she'd asked.

"My security team, Pedro and Tim, and then Crystal joined us in Brazil. You remember her from that night at Ram's Head. She speaks fluent Portuguese…"

"Yes, I remember Crystal." She had liked Crystal. She remembered Crystal's carefree live-and-let-live manner. She remembered her good figure and cute smile. She remembered thinking that Crystal was his fuck buddy… Was she providing that service on this trip?

Leslie tried not to let the jealousy overtake her, but the next words had slipped out of her mouth, and she couldn't take them back.

"So, you're back with Crystal?"

"What?" he'd asked the confusion in his voice discernible.

"Well, I know you were close."

"Leslie, how could you think that?" he'd asked, the surprise attack registering with him even as his phone started to cut out.

"I'm just wondering why she is with you and I'm not."

"She speaks Portuguese. I've given you no reason not to trust me. But I'll give you a little time to think about this. I'll see you in a few weeks."

The line went dead.

What had she done? Why, why, why had she done that?

She'd reacted like a jealous woman. She'd let the ghosts of the past potentially mess up her future. Was she truly so jaded that she now messed good things up before they had a chance?

She needed to let the dress go.

She needed to let him go.

And if he came back to her, she'd apologize and hope that if they were meant to be together, they would be.

Present Day

The Silver Linings Wedding Dress Auction

"You look hot, if I do say so myself," Suede said, his hands in his tuxedo pockets as he surveyed Leslie's outfit, which he had picked out the previous afternoon. He'd found her a sleeveless, deep v-neckline, high-low dress in a silver silk that perfectly set off her coloring. He'd paired it with a clear crystal necklace and strappy silver Swarovski-bejeweled high heeled sandals. She wore her aquamarine studs in her ears and silver cuff bracelets on her wrists. The Sunstone clashed a little, but it never left her finger, so she didn't care.

"I feel like Wonder Woman meets the Tin Man from the Wizard of Oz," she said, looking in the mirror.

"Well, you look sexy hot," Milan said as he entered the living room carrying a bottle of champagne to refill glasses. "I think we should add stylist to our services, Suede. With you doing transformations like this, we could make a mint. What do you think?"

"We don't need the money, but it is a lot of fun to bring out the pretty. Maybe we should."

They said goodbye to their puppies who were having a play date at Leslie's house and drove to the Portland Art Museum.

Suzie, wearing a strapless black silk taffeta gown, greeted them at the front door and gave them their table assignment, number one, reserved for special guests, right up in front of the thousand-person room. Leslie protested, preferring a table in the middle that was unclaimed by any of the sponsors.

"We aren't hiding you," Suede said, as he grabbed her hand and headed to their table.

"Thank you, Suede," Suzie called after him. "She looks great by the way! Good job!"

Leslie sat with her back to the crowd, facing the stage. Just as she picked up the surprisingly beautiful catalog that showed a color photo of each dress on a mannequin and gave a description, reporter Hannah bumped into her chair from behind.

Having found her, the reporter immediately stuck a microphone in Leslie's face as she asked, "Leslie Westcott, it is reported that you have at least five dresses in the auction tonight. Can you share with us a personal story or two as well as which numbers they are in the catalog?"

Suede, who had taken the seat next to her, stood to his full height and said, "I'm Miss Westcott's attorney. She will not be offering any comments on the auction or her dresses this evening."

"Hello," the reporter said, turning her focus to Suede. "Can you tell me your name and what brings you to the auction this evening? Are you Miss Westcott's date? Are you shopping for another dress for her tonight?"

"I'm headed to the bar," Suede said to Leslie and Milan, ignoring the reporter. "Martinis?"

"Yes, please," Leslie said and watched as the reporter followed Suede, the pied piper to women everywhere.

Feeling her cell phone vibrate, she glanced at the screen hoping to see Charlie's number. Of course, it wasn't Charlie. It was an automated call confirming her massage the next day. Each time she got a call, she grabbed her phone only to feel disappointed that it wasn't the one person she wanted to hear from. She thought about asking his parents if he was alright, but if he were unaccounted for or injured, she'd have heard. No, he was obviously sending her a message she didn't want to hear. Heck, maybe her little over reaction on the phone had sent him right into Crystal's arms. Wouldn't that be ironic? And devastating.

Turning the phone off, she focused on the impressive program for the evening ahead. They were going to have opening remarks by a representative for Rachel's House and then Aunt Trudel. Three wedding planners, including Suede, would start auctioning off the dresses, rotating the duties throughout the evening. They'd auction off ten dresses, have the salad course, auction off another group, then have dinner, auction off a few more, and then have dessert. After dessert, they would auction off the final lot. A silent auction in the adjacent room offered the assorted goodies like wedding flower packages, jewelry from Sauveterre, and other items from high-end jewelers, honeymoon trip planners, and photography packages.

"Do you want to look at the silent auction items?" Milan asked.

"No, but feel free to go," she said, thinking that she did not want to see any additional jewelry designed by Charlie this evening.

Suede returned with their drinks, and Leslie asked him how he'd gotten rid of the reporter. "I sicked her on the straight wedding planner with the strong British accent. They are meant for each other."

"Here we go," Suede whispered as the room darkened and the opening speeches began.

Leslie had to hand it to Aunt Trudel—she was a natural born showman. In another life, she was probably a carny under the big top or encouraging people to see the Yak Boy.

Leslie wished her father and Denice weren't in Palm Springs. They would've enjoyed this event seeing some good coming from all of Leslie's dresses.

She knew the Sauveterres were in the room because they'd donated several sets of pearl earrings and necklaces to the silent auction as well as a wedding ring set that was quite valuable. For that donation, Suzie had given them complimentary tickets to attend. Leslie felt close to Caroline after their conversation which had kept her from making one of the largest mistakes of her life. But what would she say to the woman now? *I think I'm in love with your son, but I might have messed it up because I'm a jaded mess.*

After all the times she'd darkened the Sauveterre Jewelers' door with fiancés, Caroline would probably laugh in her face and tell her to stay the Hell away from Charlie. Leslie couldn't risk the possible humiliation, so she kept her eyes staring straight ahead at the stage oblivious to everything around her.

Suede was the first presenter. They brought the first ball gown out on a mannequin, and Leslie could hear people discussing the pretty dress. Leslie did very well until Suede got to dress number seven, her James Casper. The dress she'd gotten for Jordan, by far one of the hardest to let go.

"Ladies and gentlemen, this is a gorgeous James Casper has been titled *Selflessness* by its generous donor, who is the epitome of this name. Holding nothing back and loving fully, this stunning mermaid silhouette James Casper gown is appropriately named for a queen. "Alexandra" has a strapless, lace corset bodice with a sweetheart neckline. The skirt is an extra heavy silk satin gathered in a sweep to form the mermaid flair. Forgo the veil, wear a tiara, and grace the shoulders with the thinnest of silk tulle wraps. This is the dress little girls dream of when they think of their weddings. Let's start the bidding at five thousand."

Leslie was stunned when the dress went for ten thousand five hundred.

Suede returned to the table part way through the salad course. He handed Leslie another martini and asked, "How are you holding up?"

"I'm glad the James Casper earned so much money," Leslie said as she picked at her salad. Why was she here? She felt like crying. Her life had just played out on stage.

Suzie sat down and smiled, "We are doing really well. Up to forty-two thousand on the first ten dresses. That is amazing!"

The next section of dresses also did well. Leslie watched as her Caroline Benson mermaid gown sold for seven thousand dollars. Twice what her father paid for it.

Dinner was served, baked salmon along with a filet mignon, which was over cooked. Leslie again picked at her food and drank her martini, thankful that she wasn't driving this evening.

"I'm watching you," Suede said.

"You and everyone else. Suzie looks ready to step in and pull me out of the room if this gets too much for me. Milan is counting my martinis. Why am I here?"

"Suzie told us how you were on Tuesday afternoon over Charlie. That isn't like you. We both know it. You need to snap out of it. If he isn't worthy, he doesn't get to be with you."

"I think I love him," she whispered, hoping she wouldn't start crying.

"Oh baby, I'm sorry," he said as he and Milan reached out to her, each giving her a hug.

"Thanks, guys. I just need to pull it together. It just kind of took me off guard. I haven't felt this way in a very long time. This dress auction is bringing up a lot of memories, many of them not pleasant. I just want it over."

"He will show up, I feel it," Milan said.

"Thank you, Milan," she said. She didn't want to hear about another one of his visions. The aquamarine beach dream was still freaking her out a bit, but the inspiration had done wonders for his design work on her house.

She looked down at her plate and made a decision. She wasn't a victim. She just didn't do victim well. If she kept drinking and not eating, they would need to carry her out of this event, and she would be embarrassed. Why, because she'd gotten messed up over some guy? Okay, Charlie wasn't just some guy. He'd always been there. She just hadn't noticed until it might have turned out to be too late.

She ate the damn salmon and the overcooked filet mignon, and she pushed her martini away.

Her white Maggie St. Clair that was more cocktail than wedding dress—she had used it as such—sold for six thousand dollars. It was an amazing gown, but she'd never wear it again, not with the memory of Mitch all over it.

The Brian Jones sold for fifteen hundred. Suzie and Trudel, who had joined them at the table, each turned and gave Leslie a knowing look.

"Okay," she said with a shrug. "Everyone hated it."

Suzie nodded, but Suede whispered, "I actually kind of liked it. For a simple dress it was very elegant."

"Thank you, Suede. I knew I could count on you to have taste," Leslie said with a smile—her first genuine smile of the evening. "You know which dress is up first in the final round?"

"Our special dress," he said and kissed her cheek. Milan looked like he might cry and said, "I wish I'd had my phone turned on. That would have made a lovely post for Facebook."

Their dessert was an ice cream concoction from Salt & Straw. They were more than halfway over. In two hours, she would be home snuggling with her puppy. She couldn't wait to crawl into bed, spoon her dog, and stick a fork in this day.

Trudel appeared and looked panicked as she knelt by Suede and whispered in his ear. "Of course," he said. "Don't worry, Trudel. It's fine. I don't mind at all."

"What's wrong?" Leslie asked.

"My introduction earlier in the evening was a hit. We lost our British wedding planner and the reporter. I need to fill in on the last set of dresses."

"Unbelievable," Leslie said as Suede made his way to the stage.

The crowd was definitely lit. The drinks were strong, and by the time Suede stood before the microphone everyone wanted to move the show along and might be willing to pay to do it. She thought that Suede introduced the dress he'd bought for Leslie with a bit more enthusiasm than he did for the other dresses, but it worked. The second James Casper sold for twelve thousand and got a standing ovation.

An hour later, they were up to her favorite dress, the Paris Germaine. She wondered if she hadn't made a mistake putting this dress in the auction. Heck, she could buy it back. It wasn't like she'd paid for it the first time. Her mind flashed on Charlie and the way he'd sounded during their last call.

"My friends, this is a special dress among special dresses," Suede said. "Lot Number Forty-Five is a Paris Germaine from New York. We call it LOVE. I happen to know the back story on this dress. It comes from the largest bridal show in the United States, the White Bliss. This dress was the grand raffle prize. It has never been worn. It does not have a tragic backstory. It is just a beautiful gown valued at over fifteen thousand dollars donated for a good cause. May the owner wear it on their dream wedding day to their one and only true love.

"Now, we only have a few dresses left. Let's blow this out of the water. I understand we are just short of half a million dollars between the dress auction and the silent auction. Let's help our friends at Rachel's House and start the bidding at ten thousand."

Six bidders immediately joined in. When the price got to twenty thousand, Leslie wondered who would win and smiled sadly at what could have been for that beautiful dress. She should have tried it on.

"We are now down to just two bidders," Suede said, his voice smooth in the stress of the moment. "We have the gentleman at the back and the lady in the center. Do I hear twenty-five thousand?"

Leslie wondered who the people were, and why they were buying the dress. She felt like looking but decided she didn't want to know.

"Well, well, we have two very generous bidders in this auction for twenty-five. Who will go twenty-eight thousand for this Paris Germaine?

"I have twenty-eight thousand from the gentleman in the back. Going once, going twice, and now going for a third and final time, SOLD! Congratulations, sir! You are the new owner of The Aqua Lady's Paris Germaine wedding dress. I'm sure you have some very interesting plans for it," he said with a wink and a smile that made Leslie so curious, she turned to see the man who was slowly, yet elegantly walking through the crowd and making his way toward the stage.

Charlie.

The Silver Linings Wedding Dress Auction

Happily Ever After

Leslie had to let the vision register. *Charlie. Charlie is here!*

Charlie, wearing a tuxedo that gave Suede a run for his money, joined Suede on the stage. They did a man hug and then turned to the audience.

Her heart hammered in her chest. The air was struggling to make it into her lungs. What was going on?

"Ladies and gentlemen," Suede said, "There will be a brief pause in the auction as I've been asked to make a special announcement. Will The Aqua Lady herself, Miss Leslie Westcott, please join us on stage?"

Next to her, Milan pulled out his chair, stood, offering her his hand.

Leslie didn't think, she just stood and let Milan lead her several steps until someone interrupted, "Thank you, Milan, but will you please allow me?" She looked up and saw her father standing before her with a large smile on his face.

"Dad?" she asked her voice breaking. "You're here?"

"We've been here the whole time," he said indicating the table behind hers. She turned and saw Denice sitting next to James and Caroline Sauveterre who were all smiling at her.

"Get up there!" Suzie said from where she stood at the side with Aunt Trudel, who looked to be in full Aunt Trouble mode.

"Let's not keep Charlie waiting," her father said as he led her to the stairs for the stage where her father handed her off to Suede who assisted her the rest of the way. Charlie smiled at her as Suede led her to him. Her jellied, wobbly legs threatened to buckle. Suddenly, Suede was gone, and it was just her and Charlie.

What was going on?

Had they all set her up for something?

When she was just close enough to Charlie that she could have reached out and touched him, he dropped to one knee and smiled up at her.

"I love you, Leslie Westcott, my Aqua Lady. I've adored you since we were kids. Will you please stop buying wedding dresses with other men in mind and marry me? I bought this dress for you. Would you wear it for our wedding?"

Pulling a ring box from his pocket, he opened it and showed her the ring. She didn't look at the ring. She looked at the man. All the doubts, all the second guesses and worries simply vanished. This was real. This was love.

His eyes never leaving hers, he took the ring from the velvet cushion and tossed the box away with dramatic flair. Gently, he reached for her quivering left hand and slipped something cool on the third finger.

Without thinking or hesitation, she spoke from her heart, "I'm in love with you, too. Yes, yes, I'll marry you!"

Later, she'd find out that the crowd went wild, standing and cheering as Charlie stood and pulled her into his arms. It was only when she was safely in his embrace that she glanced at the ring, a large, square cut aquamarine with just a hint of green. It had large, channel set diamonds on either side of it, set in platinum, making it deco inspired and perfect.

"When I didn't hear from you, I worried," she whispered in his ear.

"I lost my phone in Myanmar. Then, I thought it was a sign that maybe I should give you a little space to decide if you loved me.

So, I decided on a grand gesture in front of a bunch of witnesses. How did it work?"

"It worked," she said through tears.

"I'm never leaving again without you by my side," he said.

Leslie was trembling as Charlie escorted her off stage. Then he found a dark corner and kissed her the way he had during their passionate night in New York.

"They were all in on it," Leslie managed between kisses. "You did all of this for me."

"Because I love you," he said. "And yes, I had a little help. Your stepmother is a force. If it was up to her, we'd be getting married tonight, but Suede and Milan want to plan the perfect wedding and reception. I can wait a little longer to be with you legally, but not like I've waited before now. The last few years almost broke me. I'm never letting you out of my sight again."

"I don't want to be away from you ever again. I'll love you more tomorrow than I love you today. And day after tomorrow, I'll love you even more," she admitted as tears streamed down her cheeks.

"I'm never going anywhere without you again. In fact, in the trunk of my car I have three pieces of luggage that I'm taking to your house along with you as soon as we can get out of here. I think there is now some room in your closet because you got rid of all those dresses that came with men who were wrong for you. By the way, that makes me Mr. Right. I don't intend on ever leaving. So, I guess you are stuck with me."

"Good. You know, you are perfect for me," she said, as she nodded, and asked, "I'm serious, when can we get married?"

"There was a discussion about a week from tomorrow. But as for tomorrow, be prepared for cappuccino and flowers in the morning because that is how Mr. Right rolls."

"So, you think I'm going to look sated tomorrow morning?" she asked as she leaned against him, remembering the conversation they had when she modeled for him.

"Count on it."

Eight Days Later

Everyone cried happy tears, including the bride who finally got a chance to walk down the aisle in her dream dress.

Leslie had traveled a long way on her journey to love. She had finally understood that the journey had changed her for the better. She had new family in the form of Suede, Milan, Charlie's parents, and Denice, who had always been there but never quite in Leslie's field of vision. Not to forget Ginger and Daisy who sat at attention on each side of the minister with gardenias and blush-colored roses in their collars. Most of all, she had found her love and he'd been there all along.

They walked together down the aisle: Leslie, her father, and her stepmother, leading her to the man she had known and loved for most of her life.

Epilogue

Six Months Later

Daisy reclined in her custom dog bed that her new daddy had bought for her and chose to ignore the noise around her. Each day that she came to "work" at The Aqua Lady gallery at Sauveterre Jewelers was a new and different experience. It still smelled like fresh wood and varnish from all the renovations.

Charlie had been able to double the size of Sauveterre Jewelers by buying the business next door and simply knocking down a wall. His realtor had demanded that her commission be paid in jewelry. He'd made her model it for him in the privacy of their bedroom.

Now, Charlie had two apprentices who helped him execute his aquamarine designs. He had orders from around the world and a two-year waiting list thanks to a national advertising campaign that featured Leslie, once again draped in aquamarine and diamonds. But everyone who'd known about the first shoot could see that this time there was something different in The Aqua Lady's eyes, an unbridled passion that hadn't been there before.

An art gallery owner in New York had asked to feature an exhibit of Leslie posing as The Aqua Lady. Leslie and Charlie planned to go to New York five or six times a year for his business, and the open invitation was both tempting and flattering. Charlie was letting it be Leslie's decision. She was still feeling shy about the exposure, this time without a mask. But they both knew she would forever be known as Sauveterre's Aqua Lady both professionally and privately. When Leslie arrived a little before noon as she usually did during the week, Daisy stood, stretched out her front paws and made a "rooing" sound that announced her favorite person had entered the store.

Caroline and James laughed and welcomed their new daughter-in-law with a warm greeting.

Charlie put down his tools and greeted his wife with a tender kiss that should have been reserved for the privacy of their bedroom, but their passion, so long denied, couldn't be cooled.

They'd gotten married in the late fall at the Portland Art Museum which had been transformed into a white floral fairy garden thanks to Milan and Suede. Leslie wore the Paris Germaine gown Charlie had bought for her and sparkled with just enough aquamarine to look ethereal.

Leslie could almost see her father, Denice, Trudel, and Suzie breathing a sigh of relief that she'd finally made use of one of her wedding gowns as they watched her pledge her love to Charlie.

Milan later told her it was his vision coming to life. "I can't believe how many beautiful pieces of aquamarine you had on your body. It was almost more glorious than my vision of a white fairytale."

"Can you ever have enough?" she asked and smiled looking down at the diamond eternity band that perfectly nuzzled her art deco aquamarine engagement ring. Charlie wore a simple band of platinum, but to Leslie that band meant more than any of her other jewelry because it meant that he belonged to her. Inside his band, she had engraved, *I'm yours forever, Your Aqua Lady.*

"My darling, I want to show you something," Charlie said before they left for lunch. He leaned down to Daisy where he attached something to the loop on her collar.

"Oh my," was all Leslie could say. Charlie had added a white gold, heart-shaped tag to Daisy's collar with the letter "D" on it that was encrusted with small diamonds and sunstones, which perfectly matched her copper fur.

"Charlie, she looks a little like a rapper's dog, all blinged out, but I love it. I can't wait to see what you do our children."

"Me neither," he said with a wink as he gently placed his hand where their baby was just starting to show with a little bump on her mother's tummy.

Leslie snapped the leash on Daisy and together with her husband, the man she had waited so long to love, they stepped out in the sunshine and started walking into their future.

The End

Thank you for reading *The Silver Linings Wedding Dress Auction*

Mary loves to hear from her readers. If you'd like to send her an email, you may do so through her website: MaryOldham.com

Coming in November 2021: *A Paris Affair*,
Book One of The Hotel Baron Series.

Sign up for Mary's Newsletter and get a sneak peek of Chapter 1!

MaryOldham.com

About the Author

Mary Oldham is a multi-award-winning author, and three-time Golden Heart Finalist with the Romance Writers of America in the areas of Contemporary Romance and Romantic Suspense. Mary resides in Portland, Oregon when she is not writing by the Pacific Ocean in scenic Yachats, The Gem of the Oregon Coast.

Acknowledgments

It has taken a team to make this happen. Sue Grimshaw was my dream editor and to have her like my book enough to work on it was an honor. Thank you for caring so much and taking me under your wing. To Brenda Chin, thank you for offering wonderful suggestions that I integrated into this book. Thank you to Lynn Andreozzi, who embraced and got excited by the project and designed a beautiful cover. To Tamara Cribley and Chris Knight at the Deliberate Page. Thank you, Tamara, for answering 1001 questions and making my baby shine, and Chris, for your detailed grammatical editing. To all my friends who became Advanced Copy Readers, your encouragement made me feel loved. And finally, to the Beta readers, Leslie, Lorinda, Miriam, Trudy, Rosie, Catherine, Tanith, Kathy, Kathie, Bonnie, Andrea, and my ever willing and faithful sister-in-law, MarySue, thank you!!!!

CPSIA information can be obtained
at www.ICGtesting.com
Printed in the USA
BVHW090504090222
628393BV00003BA/99